THE FRENCH GIRL

JC RYAN

VINCI
BOOKS

By JC Ryan

Rex Dalton K9 Thrillers

Dedicated to my good friend Mitch Pender, a military dog trainer, for giving me the idea for this series and guiding me through the intricate and amazing capabilities and psychology of those majestic four-legged soldiers.

Mitch has a lifetime of experience and exceptional depth of knowledge as a military dog handler and trainer.

Vinci Books

vinci-books.com

Published by Vinci Books Ltd in 2025

1

About The French Girl

Rex Dalton and his best friend, Digger, the former military dog, are vacationing on the idyllic islands of Vanuatu in the South Pacific. Swimming, playing on the beach, fishing, and hikes. Nothing but the laid-back lifestyle for the two of them.

Digger decides that Rex needed some human company and must meet this beautiful French girl. Therefore, he introduces Rex to her. Not once, but twice. Before long Rex and the girl become good friends.

But the French girl carries a secret, which if exposed, would have major ramifications for France, the European Union, and NATO. She believes that she is the only one who knows the secret, but she's not.

Then the French girl disappears, and Rex finds himself accused of having something to do with it. He manages to persuade the police he is innocent.

The police eventually conclude that the girl has drowned, her body devoured by sharks and saltwater crocodiles. Case closed

But Rex and Digger don't agree, and they launch their own investigation and find her, but then discover that she is in grave danger, and she is totally oblivious about it until Rex tells her.

She realizes she must get away and asks Rex to help.

Thus, begins a harrowing journey to find a safe haven, away from the claws of those who know her secret and are bent on getting her into their hands.

Chapter One

Paris, France

French President Giles Raphael Aguillard raised his arms, one hand linked to that of his patrician wife's and the other to Lucien Laurent's, his newly-appointed Prime Minister. The Presidency not only bestowed the power as head of state of the French Republic on him, *ex-officio* he was now also the Co-Prince of Andorra, honorary proto-canon of the Basilica of St. John Lateran in Rome, and Grand Master of the *Légion d'honneur* and the National Order of Merit.

His triumphant smile marked the occasion—a rally and celebration following his election ten days before and today's accession to office. His teenaged and young adult children stood to their mother's side, and the Prime Minister's wife, along with several high-ranking ministers, stood to his. It was an illustrious occasion marred only by gray skies and drizzle, as the notorious wet and cold Paris January was barely begun.

1

Among the ministers and high-ranking officials stood a figure that had become a well-known accompaniment of the President before his election, and a frequent spokesperson since. It was the young, dark-haired, uber-intelligent head of Aguillard's communications team, Margot Lemaire, who'd engineered his resounding victory. The person who, in preparation for this occasion, rehearsed with the President until his speech was not only letter-perfect, but also pitch-perfect. Not that the new President would sing the speech—it was honed to precision to reflect the same public sentiment that had swept the President to victory in the special election.

His predecessor had served only two and a half years of his second and final five-year term when a diagnosis of aggressive brain cancer forced his imminent resignation and triggered the need for an early and abrupt election. There'd been hardly any time to campaign, but Aguillard's status as the hand-picked successor had overwhelmed the opposition party. His solemn promise to continue in the footsteps of his ill-fated predecessor, one of the most popular presidents in recent memory, and continue the most popular of his policies hadn't hurt any, either.

Margot Lemaire was content, actually, she welcomed this rare occasion to let others occupy the limelight today. She was confident of her importance to the President and of her bright future. Neither arrogant about her assets nor unaware of them, Margot was beautiful, though not spectacularly so, not at first sight. She was one of those women whose beauty proliferated the more time you spent with her. Single, friendly, and outgoing, and from a wealthy family, she moved with equal grace in the circles of the elite, the middle class, and the poor, which was what made her an excellent choice as Aguillard's campaign manager. Margot held a double PhD in political science and international affairs.

During the campaign, it had been she who graced the President's right side, where the Prime Minister stood today, while the wife and children occupied the left, closest to the President's heart as the campaign had subtly emphasized. The main planks in his brief campaign were family values and the promise that the electorate's wishes when they'd elected his predecessor for a second term would be honored; the most important of which were ambitious plans to address France's economic and immigration woes.

From the beginning, the people liked her. Before the campaign wound down, journalists and bloggers alike were writing about her elegance and unflappable demeanor under pressure, her quick understanding of any situation that might impact the campaign, and her firm grasp of the conservative principles of the prevailing party. A few bold pundits predicted that she'd be given a ministerial role in the new administration, but she herself knew she wasn't ready for that.

As the crowd roared, Margot bent down to attend to the distinguished guest seated in a wheelchair in front of her, who'd left his hospice bed to attend the inauguration of his successor.

"He makes a handsome figure, does he not?" she remarked.

"I chose well," the older gentleman said, nodding. "And you helped the people to accept that choice. Well done, my dear. Now, if you don't mind..."

"Of course." Margot's face showed sympathy and concern as she backed the wheelchair toward the stage's exit. It was too cold, and certainly too wet, for the former President. It was her responsibility to get him out of the weather and back into the hands of his caregivers, who met her in the wings.

Rather than disrupt the speech, which was going well if the roars of the crowd were any indication, she stayed in the wings.

She shivered slightly when a light gust of ice-cold air hit her face. *It's cold. I wonder if he would allow me to take a holiday? I need it… and I think I deserve it. Somewhere nice and warm.*

As if Aguillard had eyes in the back of his head, he was aware, even as he continued his well-rehearsed speech, that Margot was leaving the stage, along with the former President.

He didn't miss a beat. Between the memorized sentences, he interrupted himself and announced, "Ladies and gentlemen, a round of applause for the able leadership of the great man who is leaving the stage. Can we all please stand and show him our support for his recovery?"

But there would be no recovery. The former President was worn out, and the doctors thought he had only weeks to live, if that. He had given everything he had to keeping a firm hand on the reins of government until the special election could be held, and Aguillard was grateful for that. He had an orderly administration to help him transition into office, though he'd shortly announce his own appointments.

Trust Margot to do the right thing. She is a gem!

After the roar of applause subsided, Aguillard went on with his speech, pausing in the right places for more applause and cheering, smiling when he imparted wit, looking fondly at his wife and children when he talked about how important they were to him, and how the nation must return to a time when family was everything. He had the crowd in the palm of his hand.

But while he spoke, Aguillard couldn't stop his mind from taking a subliminal detour to Margot. She had steered his campaign with the brilliance of a life-long politico. But unlike many campaign managers, who were at heart marketers and spin doctors, instead of attacking the opposition and making promises that could never be fulfilled, Margot promoted the principles of the party with conviction. It was a fresh new breeze in French politics, and the voters loved it.

When the election went exactly as planned, he'd offered her a junior minister position, and when she declined that on the admirable grounds that she was not yet experienced enough, he'd offered her an assistant role to a new position he was creating, like that of the Chief of Staff that American presidents relied upon. In a remarkable display of intelligence, she'd declined that, too, on the same grounds. In fact, it was she who suggested Communications was the more appropriate place for her, for now. There would be plenty of time for a ministerial assignment later.

Slightly taller than the President himself, she carried herself with the style and confidence befitting a member of the aristocracy. She dressed impeccably, as well. Unlike his wife, who'd been lovely in her youth but was now putting on weight around her middle and dressed like a dowager, Margot's attire was always at the height of fashion but appropriate for every occasion.

The sight of her long legs striding down a corridor with enough speed to lift her mid-neck length, dark, silky hair in the breeze set his heart racing. He couldn't help himself gazing at length upon her regular features—the strong, straight, well-shaped nose above full lips with just the right amount of pout, the high cheekbones leading one's attention to the wide-spaced, brown eyes and high forehead. The square chin, with just enough softness to it to make it feminine. The ear just peeking from the casual hairstyle…

He forced himself to concentrate on the speech, before he lost track of where he was. His eyes strayed back to the teleprompter.

Some of the media described Margot as part of the hope for the future of the party and France. The public and the other party leaders alike expected her to soon become one of the youngest ever junior ministers in the history of the French Republic, definitely a senior minister (*Ministre*) in the not too distant future, and some even predicted her to one day be the first woman President of France.

The only woman who'd ever come close to the position of President was Édith Cresson, who was the first and only French female Prime Minister, appointed by Francois Mitterrand in May 1991. She'd made a very bad job of her tenure and ended her career in April 1992 in a scandal of corruption within 11 months of taking office.

But this young woman was different. She was not going to disappoint the electorate. They loved her. Therefore, a cheer went up from the crowd when the President announced her appointment as his advisor in charge of press relations. Even the press loved her, as she was always good for a pithy quip, and of course, she was photogenic.

Therefore, at the first press conference after the inauguration, it was with surprise and disappointment that members of the press looked up at the podium to see, not their favorite, Margo Lemaire, but her first assistant, a decidedly less-photogenic young man.

Before he could even get the written remarks started, journalists were calling, "Where's Margot?"

"Is Margot ill? What's going on?"

The assistant was forced to answer before he could make the important announcement of several new appointments to various ministries. "Mademoiselle Lemaire is not ill. However, President Aguillard has granted her a holiday to recover from the strain of the campaign and election. Please allow her the well-deserved rest, and respect her privacy."

Some of the audience settled down. Others, employed by gossip rags, rushed out of the room to write their scoops: *Lemaire Exhausted by Campaign*, *Mystery Holiday for Lemaire*, and other headlines.

Meanwhile, Margot, dressed casually, wearing makeup different from her usual, large sunglasses, and a wide-brimmed hat that dipped below her eye level, boarded a Eurail train for Lyon for a brief visit to her brother before going to Italy, thence to her destination for the month-long holiday she'd negotiated with the President.

A faint smile made her expression pleasant as she handed her Eurail Pass to the conductor. He returned the smile, even though it had not been for him. Margot was thinking about her meeting with the President to request the holiday. At first, it had been contentious. He rightly pointed out that she'd only just begun her duties as his Press Secretary. However, she had made a persuasive argument, and in the end, he'd said only, "We will miss you. Come back well-rested."

She had given him her broadest smile.

"The press will not tolerate your assistant for long."

"He is completely capable. They will have nothing to complain about."

"Capable, yes. But not so pleasing on the eyes."

"Mon Président! You forget yourself!"

Chapter Two

Mumbai, India

Rex Dalton stepped into the baggage claim area in Mumbai's Chhatrapati Shivaji Maharaj International Airport to collect his best pal, his military-trained dog, Digger. Digger was a good traveler. It seemed as if he knew whenever he was put into a cage like that it was the beginning of a new adventure. So, Rex found him in good shape, not at all anxious. In fact, he was busy flirting with a member of the airport staff, who was showing him bits of something Rex was sure wouldn't be good for him. Digger didn't care about a healthy diet—as long as it smelled good, he gulped it up.

"Digger!"

Digger's head dipped guiltily, and he turned eyes full of innocence on Rex, who didn't buy it for a minute.

"You know better than to accept food from strangers," Rex scolded. Digger's happy smile seemed to say, "But surely this pretty lady is an exception." Rex frowned at him and then turned away before the smile could give away his amusement.

To the pretty lady in question, Rex explained in flawless Hindi that the dog was trained not to accept food from strangers, but that he only observed the rule when his master was in sight, and she was not to blame for the dog's disobedience. Nevertheless, she apologized and sent a look of regret toward the charming animal as she moved to another duty after inspecting the claim ticket.

Rex let Digger out of the cage immediately and put him on leash right away. Digger would have been perfectly well-behaved traveling through the busy airport off-leash, but the leash was required, and Digger didn't care.

"We are seriously going to have to get back to your training regimen, you hooligan," Rex said to Digger. The only word the dog understood was training, and Rex was sure he was intelligent enough to know it had been uttered in reference to his attempt at scrounging an illicit snack from that caring lady. His ears drooped momentarily. But he was soon his happy self again, as the familiar scents of Mumbai let him know where they were and maybe also realizing that he was soon to see one of his favorite human friends, Rehka, again.

Rex kept a small pied-à-terre in Mumbai as he had frequent business there. If he could be said to have a home, this was it, though he didn't think of it as such. It was merely the city where his financial administrator and IT specialist, Rehka Gyan, was based. How that had come about was a long story.

Rex could be referred to as a secret agent or special operations operative or an assassin or a spy. It was less than eighteen months ago when he still worked for a black ops outfit that went by the name of CRC – Crisis Response

Consultancy. Nominally commanded by the CIA, it was actually a private company under the command of the Old Man – John Brandt – who called himself a private military contractor. Rex was their most coveted of assets – a stone-cold killer with a grudge against bad guys, especially Middle Eastern terrorists, who had killed his family when they blew up a train in Barcelona in 2004. But no one, least of all John Brandt, doubted Rex was his own man. Rex had his own definition of the 'liberty' aspect of 'life, liberty, and the pursuit of happiness'. And it didn't always coincide with his stated orders.

While Rex was on a mission in Afghanistan, Usama (the Lion), an Afghani drug lord, arranged an ambush that killed Rex's entire team, except Digger, the military dog trained and owned by the former Australian SAS operative, Trevor Madigan, Rex's good friend. Digger was now Rex's trusted companion because of a promise Trevor extracted as he lay dying.

Rex and Digger teamed up in the aftermath of the ambush and went in pursuit of those responsible. They soon caught up with them, and from the interrogation of Usama and his cohorts, Rex gathered enough information to conclude that the strings were pulled from America to get Usama to arrange the ambush. Rex also extracted from them the confession that the ambush was set up with the sole purpose to kill him and that he was presumed dead in the attack. Therefore, he'd elected to stay 'dead', take an extended vacation, and eventually determine who did it and why. He'd take care of that grudge later, when he knew more, and that was where Rehka's computer skills and Usama's money came in.

Soon after walking off the reservation and starting a new life in India, another bad guy, Prince Mutaib bin Faisal bin Saud, had offended Rex's sensibilities by buying plea-sure wives on the human trafficking market. Rehka, in fact, was one of the victims. Rex had learned of her possible fate from her father, whom Rex had met by chance. Rex had investigated, found her, and taken her out of Saudi Arabia after dispatching Mutaib, who was not only into human trafficking but also an unscrupulous international weapons dealer.

During her rescue, Rex learned that Rehka was an IT specialist, and after he'd returned her to her family, he proposed to hire her to break into the hard drives, locate and secure the cash hidden in secure accounts all over the world, and help him administer it for the benefit of the victims of both bad guys.

Some of the hard drives he acquired from Usama and Mutaib contained the information about their business deal-ings including the names and details of their contacts. Those hard drives he'd placed in safe deposit boxes in a few banks in Mumbai.

Rehka had contacted him just as his previous adventure in Thailand was winding down and reported that she'd found and secured all the ill-gotten money from both Usama's and Mutaib's records. Now, what did he want her to do with it?

From Usama, Rex had liberated cash, gold, gemstones, and computer hard drives containing the whereabouts and keys to retrieving secure bank accounts. He had no idea how much money was in Usama's or Mutaib's accounts.

Tonight, after depositing his luggage and Digger's gear at the studio apartment where he stayed, he intended to lay in some food and other supplies, take Rehka out to a nice dinner, and then get down to business the next day.

A few hours later, Rex and Rehka were enjoying the planned dinner, while Digger had been left at the apartment with his favorite toy, a Kong. The Kong was a hard-rubber item shaped a little like a snowman, with a hole running from the top of the snowman's head to the bottom. The hole could be stuffed with treats, and when Digger had finished teasing those out, he would pick the Kong up with his mouth and toss it. Because of its unusual shape, it bounced unpredictably, which delighted Digger as he chased and pounced on it. It would be good enough to keep him occupied until Rex had returned Rehka to her apartment after their dinner and gone back to his own in time for Digger's last walk of the night.

At dinner, Rex and Rehka caught up with the minutia of their lives. Rehka asked how he'd enjoyed Thailand, and Rex asked after their mutual friend, Aarav Patel, a Mumbai policeman who'd helped him while he was searching for Rehka's whereabouts. Rex watched her closely as she gave an animated anecdote about Aarav's children. She and Aarav's wife had become fast friends on her return to Mumbai, and the couple frequently had her over for dinner. He was happy to see how well she was doing emotionally after her ordeal in Saudi Arabia.

Rehka explained that she hadn't felt competent to advise Rex on the investment and distribution of his newly-gained wealth. She knew a little of what he wanted to do with it, because they'd discussed it before. But, acting independently as he expected her to, she'd researched until she found a discreet attorney who was also a financial planner.

"I haven't contacted him yet. I've been waiting for your

arrival so that I can show you what I've found, and after that, if you want to talk to him, I'll set up a meeting."

Rex appreciated her initiative and told her so. She was shaping up to be one of the best support assets he'd ever had, and that included the members of the CRC team that had backed him up on missions. When he'd 'gone rogue', his intention was to leave his profession behind, and he hadn't anticipated the need for his own team ever again.

Later, when he got back to his apartment and went walking with Digger along the dark streets to a nearby park where he could let his buddy off leash to run and do his thing, Rex reflected on the events of the past year. Nothing could have prepared him for the life he had now. He'd been afraid of dogs—a closely-held secret rooted in his child-hood. He'd been a highly-efficient black ops operator for CRC. Then he'd become a vagrant, but as much as he was not looking for it, it seems as if trouble had a habit of finding him.

He was enjoying his newfound freedom and his friend-ship with Digger. But in the back of his mind he knew at some stage he would have to leave his new life behind. He was not in a hurry to do it, but finally he would have to contact the Old Man and admit he was alive. If he did that, did it mean he'd go back to doing what he was best at in behalf of a country that might have betrayed him?

Digger interrupted his thoughts by returning from his own mission and leading Rex to the evidence, which Rex picked up in a plastic bag and deposited in the nearest waste receptacle on the way back to his apartment.

Well, I guess I'll think about that tomorrow.

Chapter Three

Mumbai, India

The next morning, he prepared a simple breakfast for himself, fed Digger his kibble mixed with some boiled eggs and a small tin of tuna in olive oil, and showed up at Rehka's apartment with Digger shortly after nine a.m.

He kissed her lightly on the cheek then unleashed Digger who immediately went over to Rehka to greet her with a wagging tail and a soft yelp as she scratched his ears. With a beaming smile, she said, "Welcome Digger. You can sit and lie anywhere you want."

She made a cup of tea for Rex and herself before they sat down, and she showed him how she used Usama and Mutaib's little notebooks in which they kept their encryption keys and pass phrases to access the hard drives and the various secret numbered offshore accounts.

She explained how, once she'd gotten access to the hard drives, it was not too difficult to get to the various secret bank accounts. Obviously, Usama and Mutaib had not been entirely paranoid about security. Maybe it was because they thought they were untouchable.

Rehka began by summarizing. There were three types of accounts.

First, money in bank accounts in their names in their own countries, i.e. Afghanistan and Saudi Arabia. That money was untouchable. There'd be tracers on the accounts against someone trying to access them, and in any case, the accounts would've been frozen while their owners' estates were being wound up.

Second, as Rex had presumed, there was money in nameless but numbered accounts in tax havens. Rehka had discovered secret accounts in financial institutions from Germany, Switzerland, and Luxembourg, none of which surprised Rex. However, there were others in such widely scattered areas as Hong Kong, Dubai, and Singapore. It seemed the demand for places where one could hide money from one's government, thanks to the globalization of economy and finance, had proliferated to include nations that weren't even dreamed of in the 1930s, when the Swiss had pioneered the strictest banking secrecy act in the world at that time.

As it turned out, from Mutaib Rex had liberated about fifty million US, which was deposited in numbered accounts to which no one without the number and security pass-phrases could get access. This was apart from the million and half US worth of gold coins and cash he took when he'd killed Mutaib.

Among Mutaib's assets were a handful of warehouses, spread across the world, packed with the stock of his trade —bullets and guns, rocket-propelled grenades, and such. These Rex would leave in place until he could go around and blow them all up. For now, leaving them to corrode away in leak-prone buildings was probably the safest option for the people living in those areas where their devious leaders, Mutaib's clients, had cornered the market on war, strife, senseless violence, drug smuggling, ethnic cleansing, and other 'peace-loving' activities.

Mutaib also had a luxury, mega-yacht cruising around the Mediterranean. This yacht, they discovered, was registered in the name of a shell company, and it took a bit of hacking and online detective work to discover that Mutaib actually owned the shell company. The company was registered in Luxembourg.

Rex was quite interested in this asset—in the back of his mind he had the idea that it would be nice to have it to cruise around Europe, off the grid. But for now, he didn't have a clue how to go about getting the ownership transferred. However, there was no urgency to get it done as it seemed Mutaib had arrangements in place with a timeshare company who had been managing and maintaining it while using it to cart people around European port cities on luxury holidays. The proceeds after costs were deposited into a secret numbered account in the Caymans.

There were also other tangible assets, some of which were inaccessible because they were publicly known, like homes and furnishings, vehicles, jewelry, and art works—all the trappings of a wealthy lifestyle.

"There might be others," Rehka said, "with possibilities for liquidation, since they'd been carefully hidden in similar fashion as the ownership of the yacht."

Rex asked her to investigate those, and unravel the complicated trail of ownership when she had some spare time. She'd discovered the assets through notes on the hard-drive records, references to this building or that warehouse full of goods. Knowing what to look for would make it easier.

As for Usama's wealth, it was mindboggling to learn that the man held in excess of forty-five million US in numbered offshore accounts. His net worth was somewhere north of seventy million, depending on how the non-cash assets were to be liquidated.

All these financial matters were a novel experience for Rex, and to be honest, utterly bewildering.

Rex had never had any other job than being a soldier, a Special Forces operator and assassin. He'd never had to worry about money. What he inherited from his parents he'd liquidated into cash and left in the bank. Most of the time, he didn't even have an idea how much money he had. He never had a need for a lot of money. The military had paid him, housed, and fed him. Later, CRC paid him, and they, too, provided food, shelter, and everything else he needed.

Save for the few thousand dollars per year he spent when he was on R and R, all of what he earned from CRC, which were not insignificant amounts, went into his savings accounts. A large part of the money he earned from CRC was placed in untraceable offshore accounts with the purpose to secure for an abundant retirement fund—if he survived the hazards of his profession for long enough to retire and enjoy it.

In short, Rex's financial experience was limited to checking his bank accounts online and withdrawing small amounts every now and then. But for security reasons, even that he hadn't done since he went rogue. By now, he had no idea exactly how much money of his own he had—by his rough calculations it could've been somewhere in the order of four million.

Nevertheless, he couldn't touch that money. Doing so would've immediately set off alarms and alerted the CIA and CRC FININT staff. Besides, there was a very good chance that all that money would have been frozen while his estate was being wound up. Having no will and no family, that money would probably end up in government's coffers once Rex had been missing long enough to be declared dead. Seven years, he thought. On more than one occasion he wanted to kick himself for not making a last will and testament when he had the chance to do so.

Damn, I could've made it plain and simple; distribute my estate in equal shares to the families of those who were killed while on missions with me. That money could've gone to the families of Frank Millard, Trevor Madigan, and the others who were slaughtered in that ambush.

Well, the US government can shove that four million into a dark place. With Usama's thirty million at my disposal I'll rectify my mistake. I'd only have to figure out how to get the money to their relatives without blowing my own cover.

He'd heard about rich people's worries being different from ordinary people's—their biggest worry being how to best use and invest their money, to make more, and to safeguard it. With all this *acquired* money and not knowing what to do with it, he was beginning to understand what the 'unfortunate' rich people had to go through.

After a few days of going through all this stuff, Rex had made up his mind. For now, there was no need to move the money out of the secured accounts. He and Rehka were the only people on the planet who would be able to get access to it.

Mutaib's money would be transferred to different banks in India and held in trust for the seven escapees, to be distributed as needed by Rehka. Her share would be handed to her in a lump sum, so she could invest it as she chose. The rest would be divided equally between the trust accounts of the remaining six women who he rescued with Rehka. The money would keep them in adequate funds for the rest of their lives.

When it came to Usama's money, Rex would take out four million and transfer it to the various accounts he'd already set up in various banks in India. This sum represented the amount he, at last check, thought he had in his American and offshore accounts. The rest he intended to distribute among the teammates who'd perished in Usama's ambush, once he could figure out how to do it without drawing any attention to himself.

Four days of studying the financial wheeling and dealing of bad guys was utterly tiring. There were times during all of it when he would have been happy to be dropped off with a fifty-pound backpack and bottle of water in the Arizona desert thirty miles from base and told to walk back, rather than sit through this. Even a few skirmishes with a bunch of terrorists had more allure than this stuff.

How the hell can any person do this stuff day in and day out and remain sane?

But, finally, he was free to continue his history tour of the world. He had to admit, it was nice to be able to spend what he wanted and not worry about where the next dollar was coming from.

After saying goodbye to Rehka while having lunch at a street café, Rex looked down at Digger and said, "My friend, you and I are going to Peru. We're going to have a look at the land of the Incas."

Digger looked at him as if to say, "Where is that?"

"Yeah, I guess you didn't pay attention in dog school during the geography lesson. But don't you worry, I'll get us there. I can promise you it's going to be much better than what you went through the last two weeks. Well, to be honest, actually anything would be better than the last two weeks."

Digger took the last piece of chicken Rex offered him, sat down, and looked down the street and back at Rex while licking his lips as if to say, "Ready when you are, buddy."

Chapter Four

Vanuatu, South Pacific

Although his sojourn in Peru was quite educational, it had turned out not to be as relaxing as Rex would have liked. Also, there was an encounter with a very beautiful Peruvian girl whom he wouldn't have minded spending more time with. But she was wise enough to show him the door once she got to know him better. Not that he did anything unseemly, but because she could see he was a restless soul who was not ready to settle down yet. Admittedly, he couldn't fault her on that. She was right—he wasn't ready to settle down yet. Not until he had dealt with those who betrayed him and his men.

In a bid to get away from anywhere that might have a potential for trouble and stress, Rex decided to stay in the southern hemisphere and visit a place that didn't even have much history to collect. A resort island, or to be exact, an island country whose only industry was tourism. From

Lima, he and Digger flew to Sydney, Australia, about six hundred miles south of Brisbane, Digger's birthplace and where he'd been reared and trained, and from there to Vanuatu.

Rex had heard of the place, knew more or less where it was, but nothing more. During his final days in Peru, while contemplating where to go next, he'd read an article online about the Vanuatu Islands and what an idyllic place it was. Swayed by the pictures and videos online, on a whim, Rex decided that's exactly what he and Digger needed—a lazy holiday on a subtropical island in the South Pacific. He did a bit of online research and learned that Vanuatu was a mostly French-speaking range of islands off the east coast of Australia, almost close enough to Digger's first home and if the wind came from the right direction, for the dog to have smelled it from there.

In the 1880s, France and the United Kingdom each claimed parts of the archipelago, resulting in some contention that was finally settled in 1906, when the two nations agreed on a framework for jointly managing the group of islands as the New Hebrides. An independence movement arose in the 1970s, and the Republic of Vanuatu was founded in 1980. The South Pacific Ocean nation was made up of roughly eighty islands stretching a little over eight-hundred miles in length.

The history of Vanuatu wasn't as interesting to Rex as his usual fare, but he'd been disappointed in previous trips as to their rest and relaxation, since everywhere he'd gone since the ambush in Afghanistan had presented him with crimes and injustices he'd felt compelled to sort out. So, he thought, *what better place to find peace than a resort destination with no reason to be of interest to terrorists and crime bosses?*

There were, however, indigenous tribes to visit and the Melanesian culture to observe. There were also opportunities to enjoy scuba diving at coral reefs, underwater caverns, and wrecks such as the WWII-era troopship SS President Coolidge. The latter was a piece of history Rex hadn't previously known of, supporting his contention that the study of history in American was sorely lacking.

He spoke fluent French. He'd get along just fine. So, on the spur of the moment, but always careful about his identity, he put his Peruvian trip's identification away and became Rowan Donnelly, effectively disappearing among the legion of South Pacific islands.

Rex had considered exploring Australia before going on to Vanuatu, but two things prevented him from doing so. First, the country was vast, the sixth largest country on earth after Canada, China, the USA, and Brazil. "We might be the smallest continent, but we are definitely the world's biggest island," the Aussies are often heard saying.

To properly explore it would involve months, probably a year to eighteen months to do it any justice. Not what he had in mind right now. Apart from the duration of such a trip, he knew by now that the longer he stayed in one place the more opportunity there was to get caught up in some drama. And then there was the fact that Australia was known as the land of 'mosts': most deadly insects, most poisonous snakes, arthropods, reptiles, and ocean dwellers. Hot enough to boil your blood in a desert where no water exists… no thanks. This was supposed to be a vacation, not a survival challenge.

"But don't despair Digger, one day I'll take you back home for a visit."

Seriously, though, he would have loved to explore Australia for a year or more. But Australia's population of twenty-four million was a fraction of India's. What were the odds he'd bump into a CRC operative who knew him? It was a silly question until he thought about the close call in India, when he'd literally nearly bumped into Josh Farley and the mysterious woman with him.

Therefore, he didn't go through customs in Sydney, in fact he didn't even leave the boarding area while waiting for the puddle-jumper to Port Vila, the capital of Vanuatu. He couldn't help but smile when one of his fellow travelers at Sydney airport told him, "Vanuatu is the place where rich Aussies go to visit their money." He learned then that Vanuatu was another one of the world's many tax havens.

He'd reserved a hut with access to a pristine beach on Fatumara Bay, just on the outskirts of town. While there'd be other people there, he didn't expect to encounter many of them—only the inhabitants of the other huts belonging to the resort.

I can deal with that.

Besides, he wasn't a sun-worshipper, though his dark-pigmented skin could take it. He was more likely to be playing with Digger in the early morning, just as the sun came up, or putting him through his training paces in the rainforest areas a few miles away. The only real chance of meeting too many people would be at the restaurants at night. But if he didn't like them, he could always use one of his many languages as a barrier.

He also thought that the island would be a good place to hone his own physical condition. Only sixteen miles from his hut to the opposite side of the island, and at its widest only about twenty-seven miles, the island would afford excellent opportunities for hikes. One of the activities he'd been looking forward to was playing hide-and-seek with Digger. Not him hiding from the dog, which would have been futile even if he blindfolded Digger and not much of a game, but training the dog to hide from him. That would be more of a challenge.

He'd started playing that game with Digger a few months ago and was stumped to see how quickly his four-legged friend caught on to how the game was played and to stay in hiding no matter how much Rex tried to bribe him to show himself.

Of course, the Kong would give both Digger and him hours of entertainment, as would the Frisbee. He'd enjoy Frisbee catch-and-fetch on the beach, hiding the Kong and letting Digger find it, even burying it and learning how deep he could bury it and Digger still finding it.

Then there was swimming. That was another eyeopener for Rex, Digger's love of water. At times when it was hot and there was a swimming pool or any open stretch of water, he had his hands full to keep Digger out of it. His favorite was a swim in the ocean. It was a treat to watch Digger bark and growl at the waves and the foam, and it was sometimes only with a lot of effort that he could persuade the dog to come out of the water again.

There were some potentially deadly hazards in the ocean, but he'd learn if the bay was all right for swimming. If not, maybe there'd be lakes or streams in the rainforest.

Rex figured he could entertain himself for at least a couple of weeks, maybe even three or four. Then he'd explore the other islands in the chain, and maybe interview some elderly indigenous people in interior villages before making the trip to Europe, specifically Italy, he'd been promising himself for some time now.

Therefore, to the question of how long he'd be staying at the resort, he'd answered, "Until further notice." They hadn't seemed to mind the imprecision.

Chapter Five

Fatumara Bay, Port Vila, Vanuatu

"Jacqui, are you up? Come on, let's walk to the market. I want to buy more jewelry."

Margot opened her eyes. "No, Ida, I'm still in bed. I'm tired. Go on without me."

Margot Lemaire hadn't understood why she was still so tired. She was always full of energy and on the go. Yes, she'd been exhausted after the whirlwind campaign, and the trip to get here had been long. She'd had to sneak out of Paris, visit with her brother long enough to be sure she'd successfully eluded the press, then travel by train to Italy, where she'd boarded a plane to Sydney. When she'd finally arrived in Port Vila, she'd slept nearly around the clock.

But that had been nearly a week ago, and she still hadn't adapted. Each day, she slept until nearly ten a.m. It simply wasn't like her—she'd always been an early riser.

Her new friend, Ida Engberg, to whom she'd given the false name, Jacqui Madrolle, under which she'd checked in, was a bundle of energy. Margot wasn't sure the woman even understood the meaning of holiday. She was always on the go, lots of fun, but Margot's energy wasn't up to par.

And now she knew why.

It was because of that, that she wanted to stay in bed forever, not face the discovery she'd made last night, but her new-found friend was going to *make* her face the day.

Maybe it's best if I'm busy, it will keep my mind off it until I can get confirmation. Are there any doctors on this island?

They'd met on the day Margot arrived. Ida was as tall as Margot, but almost the opposite in every other physical aspect. Her hair was the palest blonde, and her eyes a shade of blue which reminded Margot of the color of the interior of an iceberg. They'd met on the beach, and she told Margot she was from Sweden.

Ida was an open book, prattling on in adequate French about a breakup with a stupid boyfriend.

"We've been living together for two years, and he still doesn't want to let me meet his parents. I've had enough. He's not serious about me. I think he's just using me for my cooking skills." Ida trailed off in a peal of laughter, but Margot was sure she could see the pain in her eyes.

It lulled her into sharing her own pain. "I understand. I'm here to think about my future, too. I also have a lover, though we can't move in together. He's married."

Ida's eyes grew big and round. "Married! Oh, my goodness, how did you get into that situation?"

Margot smiled, unwilling to get into the details. "Stupid, isn't it? Let's talk about something else. It's too depressing. We are in paradise, let's make the best of it."

"What shall we do?" Ida asked.

That had been the beginning of a holiday friendship. Margot didn't suppose it would last beyond the vacation, but it was pleasant to have girl talk for the duration. She'd had little opportunity for that in her capacity as a campaign manager and knew it wouldn't be any different when she went back to her duties in France.

Her thoughts returned to Ida's urging that she get up and go to the market. By now, Ida had marched into her bedroom and pulled away the mosquito net. "Come on, lie abed. The day is getting hotter. I want to go while it's still cool. Up with you, now."

Margot was laughing and trying to cover herself with her sheet, while Ida pulled at it with surprising strength. Finally, Ida let go and said, "I'm going to start your shower. Get. Up."

"Slave driver. Okay, okay, I'm getting up."

———

Ida laughed again and stepped into the adjacent bathroom, quickly scanning the room as she turned on the water.

Ida was also not who she pretended to be, and her story of a breakup with a stupid boyfriend was just that—a story. She didn't have a boyfriend, not for a very long time. Truth be told, anyone who had been in a relationship with her for any length of time was inclined to put running shoes on and go for a long run and never come back.

Ida's heart started racing when she spotted the little blue and white box in the wastebasket. She stepped to it quickly and gingerly pulled out the little cylindrical item that told the rest of the story that Jacqui had not divulged. She could not believe her fortune. An evil grin broke across her lips.

Margot Lemaire aka Jacqui Madrolle is pregnant.

Ida knew much more about Margot than she could've imagined. Margot would've been horrified to know not only did Ida know her real name, she also knew Margot was the brilliant campaign manager who'd steered Giles Aguillard into office. Ida's employers' body language experts made an in-depth study of the interactions between Margot and Giles Aguillard during the campaign and were convinced there was more than just a working relationship between the two of them. By tapping her phone, they learned about Margot's Vanuatu holiday plans and tasked Ida to get tangible evidence of the relationship, which they intended to use to blackmail the new President of France.

When Ida was sent to get more information, her employer knew it was a long shot but was prepared to spend the money on it. He hoped to get an incriminating recording at best. What Ida was staring at was so much more than a taped slip of the tongue, this was the ultimate proof.

Pregnant! How juicy! Aguillard the family man, an adulterer. How will he spin this one? This is better than I could have hoped for, and it explains why she sleeps all the time.

She slipped the testing kit into her pocket but left the wrapping in the bin. Women who were happy about their pregnancies usually keep it as a memento. Lemaire had thrown hers away.

If I can now just get her to bare her soul to me and tell me herself that Aguillard is the father so that I can record it… Well, I can only try…

"Come on, Lazy! Your bath awaits," she called, giggling. The giggle was genuine, but the reason was wicked.

Margot showered while Ida waited outside the hut on a covered veranda that was bigger than the dwelling and served as a gathering space for guests, since the hut itself consisted of the bedroom, attached bath, and a tiny kitchen. The tropical climate of Vanuatu lent itself to such a casual arrangement, averaging between eighty and eighty-eight Fahrenheit for a high temperature, and never lower than sixty for a low. Ocean breezes kept it cool in the hottest part of the day, and the thatched roof kept off the frequent rain. One could not have asked for a more perfect year-round climate.

When Margot finally appeared, dressed in a strapless sundress and wearing a big, floppy, straw hat she'd bought at the market on her first day, Ida gazed at her closely.

No sign of distress. I wonder if he told her he'd leave his wife for her. They always do. Or maybe she intends to stay here until the child is born?

Ida chattered about this and that as they strolled to the market, looking for her opportunity to learn more about Margot's pregnancy and her plans. The opportunity came as they wandered among the stalls. A young island woman was nearby, with her newborn baby carried in a sling tied in front of her. Ida started a conversation with the woman.

"Your baby is so sweet," she cooed.

"*Merci beaucoup, Mademoiselle,*" the woman said, with a shy duck of her head and a fond gaze at her baby. "She is two weeks old today."

Ida glanced at Margot. "I just love babies," she remarked. "Would you… May I…?"

"Of course," the young mother said. She cradled the baby in one arm and untied the sling with the opposite hand. When she had the sling loose, she scooped the baby into Ida's waiting arms.

Ida, who in fact loathed babies, nevertheless gave a credible performance, smiling at the infant and making silly baby talk. She handed Margot her cellphone and asked her to take a photo.

She turned to Margot. "Don't you want to hold her?

She's so sweet! Give me your phone, I'll take a photo of you two."

Margot had turned pale and appeared to be in discomfort. "I... No, I don't think so. Sorry, I don't feel well. I don't know what it is, but I don't want to infect the baby with it."

Ida pretended to be reluctant to hand the baby back, but finally did, and she slipped her hand into her market bag and brought out a handful of Vatu, the local currency. As the woman retied the sling, Ida stuffed the cash in with the baby, earning a smile from the young mother.

"For her wedding someday. Thanks for letting me hold your baby, she is so *cute*," Ida said.

As they turned away, Ida asked with apparent innocence, "Don't you like babies?"

Margot answered, "Yes, I do, but as I said, I may be coming down with something. I probably need to go and see a doctor. I hope there's one here that will see me."

Ida had to use a lot of restraint to contain her sudden urge to laugh and tell Margot that pregnancy was not contagious.

Before they returned to their huts for a midday siesta, the two women asked a passer-by and were referred to a women's health clinic located conveniently on the way back to the resort. Margot urged Ida to go ahead while she ducked in to make an appointment.

Ida protested she'd wait, but Margot insisted, and finally Ida had to go to avoid inciting suspicion. After all, they'd been friends for only four days. Too much concern would be overkill. She waved cheerily and said she hoped the doctor would see her and that she would feel better soon.

At the clinic, Margot was disappointed to learn that unless it was an emergency, she'd have to make an appointment and come back. The doctor was fully booked for almost a week. She was anxious to get to the bottom of this, though the test and her lack of energy should have been enough confirmation. She was pregnant, but it wouldn't be official until a doctor had said so—until then, she'd prefer to live in denial.

Only five minutes behind Ida, she trudged back to the resort, head down, lost in thought.

What will I do if it's true? Giles will be destroyed, his marriage will be destroyed, the party will be destroyed. We've campaigned on family values. Hypocrites! Both of us. And infinitely stupid.

She began to weep silently as she walked with a duel raging in her mind.

It's a disaster!

If it became public, it would certainly cost her the career she'd dreamed of, and it would certainly bring down Giles' presidency. Giles was the right man for the job. She believed that. He would carry out his predecessor's promises, the ones she'd believed so fervently were necessary for the good of France.

The other party… No, I couldn't do anything to harm Giles. Abortion?

I'm a Catholic, a Christian, I will not kill my child… no matter what, that's not the answer. But what is?

Stop fretting and wait until the doctor tells you you're pregnant or not. Maybe it's nothing. The strain of the campaign, the travel. Those DIY tests are notoriously inaccurate. Maybe I'm coming down with the flu.

A sudden urge had her turning into the tall brush beside the path, where she vomited.

Yes, that could be flu. It could also be… No, don't go there.

She felt a little better after that, though her mouth tasted awful. Margot quickened her step. The only relief for the sour taste in her mouth was a good tooth-brushing and some cool water.

I'd better not try to tan this afternoon. But Ida will demand to know why not. I'd better rest, and maybe it's best not to eat lunch. Maybe I'll feel better later.

The only saving grace is I am the only one who knows about it and who knows who the father is.

Chapter Six

Fatumara Bay, Port Vila, Vanuatu

Nearly a week after Margot had arrived at Port Vila, she and Ida were getting along very well. Just last night, Ida was crying in Margot's arms. The boyfriend she'd run away from and planned to break up with when she got home had dumped her, by text message, no less, the brute! It was one thing to be the dumper, and quite a different thing to be the dump-*ee*.

Ida was devastated.

Margot had cried empathetic tears and comforted her new friend the best way she could, with soft words of encouragement and wine. Pleading she still wasn't feeling well, Margot herself had abstained from the wine. She blamed it on unfamiliar food and a delicate stomach.

"Ida, maybe he had a feeling you were going to break up with him, and he just did it first to feel better about himself. You know you're too good for him. Why be hurt over this? Look at the positive side. It saves you from a painful meeting with him."

"But no one has ever broken up with me before. This feels awful, Jacqui. How can I look my friends in the face when I go home?"

"Just tell them you broke up with him. How are they to know it isn't the truth?"

Ida made a sour face. "Because he'll tell them, the bastard. He'll turn all my friends against me. I can't ever go home."

Margot had laughed, earning a look of near-hatred from the distraught Ida. She backpedaled quickly. "I'm sure you'll be able to go home. But why would you want to? This is paradise, truly. I may stay here myself."

Ida's tears had dried in an instant. "Truly? You'd give up your home and live here?"

Margot had told her part of the truth about her family, only keeping the names consistent with what she'd said before. Ida knew she was from a wealthy family, the only daughter of parents who'd inherited vineyards and two wineries from *their* parents, uniting two winegrowing families who'd been neighbors for more than a century. She'd mentioned that she'd studied for a career, since it was her brother who would inherit the operations and even now ran them. She'd told Ida that she and her brother were very close and implied that they, she and her brother, were both well to do.

Ida had been reticent about her family, though. Margot thought it might be because Ida's family was not distinguished like hers. It didn't matter to her. She was egalitarian, not snobbish about the lower economic classes at all.

Ida wasn't on the beach this morning. *Must be an errand in town*, Margot thought. Ida's company had been so constant that she'd had no opportunity to read the books she'd brought with her. Fortunately, they were all on her eReader, so no one would have to wonder why a young woman on holiday in a tropical paradise was reading an economics book by a French author—in English.

Once she had the shade situated so the eReader's screen wouldn't have too much glare, Margot leaned back in her chaise lounge and propped one elbow on a wooden armrest. Next to her, just outside her peripheral vision, was a tiny redwood folding table, just the right size for the cheese, grapes, and sparkling water she'd brought out for a snack. Deeply immersed in her reading, oblivious to her surroundings, she reached for the water without looking and shrieked when her hand encountered something furry.

With arms and legs flailing, she tried to scramble out of the chaise, upsetting it sideways in the process. She dropped her eReader and oriented herself on hands and knees. A glance in the direction of the little table showed the reason for her scare—a big, shaggy, black dog gulping down the last bit of cheese on the plate, readying itself to go for the grapes. When the dog saw her looking at it, it sat down nicely and offered her a big dog-style grin, with mouth open wide and tongue lolling out. The look on its face was so happy, she couldn't help but laugh.

"Well, hello, *Monsieur Chien*! Who are you, and who invited you to my party?"

She pushed herself to her feet and walked toward the dog, who remained seated and tracked her approach with intelligent eyes. When she could reach him, she dropped again to her knees and petted him with her right hand, while her left dug in vain in the thick fur for a collar and tag. She sat back on her folded knees in the sand and asked, "What shall I do with you, *eh*? You are a handsome fellow. Someone must be looking for you, though. You don't seem to be a stray. And by the way," she remarked more severely, "are you supposed to be eating cheese and grapes? I've heard it isn't good for dogs. Well, I actually know for French dogs, it's bad. But then, you don't look French to me."

That was when a deep voice said from behind her, "Only if they're lactose intolerant. But this rascal knows better than to beg food, let alone steal it."

She looked up in surprise, then quickly turned her face away. The fellow had spoken in flawless French. He could be paparazzi. Her anonymity was in danger!

"I'm sorry about this, miss." The man was righting her chair and dusting the sand off her eReader. Then he scolded the dog. "Digger, for shame! Apologize to the lady!"

To her amusement, the dog hung its head and belly-crawled toward her, putting its chin on her leg.

"Apologies do not come with drool, Digger. Get your head off her."

The dog moved its head, crawled a few inches closer, and stuck his nose under her arm. She laughed out loud.

"Monsieur, I think your dog is laughing at you. Or perhaps at me."

"He's definitely having a good time. My apologies again. He's usually better behaved. He must sense that you like dogs."

"Indeed, I do. I was raised with Briards. This fellow reminds me a bit of my own dog, except that my Hugo was blond, not black, and he had longer fur."

"Digger's a Dutch Shepherd. Believe it or not, he's well-trained. I don't know what came over him."

Margot accepted the man's extended hand to pull her to her feet. "Rowan Donnelly," he said.

He politely let go of her hand, but his gaze stayed on her face. She detected no recognition.

"Jacqui Madrolle. Where are you from, Monsieur Donnelly? Your French is excellent, but that is not a French name."

"My ancestors are from Ireland. It's an old family name. Not so common anymore. I'm told it used to be O'Donnelly, but you know what it's like these days—everything gets abbreviated or 'acronymed', so I might end up with the surname OD or just D sometime in the future."

She started giggling.

He hadn't exactly told her where he was from, but she had either not noticed the evasion, or noticed it and over-looked it, or noticed it but didn't care.

"Have you studied in France?"

"You're referring to my accent, I assume. I've never been to France. I can't explain it, but when I learn a language, I take on the accent of my teacher."

"What an amazing trait. I wish I was able to do that. I am told my English and Italian accents are horrible."

With his last statement, Rex Dalton lied with equanimity. He'd been to France, all right, but never in an official capacity. He'd done nothing there that he could discuss with the pretty woman Digger had introduced him to. Giving her a false name as well, was for security—he didn't consider it a lie.

Rex would have liked to stay and talk with the woman. She wasn't as stunning as some of the women he'd met on his adventures, but something about her led him to believe she'd be interesting. Her eyes kept flicking to her chaise and the eReader he'd placed on it when he picked them up.

"Again, I apologize for my dog. Perhaps we can chat another time?" He made the overture a question with a slight rise in tone, probing for the reaction that would let him know whether she cared to become acquainted or not.

"That would be nice." When she smiled, her eyes lit up, and it transformed her facial features into something very attractive.

"I hope to see you soon, then." Rex pointed at Digger and said, "You. Home. You're in trouble, mister."

Digger got up, shook off the sand, all over Jacqui and Rex, and trotted away, leaving them open-mouthed in astonishment, and in Rex's case, indignation.

"I'm so sorry, I don't know what to say," Rex muttered. "It looks like he's set on embarrassing me today."

"It's nothing. Please don't worry. I love dogs." to Rex's amazement, Jacqui was still smiling. She gave a wave goodbye as she picked up her chair and eReader and headed toward one of the little huts in the resort. Rex made a note of which one, before turning to catch up with Digger.

When he did, he stopped the dog and made Digger turn to face him. He waved his index finger at him. "What was that all about, you scoundrel? You have never behaved that way before. You've humiliated me."

Digger must have sensed that this rebuke was not a serious one, so, his only response was a grin that Rex imagined was smug, as if he were saying, "Well, you needed to meet a nice girl, didn't you?"

Answering the imagined question, Rex said aloud, "No, I didn't."

Digger tilted his head. That definitely meant, "What are you on about? I can't read your mind, stupid."

Rex determined that there was simply no way to punish

the dog. In the first place, the incident was now in the past, and Digger wouldn't associate it with any punishment, that was beside the fact that Digger's body language told Rex he believed he did nothing wrong.

Secondly, there was no kind of punishment he could think of that would fit the 'crime'. That's if it was a crime to begin with—to be guilty of a crime one has to have a guilty conscience, and Digger didn't display any of that. On the contrary, what he displayed was that he'd engineered a brilliant plan to introduce the leader of his pack to the nice woman on the beach and that was deserving of praise, not reprimand.

At the end of his musings Rex looked at Digger and said, "Well, okay, you're off the hook, but next time, let's plan it together. You have to understand humans are a bit more subtle than canines. Okay?"

Digger just smiled.

Chapter Seven

Fatumara Bay, Port Vila, Vanuatu

For the next morning, Rex had planned a hike to the interior and another game of hide and seek. Digger was getting better at coming out of hiding when called, even if Rex hadn't found him. Sometimes Rex had the Kong for him, and sometimes not. The secret to training a working dog was to make praise the reward, not food and treats. Rex always made sure to give Digger lavish praise and wait long enough so that Digger couldn't make a connection between his performance and getting a treat.

Though there were plenty of paths to get inland from his hut, Rex wittingly chose the one that led past Jacqui's veranda. He didn't expect to see her out, as it was quite early, but to his delight, she was sitting there with a blonde woman who was about the same age or slightly younger. Both had large mugs in their hands, coffee, he presumed. Jacqui smiled and waved, while the other woman turned to look curiously at him.

He could just imagine what was being said as he and Digger went past, Digger on leash for the trek through the populated areas before they reached the bush. "Who's that?" the blonde woman would be saying. And Jacqui would answer, "Oh, just some man with a rowdy dog. We met on the beach yesterday when his dog helped himself to my food." They would laugh or shake their heads at the thought of the misbehaving dog, and that would be the end of it.

But maybe a game of Frisbee at this end of the beach tomorrow would be entertaining.

Tired from a fifteen-mile round trip and a few hours playing hide and seek in the jungle, Rex and Digger turned in as soon as darkness fell that night.

Rex was now convinced Digger would perform the hiding act perfectly if the need arose. He hadn't been able to find the dog in any of the places he'd hidden. Digger even upped the ante on the game without being told, by climbing a tree and hiding in its broad leaves. Rex had been astonished, but Digger just gave him a look that said, "Well, what else did you expect from a dog genius?"

Digger's talent for climbing trees was one of the things that charmed Rex enough to overcome his childhood fear of dogs, back when Digger was Trevor Madigan's team-mate. It was not as if he could climb trees like a cat or a monkey, but if there were enough low hanging branches and support for him, he did it with relative ease. It had come in handy in several of Rex's adventures since then, and now had a new use. That he'd thought to do it on his own without being commanded to do so gave Rex another level of respect for the dog's intelligence.

"Hmm, Digger, I had my doubts, but now I'm one

hundred percent sure you contrived that 'introduction' to the lovely Jacqui Madrolle on purpose. Didn't you?"

The sigh coming from Digger could only have meant, "Of course I did."

Rex had determined that the bay on which the resort was located was safe, and because of the shark nets, had none of the deadly sea-dwellers of the open ocean on the beachside of the nets. It was time to implement his plans to 'accidentally' bump into Jacqui, so he took the Frisbee and headed with Digger to her end of the beach. Digger insisted on barking at the waves and chasing the receding foam as Rex jogged in the firm sand close to the tide line. But he didn't need to be invited twice to run into the waves with Rex when they came to a likely spot.

Rex laughed out loud at Digger's antics. He'd chase the water as it drew back, and then bark and splash noisily when the next wave lifted him off his feet and deposited him back on the shore. The surf was high enough today that Rex didn't worry about Digger swimming too far out. He always came floating back on the wave, only to run out again, barking madly, as if the sea were taunting him.

After an hour of that kind of fun, Rex had all but forgotten his ulterior motive, even when he enticed Digger out of the water with the Frisbee. He threw it a few times, and Digger dutifully brought it back. On the fourth or fifth throw, though, the wind caught it. Digger was racing to catch it, and Rex caught his breath as he saw the impending disaster—Digger rushing forward, his eyes fixated on the prize.

"Damn, not how I envisaged *this* meeting," Rex mumbled. "I didn't literally mean bump into her…"

It looked as if Digger was unaware of what was about to happen as he took a flying leap at the Frisbee and crashed headlong into Jacqui, who'd come down to the beach, probably to see what all the noise was about.

Jacqui landed flat on her back and Digger on his feet, like a cat. He immediately began wagging his tail, whining, and licking her face, joyful to see his new friend and apologetic all at once. Rex saw the whole thing from twenty yards away and came running through the shifting sand, losing one of his flip-flops in the process.

When he got to her, she said to Digger, "We have to stop meeting like this," and burst into laughter. She was still flat on her back, trying to fend off the sixty-pound Digger, who was determined to show how sorry he was by kissing and licking her face while letting out soft whines.

"Digger!" Rex shouted. To Jacqui, he said as he extended a hand to help her up for the second time in two days, "I really don't have any explanation for this. I'm so sorry."

"Don't blame Digger. He was watching the Frisbee and didn't see me," she told him. "And speaking of which, where did it go?"

Rex looked around and spotted the bright red object lying a few yards away. "Digger, fetch the Frisbee."

Digger trotted off and came back with the disc in his mouth, dropped it at Rex's feet, and gave a soft *woof*. Then, unbidden, he went after the lost flip-flop and brought it, too.

"Are you all right? You took quite a spill," Rex said.

"I'm fine, just a bit shaken up. Maybe I need to walk a bit to see if everything works right." She smiled as she said it, to let him know she was joking.

Rex slipped his foot back into a slobbery flip-flop. As if in accord, he and Jacqui turned and started walking down the beach, toward Rex's hut, with Digger dancing around them in obvious delight. He could see Digger taking Jacqui's feet out from under her again in his enthusiasm.

As they walked with a more sedate Digger at Rex's side and Jacqui on the other, nearer the bay, they chatted about the weather, about Digger's boundless energy, and about when they'd each arrived and what sights they'd seen so far. Jacqui was fascinated by Rex's story of his hike to the center of the island and back the previous day.

"Why hike? Why not just drive?" she asked.

Rex smiled broadly. "For one thing, I haven't rented a car. And for another, I like to hike. And Digger needs the exercise. As you can see, he's a highly energetic dog."

"Indeed. I'm afraid I wouldn't be able to keep up with him. Maybe my friend Ida would, though. She's got lots of energy, which I seem to be lacking." She stopped talking abruptly and then changed the subject, asking Rex what he did when he wasn't vacationing.

"I'm a history teacher on sabbatical, collecting oral history from indigenous people for a travelogue, I think," he said.

"You think?"

"Well, I came into a little money recently, and I've been bumming around, telling myself I'm doing research. But I really have nothing to research for such as a PHD or Masters, unless I write it up for my own pleasure.

"What do you do?"

She looked away from him, across the bay. After a few moments, she said, "I'm thinking about whether to continue in my job or take some time off."

Rex was trained to detect when people were lying, and

that was exactly what Jacqui was doing, at the very least she sidestepped his question. But he was definitely not going to confront her about it. He could only wonder why she did. Besides, he just lied to her, she probably had the right to return the favor, although he didn't get the impression that she picked up on his lie.

Rex smiled, "I can highly recommend time off, if you can afford it," he answered. Then he added, "Sorry, I don't mean to pry."

"It's okay. I do need to work. I can afford a little time off."

Instead of sharing more of her background with him, she immediately began to talk about her friend Ida.

"You must meet her. Sweet girl. She escaped to Vanuatu to contemplate a break up with a boyfriend, and then the poor thing gets a text from the jerk that he's breaking up with her." She hesitated for a moment and then continued. "I'm not telling you anything she wouldn't tell you herself. The girl simply has no filters. She told me about her plan on the first day we met."

Rex thought this Ida was probably much less interesting than Jacqui, but he agreed to have lunch with the two of them the next day. By that time, they'd walked to the rickety fence that separated the resort's private beach from the public beach beyond, turned, and walked back almost to Jacqui's hut.

"I think I'll go in and have some breakfast," she said. "See you tomorrow? You'll come here between one and two?"

"I will," he said, marveling at the casual, hour-long range she'd given him. *Island time*, he thought, *a true laid-back lifestyle*, and he had no problem with it. It was the first time in a long time that he felt relaxed.

He stood there, watching Jacqui's progress toward her hut, until Digger called him back to the present with a soft, questioning *woof.*

"Oh, right. We haven't had breakfast either, have we, boy? Let's go get some."

Digger took off at an easy lope, inviting Rex to chase him. Rex kicked off his flip-flops, paused to pick them up, and then pelted toward Digger as fast as he could in the sand. Digger looked back, saw him coming, and put on speed. Rex was too out of breath to laugh when they reached his hut, but the sight of Digger skidding to a halt and then sitting down as if he'd been waiting for a long time made him laugh anyway.

"Well, mission accomplished," he remarked to Digger, setting down his bowl of kibble and scrambled eggs. "We've met the girl, and she *is* interesting. I wonder what her story is? She's almost as reticent as I am."

Digger made no reply, obviously because he felt he'd done his bit to introduce them, on two occasions. It was for Rex to step up to the plate now.

Chapter Eight

Port Vila, Vanuatu

Rex and Jacqui and Digger, sometimes accompanied by Ida, got to know each other. Jacqui told Rex she was a government employee in France, but she didn't elaborate. Rex sensed it was a bit more revealing than the first day but still not much more, and he kept on wondering what she was hiding and why. Although the thought crossed his mind fleetingly, there was no compelling reason for him to Google her name or ask Rehka to do background research on her.

Rex liked it best when Ida wasn't present, not because he wanted Jacqui all to himself, he just didn't click as well with Ida. And Digger seemed to feel the same about the Swedish woman, preferring Jacqui's attention above Ida's.

Rex introduced Jacqui to reef fishing. Ida wasn't interested, so they were alone out on the boat other than the guide that day. The conversation ranged from Digger, how to fish, the preparation of the catch, and anything else but personal revelations about their backgrounds from either of them. Digger provided plenty of entertainment by barking and snapping at the fish they pulled in. Or rather, that Rex pulled in, because try as she might, Jacqui couldn't land one. She got bites, even hooked a few, but they all got away.

She pouted her lips in mock dejection, "It looks so easy when you do it. Why can't I get it right? Maybe the fish don't like me."

Rex laughed. "What's not to like? I don't think that's the problem. Don't worry, you'll do much better when we go out to a crater lake tomorrow and fish for eel or prawns."

Jacqui immediately latched onto that and told him about all the culinary pleasures she could prepare with either. Rex's catch of the day, a yellowfin tuna, was tagged and released, and the other fish he'd caught would be given to local villagers, as was the custom.

The one thing Jacqui would not do, no matter how Rex and even Ida cajoled and reassured her, was go in the water for a swim. She had an irrational fear of the sea creatures she'd been told about and would not believe that the shark nets offered protection. She told Rex she couldn't bear the anxiety she felt when any of them were in the water.

Rex couldn't remember when the last time was that he'd felt so relaxed and carefree. The days felt as if they flowed into each other as there was always something exciting or relaxing for them to do, including lunch or dinner, or sometimes both, either at restaurants or at Jacqui's little hut. Rex was amazed at Jacqui's ability to put together a gourmet meal with the minimal equipment provided in the hut kitchens. He gained a new appreciation for French cuisine after their successful eel and prawn fishing trip.

Ida joined them often, but from her side also never warmed up to Rex or Digger. The fact that Digger didn't like her much, either, put Rex on alert. Digger was a remarkably good judge of character and Rex knew not to ignore it. So, he decided it would be sensible to remain attentive when she was around.

On the fifth day after Digger knocked Jacqui down while playing Frisbee, Rex learned she wasn't a good sailor. The four of them, including Digger, had booked a yacht to visit one of the nearby islets for a picnic. Jacqui had insisted it was her turn to treat after Rex had taken her on his fishing expeditions.

But unfortunately, the poor woman spent most of the short trip in the head retching her guts out, too embarrassed to just lean over the rail. By the time they landed, she was pale, and a fine sweat shone at her hairline.

"I'm so sorry," she gasped as they went ashore. "I've never had that reaction to a boat ride before." She pressed her lips together and gamely kept up with them, though she appeared to be dreading the trip back. Rex wished they'd gone to a different island, one with air service back to Port Vila. He'd have put her on a plane to spare her the uncomfortable trip back.

Rex was a bit taken aback by Ida's apparent heartlessness. Jacqui's supposed friend paid no attention to her discomfort and made no effort to try and comfort her. He tried to strike a balance between watching out for Jacqui's well-being and not being intrusive about it because of her obvious discomfort about it.

Digger didn't have any such compunction. He stayed at Jacqui's side all day, leaning against her when she was sitting down and staying closely at heel when she was moving. At the picnic, he refused to come to Rex for a treat, which was a first in Rex's memory. Digger was never off his food, but he appeared to be sharing Jacqui's malaise today.

Rex put it down to the dog's remarkable empathy and didn't worry about it.

On the trip back, Jacqui wasn't quite as bad, and she was able to stay on deck and enjoy the breeze. However, she excused herself from their dinner plans, leaving Rex and Ida to share an uneasy dinner together rather than either admitting they'd rather eat alone. At the restaurant, they found little to say to each other, and Ida seemed put out that they'd be seated outdoors to accommodate Digger. For his part, Rex couldn't imagine why anyone would want to be indoors, dog or no dog. He didn't apologize for it.

The next day, Rex and Digger went out for a good long run and to play on the beach in the morning, as had become their habit. Rex spotted Jacqui leaving the hut, but instead of turning toward the beach, she walked off toward town.

Must be market day or something. I wonder why she didn't invite Ida or me for company?

The idle thought was soon lost in the morning's fun. He and Digger went for a swim as usual, and then air-dried as they enjoyed a vigorous game of Frisbee. When the sun grew warm, they headed back to Rex's hut, where they had breakfast, and then Rex checked his email and read for a while.

Digger had a nap.

The plan for the evening was for Rex to provide the meal, but considering Jacqui's expertise in the kitchen, and his cooking skills limited to opening cans and heating stuff in microwaves, he decided not to embarrass himself and rather have it catered, after a fashion.

When he'd showered and let Digger sleep for a while, he went to the market and found a woman from whom he'd purchased prepared food before. He knew it was good, so he asked her to provide a full meal of native dishes and bring it to his hut just before Jacqui was to arrive. Ida had declined the invitation, so it would be just the two of them and Digger.

He was looking forward to the evening. Jacqui had shown herself to be intelligent, witty, and sophisticated. She was good company.

Maybe she'll share a little more about herself. I wouldn't mind learning more. She's someone I could be friends with, not just vacation buddies.

When Jacqui arrived, both Rex and Digger immediately saw something was not right with her. Her eyes were red and swollen, obviously from crying. Digger made a few soft whining sounds and cozied up to her right away.

Clear that she was not her usual sparkling self, Rex asked if everything was all right, but immediately regretted asking.

Stupid question. He chastised himself. It's obvious there is something wrong—why do you even ask?

"Yes, I'm fine," was all she would say.

There you have it. Stupid questions deserve stupid answers.

She reclined in one of the lounge chairs on the veranda while Rex set out the food that had been delivered hot just a few minutes before. As she idly petted Digger and scratched him behind his ears, he showed less attention to the food than he normally would. Instead, he put his head down on her lap and leaned into the chaise, the picture of dejection.

Digger soon had Jacqui smiling, though to Rex it seemed as if the smiles overlaid a deep disquiet she was trying to hide. Digger's behavior lent credence to his theory. The dog kept shifting closer until he was all but lying in her lap, but she didn't seem to mind. From what Rex observed, it seemed as if she found some solace in it.

He couldn't help but wonder if this was a signal from Digger that he'd 'approve' of her as a romantic interest? The dog had his own idiosyncrasies about Rex's relationships, as if he was responsible for screening and approving or disapproving Rex's relationships. For instance, he hadn't shown any such favor to a girl in Thailand with whom Rex wanted to become romantically involved. In fact, he did everything possible to prevent it from happening. The girl in Peru, on the other hand, was a different story, Digger had no problems with her, but *that* girl had ended the relationship herself.

With Digger as a barometer, Rex having learned that it was very important to take note of his canine friend's 'first impressions' of people, he seldom had any issues choosing to be friends only or pursue deeper relationships. That was despite butting heads with the stubborn animal in Thailand. However, this time seemed different. Jacqui hadn't shown any interest in anything more than a casual, vacation friendship. Right from the first day, although always friendly and spontaneous, there was a tacit message from her, 'I'm not available'. Rex didn't press the matter—they'd probably never see each other again after they left Vanuatu, which he felt would be a shame. Not since Italy had he met such a fascinating woman. Still, she seemed so much more distant tonight than on any other occasion. Something was definitely bothering her, despite her assurances that it was not the case.

Rex resolved not to think about women and romance anymore, or anything but the delicious food and tonight's company. He cast about in his mind for something to talk about and hit on the subject of French wine. He'd never seen Jacqui take a drink of wine or anything else alcoholic. To his mind, this was an anomaly—French and no wine was too much of an oxymoron to let it go by without mention. It was like being American without turkey for Thanksgiving.

When he had the table arranged to his satisfaction, he invited Jacqui to move to a chair at the table. Before he sat down, he asked if she cared for anything to drink.

"I have a nice Bordeaux cabernet sauvignon, or juice made with pomelo and naus fruit. Or sparkling water, of course. I don't suppose you'd be interested in beer."

Jacqui smiled, "No, I'm not fond of beer. I'll have the juice, if that's all right."

"Of course."

Rex went into the kitchen and poured a glass of the chilled tropical juice. As he returned and set it down in front of her, he remarked, "Isn't it unusual for a Frenchwoman not to drink wine?"

Jacqui blushed. "I'm trying to cut down," she quipped. "Seriously, though, I've had a bit of an upset stomach since I got here. I thought it was best not to mix wine in with whatever is causing it."

Rex remembered just how upset her stomach had been the day before, on the boat. He didn't think it polite to bring it up or comment any further on it. "I just hope this local meal will agree with you."

"It looks delicious. I'm sure I'll be okay."

Rex changed the subject. "You mentioned you weren't raised in Paris. Did your family live in wine country?"

"Yes, I was raised amidst vineyards. My family have been vintners for centuries. My brother runs the winery now."

It was more than she'd shared before, and Rex congratulated himself on thinking of a subject to carry the conversation for hours.

"How interesting! Tell me more."

While Jacqui regaled Rex with escapades from her childhood, mostly perpetrated by her brother, something mysterious was going on in town without the knowledge of either.

A shadowy figure dressed in black right down to the balaclava that was completely inappropriate for the climate, expertly picked the lock at the women's clinic. The person quickly found the patient records, filed in manila folders with color-coded tabs. A grunt of satisfaction accompanied the discovery. The task would have taken a bit longer if computer hacking had been required, but this doctor apparently hadn't moved to the computerized records that most were now using.

A rapid search through the files revealed the filing system, and after that the record the person was looking for was easily found. While waiting for the copy machine to warm up, the person riffled through the file and found what was needed and took photos of all on his mobile phone before copying them. Each page was carefully put back in order, and the file placed back in the original spot.

The individual even re-locked the door after leaving.

Chapter Nine

Fatumara Bay, Port Vila, Vanuatu

Rex thought he'd successfully brought Jacqui out of her somber mood by the time she was ready to leave. They'd been laughing about her brother's misfortunes as a teen, and even Digger had relaxed a bit. All the signals said she was now okay, at least for the night.

Digger clearly wanted to accompany her back to her hut, but when Rex offered to walk with her, she insisted she'd be fine.

"The moon is so bright, I don't think I'll have any problems. Please don't bother. Thank you for a lovely evening."

"Let Digger walk with you, then. What kind of gentleman would let a lady walk home alone at this time of night?"

"The kind that knows how to take no for an answer," she quipped.

Rex couldn't argue with that. Pressing her any more would be awkward at best, if not a little creepy.

"I'll keep Digger inside, because he's never known how to take no for an answer." He grinned to show he was joking, and Jacqui laughed as she set out.

"*Au revoir*," she called over her shoulder.

"Next time," Rex answered, in English.

The next morning, when Rex woke, his thoughts went to Jacqui immediately. Despite the fact that she seemed to be in better spirits when she left last night, whatever troubled her had not been resolved. He wanted to see for himself whether she'd truly come out of her funk, or if not, whether there was something he could do to help her, but at the same time he was hesitant to put his nose in her business and become a nuisance.

You came here for relaxation, not to interfere in other people's personal matters.

Bullshit. In the past when someone was in trouble, you helped. What's stopping you now?

His better nature won. Digger was restless, too, so even though it was early, Rex called Jacqui to invite her for a walk on the beach. The phone rang but there was no answer. *Maybe the phone is on silent.* He took it as sign that she wanted to be left alone. Nevertheless, he left a message that he was concerned, wondering if she was okay, and asked her to call or text back.

Rex cooled his heels for a while and then bowed to Digger's insistence and went for their run on the beach. On the way back, they went to Jacqui's hut and found no one at home. While standing just outside, he sent her a text.

"You okay? Dinner tonight?"

Still no answer.

Rex took Digger back to his hut and spent the rest of the day reading and brushing up on his Russian and Cantonese by working through a few audio lessons. He waited for a return call or text in vain. He considered calling Ida but reasoned that if Ida hadn't seen or heard from Jacqui either, she probably would have called him. Chances were, they were together, and he'd just be intruding. Finally, still troubled, he and Digger went to sleep.

The next morning, he noticed a text had come in overnight from Jacqui. He was relieved to get a message from her but wanted to kick himself for not hearing the message come in, until he read it and realized it would have made no difference.

"I'll be out of touch for a few days, just taking some time for myself. Please don't worry. I'm keeping my phone switched off. I'll be in touch when I get back."

Rex nodded slowly as the thought crossed his mind, *well, what's a Vanuatu vacation if not taking time for yourself?*

Although he tried to convince himself all was okay with her, he knew something was amiss, and being completely out of touch didn't help either. It was a bit vexing that there was nothing he could do about it. It was her business, and her choice not to accept his offer to help. He had no way to reach her and trying to find her would definitely be stalkerish.

Back and forth his thoughts went, as he paced to match them.

I have no real influence. She's a friend who has something heavy on her mind and doesn't want to talk about it. So, for now, none of your business.

"She's fine, right, Digger?"

But Digger's soft whine was no consolation. In fact, it only served to urge Rex to reason it out and eventually concluded he'd been right in the first place. It was none of his business. Rex was not a fretful person. He couldn't remember when the last time was that he was so restless about anything—not since his teenage years.

Maybe she'd even gone to get away from me. Maybe I'd pried too much.

"You think that's it, Digger? She wanted to get away from us? Or, probably not you, probably just me. I should mind my own business."

Digger responded by getting out his Kong and dropping it at Rex's feet. It took an eccentric bounce and Digger pounced on it as if it had been a rabbit. Rex reached for it to put a treat in it, but Digger grabbed it in his mouth and ran behind the bed.

"Oh, so you want to play keep-away?" Rex grinned and dived under the bed, but Digger was much quicker. He ran back around, tugged on the hem of Rex's shirt, and then dodged out of the way before Rex could grab him.

"Let's take this outside, before we break the people's furniture."

All Digger must've heard was 'outside', and the next thing Rex knew, Digger had bumped his way out the door, running at top speed.

By the time Rex caught up, Digger was rolling in something in the sand. Something stinky, more than likely. Rex said, "What's got into you?"

Digger rolled over on his belly, back legs out, front legs propping him up, and grinned.

That was when Rex finally understood. His goofy dog was trying to distract him from Jacqui. Or more likely, from whatever was bothering him, because Digger couldn't possibly understand it was Jacqui's text that worried him. Could he?

Chapter Ten

Lamap, Malekula Island, Vanuatu

Margot lay on a comfortable bed, with window coverings drawn enough to keep the room semi-dark. The bed was in a room in a guesthouse in Lamap. For the past twenty-four hours or more she didn't get any sleep, her mind had been flooded with thoughts about what she should do. The day before, she couldn't think—her new friends were too present, and too curious, too much of a distraction to think clearly.

She'd finally seen the doctor, and now there was no escaping the knowledge. She was pregnant, with the baby of the French President, Giles Raphael Aguillard, about two and a half months, as she'd calculated. The hectic campaign activities had distracted from the first indication, and she hadn't even noticed. But when she'd noticed the calendar and thought back, she'd bought the test kit. She had to admit to herself now, in her subconscious mind she'd known for a while that she was pregnant, but in the same subconscious mind she was living in denial as if it would undo it.

A bit like trying to 'unring' a bell, she thought and grinned glumly.

She wasn't showing yet, but she soon would, and unless she did something about it, all hell would break loose.

Although it was true that in the modern society it was no longer unusual or even a reason for shame when a woman her age became pregnant out of wedlock. Many who hadn't found a suitable mate but still wanted children turned to other means—artificial insemination or in vitro. Some of them adopted. But in her case, it would be unusual, it would immediately be the main topic of media gossip and speculation. And although the media could be given the silent treatment, if the name of the father became known, a scandal of epic proportions would erupt.

The fact that she had no one to talk to only added to her overwrought condition as her mind was attacked by wave after wave of ideas—none of which presented a solution.

Go into hiding and give the baby up for adoption after birth?

It was only a fleeting thought, and it made her nauseous just to think about it—not an option.

Abortion?

She'd spent even less time on that one—would never have considered it at all if it hadn't come unbidden into her thoughts in her panic.

By now she was absolutely sure she was going to keep the baby—that was the easiest part of it all. She'd simply have to take a leave of absence, maternity leave, for a few months, but her place would be waiting for her when she returned. She was confident of that. Unless Giles decided it would be too dangerous for *his* career to keep her around.

That brought her to the next thought. Giles was totally unaware of the situation. The question was, should he be made aware of it or not? Did he even have a right to know? He'd never indicated he'd leave his wife for her. He'd never given her any illusions that he loved her.

How could I be so foolish? Star-struck, or just plain stupidity? Probably both.

Star-struck felt less self-judgmental. Yes, she could go with star-struck. He was handsome, sophisticated, and so lavish with his praise of her work. Too much wine one night over a thorny campaign issue, and it had just happened.

Isn't that what everyone says when they're caught red-handed? It just happened? Yes, it just happened, because stupidity just happens. It's never planned.

But then, it had happened again and again, for more than three months.

Serial stupidity?

They couldn't get enough of each other. Thinking back on it, Margot was surprised they hadn't been outed before by some other staff member. Surely there were other people who knew of the affair.

Keeping the baby would seal his fate as well as hers—if the truth became known. His career would be ruined, France would be embarrassed, his party would be ruined, and probably his marriage, too. Margot had no love for his wife, but his children were innocent bystanders. Whatever the troubles between him and his wife that led to his infidelity, the children weren't to blame.

No, you'd have to keep this to yourself, one way or another. There is too much at stake, it's not just you and Giles.

Slowly but surely, she came to the conclusion that the only way to do that was to disappear until after the baby was born. Time enough to think about the future while she waited.

After two days of self-reflection and self-recrimination, and making no more progress, Margot reached the point where she knew she had no choice but to take the step she had been dreading—call her brother. She'd been telling herself that she'd been putting the call off because no phone calls were private anymore, someone could be listening. But she knew the real reason was the disgrace it would bring to the Lemaire family name.

"Bertrand, I'm in trouble. I need your help." She blurted without greeting when he answered his phone.

"Margot! What's wrong? Are you in danger? What..."

"I am safe. You don't have to worry about that. But I have a major crisis, and I am at wits' end. I have no one else to turn to..."

"What's it Margot? Tell me. Do you want me to come to you?"

"No, no, that's not necessary... Bert, I can't tell you much more over the phone, it's not safe to discuss the details over the phone."

"Damn, Margot. What am I to do if I don't know what's going on?"

"Bert, I'm... I... I'm pregnant... I..."

"Congrat... no, wait. It's a crisis that you're pregnant? Why? Hang on... who is..."

"We can't talk about it over the phone, Bert."

"Okay, let me see if I understand what I've heard so far. You're pregnant, it's a major crisis for you, and you can't talk about it over the phone. Right?"

"Yes, that's correct."

"And you can't tell me who ... oh, wait a minute... now I get it." Bert said as he felt the bile rising in his throat when he remembered how furious he was about the gossip in the pony press about his sister and Aguillard a few months ago. Margot told him it was just that, gossip, without doubt seeded by the opposition. But now it seems there was truth to it. "That's the crisis. Is it not?"

"Yes, Bert, that's the crisis."

"Mon Dieu," Bert whispered in shock. But he soon got his composure back and said, "What did you have in mind?"

"I need to disappear for a while. As in without a trace… No one must be able to find me… I… I think that'd be the best option right now…"

Bert was a few years older than Margot. He loved her unconditionally; he had always been very protective of her and very proud of her accomplishments. "Margot, I can only imagine the stress you're under right now. But I want you to know I'll do everything in my power to help you. So, the first thing that comes to mind is to find a way to get you out of there unnoticed and bring you to the farm… we can…"

"No! Sorry Bert. No, that won't work. I can't go back to France, not until after the baby is born. It's too much of a risk. We need to think of another place, out of sight, away from prying eyes and snooping media. A private clinic somewhere… a place where I can arrive and stay incognito for the duration."

"How far along are you?"

"About two and a half months, by my calculations."

"We will get through this, Margot. Where are you now?"

"I have a hut near Port Vila, but right now I'm in Lamap."

"Stay right there. I'll get back to you in an hour or two with a plan. Are you safe there?"

Margot smiled faintly, that was Bert, always concerned about her safety and well-being. "Yes, Bert, don't worry about that. I'm quite safe here."

"Good. I'll call you soon. I love you."

"Love you, too, and thank you."

Margot spent the next couple of hours trying to visualize the future. She could always go home, raise her baby with her brother acting as a surrogate father to the child. By now she'd surmised that to keep it all under wraps, whatever she did, it was important to keep distance between her and the President until after the baby was born. The reality of her pregnancy settled in, and like most newly-pregnant women, she already loved the tiny life growing within her.

Three hours later, her phone rang. She checked the caller ID, it was her brother.

"When can you get back to Port Vila?"

"I can be there tonight, if I'm quick to catch the afternoon flight. What do you have in mind?"

"Get the flight and then call me back. I'll have the details by the time you're back."

"All right, I'm on it. Thank you, Bert."

"It's nothing, a little sleight of hand, is all. Just make sure you catch that flight to Port Vila. I'll talk to you tonight."

Bertrand had thought of everything and did a magnificent job in only a few hours. His solution was brilliant, though it would present some difficulties later. But there'd be plenty of time to sort those out.

She wouldn't have gone back to Port Vila at all, if there hadn't been incriminating evidence among her possessions she had to get rid of.

When she got back to her hut, she packed a small bag with the few mementos she had of her and Giles' affair. They were too dangerous to leave behind, though she wouldn't keep them. She'd tear up the pictures of them together in attitudes of affection and give the pieces to the ocean, and she'd sell the few pieces of jewelry in the Philippines or Singapore when they stopped to get the false travel documents her brother would have waiting. She packed a negligee that was one of her favorites and one of his, too. It was the only thing she'd keep as a memento of their time together, other than the baby.

Everything else—her clothing, luggage, books, even her passport, she'd leave behind. That way, it would look like she'd simply vanished. With no evidence of foul play, everyone would assume she'd gone for a swim and been taken by one of the creatures of the sea or drowned. There'd be no need for lengthy goodbyes, offers to stay in touch, or unanswered questions. She'd just be gone.

When everything was in readiness, she sent Rowan a text. *"Dinner invitation still open?"*

Chapter Eleven

Fatumara Bay, Port Vila, Vanuatu

Rex texted back, "Yes. Absolutely. Meet you at eight at our favorite place?" He didn't know whether to expect Ida to join them, and he didn't care. He was just happy Jacqui was okay. Ida or no Ida, when he saw Jacqui, he'd be able to judge for himself whether she had resolved her problem or not.

As it turned out, Ida was there for a while, and Rex was frustrated to see that Jacqui was keeping up a façade. Though she was trying to be carefree and breezy like always. Quintessentially French, she always displayed a good measure of *joie de vivre*, but Rex was not fooled by it. If anything, dark shadows under her eyes, ineffectually covered with makeup, gave away that she was even more strained than the last time he saw her.

She didn't mention anything, and Ida seemed completely unaware she'd even been gone.

However, despite the stress signals Jacqui gave off, Rex

got the feeling that she'd come to some kind of decision about her problem. He kept up his own façade, responding to her as she clearly wished, without mentioning his disquiet. Even if he'd felt he could press more, he didn't want to do it with Ida there. She didn't seem to be in the loop at all, or maybe she was but didn't care.

Digger wasn't buying any of it. He kept looking at Rex as if to ask why he wasn't doing something about Jacqui's distress, though Rex couldn't fathom what the dog would have him do. In the end, with Rex not taking action, as if to make up for Rex's lapse, Digger spent more time at Jacqui's side than at Rex's, though to be fair, it might have been because she kept sneaking the dog bites of her dinner. So much so that Rex didn't think she ate much at all. He made no mention of it.

Ida excused herself early, and Jacqui stood to give her an air kiss on each side of her face. "*Adieu*," she said.

"*Au revoir*," she answered. "See you later."

Again, Rex didn't mention that he found it strange she used the word *adieu* like in a final goodbye, but he was now alert to any signals Jacqui inadvertently gave.

She picked at her dessert and soon grew restless. When he'd finally finished his, Jacqui put her hand on his arm and leaned toward him.

"Rowan, thank you for being my friend while I'm here. You and Digger have been a pleasure."

Rex smiled, because she'd given him an opening. He said, "That sounds almost like goodbye. Are you planning on leaving soon?"

"No, no. I'm just feeling a little emotional. I've been going through some personal problems, but everything will work out. I'm afraid I'm not very good company tonight, though, and I'm a little tired. I may just vegetate and sulk in my cabin for a couple of days. Why don't you come by day after tomorrow and I'll treat you to a nice breakfast?"

It was a clear signal that she wanted to be left alone for a while longer. As he searched her face, he could see no indication she was lying about everything working out. As a highly trained special agent, he was adept at reading the micro expressions and body language of people. It was evident there was still something she was holding back, but he didn't get the impression she felt stranded or hopeless. He left it at that because he was sure she wouldn't harm herself.

As they walked together back toward the resort, Jacqui remarked, as she had before, on the number of visible stars. "We don't have so many in Paris," she said.

"You have them. You just can't see them," he answered, with a straight face.

She turned to him, saw him trying not to laugh, and then lightly punched his arm. "You knew what I meant, silly."

Then she laughed, and he couldn't hold his in anymore. Digger, trotting along between them, looked up at each of them and broke into a grin, but Rex didn't think it was because he got the joke. He was just happy to see his human and the pretty girl laughing for a change.

When they came to the fork in the path that led one way to her hut and the opposite way to his, they paused. Rex wanted to take her hand and tell her he was there for her if she needed anything, but her posture indicated a touch wouldn't be appropriate. Instead, he said, "Good night, Jacqui. I'll see you day after tomorrow. Text me when you're ready for me to come over."

"I will." She turned to go, and Rex watched her walk a few yards. Digger was on leash, since they'd been to town, and he almost pulled Rex off his feet trying to follow her.

"No, Digger. I know she's not okay, but she wants to be left alone."

Digger whined, sat down, and didn't take his eyes off Jacqui's retreating back until Rex said, "Come on, boy. Let's go home."

Chapter Twelve

Fatumara Bay, Port Vila, Vanuatu

It was shortly after midnight when Margot sneaked through town, keeping to the shadows and making sure to avoid being seen by anyone on her way to the marina. There she was met by a lanky, gray-haired, man aged between fifty and seventy—it was too difficult to tell his age in the semi-darkness. They had a short, whispered conversation before he led her to a small rowboat and helped her in. She had no luggage. He rowed the little boat in near silence to a yacht that was anchored about three-hundred yards away.

As they approached, Margot could make out the name on the side of the mega-yacht—Java Princess.

Bertrand had arranged passage on it, booking the entire yacht for her privacy. He'd paid the owner handsomely to ask no questions and require no passport. It was a small risk. There'd be little worry of being stopped by any authorities before Margot had the opportunity to retrieve the false passport that would be waiting for her in Singapore. She trusted

Bertrand to smooth the way for that errand, because he'd thought of literally everything else.

On board, the yacht owner greeted her personally and showed both discretion and willingness to let her have as much privacy as she wished for the voyage. He asked if she would join him for meals or prefer to have them in her cabin. She answered that it would be nice to join him at mealtimes. Then he showed her to her cabin.

She found it already stocked with everything she'd need for the voyage but had to leave behind. Her favorite brands of personal hygiene items, from shampoo to body lotion, plenty of clothing in her size, even lingerie. She wondered who'd done the shopping, because the items were tasteful and closely reflected her usual style.

When she turned to thank the owner, he had already gone.

Discreet indeed. I wonder how Bertrand knows him?

She was not to discover the answer to that question, nor the others that crossed her mind on the voyage. All she learned was that his name was Henri, apparently in his sixties, he spoke passable French with a provincial accent she couldn't identify, and he was kind and respected her desire for privacy and kept his distance.

After the strain of seeing her friends again and saying goodbye without saying it, she was exhausted. Worst of all was lying to Rowan about their breakfast date. It had been Bertrand's idea that the discovery of her gone missing should not be *too* soon, hence the ruse to invite Rowan for breakfast on the second day after their dinner.

Not long after she went to bed, the movement of the boat lulled her to sleep. She didn't hear the engines start or feel the movement as the yacht left the harbor and set a course that would take them between Australia and Papua

New Guinea before threading through the outer islands of Indonesia, through the Java Sea, and finally to Singapore. There she would become someone else before traveling the final leg of the journey to Vietnam where she would spend the next few months. The boat's movement didn't make her sick, and she spent the most restful night she'd had in almost a week.

Henri, who was also the captain, turned the wheel over to his first mate, Enrico, an Indonesian man who'd been with him for years, serving as cook and the only other person needed to operate the yacht. They'd plied their trade on these seas together for almost thirty years, usually with some kind of contraband including humans, endangered tropical birds or small animals bound for a very secret private zoo, drugs, or anything else someone wanted transported quietly, quickly, and with no questions asked.

The penalty for transporting a paperless individual on the high seas, he didn't know. It was not really his problem. It was on his passenger if she entered a country illegally. Much safer than a cargo of illegal drugs, birds, or animals, though, and therefore he was very happy with this charter. He left the reporting of their departure to Enrico. The port authorities knew him and never hassled him about anything. This yacht came and went on an irregular schedule, and the only ones aboard, as far as the authorities knew, were her owner and the lackadaisical but affable first mate.

Chapter Thirteen

Fatumara Bay, Port Vila, Vanuatu

At about nine in the morning on the second day after the dinner date, Rex was wondering if Jacqui had forgotten inviting him. Or maybe he'd misunderstood the plan. She was supposed to text him when to come over, but no text had come. It was getting late for breakfast. Digger had already had his and was enjoying a nap in the sun just outside the veranda cover.

Was I supposed to just show up?

An hour later, he decided that must have been it, and she must have had brunch in mind, not breakfast; otherwise she'd have called wondering where he was.

He woke Digger, and they walked to her cabin, but no one was there.

Rex thought about an old movie he'd seen called Groundhog Day, where the main character kept waking up and doing the same things over and over, until he finally got it right and broke the pattern. This morning was a reprise of the day a week ago, when she'd left unexpectedly without notifying anyone. But what was it he was supposed to get right to keep from repeating this pattern?

However, she'd been very specific about the day, and she hadn't canceled. She wasn't answering her phone or responding to texts again, just like before. But before, she'd let him know the next day. As frustrating and bewildering as it was, he decided to go back to his hut and wait for her to do so again.

His stomach growled. Somewhat put out by Jacqui's erratic behavior, he turned to retrace his steps. Digger followed reluctantly, unable to understand why they weren't playing on the beach this morning.

When they got back to the hut, Rex made his breakfast, keeping up a running one-way conversation with Digger. "This is getting old. I'm wondering if we both haven't been taken in by a drama queen. She seems genuine, but what's this silly game she plays of acting like she wants to be alone and then disappearing. Women, I tell you. The book about understanding them has not been written yet."

Digger tracked Rex's movements and paid attention to his words, or so he pretended to do. Rex knew he was talking to an animal, though. One who couldn't understand the conversation, much less respond, unless it included certain words he knew. He was probably waiting for Rex to give him more food and only pretending to be interested in the conversation to achieve that objective.

As the day wore on, Rex kept his phone close at hand, but he didn't hear anything from Jacqui. Nor from Ida, though that was less surprising. She never initiated a call to him.

Chapter Fourteen

Fatumara Bay, Port Vila, Vanuatu

The next morning, Rex woke with a sense of anticipation—this would be the day Jacqui would send him the belated text to explain her absence, like she did before. But again, as the day wore on without word, the continued silence started to feel permanent.

He went to the market late in the afternoon to get some food and bumped into Ida.

"Have you heard from Jacqui?" he asked.

"No, I haven't. And it's strange. After dinner the other night, she said to come over for breakfast, yesterday that would've been. But she wasn't home when I went over, so I thought she must have forgotten about it and went on a trip to one of the other islands."

But then Rex recalled the formal form of goodbye Jacqui had given Ida when she left them at dinner, *adieu*. And the expression of gratitude for his and Digger's friendship. It struck him that this wasn't the same as the previous time at all. Jacqui had hinted at a decision, and now he became worried about what that decision was.

Damn. I should've picked that up.

"I think we should report her missing," he said.

"Surely it's too early for that," Ida replied. "She'll probably turn up at some stage. I'm not worried, and she's old enough to take care of herself."

Not for the first time, Rex reflected on how self-centered Ida was. She never seemed to have a care in the world for anyone but herself.

His first thoughts turned to kidnapping, admittedly because of his own experiences in the not-too-distant past. But why would anyone kidnap her, a low-level government employee? She'd all but said her family wasn't wealthy, despite owning a French winery. In the end, it was her melancholy the last few times he'd seen her that worried him. He couldn't shake the feeling that she was vulnerable, though he couldn't guess the reason.

"Ida, would you come with me to her hut now? I think something's wrong. And if it's bad news, we should be together when we discover it."

"What bad news are you talking about?"

"Let's not borrow trouble. Just please, come with me, okay?"

Ida put on a pout, but she followed him out of the narrow aisles of the market and then walked beside him back to the resort. They had little to say to each other. Rex noticed Digger walked on his opposite side, as if to avoid the sullen woman. She wasn't his first choice of companion on this errand, either, but he had a bad feeling, and his reasoning about having a witness was sound.

However, when they got to the hut, they peeked in the windows and didn't see any sign of Jacqui. The door was unlocked. They entered, but there was still no Jacqui inside. As far as he could see, all her stuff was there, as if she had just gone out for a short while.

"What do you want to do now?" Ida asked. "She isn't here. So, what?"

Disgusted with her lack of concern, Rex answered that he'd report Jacqui missing to the resort manager, and Ida could go on back to her own pursuits if she wanted. She regarded him with a blank stare and then left without another word.

"Weird woman," Rex said to Digger when she was out of earshot.

Digger woofed in apparent agreement. He'd never liked Ida, but it was obvious the feeling was manifestly mutual.

Rex trudged back to the resort offices and reported to the manager what he'd found and his worries about it. He explained they'd had a breakfast date the day before, but Jacqui hadn't been at home and hadn't been seen since. The manager reassured him she'd probably just gone island-hopping and forgotten the date. He promised to check on her later, though.

That's the trouble with places like this. Always so laid-back. Nothing that can't wait a week is worth doing.

In his concern, Rex had forgotten that was exactly what he'd been looking for when he got there—a laid-back life-style for a few weeks.

Chapter Fifteen

The Coral Sea, off the East Coast of Australia

Margot stretched luxuriously in her cabin on the yacht. Bertrand had outdone himself, though she'd been trepidatious about an ocean voyage with her morning sickness. As it turned out, the yacht was large enough that the movement of the waves didn't bother her much. She'd acclimated to the gentle rocking quickly and hadn't suffered nearly as much as she'd done on the trip between islands in the little motor launch she'd taken with her friends a couple weeks ago.

The captain, Henri, was clearly a rogue, but a charming one. In the two days since they departed Vanuatu, he'd regaled her with tales of his adventures on these seas. He never named names. She was reassured that they could trust him not to reveal *her* name or whereabouts when he'd delivered her to Vietnam.

His company distracted her from the decision she'd made, which was to give up everything she'd ever wanted before and raise this baby incognito. A baby changed everything, she reflected. How could she be a good mother and be in politics, too? It wouldn't work. She'd be away from the child for long hours every day. A nanny would be raising *her* child. How could she bear that? She had rich, happy memories of her own mother. Her child would barely know her if she returned to her position.

Still, it was a bittersweet thought that she'd worked so hard for her dream job and then thrown it away in the arms of a man who didn't love her.

What was I thinking? Well, obviously I wasn't thinking. I betrayed my own philosophy, my morals, and the party's stance on family values for a few moments of pleasure and a career in politics. That's the kind of woman I've become. I don't even recognize myself.

She soon realized she would find no comfort in castigation. What had happened, happened, and at some stage in the future she'd probably look back at this time in her life and admit it was for the best. Now it was up to her to save the party and Giles' presidency, as well as his marriage, by staying away. She couldn't blame him. He wasn't a monster. If she'd only said no, none of this would have happened. It was all her fault.

"Stop it!" she commanded herself, speaking aloud. "Go and find something pleasant to do and stop this endless negative talk. You're going to have a baby, and you're going to be the best mother there can be. Your baby is going to be a happy baby, because you are going to be a happy mother."

She gave a decisive nod while looking herself in the eye in the mirror. She would put on a swimsuit, while hers still fit, and lie in the sun on deck. When she got to the convent in Vietnam, there would be no such pleasures, so she should enjoy them while she could.

Chapter Sixteen

Port Vila, Vanuatu

The next afternoon, Rex was writing a blog post about Vanuatu's attractions when Digger started growling, and soon after, a shout from outside brought him to his feet. Digger had scrambled to his feet as well, and stood with hackles up, looking at the door. Rex quickly walked over and opened it cautiously to see what was going on.

Outside, three men, police, judging from their uniforms, stood in attitudes of caution. The one in the middle had his hand on what appeared to be a weapon at his hip.

"Come out with your hands up!"

What the...

Rex nudged the door the rest of the way, raised his hands, and told his growling companion to stay. When he got outside, he stopped several feet from the officers.

"What's this about?" he called to them.

"You are wanted for questioning in the disappearance of Margot Lemaire," was the answer.

Rex felt his expression dissolve from caution to confusion. "Who's Margo Lemaire?"

"We'll ask the questions. You'll give the answers. Step forward. And command your dog to lie still, or we'll shoot it."

Apart from the alarm bells that went off in Rex's head, he felt the anger rising, not only because of the threat to harm Digger but also the policeman's rudeness. However, he kept it under control. "Digger, lie down. Stay," he said sharply. Without looking back to the dog, he knew Digger would obey, even though he now registered that the low growl meant the dog viewed the policemen as enemies.

"I'm sure there's been some mistake, but I'll accompany you peacefully. My dog is a trained service animal. I need him to be with me. I'll put him on leash."

A short consultation among the three men resulted. The apparently trigger-happy officer who'd threatened to shoot Digger gesticulated, but the others must have prevailed.

"Where is the leash?"

"Inside."

One of the policemen stepped forward, and Rex kept his hands in the air until he got inside, lowering one only to pick up his passport and wallet. He nodded at the leash, and the cop picked it up.

"Digger, let the man put your leash on," he said, hoping the dog got the gist of the command, which he had never used before.

If Digger can play along and be nice, it will help to calm these cops down.

Digger flattened his ears and ducked when the officer approached, but Rex said, "Friend." Digger stopped growling, looked at Rex for a second or two, and then allowed the officer to attach the leash. Rex then submitted to being handcuffed, in front so he could handle the leash. Together, the three exited the hut again, and Rex was relieved to see the aggressive officer relax.

They all squeezed into a too-small car, which would have been adequate without Digger. The dog rested uncomfortably on Rex's lap, overflowing onto the lap of the officer who'd leashed him. *At least,* Rex reflected, *he's stopped showing aggression.* That was the most dangerous thing Digger could have done under the circumstances. It went against his nature to allow Rex to be captured like this, but fortunately he'd obeyed Rex's commands.

Poor Digger, he must be completely confused, probably just as much as I am.

At the station, Rex was told to put Digger in a holding cell. From Rex's perspective, it was not ideal, but there was nothing to be done about it. For now, he had no reason to plan an escape, and even if he could, where would he go? The best course of action was to remain calm and cooperate until he knew what was going on and whether he and Digger were in any kind of danger. Rex, however, warned the officers that he couldn't control the dog if they were separated and asked them to please not approach the dog if he was not present.

"He's only trying to protect me, and he doesn't understand what's happening. I promise I can control him if you keep us together."

"That will not be possible. It's for our safety."

"Your safety would be better served if you let me keep him close, under my control." Rex tried again to persuade them to let Digger be with him, to no avail. But in the end, in order to not escalate an already explosive situation, Rex very reluctantly agreed to allow Digger to be locked up. He was worried that Digger might injure an officer while trying to get to him, so, Rex kneeled next to him and spoke softly. "It's okay, Digger. Be calm. I'm okay. Stay. I will be back soon. Good boy."

Digger was making soft growls and whines, but after a minute or so of Rex's reassurances, he calmed down and was quiet when Rex was led away and placed in an interrogation room.

Rex resisted looking back at the dog as he was led away, lest Digger interpret the look as a signal for help.

In the interrogation room, Rex was offered a chair and a bottle of water, both of which he accepted. They didn't remove the cuffs, but Rex was not too worried about that for now. If need be, he could get out of them in less than five seconds. When the three officers who had picked him up left, Rex resigned himself to wait. He knew the rituals of interrogation well. The first step was to leave the prisoner alone and let him worry for an hour or so.

Rex looked at his watch and took note of the time. He had no doubt somewhere in the room they would have some concealed surveillance apparatus. He didn't look for them—he didn't want to let them know that he probably had more knowledge about interrogations in his pinkie than they had in their combined heads.

He remained in the chair, putting up a front of someone who had nothing to worry about. He took small sips of water every now and then and practiced calming breathing techniques; slow long breaths through his nose filling first his lower, then his upper lungs. Then he held his breath for a five-count before slowly exhaling through his mouth while he concentrated on relaxing the muscles in his face, jaw, shoulders, and stomach.

To his observers, it could've looked like he had fallen asleep.

The breathing helped him to relax but didn't take his mind off Digger. He simply didn't know how long Digger would tolerate the circumstances that were strange to him.

Rex knew he just had to keep up the façade of calmness, and it would soon wear the police down. He knew how to wait—in fact, he was trained in the art of waiting. The life of a black ops field operator, they were told during their training, was one of endless traveling from one location to another, followed by extended spells of mind-numbing tedium, every now and then punctuated by bursts of absolute violence and terror.

And then there was the waiting. Waiting for the target or a contact to turn up, waiting for the target to make a move, waiting for someone to complete a task before the next one could begin, waiting for the right time, waiting, waiting, and more waiting, and then quick action—get the job done, get out of the area, and go home. Then waiting again for the next mission.

Over the years, Rex had schooled himself and had learned to fill his waiting time by reading history and learning new languages. He always had an eReader device to read books and an MP3 player with him, so he could perfect his accents and improve his vocabulary by listening to native speakers of whatever new language he was learning.

But this time he didn't have his eReader or audio player with him.

Nevertheless, he expected the cops to give up, sometime between thirty and forty-five minutes. Then he would hear what had landed him here.

In the meantime, he allowed his mind to wander. They'd said they wanted to question him in the disappearance of Margot something. He didn't know anyone by the name of Margot, not on Vanuatu, but he did know someone who'd disappeared. Could that be Jacqui? If so, was Jacqui her nickname or had she been using a false name all along?

We'll know as soon as the cops have had enough of looking at a man who's sleeping in their interrogation room instead of biting his fingernails.

He'd met only a few people to speak to: the resort manager, Jacqui, Ida, the captain of the fishing boat, a few servers at the restaurants, a few shop owners in the market, and the woman who'd catered the dinner for him and Jacqui a while ago. But they never exchanged names. Was *that* perhaps Margot whatever?

It was fruitless to speculate further, until he knew who they were talking about. He occupied some of the time he had to wait by counting the acoustic tiles in the ceiling.

Eventually his wait came to an end. The cops lasted exactly twenty-eight minutes. A portly officer with stripes on his uniform sleeves indicating he was a sergeant came in, carefully closed the door, and sat down opposite Rex, across the scratched and wobbly small table from him. He put his hands atop the table and folded them together, then leaned forward, causing the table to creak under his weight.

"What have you done with Mademoiselle Lemaire?"

Lemaire. Margot Lemaire, that was the name.

Politely, he answered. "I'm sorry, but I don't know who that is."

"We have it on good authority you had dinner with Mademoiselle Lemaire night before last, and you were the last person to see her."

Understanding dawned on Rex, and not only understanding that they were indeed talking about Jacqui, but that this interrogation had something to do with what Ida had told them—she was the last one to see them together. Nevertheless, he kept his face neutral. Something was going on that he didn't yet understand, and if he was to get to the bottom of it, he'd have to keep his wits about him.

He answered carefully. "Night before last, I had dinner with two ladies I know as Jacqui Madrolle and Ida Engberg. We are casual friends, met here on the island for the first time, all staying at the same resort. I do not know a Margot Lemaire."

"This Ida Engberg you speak of is the witness who told us you were the last to be seen with Mademoiselle Lemaire. She said the three of you had dinner, and then she left, leaving you and Mademoiselle Lemaire together."

"Unless Mademoiselle Lemaire is the person I know as Jacqui Madrolle, that is a false statement."

"Then perhaps you'd care to explain why the resort manager also reported Mademoiselle Lemaire missing and that you were the one to alert him to that fact."

"I alerted him to the fact that *Jacqui Madrolle* was missing, I never used the name Mademoiselle Lemaire, simply because I don't know anyone by that name. But I'm going to assume at this point that Mademoiselle Lemaire and Jacqui Madrolle are one and the same person. However, I have to say I'm perplexed as to why she would give me a false name.

"Be that as it may, of course I am concerned that she's missing. We had an appointment for breakfast yesterday morning, and she wasn't there when I called for her. I asked Ida to accompany me to her hut to see if we could find her, and when we didn't, I reported her absence to the manager.

"However, this is not the first time it's happened. She went to Lamap before, and she turned up just fine a few days later. But that time, she sent me a text that she was okay and would be out of contact for a few days. This time she didn't. Why are the police now involved? And why the heavy-handedness in questioning me?"

"Mademoiselle Engberg indicated you might be a danger to Mademoiselle Lemaire."

Ah that explains why they cuffed me.

"Sergeant, I take it she also told you exactly how I endangered Mademoiselle Lemaire, and you're burning to tell me?" Rex raised his eyebrows questioningly.

The sergeant made no reply.

"No? You didn't ask?"

The sergeant made no reply.

"So, let me just see if I understand the situation correctly." He didn't wait for a response, as it was not a question. "You spoke to Mademoiselle Engberg, she confirmed we had dinner with the person we, Ida and I, have come to know as Jacqui Madrolle, who you say goes by the name of Margot Lemaire. Right?"

The sergeant nodded.

"Good. Then Ida told you I was the last person to see her the night we had dinner together?"

The sergeant nodded.

"Did she say that, or did she say when she left, we were together?"

The sergeant blushed. "She said she left the two of you together."

"I see. Okay, then she told you I am a danger to Mademoiselle Lemaire. But you never questioned her as to what kind of danger I would pose to this woman. Right?"

The sergeant cleared his throat and shuffled on his chair.

"Sergeant, I don't know how the laws of Vanuatu work, but I suspect it's not entirely different from the laws of

France or America or other civilized countries. In other words, it's illegal for the police to make up false charges against people..."

"Wait a minute. What are you insinuating? That I am making up..."

"Yes, sergeant that's exactly what I'm saying. You know why? Because you know as well as I do you don't have a case. You don't have a lead. If you think you have a case against me, go ahead and charge me now, so I can get myself a lawyer.

"I take it in your country people *are* entitled to representation?"

"Yes, of course they are..."

"The alternative is of course that you can stop this farce, and you can listen to what I have to say. I *am* worried about Jacqui, sorry, Margot's disappearance. We've become friends during our vacation here. That's why I reported her missing."

The sergeant stared at Rex for a while, probably considering his options and maybe wondering how this guy managed to turn the tables on him so effortlessly.

"Well what's it going to be? Am I under arrest or not?"

"No, you're not." The sergeant whispered.

"Good. So, do you want to hear my side of the story or not?"

"Yes, please continue," the sergeant said as he opened his notebook and retrieved a pen from the inner pocket of his jacket.

"Before we start, I guess this is not necessary anymore?" Rex held his hands out in a gesture for the cuffs to be removed.

The sergeant nodded, took the keys out of his pocket, and unlocked the cuffs. It was clear he was not really in the mood to apologize about the rough treatment, and Rex didn't care about it.

"That feels a lot better," Rex smiled and rubbed his wrists. "Now, I need to get my dog first. I take it that's not going to be an issue?"

The sergeant nodded. He got up and led Rex to the holding cell where Digger was pacing nervously. When Digger saw him, he lifted himself onto his hind legs, put the front paws on the cross-bar of the cell door, and whined piteously.

"It's okay, boy. I'm here. We're going to get you out."

The moment the door swung open, Digger rushed at Rex and did something he almost never did. He stood on hind legs, stretched to his full length, dropped his paws on Rex's shoulders, and licked his face.

"Okay, boy. That's enough. I know you love me. Off. Get off now."

Digger dropped to all fours.

"Thank you, Sergeant. Now, we can talk about what I know and if there's anything I can do to help find Mademoiselle Lemaire."

In the conversation that followed, Rex told him how he met Margot first. He deliberately made a point of elaborating about the role Digger played in the introduction. That had the sergeant smiling from ear to ear, which was exactly what Rex wanted to achieve. That bit of humor broke the ice, and the sergeant was a lot less stressed from that point onward.

Rex continued to tell him how Margot introduced Ida to him later, how they became holiday friends, and the things they did together. He also told him that lately it became obvious to him that something was bothering Margot but that she didn't want to talk about it. He described his observation that she'd been crying before she went to Lamap, and on her return he got the impression, when they had dinner with Ida two nights before, that Margot had made some sort of decision about her problem while she was away.

"She claimed she was fine, but I had the impression she was holding back."

"The impression." The sergeant's tone indicated skepticism.

"Yes, the impression." Rex replied. "That's all I can say. She didn't share any of it with me—only that she was fine."

"So, you don't think she went on another retreat like the first one."

Rex shrugged. "I couldn't say for certain. The first time, she let me know. This time, she didn't. As I've said before, we only met when I arrived at the resort, so I don't know her *that* well. She and Ida were here before me. Maybe you could question Ida about that. And while you're at it, please find out why she would say I was a danger to Jac... Margot. I can't imagine why she would think that."

"All right, Mr. Donnelly. You are free to go. I'll be in touch if I have more questions. I take it you are planning to stay a while longer on our beautiful island?"

"Yes, I haven't decided when I'll be leaving yet. I'm still enjoying it. If I do decide to leave, I'll make sure to let you know."

"That'll be good. I think the whole matter will be cleared up in a day or two at the most," the sergeant said.

———

Back at his hut, to which he hadn't been offered a ride, Rex considered the whole episode. He wasn't at all sure that the matter would be cleared in a day or two. He'd stay out of the way, but he'd watch what they did to investigate, and he'd clean up behind them if he thought it necessary.

Jacqui Madrolle is Mademoiselle Margot Lemaire. Why the false name? What is she hiding? Rex was contemplating it from all angles when it dawned on him that he didn't have the monopoly on anonymity through false identities. The only question that remained was what was Margot's reason?

Rex went through his usual routines to activate a network of proxy servers to disguise his location and identity, before he started Googling the name Margot Lemaire. Thousands of hits came back. Reading about her real life was a revelation.

It turned out that the 'low-level government employee', Jacqui Madrolle, was actually a confidant to the newly-elected President of France himself—his campaign manager, and apparently a brilliant one, as he'd won handily. She'd recently been appointed his Press Secretary.

That explained the false name. He supposed she couldn't go anywhere that paid attention to French politics under her own name and still expect any privacy. A few entries down, he found the story about her assistant being almost booed off the podium until he explained that Margot had taken a vacation to recover from the rigors of the campaign.

So, that explains what she was doing here. R and R, like me. So now, what's happened to her? Could it have something to do with her position?

And why the hell didn't I pick up on any of this? Why didn't Digger? But how was Digger supposed to know she's using a false name? He smells or senses deceit in people not their names.

He looked at Digger and said, "Sorry buddy. This was my mistake, not yours."

Digger didn't even open his eyes. He just moved his ears, slightly.

I really need to keep my guard up and be less trusting. Too much leisure is making me rusty.

A few hours later, Digger was unsettled. Rex took the Frisbee and invited Digger to go for a moonlit run on the beach. He didn't have to say it twice. Digger raced him out the door.

Chapter Seventeen

Fatumara Bay, Port Vila, Vanuatu

The next morning, Rex was up early and gave Digger his beach run and a short swim at dawn. By the time the market opened, they were waiting for the booths to open their shutters. Rex spent the morning poring over the wares and keeping his ears open. He was still fuming about what Ida allegedly said to the police and intended to confront her with that the moment he saw her.

Later in the afternoon, Rex was back at his hut when the sergeant dropped by in person. Rex offered him a seat on the veranda and some tropical fruit juice, which the sergeant gratefully accepted. When Rex set the tray with a pitcher and two full glasses down, the sergeant reached for one and drank nearly half of it in a few gulps, before speaking.

"Mademoiselle Engbert has left Vanuatu."

"When?" Rex asked.

"While you and I were conversing yesterday, she

boarded a plane for Australia. We have put a wanted bulletin out on her, but so far, no sign of her."

Rex just nodded. He didn't much care for the woman, even more so since he learned she'd badmouthed him to the police, but he didn't get the idea she was physically dangerous to anyone. However, he didn't share his thoughts with the policeman.

"We don't know whether it was coincidence or not. The timing just seemed strange, though we didn't tell her to stay on the island."

Rex said, "Come to think of it, she *did* tell me she was leaving in a day or two, the morning I decided to look for Jacqui instead of waiting for her to contact me. Excuse me, I mean Margot. Maybe it was just coincidence."

"Perhaps so. Nevertheless, we have inquiries out. Have you thought of anything else? Could Mademoiselle Lemaire have been involved in a swimming accident, for example?"

Aha, so, that's the real reason for the visit.

"Not unless someone dragged her into the water or she landed in it by some accident. She wouldn't go near the water. She was afraid of the deadly creatures you have around here." If Rex had been speaking English, he'd have used the word 'critters'. That was the word that came to mind. He didn't know of a French equivalent, though. "Maybe you can tell me why you're thinking it could have been a swimming accident?"

The sergeant hesitated, then apparently remembered Rex was no longer a suspect. "We have checked her hut. Her passport and pocketbook are still there, along with her clothes, her laptop, cellphone, and Kindle reader. If she had gone to one of the other islands, she'd have taken at least some of that. At a minimum, her cellphone, passport, and pocketbook.

"Inquiries to the other islands have not turned up any evidence that she was there recently. Her trip to Lamap, yes. Thank you for that lead. But that was before she had dinner with you and Mademoiselle Engbert.

"That's why we're thinking perhaps she met with an accident while swimming alone. It has been known to happen. Tourists don't always understand the inherent dangers in these waters. If they swim outside the shark nets…" He trailed off, leaving the rest of the sentence to Rex's imagination.

Rex shuddered. But he was resolute when he answered. "She would not have gone into the water of her own volition."

"Unless the decision you mentioned her making was to end her own life," the sergeant said.

Rex was quiet while he considered whether she would have committed suicide. He hadn't gotten that vibe. If he had, he would have pressed harder for answers when he thought she was troubled.

Did I miss it?

But no, that didn't feel right, and he said so.

"With all due respect, Mr. Donnelly, we will make that determination. You are not a trained investigator, though I do appreciate your cooperation and impressions."

Rex didn't reply. He didn't want to get into an argument with the man, although he strongly disagreed with him.

The sergeant smiled as he got up. "Thank you for the juice."

Rex thought that would be the end of it, believing the sergeant had already settled on suicide as the reason for her disappearance. He would find out the next day that it wasn't nearly so simple.

Chapter Eighteen

Sydney, Australia

Ida knew exactly where Margot had gone.

Her assignment had been to get leverage on Margot Lemaire so that her employer could blackmail Lemaire's illicit lover, the French President, Giles Aguillard, into renouncing his campaign promises to continue his predecessor's policies. Specifically, the policy of standing firm on not allowing a Russian gas pipeline to be built through the French countryside to Paris.

The French people had been against the idea, though there were some in Paris who would welcome cheaper gas. The cost, however, would be great—the construction of the pipeline would destroy hundreds of hectares of beautiful French countryside, disrupt the wine industry, expose the people to potentially hazardous conditions, and worst of all, make them dependent on Russia for much of their gas usage. The latter didn't sit well with the majority of the French people, irrespective of their political affiliations.

It would take quite a threat to the President to make him recant his campaign promise, and the serendipitous find of his paramour's positive pregnancy test would be just that threat. A day later, Ida's report had brought two more agents to surveil Margot's movements, and the confirmation found in her medical records at the clinic sealed the strategy.

When Margot flew to Lamap, Ida wasn't concerned, because she had the other two on her tail there. And when she left on the yacht, Ida knew where she was going thanks to telephone taps her agency had on Margot's cell phone and now her brother's land lines and cell phone as well.

They'd pick up her trail in Vietnam, because to effectively blackmail Aguillard, they had to be able to capture her at any time he proved uncooperative. Until then, Margot was free to roam where she wanted, so long as Ida's crew knew where that was.

Ida and her crew would be in Vietnam before Margot got there, but Ida had stayed longer on Vanuatu to wrap up the unexpected complication of one Rowan Donnelly—a too-nosy man Margot had made friends with while she was there. She bargained on it that the cops would keep Donnelly from interfering. She'd made sure of that when she told the police Donnelly was the last one to see her and that she got the impression Margot felt uncomfortable in his presence. "I'm not sure why. Maybe she felt he posed some kind of danger to her," she'd said when the policeman questioned her.

As soon as she'd planted that seed, Ida and her crew flew by private charter to Australia, where they would be boarding a plane for Vietnam in about ten days' time, a day or so before Margot would arrive in Ho Chi Minh City.

Chapter Nineteen

Fatumara Bay, Port Vila, Vanuatu

Rex was awakened before dawn by Digger's barking and a racket outside.

Don't tell me the cops have changed their minds again.

If he were honest with himself, Rex wouldn't have been surprised if they had. The police theories had holes in them you could drive a Humvee through. They had nothing but his word that he hadn't murdered Jacqui/Margot and fed her body to the sharks. They'd let Ida Engberg get away with only the most cursory of questioning. Had they even tried to track Margot's movements? Did they have a bloodhound on the island?

The last thought gave him an idea. As soon as he'd discovered the source of the noise outside, he'd see about offering Digger's services for the tracking. If Digger could track her from her hut to the ocean, maybe he could accept that she'd committed suicide. Because she damn well wouldn't have gone swimming for any other reason. Unless, of course, her fear of the water was a ruse, the same as the name Jacqui Madrolle.

Nonetheless, there are at least ten easier ways to kill oneself than dishing yourself up to the sharks. Jacqui or Margot or whatever was worried and stressed, not suicidal.

He dressed quickly and snatched his door open. And then dropped his jaw. Camped out in view of his veranda were a gaggle of news cameras with their operators, crews, people dressed in business suits, and vans with satellite dishes on top of them. When he appeared, the suits surged at him.

Digger started barking furiously, causing the men in suits to hesitate. But eventually the bravest of them extended his arms in front of him, hands patting the air as he approached.

"Quiet, boy. Sit," Rex told Digger.

Rex crossed his arms and took a step back into the darkness of his hut. He wasn't inclined to talk to reporters, and he certainly didn't want his face on the air. He turned slightly to present a profile to the camera and waited for the reporter to get within talking distance. He'd send the guy packing and then get busy on his quest.

"Mr. Donnelly, may we have a moment of your time?"

"What do you want?"

"I'm sure you are aware that the disappearance of Margot Lemaire is of national concern in France. We'd like to talk to you about your last meal with her."

"Why would it be of national concern?" Rex asked, still with his arms crossed. He was not going to give them any information to leech onto. "If you turn those cameras on or are broadcasting without my permission, I'll let my dog loose on you, and then I'll sue your stations into oblivion."

"No, no. They aren't broadcasting. Not yet."

"And that's the way it's going to stay until I tell you different," Rex said in a measured tone.

The reporter caught the look in Rex's eyes, spun around to the cameraman and told him to keep the camera off and to back off as well. Then he turned back to Rex and said, "You must be joking about why Margot's disappearance is newsworthy."

"Not at all. Until day before yesterday, I'd never heard that name. What's this about?"

The reporter looked behind him, saw, as Rex could see, that the others had tacitly elected him their spokesperson, and came even nearer. He looked apprehensively at Digger and then dropped his bombshell.

"She didn't tell you that she was President Aguillard's campaign director, and that she had a very bright future in the French government?"

Rex's jaw worked. The ever-so-charming Jacqui had snookered him, but good. That much he'd figured out already.

He brought himself up short as he remembered his thoughts of the day before. He had no room to be angry at deception or a false name. He was traveling with false papers himself, and he never shared his true past with anyone. Not even his most trusted employee and friend, Rehka Gyan. Speaking of whom, this would mean contacting her, because the stakes just got a lot higher for Mademoiselle Margot Lemaire. Suddenly, he was aware of quite a few other possible explanations for her disappearance—none of them involving suicide.

"No, she didn't share that with me. Along with her true name. So, as you can see, I didn't know her at all. Now, if you'll excuse me, I have work to do. And I have no comment about Mademoiselle Lemaire. None."

It was the reporter's turn to be nonplussed. "But, but, but…" he sputtered.

"Digger, if this man isn't out of my sight in thirty seconds, you may have him for a snack," Rex said, looking at the reporter rather than the dog.

The reporter noted Digger's sudden alertness and beat a hasty retreat, yelling at the others to hurry and leave immediately. He must have been well respected among them, Rex reflected, because in less than five minutes they'd packed up their gear and cleared the beach.

Irritating as the unwelcome media visit was, it served a purpose in that it got Rex to sit down and think carefully through the events from the last time he saw Jacqui up till now. Stepping through it all, it brought him to the point where he recalled when she said goodbye to Ida using the word *adieu* like in a final goodbye and that he thought it strange. Then later, she thanked him for the friendship, and the impression he got was that it was as if she was saying it because she was leaving. He recalled the sergeant mentioning all her stuff was still in her hut including her cellphone, and that was the main reason they thought she went for a swim and died either by accident or suicide.

But what if she had another cellphone? The one she used here, the number she gave me could've been a burner phone, bought solely for use while on holiday while she kept her official phone off. After all, it's clear she was trying to escape attention while on holiday. The most important question is still, why did she disappear? Was it planned or was she somehow forced?

Next task: get some clothes from Margot's hut and see if Digger can still detect where she went. After that, depending on what Digger finds, I'll have a word with the resort owner about letting reporters hassle his guests.

Rex didn't give Digger his beach run that morning. He

figured the jog to town would suffice, and with the gaggle of reporters around somewhere, he didn't want to be photographed, even at a distance, at play with his dog in circumstances like these. As soon as he'd explained as best he could to the disappointed dog and got ready, he leashed Digger and they made their way to the police station to ask for the sergeant he'd spoken to the previous day.

The sergeant came out of his office with a tall, sinewy man in street clothes whose bearing labeled him a cop to anyone with half a brain.

"Oh, good to see you, Monsieur Donnelly. You saved me a trip to the resort. This is Detective Caron, from Paris. He is taking over the investigation and would like to speak with you."

"Happy to. But I came here to offer my dog's ability to track, if you haven't already tried that. I need a piece of Mademoiselle Lemaire's clothing. Perhaps you'd care to speak with me while we go to her hut and get it."

The French detective's eyebrows went up in a gesture of astonishment. Rex couldn't be bothered with protocol, though. It had already been hours, and the scents were fading. He wasn't entirely sure how long afterward Digger would still be able to pick it up and follow it.

The sergeant, who'd been looking at Rex as he spoke, swung his eyes back to the French detective and gave a nervous chuckle. "I have already cleared Monsieur Donnelly, Detective Caron. He was free to go, but he has stayed and is offering help. I think we should accept his offer. We have no such ability present, to track Mademoiselle Lemaire."

The detective allowed his face to fall into a neutral aspect and nodded slowly. "Of course, that is what we should do. Come, Monsieur Donnelly, let us get that piece of clothing for you and let your dog try to sort out the many times Mademoiselle Lemaire must have left her hut since she arrived."

The sarcasm wasn't lost on Rex. However, he didn't feel the need to try to explain that the strongest of the scents would be the latest journey and that Digger would know what is expected of him. He didn't know whether Digger could pick up a scent from two days ago at all. He just thought it was worth a try.

The trip back to the resort, in the little car, wasn't much faster than Rex and Digger had made it to town when they were jogging. It seemed the island's native population, as well as every tourist there, were milling around trying to get the reporters to interview them. Rex shook his head.

Well, at least they're keeping them out of my face.

When they reached Margot's hut, Rex noted the crime scene tape around it. The sergeant explained they'd put it there to discourage souvenir hunters. He was still convinced Margot had gone for a midnight swim, despite Rex's claims she wouldn't have, and wanted to preserve the woman's effects for next of kin when the investigation was closed and Mademoiselle Lemaire presumed dead.

Rex tried once more. "I'm telling you, sergeant. She told me she wasn't a good swimmer, and besides, she was afraid of the creatures in the sea. In fact, this is what she said, verbatim, 'Rowan, I have made a pact with them. I will stay out of their habitat if they will stay off mine'. She made a joke of it, you see."

But the sergeant didn't appreciate the humor. "Monsieur Donnelly, she didn't tell you who she was or even her real first name. Why wouldn't she lie about her aversion to the water? You, of course, wouldn't first think of deception when you meet a pretty woman. As a trained policeman, that is my first thought."

Rex suppressed his smile. In fact, there was a time when he thought of deception when he first met anyone—it was second nature, and it had kept him alive. Since teaming up with Digger, he had extra help on that front. Digger was more adept at detecting deceptive people than any human could ever dream to be. Digger had exhibited affection and concern for Margot, not distrust. There was no point, and considerable danger in getting into a pissing contest with the sergeant over who was the better trained investigator, though.

In short order, they entered the hut. Rex pointed to a nightgown tossed casually on the bed. "That was probably the last thing she wore before disappearing," he said.

The detective nodded gravely. "You are most assuredly correct. Your dog may sniff it."

Rex picked it up gingerly and held it out to Digger, who sniffed it curiously and then whined.

"Seek. Find Jacqui, boy."

The detective frowned. "Her name is Margot."

"Yes, sir. I know that. But Digger knew her as Jacqui, the name she gave me. And I'm not so sure he even cares about the name. He knows her scent, and that's what's important, otherwise I could've told him to find Jacqui and not bothered to come here."

Digger was ignoring the exchange. He was already following his nose out to the veranda and down the trail. To everyone's surprise, he turned toward town rather than the beach.

"It is of no use," the sergeant complained. "This is a waste of time. He is going toward the town, not the beach."

When the French detective concurred, Rex understood

that he, too, had concluded Margot had drowned. Their minds were made up, and nothing he could do or say would change them.

Rex made up his own mind, adopted an attitude of defeat, and said, "I'm sorry, gentlemen. I thought he could do it. I'm sorry to have wasted your time."

The sergeant generously stated it wasn't his fault, he was only trying to help, and other conciliatory statements.

The French detective was fidgeting, obviously anxious to get back to the station and do the paperwork that would get him off this island and back to Paris.

Rex was itching to follow Digger, who was now nearly out of sight on a side trail, but still heading in the general direction of the town.

Chapter Twenty

Port Vila, Vanuatu

As soon as the policemen left, Rex hurried after Digger. The dog still had his nose alternately to the ground and in the air. It gave Rex reassurance that Digger was still working, still following Margot's scent. The only puzzle was that it led toward town, which refuted the theory the police were working on. Rex knew the fallacy of determining a theory and then working to prove it, rather than investigating thoroughly before forming an opinion. He struggled to keep his mind open and not try to figure out where the scent would lead before they got there.

When had Margot last taken this road to town? He'd seen her home along the same route after dinner three nights before. He'd taken it to the market yesterday. If she'd still been here then, and just hiding rather than having gone somewhere, he might have seen her at the market or along the way. Logic told him she'd gone before the day he was supposed to go to her place for breakfast, so the scent couldn't have been strong. Nonetheless, Digger was moving quickly and confidently. Rex started wondering if Digger had lost her trail and was now following theirs of earlier in the day.

But then, just before they came to the neatly laid-out blocks of the town, Digger veered sharply left along Wharf Road. Rex hadn't explored that shoreline, a north-facing aspect of Mele Bay, protected by Ifira Island from the rest of the bay. It was where the cruise ships docked, he knew. He doubted she could have boarded a cruise ship. What else might be down there? He could only follow Digger's lead and see for himself.

The road meandered along the shoreline, and Rex could see a cruise ship in port, dwarfing everything around it. He passed what looked like several warehouses in an area that had been built out into the bay, with unnatural straight lines and angles.

Must be a commercial dock for cargo ships.

Digger ignored that area and continued toward the cruise ship, causing Rex to doubt the plan again. But they were soon past the enormous ship, and now he could see smaller docks in the distance, some empty, some occupied by everything from luxury yachts to disreputable-looking fishing boats. Beyond them, in the bay itself, were skiers and jet-skiers, roughing up the water.

Rex lengthened his stride when he saw Digger, about fifty yards ahead, step onto a floating dock.

"Digger, stop!" he called. But his words were swept away by the wind. Digger kept on going as Rex began to jog. At the end of the dock, he stopped and looked out to the bay, taking in the picture of forlornness. When Rex caught up to him, Digger looked at him and lifted his chin in an eerie howl.

"What is it, boy? What's wrong?"

Digger leaned against him, shaking. Rex didn't know how to interpret that. Was Digger telling him Margot had gone into the water here? It made no sense. Not only did Rex believe she'd been telling the truth about her terror of the sea and all its inhabitants, but the water here was oily, definitely unappealing to a swimmer.

Maybe Digger is just upset that his quest has come to a dead end without finding his target. Or maybe he's sensed something about where she went from here. Onto a boat? Perhaps unwillingly?

Rex looked around and noticed the activity around the dock for the first time. There were plenty of potential witnesses, if he could only find those who'd been present when Margot passed this way.

Rex stopped the first stevedore he saw and questioned him. Had he seen a pretty lady here any time in the past three days? He described Margot, but the man he was questioning showed him a blank face and just shook his head. Rex let him go and looked around. This was going to take a major effort. He pulled out his cell phone and called the police station. The sergeant was with an important official from France, he was told, and could not be interrupted.

He left a message that he'd traced Margot to this dock, describing how far past the cruise ship they'd gone, and how many docks were in between. "Please have him send help to question the possible witnesses to a kidnapping." He hung up while the person who'd taken his call was still sputtering.

Witnesses were notoriously unreliable. Ten people could witness the same incident, and each swear on a stack of bibles that the victim was tall, short, black, white, a man, or a woman, and any combination of those attributes. Even so, he had to try. At the end of two hours, he was convinced that Margot had either come here to board a yacht voluntarily or had been taken aboard by force. He had witnesses who swore to both. He got the impression that there was illicit activity going on around the dock, and those who knew anything had been overcome by a sudden bout of amnesia.

Those who said she boarded a yacht couldn't remember the name, nor its destination. And like with all unenthusiastic eyewitnesses, their description of the yacht varied from that of an express cruiser or sports cruiser to a triple-decker mega-yacht and everything in between.

One thing was agreed by everyone, though. It had been after midnight on the night of their last dinner.

To trace the yacht, Rex would have to involve his IT specialist, Rehka Gyan. If she could determine what had departed that night and where it was going, he could intercept it at its destination and be sure Margot was all right.

Does that mean I am a stalker? Maybe she'll think so, but what if she's in trouble?

The choice was clear.

Without bothering to call the sergeant back, Rex found a trail that cut across the peninsula and urged Digger homeward. There was no time to waste.

Chapter Twenty-One

Port Vila, Vanuatu

By the time Rex returned to his hut, he had a string of requests in mind for Rehka to investigate. The first would be to have her check the records for what vessels had left Vanuatu during the time from when he'd dropped Margot at her hut after their last dinner together until this morning. With luck, they'd have filed itineraries. With even more luck, Rehka could tap into their communications and they could narrow down which one Margot might have left on.

Next, he'd ask her to try to trace Margot's cell phone number to a carrier, and then hack into the carrier's records for a list of phone numbers she'd called since arriving in Vanuatu. Maybe she'd called someone else to tell them where she was going. And if she hadn't gone voluntarily, maybe someone on that list had received a ransom demand. He'd call every number until he found something to go on.

When he found where she'd gone or found who had her, he hoped to have enough information to decide whether she had gone voluntarily or been forced, and from there to decide whether his help was needed or not. He wouldn't track her down just to ask for an explanation, but he couldn't abandon her to whatever fate awaited her if she was under duress or worse. If she thought him a stalker, so be it. He could explain.

Finally, Rehka could help him get wherever he needed to go in the most expeditious time. Much more easily than he could arrange the travel, especially if he needed yet another set of identification papers. Digger would also require false papers if the destinations were other than India, Thailand, or Peru, where he'd been recently. All that took time, and he might not have much time.

He arrived at the hut a step behind Digger, who'd figured out their destination several hundred yards ago. He took the time to praise Digger and let him out of his harness, give him some water, and stuff the Kong with dried fish nibbles to keep the dog occupied. Then he called Rehka.

Rehka had equipped them both with encrypted satellite phones. Rex's phone was encased in a shockproof and waterproof casing, because he would be out and about in nature and some rough places with his phone. Hers was daintier and looked like a normal mobile phone.

The phones' ringers were set to sound like a normal smartphone. On close inspection of the two phones, however, it was evident that the phones were programmed with only the other phone's number. Rehka had only Rex's number on her phone, and Rex had only Rehka's number on his.

If someone were really, really technical, understood the latest and greatest in secure communications and encryptions, and had a lot of time, he might have been able to figure out that every call made through these phones were end-to-end protected. Each phone had an encryption app, developed by Rehka, running on it. Each app had encryption keys, and they expected and accepted only keys from the app on the other phone. In other words, it was impossible for a man-in-the-middle attack to be successful.

Apart from the encryption, the signals from the phones were digitized and sent over the internet through a heavily encrypted virtual private network tunnel, which was routed and rerouted through no less than twelve virtual telephone switches located across the globe. Only after a worldwide tour through a maze of virtual telephone-switch destinations did the signal arrive at the sender's or receiver's phone, though the trip took less than a second.

It was not impossible to tap into their conversations, but to do it someone would need one of the phones in his hand, he'd need the password to unlock the phone, and he'd need to know the passphrases, which Rex and Rehka had agreed beforehand. He'd have to give that passphrase to the other party when they made the connection and before they would say anything. The passphrases were set up to sound like a normal greeting between two normal people about to have a normal conversation, but certain words in the phrases would signal if the other party was under duress or not. That is, any mention of weather meant things were okay. No mention of the weather meant things were not okay.

"Good afternoon, boss," she answered with her usual cheer. "What can I do for you?"

Rex started by telling her how great the weather was in Vanuatu. Rehka responded with, "You know what Mumbai's weather is like. Always the same. Hot and lots of rain."

With the security checks out of the way, Rex explained as succinctly as he could, giving Rehka the assignments in the order he wanted them completed. When he was done, he asked her to repeat it back to him, to be sure she'd missed nothing. Her repetition was letter perfect.

"How soon can you get all this?"

"I'm not sure, but I'll update you in an hour or so with progress and give you an estimate of how long it will take."

"Great! I'll wait up for your call."

Rex sighed as he ended the call. For the next hour, there was nothing at all he could do about Margot. He began pacing.

Maybe I should take Digger for another play on the beach? He's earned it.

116

Chapter Twenty-Two

Paris, France

In the aftermath of the elections, President Aguillard had gone about his business after Margot left, and he'd been too busy to notice her vacation had extended beyond what they'd discussed. However, when Paris police were notified of her disappearance, and they informed him, his attention was forced back to her.

Maybe she'd been found by reporters and took off where they couldn't find her again?

However, a few days later, things took a turn for the worse when the senior detective who'd gone to investigate the disappearance phoned and gave the news to Aguillard and his best friend, the Prime Minister, of the conclusion that she'd most likely drowned in a swimming accident. He delicately hinted that there would be no way to recover a body in those waters, without outright saying that predators would have consumed it. Aguillard was an intelligent man, though, and he managed to contain his horror and grief, presenting only a mask of the correct measure of sorrow that a close and trusted colleague had died.

He wasted no time in assigning the assistant as temporary Press Secretary while he sought out a more appropriate person to succeed Margot. Only after the day had ended and his wife had gone to bed did he give way to his real feelings. But to his surprise, they weren't as deep as he'd thought. The dalliance with Margot had been a convenient outlet for his stress during the campaign. She was a beautiful woman, certainly, but nothing could come of their relationship, especially now that he was in office.

Public knowledge of the relationship would be disastrous, not only on a personal level, given his wife's family money and its importance in his ambitions, but also within the party. The French people might forgive him—after all, l'amour was as stereotypically French as the Eiffel Tower or cheese and wine. But the party had certain standards of morality that they advocated, and that he'd acclaimed from every podium for years—the party would forsake him over something like that in a heartbeat.

With the party's support, he could look forward to ten secure years as President—two terms, followed by a lucrative career as a highly-paid speaker. His autobiography would sell, along with any political treatise he wrote thereafter. Oh, yes, his life would be charmed, but only if this indiscretion of his remained a secret. Now that he thought of it, sad as it was, Margot's death might turn out to be a blessing in disguise. He'd had his regrets about his inanity, letting his hormones dictate his judgment, and often he'd been agonizing over the possibility that she might tell all in an act of revenge someday. These types of improprieties, sooner or later, always found their way to the surface. But this way, heartbreaking as it was, there'd be no messy ending of the relationship, and no chance of it being discovered.

He turned out his study lamp and made his way to the bedroom where his wife lay sleeping. As a sop to his guilty conscience, he kissed her forehead as he settled in to sleep.

Had he known it was the calm before the storm, he would not have closed his eyes that night. Not that it would have helped much.

Once the report about Margot Lemaire's presumed death reached the news media in Vanuatu, an alert news desk clerk for France24, a major TV station, who was assigned to watch international news for items of interest to France, picked up the tidbit and reported to his immediate supervisor. The supervisor recognized they had only a few minutes, at most, for a scoop. He pitched it to the news anchor, who instructed his assistant to phone the detective he recognized from the Vanuatuan news clips.

Less than half an hour later, TV programming was interrupted with the familiar *Breaking News* banners. In shopping districts where TVs were displayed, pandemonium ensued. Margot Lemaire was a popular figure in France, and particularly in Paris, where her face was as familiar to viewers as their own in the mirror.

Reporters flocked to the Élysée Palace demanding to know why they hadn't been notified of the death, and the President was forced to declare a day of mourning, with flags lowered to half-mast. For a minor government official who hadn't yet done anything of distinction except get a popular man elected as President, it was unprecedented.

Speculation about the circumstances would continue for

weeks, until another juicy news story came along, and then, like people everywhere, most simply forgot about Margot Lemaire.

Chapter Twenty-Three

Port Vila, Vanuatu

True to her word, Rehka called back in an hour. Rex was strolling back to the hut in the moonlight, Digger happily at his heels after a night time frolic on the beach. Unsure when she would call, Rex had taken the phone with him despite the weight in his beach shorts pocket.

After the usual weather passphrase followed by banter that indicated both were alone and not under duress, she got right down to business, first explaining that he had an early morning flight to Brisbane, Australia, thence to Mumbai.

"I'm sure you're aware there are several private enterprises as well as government agencies that track shipping traffic across the globe. I've managed to document every vessel that was in Vanuatu on the last day you saw your friend and for now limited my search to those that have left on that day and the day after. I'm going through the satellite feeds now. By the time you get here, I'll have it narrowed down enough to hack into their communications. When you're here, you can help determine which one has your friend aboard."

"Excellent work, Rehka. Remind me to give you a raise."

Her tinkle of a laugh echoed down the link. "You gave me a raise last time."

"Well, it's time for another. Okay, I take it my boarding pass is at will-call?"

"Yes."

"Thanks. I'll start packing. It won't take long. Traveling light, you know." 'Light' was a relative term. What with Digger, his travel crate, dishes, harness and leashes, and the coms gear that went everywhere with them, there wasn't much room left for items he could always pick up or borrow if he needed them only rarely.

"See you soon," she said, giving Rex the impression she was anxious to get back to work.

"Yes, see you soon. Digger will be happy to see you."

"And you won't?" she teased.

"Of course, I will. Bye."

Rex was grinning as he ended the call. Rehka had that effect on him. She was always a breath of fresh air when the situations he sometimes found himself in stank.

Rex hurried back to the hut to pack. Digger's excitement made it clear that he has sensed a new adventure coming.

That night, Rex slept better than he had in the past week. Thanks to Rehka, he had a solid chance of finding Margot and getting to the bottom of this mystery.

Chapter Twenty-Four

Mumbai, India

While she waited for her boss to arrive, Rehka wasted no time. The man she knew as Ruan Daniels, her friend and rescuer, was an exacting but very fair employer. Some things he told her, others she surmised. He was a mysterious man, but one she respected and admired greatly. And one she didn't want to disappoint.

Before she picked him up at the airport, Rehka wanted to have the fourteen vessels that had left Port Vila narrowed to no more than a handful for the SIGINT surveillance she and Rex would need to conduct if they were to find this woman he was determined to locate. Rex had told her that the witnesses all said it was a yacht she boarded, though the descriptions varied. Therefore, she eliminated the cruise ship and cargo vessels that had departed.

That brought the number down to an even dozen. Of those, two were too small to be ocean-going. They were probably pleasure yachts owned by locals that had departed for other islands in the Vanuatu archipelago. She eliminated those on the grounds that the other islands had been searched for the woman and came up empty.

That left ten, twice as many as she wanted to present to Rex by the time he touched down in Mumbai. She was able to determine through ownership records and specs on the yacht features that only eight of the remaining vessels had internet capability. The other two she set aside for later investigation in case the woman wasn't aboard one of those whose communications she could tap into.

Rehka put in a solid few hours of work after speaking with Rex, and then went to bed, knowing that once he left Brisbane, Australia, at nine a.m. the following morning, she'd have fifteen hours before he arrived locally. Admittedly, two or three of those hours would be devoted to finishing her night's sleep. But that was plenty of time.

Rehka had routed Rex through Singapore, saving up to an hour over other routes. That was in case time became an issue, though if the woman was being taken almost anywhere in this part of the world, Rex would arrive days beforehand. Logic told her no one would be sailing east, as that would be a journey of almost six-thousand miles to a major land mass such as South or North America.

Just as well, too. Tracking a yacht in that vastness wouldn't be easy.

The next morning, she got an early start and established that two of the yachts would stop in Australia where they would dock to undergo maintenance as their owners and guests departed to explore Australia for a month. She tracked each passenger through credit card usage and determined that it was unlikely Margot Lemaire was one of them. It was *possible* she was using a different name and a credit card established in that name, but it was improbable under the circumstances Rex had described.

That left six more for her to find through vulnerabilities in their communications networks and establish listening posts. Six was a stretch in the hours between then and the time she was to pick up Rex. Even if all she did was get the hacks set up and start recording them, it would be a big head start when Rex joined her to help her listen in.

———

Rex took a moment to stretch his legs upon disembarking from the plane. They'd stopped in Singapore, but head-winds had delayed their arrival, so the crew requested anyone traveling on to Mumbai remain on the aircraft. Rex could barely stand in the aisle for the few minutes between the other passengers getting off and new passengers getting on.

He could only imagine Digger's discomfort. As soon as he'd restored circulation to his legs, he hurried to the cargo area to retrieve his dog. Digger was so glad to see him. He had to command him to sit twice before Digger settled down. It was all Rex could do to calm him before opening the cage door. The first time, Digger sat, but sprang up again as soon as Rex's hand went to the catch on the door. Rex didn't want him charging through the door and startling other passengers.

"I'm glad to see you, too, boy. Let's get you some food and a chance to run."

Digger's behavior indicated he'd understood and agreed, but maybe the priority was reversed.

Rex knew Rehka would be in the terminal somewhere to meet him, and he called to let her know where he and

Digger were waiting for his other luggage. In a few minutes, she arrived, breathless, and Rex had his hands full to keep Digger from jerking the leash out of his hand in his eagerness to get to Rehka when he saw her.

She gave Digger an enthusiastic hug through his licking, yelps, and whines of excitement. Finally, when Digger calmed down, she was able to hug Rex and kiss him on the cheek. She offered to take Digger to find a spot for his relief, while Rex continued to wait for the carousel to start disgorging bags, and Digger was more than happy to go with her.

Sucker for beautiful women—just like his master. Rex smiled as the thought crossed his mind.

It was not quite dinnertime, but the flight had been long, and Rex wanted to decompress before hearing Rehka's report. He suggested she drive him to his studio apartment, where he could unpack, freshen up, and then join her at her apartment where she could show him her progress. Then they'd go out for dinner, leaving Digger in the apartment. After dinner, they'd begin combing the data her passive listening had picked up to see if they could narrow the six yachts to fewer. One way or another, they'd have to work through the recordings as quickly as possible, until they found the right yacht or caught up with real time communications.

Rex couldn't fault her logic that the yacht wouldn't have reached its destination yet, but they had no idea on which yacht she was and where it was headed, neither did they have any idea if Margot was in danger or not.

As far as Rex was concerned, and Rehka agreed, they were up against the clock.

Chapter Twenty-Five

Mumbai, India

Early the next morning, Rex kicked lightly at Rehka's apartment door. He was juggling a box of Indian pastries, one large takeaway coffee for himself and an Indian masala chai tea made from cloves, cardamom, cinnamon, black tea, sugar and milk for Rehka. He also had Digger's lunch, a roasted chicken, and his harness and leash, which he'd brought along for breaks, so they could walk Digger in a nearby park.

Rehka opened the door, laughed out loud at Rex's predicament, and took the drinks off his hands, freeing him from the imminent danger of scalding his feet if he dropped them. She stood aside for him to enter the apartment and shouldered the door shut after Digger followed him in.

Setting the drinks on a nearby table, she bent to greet Digger, who returned the gesture with great enthusiasm. Rehka laughed again at his antics.

"Any news?" Rex asked. He assumed she'd have been up

for an hour or more, and her answer confirmed he was correct.

"I've been able to eliminate two more of the signals I've been tracking. One was from a flybridge that I thought was marginal in the first place. This morning I confirmed it is occupied by a retired couple, who have stopped for some fishing in the Gulf of Carpentaria."

The Gulf of Carpentaria was the shallow sea off the coast of northern Australia between Australia and Papua New Guinea.

"Okay, yeah, sounds like that isn't the one."

"The other turned south and is headed along the southern coast of Australia toward Melbourne."

"Why did you eliminate that one?"

"Gut feeling, mostly. It appears to be a party of old friends, three couples, who are playing poker, drinking, and talking about sailing all the way around Australia."

"That's going to take them a while, it's an enormous country." Rex smiled. "And I'd say your gut feeling is right. That one wouldn't be carrying her, either."

"So, that leaves four, and I think with the two of us listening to the communications now, we'll pick her trail up sooner. I've set up a spare monitor and headphones for you in the office, where you can plug in your laptop, and I'll work here in the kitchen."

"Sounds good," he affirmed. "Have a pastry."

She grinned at him. "It's always about food with you, isn't it Ruan?"

"My motto is eat and sleep when you have a chance, because you don't know when you'll have time for it again." He didn't tell her that it was a motto drilled into him during his Delta Force and CRC training.

"And to be honest, I think that's Digger's motto, too.

Although, Digger seems to be hungry all the time. Did you look at him after he had half of that chicken just now? Don't you think that look on his face said, 'So, when am I going to get something to eat in this place?'"

Rehka laughed. "Yes, that's exactly what it looked like."

Rex looked at his dog, who'd made himself comfortable and was now sleeping in the center of the room. His ears twitched now and then. Rex had no doubt he'd heard his name, even while he slept, and was alert to hear more, especially when it had anything to do with food.

Rex collected the dishes, carried them over to the sink, washed them, and placed them in the drip tray, then turned to Rehka and said, "Shall we get to work?"

She led him to the spare bedroom she'd converted to an office space and showed him where she'd prepared the spot for his laptop. Since they were monitoring all real-time communications and listening to recordings from two yachts each, they got busy and didn't speak until Rex declared break time.

Rehka made sure the recorders were operational before they took Digger out for a run at a nearby park while they stretched their legs.

It was late in the afternoon when Rehka shouted, "Got it!"

Rex ripped the headphones from his ears and waited for her to elaborate.

"Someone on this one, the mega-yacht "Java Princess", had been googling Margot Lemaire. I'd bet that's someone trying to determine what's been reported about her disappearance."

"Yep, you could be right," he said. "Give me the details, and I'll check the yacht's bearing. You keep analyzing the internet searches coming from that yacht."

Rekha gave him the information he wanted, and they both listened and watched intently for anything else. Hours later, after a delivery dinner they both ate while maintaining their watch, Rex determined the yacht was changing directions as it prepared to pass between Papua New Guinea and the northernmost tip of Queensland, Australia.

"Looks like they're headed in the direction of Indonesia for now," he guessed.

"That's going to take a while. Let me pull up the specs for the Java Princess," she answered,

A moment later, she had them. "Cruising speed is fourteen knots, maximum twenty-two."

"I don't think they'll be going at the maximum." He compared a few of the GPS coordinates they'd collected, did a quick calculation in his head and said, "They're averaging sixteen. Yes, that's going to take a while to get to Indonesia. I think we can afford to take a break, have some dinner, and pick them up in the morning."

Digger, who'd spent most of the afternoon sleeping, sprang to his feet. The words dinner, breakfast, lunch, food, eat, and such would do it every time—without fail.

Chapter Twenty-Six

Arafura Sea, north of Darwin, Australia.

Margot took advantage of the king-sized lounge on the open deck aft for the first several days of the trip. The weather was great, the sea was calm, and she lay there in the early morning until time for lunch, and then again after the sun had descended far enough not to bake her. To keep herself busy, sometimes she read on an eReader with thousands of books on it, provided by Henri, sometimes she slept, or stared out at the endless sea or distant landforms. She'd never been indolent, and this felt like complete luxury, to just drift through the days with no duties pressing on her.

The captain had told her it would take almost twelve full days to reach Singapore, unless she was in a hurry. If necessary, the yacht could do it in eight or nine, but running her at top speed was hard on the engines, and they'd have to refuel somewhere, probably somewhere in Indonesia.

"You won't have to leave your cabin there," he assured her.

"It's all right. I'm in no hurry."

"We can of course stop whenever and wherever you'd like if you want to dive some coral reefs or swim," the captain added.

Margot shuddered. "No thank you. I have no desire to swim in the sea."

That had been nearly a week ago, and Margot was now brown as a berry and thankfully didn't suffer any sea sickness. Only occasionally was she plagued by morning sickness, and it was getting less and less frequent. In fact, she felt healthier and happier than she had in years.

Being pregnant agreed with her, it seemed.

She had fully accepted that she would raise her baby out of the public eye and on her own, though she hadn't ruled out the possibility that there could be a stepfather for the child in the future. She was sure it was a girl, though she couldn't have said why she felt it.

There was however something that bothered her. Up till now, her criminal record existed only in her mind. It would never have come to the attention of the police. Jaywalking, drinking a bit too much when she was a student, parking in the wrong space or for too long were not on the police radar and would not give her a criminal record. But now, within a bit more than a week, she had already committed one serious offense by leaving Vanuatu without going through customs, and that was minor compared to the string of crimes she was planning to commit next. Meeting with some unsavory character in Singapore to collect her new but forged passport and using that to enter Vietnam under a false name—she didn't want to count how many laws she would've broken and still intended to break by the time she left Vietnam after the baby's birth.

Her brother had said the captain would bring the fellow

to the yacht to deliver the goods. Henri had been most kind and quite discreet, never mentioning her delicate condition, if he knew about it, sharing his table with her graciously, and always striving to entertain and keep her from being too bored.

Some of the time she spent doing research, thanks to the tablet PC with a satellite internet connection her brother had the captain provide for her as part of the service. She was somewhat horrified by the descriptions of how her body was going to change in the fourth month of pregnancy, and she was thankful she hadn't had any of those symptoms yet, except her bikini tops seemed to be shrinking. After she caught the first mate staring at her, she began wearing her cover-up whenever she moved from her sunning bed to the interior of the yacht. She hadn't felt the baby move yet but was reassured that it was perfectly normal for a first-time mother not to feel any movement for another month or even two.

She supposed she'd soon start 'showing', though for now her belly was almost as flat as ever. Over the next week, however, it developed a slight curve and the bikinis were now positively obscene. She gave up sunbathing and did her reading in the spacious and lavish lounge of the yacht.

She'd grown accustomed to the luxury in her stateroom. She had the master, the captain explained. He had one of the other king staterooms, and the first mate was belowdecks in a very nice stateroom of his own.

The first time she'd taken a shower, she was almost baffled by the complex set of controls. But she quickly got used to it, and by now, she was enamored of the variety they afforded and vowed she'd have a shower just like it when she set up a home for her and her baby.

Margot often thought about Ida and Rowan and

couldn't help but feeling ashamed about how she deceived them. She and Ida got on well, but admittedly she felt a lot more endearing toward Rowan and of course Digger. It was so much fun until she discovered her pregnancy. But even then, when she was miserable, Rowan and Digger always cheered her up. He was such a gentleman. She was really going to miss the two of them, not Ida so much.

Not long after they'd met, she got the distinct impression that Rowan Donnelly was not a history teacher, and there were times when she wanted to confront him with that but held back when she realized she was also not who she said she was.

Since she got on the yacht, there were many days that she wondered if she should not have taken him into her confidence and asked him to help her. She didn't have to tell him everything. He had been so caring when he'd realized something was wrong with her, she was almost sure he would've gone out of his way to help her.

Can't turn back the clock now. Can I?

Chapter Twenty-Seven

Paris, France

The Prime Minister, Lucien Laurent, was getting ready for bed. His wife had gone to bed early and was already asleep. His heart was heavy with grief for his family friend Margot Lemaire, and he'd stayed up later than he normally did. Then he heard his doorbell ring. He paused as he heard the in-house security guard making his way to the front door. A few minutes later, a light knock at his bedroom door summoned him in his pajamas and robe to accept the package held out to him.

"Who delivered this?" he asked, now holding the package gingerly.

"One of the security detail outside, sir" he said.

The Prime Minister suppressed his irritable reaction. "He didn't stay to explain?"

"No, sir."

"Thank you."

His security team would not have wanted him to handle

a package and certainly not to open it without precautions being taken. He was confident they had done what was necessary to insure it wasn't dangerous.

He opened the package and read the note of explanation addressed to him.

"Merde!"

The Prime Minister had turned pale. His hands were shaking as he walked to his study, closed the door behind him, and sat down behind the oak desk. He seized the decanter of cognac on the credenza behind him and read the note again.

He'd made no mistake the first time. The unknown sender of the package had made a serious threat against the government of France, not to mention the threat to his old friend's daughter.

Monsieur Prime Minister, your loyalty to your friend, President Aguillard, is admirable but misguided. Enclosed is proof that he is a philanderer, contrary to his public façade. We have chosen you, as a family friend of the woman he has impregnated, to confront him with this knowledge and challenge him to save his Presidency by complying with our demands.

Margot Lemaire is alive. We know her whereabouts. We assure you no harm will come to her unless President Aguillard fails to meet the terms of our demands.

We know you hold sway over the President and that you are a reasonable man. It is our expectation that you will use your influence to encourage the President to do the right thing and not embarrass France and the EU.

The clock is ticking.

The second reading sent his anxiety up another notch.

He pushed the flash drive that came with the package into the USB port of his laptop.

He began with the Word file. It was named 'The Aguillard-Lemaire Affair.docx'.

MR. PRESIDENT YOUR PREDECESSOR REFUSED TO SIGN THE PROPOSED GAS PIPELINE AGREEMENT. DESPITE THE FACT THAT YOU HAVE SAID YOU WOULD CONTINUE HIS POLICIES, WE LIKED YOU RIGHT FROM THE BEGINNING AND SUPPORTED YOUR CAMPAIGN IN ANY WAY WE COULD. YOU CAN THANK US FOR GETTING YOU ELECTED.

THEREFORE, WE ARE SURE, OUT OF GRATITUDE FOR OUR HELP, YOU WOULD WANT TO SIGN THE OIL PIPELINE AGREEMENT. OF COURSE, IF YOU DON'T WANT TO DO SO THAT'S YOUR PREROGATIVE.

HOWEVER, WE WOULD LIKE YOU TO SERIOUSLY CONSIDER DOING SO, AS WE HAVE CERTAIN INFORMATION ABOUT YOUR PECCADILLOS, WHICH IF WE RELEASE IT, WILL DESTROY YOUR REPUTATION, YOUR MARRIAGE, YOUR PARTY, AND YOUR COUNTRY. JUST LOOK AT AND LISTEN TO THE REST OF THE FILES ON THE FLASHDRIVE THAT CAME WITH THIS LETTER. WE ARE CONFIDENT THAT YOU WILL MAKE THE RIGHT DECISION FOR YOUR REPUTATION, YOUR MARRIAGE, YOUR PARTY, AND YOUR COUNTRY.

"How curious," the Prime Minister remarked aloud. The

threats to the President were much more subtle than in the note addressed to him. It appeared he'd been elected to deliver the worst of them. The next file was the image, named 'Blood-tests-Don't-Lie.jpeg', so he opened that. At first, he wasn't sure what he was seeing. A closer look, after he enlarged the image on the monitor, made him shout, "The rumors are true then!"

Before he opened the last file, an audio file named 'Listen-To-This.mp3', which by now he feared could be the worst of all, he poured himself a two-finger shot of cognac and downed it in one gulp, then poured another.

Steeling himself to hear whatever was on the file—*please God, don't let it be them in flagrante*—he listened to Margot Lemaire talking to her brother on the phone. *Thank God!*

However, his relief was short-lived.

The conversation was exactly fifteen minutes and thirty-four seconds long, and the sound quality was impeccable. There could be no misunderstanding or doubt about who was talking and what was said. During the time he listened, he downed three more double-finger cognacs.

In his disquiet over the rest of the message, he'd momentarily forgotten that just this afternoon he'd thought Margot dead. He had a fondness for her based on the life-long friendship he'd enjoyed with her father.

Thank God, she's alive.

But again, his relief was short-lived as the gravity of the situation dawned on him. What he'd seen and heard was a political nuclear bomb with a ticking timer, and he was only able to deal with the knowledge without breaking into a destructive rage because he was by then very drunk.

Mon Dieu! What a disaster! If Giles were not the President, and if it were not the twenty-first century, I'd go over there and slap him across the face with a white glove! What was he thinking?

Well, it was obvious he'd not been using his brain.

The same goes for Margot.

Though the text was blurring, the combined effect of being awake the whole night and finishing the entire decanter of cognac, he gave the Word file with the message to the President one more read and looked at the scanned image of Margot's pregnancy test. Though he was disappointed in her rather than enraged, as he was with the President, he couldn't help but think she'd been irresponsible.

Had the woman never heard of birth control? But I guess I could ask the same question of the President.

Often, issues had a way of resolving themselves without the need for action. This was not one of those; it was wishful thinking to keep it all to himself or hope it would go away if he ignored it. It was incumbent upon him to do what he must to protect the party and the President, not to mention Margot and her baby. And France. And the EU. And NATO.

Too many interests to protect. Somewhere, something is bound to give. And I'm not even the one who caused this mess.

The letter had held a vague hint that the President must sign the accursed agreement soon, and any delay would trigger the obvious threat contained in the files accompanying the letter of demand.

Thinking of that led him to the obvious question he'd not asked so far; *Why me? Why did they pick me? Holding sway over the President? My ass. If it is so, it was obviously not enough to keep him from adultery with a woman who is young enough to be his daughter.*

Does the fact that I know now make me complicit in this ethical dilemma? Probably not, but if I become involved in the obfuscation thereof, the President and I will, on the same day, be packing our tchotchkes in cardboard boxes in the presence of security staff before we're escorted off government premises—in one of the biggest scandals in French political history.

I wish I had never read this.

But contrary to the software on his computer, his brain didn't have an 'undo' button. There were many reasons he could think of why he'd been selected, and none of them had anything to do with the so-called 'sway' he held over the President. What came to mind were several: to sow distrust and discord in the government first, to destroy the good relationship between him and the President, to destroy him and the President so thoroughly they'd never have a say in government again, to shock the French people into voting for another party, one that would allow the cursed pipeline to be built.

The solution?

I don't have an idea, but we need one, and a few backup solutions, and we need them immediately.

Though it was three-thirty in the morning, at least two hours before the President would normally be awake, he made a call to the President's aide and insisted on seeing the President immediately. Then he summoned his assistant to call his driver while he took a shower and got ready to face the worst day of his life.

Chapter Twenty-Eight

Paris, France

Giles Aguillard and Lucien Laurent had known each other since their university days, and over the years they'd become very close friends who trusted and respected each other. Nonetheless, Aguillard was enraged at being awakened at the ungodly hour of three-forty-five a.m.

This had better be good.

His anger escalated to just short of a screaming rage when he entered his study and found his Prime Minister in an obvious state of inebriation, speech slurring, and unsteady on his feet.

"What is the meaning of this, Lucien?"

Laurent thrust a piece of paper into his hand and countered, "Why don't you rather tell me what the hell's the meaning of *this*?" It was the letter that came with the flash drive.

Aguillard studied the paper with confusion and looked up, his expression troubled. "Where did you get this?"

"That letter and this flash drive were delivered to my quarters late last night."

The President handed the paper back. His face had gone ashen, and he didn't say anything as he held out his hand to Lauren in a gesture to give him the flash drive.

Aguillard sat down behind his desk, turned on his computer, and inserted the drive. He didn't consider whether it might be infected with a malicious program, if the Prime Minister had opened it, it must have been vetted by security. He opened the drive directory and clicked on the image file, Bloodtests-Don't-Lie.jpeg, and stared at the medical record that indicated Margot had been pregnant.

The next file he opened was the letter, The Aguillard-Lemaire Affair.docx. His jaw worked as he read it and recognized it for what it was—a blackmail attempt.

So, someone knew of the affair, and put two and two together to make five. It doesn't constitute proof that I am the father of this inconvenient child of Margot's though... our child.

But what's this last file?

Obviously, it was an audio file. He looked around nervously and saw that it was still only him and Laurent in his office, the security team just outside the double doors, presumably. The doors were shut. It was safe to listen to the file so long as the volume was down. He clicked to open the file and immediately lowered the volume when the sound started.

Margot's familiar voice came through the speakers, and it soon became clear she was speaking to a man she trusted implicitly. Bertrand... wasn't that her brother?

Aguillard listened with growing alarm as he heard Margot telling her brother she was in trouble and needed his help. Though she never said his name, Aguillard recognized she was determined to protect the identity of the baby's father and had engineered her disappearance to make it unlikely anyone would look for her.

Good girl.

But it was also blatantly obvious that her brother had reached a conclusion about who the father was, although he also didn't say it.

Well, he was still technically in the clear, though anyone who'd heard the rumors, among which counted his wife and God knew how many others with half a brain, including her brother, would be able to put two and two together, as the blackmailers clearly had. And if the media discovered this, Margot would be put under merciless pressure to come clean.

It was only a matter of time.

He returned to the demand letter and read it again.

Merde, this is a double-edged sword. I'll be out of office in days if this comes out, and the next President will let the Russians have their pipeline.

Now he knew why his Prime Minister had been so angry and so drunk. Aguillard recalled the friendship between the families. The only choice he had now was to involve his friend in the cover-up, because a cover-up would be imperative. In fact, come to think of it, the Prime Minister had de facto become involved when he'd read that letter and the rest of the files on the flash drive. If he only remained silent about it and did nothing else, he *would* be complicit.

Aguillard had not risen to the top of his calling because he was stupid, though he recognized, not for the first time, that having an affair with a much younger woman who was also his employee could only be described as short-sighted. And if he had to be honest with himself, as he had every so often been over the past

few months, he'd have to admit, also stupid and irresponsible.

Even so, his mind immediately went to work on what he
would need to do next. First was to extract an oath of
silence from Laurent. But the man was more than just a
little drunk, more like three sheets to the wind.

Aguillard paced as he considered the dilemmas he
faced. Had he been a less experienced politician, they would
have been heart-stopping. As it was, they required some
finesse, and panicking would do him no good.

He needed time, and the blackmailers, obviously
Russians, though he didn't yet know whether it was a
private enterprise or the government he was dealing with,
had hinted there was none to waste. But he had no doubts
that someone in the Russian government would be found at
the bottom of this. However, he couldn't sign the agreement
they wanted without bringing his constituents down on him,
not to mention the entire European Union and NATO.

France was already dependent on Russia for a large
percentage of their gas. Russia, for years, had been drooling
at the prospect of increasing that dependency. They already
had most of Western Europe tied up in increasingly expen-
sive dependency on their product.

The Americans wouldn't like it either, for both strategic
and economic reasons. Not that he personally gave one whit
about whether the Americans approved of his actions or
not. The issue was that America was a powerful ally,
powerful being the operative word. This early in his presidency, he couldn't afford to alienate them.

Those were the international political repercussions.

In France, although not openly admitted, it was hardly a
cardinal sin to have a mistress. What *was* a big deal was
being caught out. And having the existence of one appear

in the headlines for a President was going to be a first. There was no telling what the French public's reaction was going to be.

His next issue would be what his wife would do if she got wind of it—she was aware of the rumors about the affair and had confronted him about it. He told her it was dirty politics from the opposition. She believed him. If she now learned he'd lied—well, the word emasculation came to mind, and not only emotional. A cold shiver ravaged his body at the thoughts that crossed his mind.

She has enough clout to get the guillotine reinstated, and I'm sure my allowance and head would not be the first things to be chopped off.

But he had no doubt, eventually his head would go as well. A scandal had to be avoided—if necessary, at all cost.

Aguillard had been in politics long enough to know that the judicial principle of innocence until proven guilty didn't operate in the court of public opinion. In that court, there was no trial, neither the right to representation, nor the right to be heard. Once accused of wrongdoing, he would be guilty. Not that he was innocent to begin with, but if he could somehow come up with a way to control the narrative, the outcome might be less excruciating than when the media controlled it.

He turned to Laurent and said, "Lucien, here's what we're going to do now. First, I'm going to order the DGSE to find Margot at any cost."

The DGSE, General Directorate for External Security, was France's external intelligence agency, the French equivalent to the United Kingdom's MI6 and the United States' CIA.

"We're going to cite the package but not tell them about all of its contents." What he didn't tell his intoxicated friend was that if he went along with this, he'd be complicit to the coverup, and they would face the same consequences if it became public.

"We'll tell them we have it on authority she is alive, in Vietnam and perhaps plotting with a foreign government. That should do it. By the time they find her, we will have figured out what to do."

The Prime Minister was just staring at him. Probably too drunk and too tired, or to shocked, or all of the above, to make a reply.

"You see, Lucien," the President continued, "securing her physically will break the stranglehold the Russians have on us."

Laurent's eyes were glazed over as he stared at Aguillard in apparent stupor and remained wordless.

"They could hardly claim she is alive if they couldn't produce her, and failing that claim, no one would believe the rest of it. But then… it would only work so long as she is prepared to deny the affair."

Aguillard continued his soliloquy for a few more minutes before he realized that his Prime Minister, although present in body, was definitely absent in mind. The lights were on, but no one was at home. He paused, fixed his gaze on Lucien, and frowned but got no response. It was infuriating, but he also knew at that moment he had only one ally, or rather potential ally, and he had to be careful not to estrange him. In the coming days and weeks, friends might very well become a scarcity.

Hmm, maybe not a good idea to expect a drunk man to come up with any brilliant ideas. He decided to continue his problem solving in silence.

Bargaining on Margot's silence was a different kettle of bouillabaisse. Aguillard had no doubt Margot was like any other woman when it came to love. The ancient saying, *Hell hath no fury like a woman scorned* was likely to come into play. He'd have to take steps to avoid that, because the moment she appeared on TV stating that she was carrying his baby, and he was trying to silence her, public opinion would sway in her favor, and he'd be in worse trouble than ever.

Should I have her killed? Insist she's a spy and must be eliminated?

No, that ruthless he was not, but he had to admit that if she were dead, then the well-known Stalin doctrine was in play – "Death solves all problems—no man (in this case woman), no problem."

Surely the interests of France, Europe, and NATO were worth more than one life?

Two his conscience interrupted his chain of thought. *One of them your own blood!*

Chapter Twenty-Nine

Paris, France

Two hours later, and with several cups of strong black coffee coursing through his system, Lucien Laurent had started to participate in the conversation.

To Aguillard's relief, it seemed as if Laurent had made up his mind and was not going to abandon him.

Laurent pointed out that the DGSE operated under the direction of the Ministry of Defense, therefore the Minister had to be read in on the matter before his agents can be sent on any mission. The only question was what was the Minister allowed to know?

They both agreed that for now, the Minister of Defense only needed to know that Margot Lemaire had become a national security risk and that it was of the utmost importance to apprehend her, bring her back to France for questioning, and to keep the whole mission top secret—strictly need to know only. The Minister had to report directly to the President and Prime Minister.

In due course, the Minister of Defense was summoned to an early morning emergency meeting with the President and Prime Minister on a matter of national security.

From the backseat of his official vehicle, when the building came into view, the Minister couldn't help but think of the history of the imposing presidential residence and office known as the Élysée Palace where the Council of Ministers held their meetings. It was built in 1722 for Louis Henri de La Tour d'Auvergne and had been in use as the office of the French President since 1848.

The name Élysée was derived from Elysian Fields, 'the place of the blessed dead' in Greek mythology.

The meeting was brief and to the point. Neither the President nor the Prime Minister would reveal the source of their information about Mademoiselle Lemaire's apparent perfidy. Yes, he understood the gravity of the situation, the need to act with speed, and the need to not discuss the details with anyone. Not even the agents he was going to assign to the mission. All they had to know was that it was a matter of national importance. He also understood that she was not to be harmed, and he had to act upon it immediately.

Word went down from the Minister of Defense to the director of the DGSE, who briefed a team of three of France's experienced field agents.

The Minister wasn't given any specific information about Lemaire's alleged treachery. He was a politician and had no experience or skills in these kinds of matters and didn't ask for more information. For him and for his career it was more than enough that the President knew the facts and wanted him to make it happen. The Director of the DGSE, on the contrary, was an experienced spook and analyst and pulsed the Minister for details. But he was told that the President had the details, was obviously not prepared to divulge them, and that should be enough for the director to act on. It was not as if it was expected of him to send his agents on a life-threatening mission. Besides, what else did the director need to know to send a few agents on a simple mission to Vietnam to apprehend Margot Lemaire?

The director knew when to stop questioning his orders if he wanted to stay in his position and hope to retire on full pension one day. So, he nodded and told the Minister he'd get onto it immediately.

The director briefed the agents with the little he knew and passed on the same sentiments passed on to him by the Minister when the agents had many questions. "This assignment comes directly from President Aguillard," he told them. "You should be honored. The President is privy to information way above your and my pay grades. So, stop second guessing me or the President for that matter. Get your asses out of here, go to Vietnam, observe Mademoiselle Lemaire, gather evidence of her indiscretions if you get the opportunity, apprehend her, and bring her back to France. How much more do you need to know in order to execute an order as simple as that?"

The three agents looked at each other, shrugged in unison, and stood to leave.

"Oh, two more things," the director said, "One, you are not to harm her in any manner. Is that understood?"

"Yes, sir," they replied in chorus.

"Good. Two, I want daily reports at the minimum. More if necessary."

"Yes, sir," they replied in chorus again.

Like the three stooges, the director couldn't help but think when they turned and left his office.

Chapter Thirty

Mumbai, India

The days became tedious for Rex, who preferred action to the eternal and insufferable waiting, but despite his preferences, waiting was familiar. He continued to track the yacht they thought bore Margot westward, listening and watching in real time to all signals emanating from it.

Meanwhile, in case they were wrong, Rehka was monitoring the other three. She had developed a method to monitor the audio signals using audio editing software that showed her the spikes of noise when someone was speaking over the radios. That way, she didn't have to do as Rex was doing and listen to long periods of silence.

It gave her the ability to keep track of three yachts while Rex focused on the one in which they were most interested. If something emerged that proved them wrong about which yacht carried Margot, they wouldn't be too far behind in tracking the others. And if their SIGINT effort produced a positive indication that she was on a different one, they'd know it soon enough to change tacks.

When Rehka hacked into the satellite links of the yachts, she also uploaded a small and unobtrusive piece of software which accessed the microphones of all electronic devices using the uplink. The software activated the microphones and kept them running with the user of the devices none the wiser. This enabled them to listen to any conversations taking place in proximity to those devices when they were switched on.

So far, they'd listened to the captain or his first mate talking on the satellite phone or on the marine radio network making daily reports or talking to other ocean-going vessels. None of the conversations made any mention of a girl on board.

It was late on the twelfth day after Rex had the last dinner with Margot that he noted the Java Princess might be heading for Singapore. Not long afterward, he got confirmation when he overheard a conversation between a male who he assumed was the captain of the yacht and a male who he assumed was in Singapore.

The conversation was brief. The presumed captain said, "Henri here. We're about three and a half hours away. Do you have everything ready?"

The Singaporean answered, "Yes. I have. Text me when you've docked. I'll meet you at the taxi rank on Sentosa Island."

Rex couldn't imagine a legitimate reason for Margot to go there willingly, lending more credence to the idea she'd been abducted, or at the very least, had not been going there by her own choice.

Or is Singapore where they're going to take her off the yacht? Hence the meeting in the parking lot. I need to get there before they dock.

He alerted Rehka to what was happening and re-tasked her to research flights from Mumbai to Singapore and get him on the first one that was available. If he lost the trail in Singapore, he might never pick it up again if she were to be taken into one of the South East Asian countries. He continued to monitor everything in real time, while Rehka divided her attention between monitoring the other yachts and making arrangements to get him and Digger to Singapore on the first available flight. It was a five and a half hour flight, but then he still had to get Digger and clear customs. He could only hope that the yacht would still be there when he arrived and hope that Margot might perchance still be aboard. If not, he'd have to persuade the captain to assist him in tracking her down if she wasn't. That was if the yacht was still there when he got to the harbor.

They agreed while Rex was en route, Rehka would continue to monitor the other yachts as before and take over the real-time observation of the Java Princess, so she could update him when he landed.

Rehka had found a flight leaving in only four hours and he had to start checking in three hours before departure. Although, he knew the airline staff would only close check-in an hour before departure, it was still going to be tight. He had less than two hours to race back to his apartment to get the rest of his and Digger's gear, quickly walk Digger, and get to the airport to check the dog into cargo before the deadline to report to his gate and board the plane.

Fortunately, he found a taxi driver who, after being handed a wad of cash equivalent to what he would earn in a week, understood the word 'hurry' to mean exactly what Rex had meant it to. The drive to the apartment was hair-raising. On arrival, Rex asked him to wait and shoved another wad of cash at him.

Fifteen minutes after he arrived at the apartment, Rex had a hastily-packed carry-on with Digger's gear, another with his minimum requirements, and an agitated Digger back in the taxi. He explained to the baffled driver that he required a stop at a nearby park for the dog before they could proceed to the airport. He didn't try to translate or explain the common American expressions 'hurry up and wait' or 'take your time as long as you do it in a hurry'.

Chapter Thirty-One

Singapore

Arriving in Singapore harbor, three hours after talking to his contact, Henri motored smoothly into a pier in the orderly slips of the yacht club. Margot would wait on the yacht while Henri fetched the forger.

Henri took a taxi to Sentosa Island and came back in the same taxi with a gentleman who looked like a successful businessman dressed in a sharp-looking suit. Not the unsavory character she'd expected. He politely shook her hand, then indicated his briefcase and asked if she would like to see the work before he left.

Henri had coached her, before leaving to fetch the man, that it was critically important for Margot not to do anything that would make this man suspicious that it could be a police sting. Difficult as it was, it meant suppressing her nerves and acting as if this were any other legitimate business transaction.

"Yes, that would be appropriate," she said, in English,

affecting cool indifference. She inspected the documents. She had no expertise in forged passports or any forged official documents for that matter, but she couldn't see any flaws. Without saying a word, she handed them to Henri for his opinion.

Henri looked at them nodded and handed it back to her.

After the forger had debarked and been driven away in the waiting taxi, she and Henri reverted to French. He declared, "These papers are serviceable, but perhaps not the best quality I've ever seen. It might have been dangerous to say so in his presence, however."

"I only need them to get me into Vietnam without raising eyebrows," she said.

"Then they will do fine."

"Thanks for your help with this, Henri. I appreciate it very much."

"My pleasure, mademoiselle. We should be on our way to Vietnam in a few hours."

Six hours after arrival in Singapore, the yacht had been refueled, supplies had been stocked, and they were on their way again.

Next stop: Ho Chi Minh City. Another day and a half at sea. Then waiting for Henri to let Bert know about our arrival and his contact to pick me up and transport me by land to the convent in Da Nang, my temporary home for the next six or so months.

She sighed, lay back on her bed, and closed her eyes.

Chapter Thirty-Two

After the mad rush to get on the plane, the usual wait between check-in time and boarding was welcome. He had time to take a deep breath, grab a bite to eat, and secure a bottle of water for the flight.

He had about ten minutes before the boarding call when his satphone rang.

"Ruan, I've got some good news. Margot, if that's her on the yacht, has not left it. She's heading for Vietnam."

"Explain quickly, please. I am about to be called to board the plane."

"I overheard a conversation between Henri, the guy who we think could be the captain and the man who he called earlier to announce their arrival and a woman. They spoke English while the man who came aboard was there, but they reverted to French after he left."

"I didn't know you spoke French," Rex interjected.

157

"I don't. I ran it through automatic transcription and then through Google's translation program."

Rex shook his head in admiration.

"Okay, what did they talk about?"

"Well, they didn't use the word passport, but from the context of the conversations, I got the impression that was what this man brought to them and what he was paid for."

"Passport you say… hmm that makes sense. She left hers in Vanuatu, and she can't get off the yacht without one. Okay, no time to wonder about that now. So, you also overheard that they're heading for Vietnam now?"

"Yes, that's what I gathered from the translation between the woman and this Henri guy. Something to the affect that she needs it to get her into Vietnam without raising suspicion. But I've made a recording of the whole conversation and sent it to your phone."

"Rehka, you're a star. Thanks for that. Okay, I guess there's no sense in trying to try and cancel my flight now. I've checked in and cleared customs, Digger is probably already on the plane. I guess the best is for me to go to Singapore and from there to Vietnam. At least that's only two hours flying."

"I agree. I have already started looking for flights from Singapore to Ho Chi Minh City."

Overhead, he heard his section number called for boarding.

"Thanks, Rehka, I've got to go now. I'll call you after I've landed."

"Okay, Ruan have a safe trip. I'll keep on listening."

Once the plane had reached cruising altitude and the hostess had served him with a packet of snacks and a soft drink, he retrieved his earphones from his bag and plugged them into his satphone.

The sound quality was poor, and it was difficult to say with one hundred percent certainty it was Margot's voice he was listening to. He'd heard her French accented English and the way she pronounced certain words when they were speaking English for Ida's benefit, and that was the one thing that made him at least ninety percent sure it was Margot's voice.

Other than that, Rex reached the same conclusions as Rehka; the meeting on the Java Princess in Singapore was about a passport or some kind of papers that would help this woman get through Vietnamese customs, and that they'd soon be en route from Singapore to Vietnam.

Vietnam? Ah, it's a former French colony. That makes some sense.

However, the big takeaway of the conversation between Henri and this woman was the tone thereof. There was no indication of antagonism between them. On the contrary, it sounded as if they were good friends. And that immediately had him in doubt about his assumption that Margot had been abducted or was even on that yacht against her wishes. Thinking about it, he had to admit that it fit much better with what he thought earlier about the way she said goodbye to him and Ida the last night they saw her.

But that meant she'd planned her disappearance.

Of course, those conclusions immediately unleashed another barrage of unanswerable questions. He sighed, pushed the button in the armrest of his chair to recline his seat, leaned back in it, and closed his eyes.

Many questions and no answers.

Chapter Thirty-Three

Singapore

It was past midnight in Singapore when his plane arrived. He called Rehka on the secure satphone for an update immediately and asked for the status of the yacht as he walked toward the cargo area to get Digger.

"The Java Princess left port two hours ago, they're going to Ho Chi Minh City. Do you want to go straight there or wait until we're sure?" she asked after the usual security routine.

"Digger needs a break from air travel, and I could use a good night's sleep. Let's wait. I'll call you when I get to a hotel."

"Way ahead of you, boss. I assumed you'd want to wait and booked a room. The hotel has a dog walking area. Their restaurant is closed now, though. You'll have to grab a snack there at the airport."

Rex thought, not for the first time, what a jewel he'd found in Rehka. "You're the best," he told her.

He could hear the smile in her voice as she thanked him. It took so little to make her happy. Her life now was charmed, compared to the circumstances in which he'd found her at first, enslaved in a Saudi harem. No wonder she was always so cheerful, at least when she interacted with him.

"Keep me in the loop," he added. "It will be at least another hour before I sack out."

"I will," she promised.

By the time he'd walked Digger, found something for them to eat, and reached his hotel room, Rehka had reported that there was virtually no SIGINT coming from the yacht. Everyone aboard, except whoever was piloting, was probably asleep. Rex told her to grab some sleep herself and call him when she woke up in the morning.

Mumbai was two and a half hours behind Singapore, so Rex didn't expect a report before he and Digger left the hotel room. Nevertheless, he got a wake-up call only five hours after he'd gone to sleep.

"She's definitely aboard," Rehka reported. "Now that we know her cell signal, I've been monitoring that. She called someone in France just a few minutes ago."

"What did they say?"

"Well, here is a piece of new information. They had a long discussion about her pregnancy and…"

"What! Did you say pregnancy?"

"Yes, Ruan, that's what I said. This woman is pregnant. Erratic as the Google translations are, it's clear that she's pregnant and that she's going to Vietnam to have the baby there…"

"Pregnant. How the hell…"

Rehka started giggling. "Ruan, don't tell me you've never had a lesson about the birds and the bees. Unless it was done artificially, there's just one way…"

"Yes, yes, that much I know, but…"

"Ruan, you're not perhaps…"

"No, Rehka you don't have to spend another second on that thought. My friendship with her is purely platonic."

"Don't worry, I believe you. Notwithstanding, she *is* pregnant and apparently going to book into a convent in Da Nang and stay there for the rest of her pregnancy."

"Okay."

"The translation software isn't very good, you know. Sometimes it comes back with something that makes no sense. But I've sent you the audio file—you can listen to it."

"Well, it's very resourceful of you to use it at all. Go ahead and get me a flight to Saigon."

"You do know it's called Ho Chi Minh City now, yes?" she asked.

Rex knew the city was renamed from Saigon to Ho Chi Minh City after the Fall of Saigon in 1975, in honor of Hồ Chí Minh, the first leader of North Vietnam. However, the informal name spelled, Sài Gòn, remained in daily speech both domestically and internationally.

"Yes, I know, just a slip of the tongue. That's the name I learned in school when we did the history of the Vietnam war. Ho Chi Minh City it is then.

Rehka said she'd get back to him with flight plans.

Rex tried to go back to sleep—it was impossible. His brain was teeming with a whole new scenario and what felt like hundreds of new questions.

Pregnant? That explains her nausea on the boat trip… and abstaining from alcohol.

He checked his phone; the audio file was there. He plugged his earphones in, sat down on the chair next to his bed, pushed the play icon on the sound app, closed his eyes, and listened.

Because this file was directly recorded from a phone, the quality was much better than the previous file. He heard her say to the man who answered the call, "Hi, just letting you know that I got my new passport, and we are on our way to Vietnam."

After listening to the first few sentences uttered by the woman on the phone, he knew with hundred percent certainty it was Margot.

Okay, that box has now finally been ticked and firmly so—she is alive.

The other box that's also been ticked firmly now is that she'd not been abducted.

He continued to listen as the man assured her everything would be okay, and they discussed the arrangements he'd made for her to go to a convent in Da Nang to have the baby.

After a few more minutes of discussing arrangements, the call ended when Margot told the man that she'd just remembered she was not supposed to use her cellphone at all.

That left Rex in frustration that he still didn't have the slightest clue as to why she was hiding her pregnancy from the world.

What could the reason be? Well, she is a famous and high-ranking person in the French government. But she never mentioned a boyfriend to me. Could it be that her pregnancy might cause some sort of scandal in France and that's what she's hiding from?

Chapter Thirty-Four

Changi Airport, Singapore

After missing the yacht in Singapore and cooling his heels overnight, Rex woke before dawn the next morning with a sense that the chase was about to end. He and Digger had a flight to Ho Chi Minh City to catch, and according to his calculations he'd be there several hours before the yacht arrived. He'd have time to take care of Digger's needs, scout, maybe get something to eat, and then be on the spot as Rehka kept him up to the moment on exactly where it would dock.

He didn't count on the string of minor disasters that began the moment he stepped out of his hotel room. There was no one at the desk, and ringing the bell several times didn't produce a person either. He could have walked out without settling the bill, not that he would ever do so. At the last possible moment before he would have had to leave to make it to the airport, a sleepy desk clerk appeared, scowling and scolding Rex roundly in Mandarin.

Rex apologized in the same language and explained quickly that he had a flight to catch. The desk clerk gave a slight bow, but not before the look of astonishment crossed his face that this *báirén* understood and addressed him in his mother tongue. He immediately switched to Singlish, the informal English-based creole spoken in Singapore, for the rest of the transaction. Rex had to suppress a smile at the clerk's embarrassment.

It was also too early for any place to be open for breakfast. Rex could handle the hunger—after all, it was only a short flight, and in any case, there'd be vending machines at the airport. However, he didn't have kibble or anything else suitable for Digger's meal. Digger was already beginning to show confusion and impatience for why his breakfast hadn't materialized as usual.

There was nothing to be done about it but head for the airport and hope a solution would present itself. But, when they arrived, the delay at the hotel had left Rex with no time before Digger had to be handed over to the baggage area. As Rex ordered Digger into the crate, his furry companion let out a mournful howl which could only have meant, "Damn, Dalton, you put me on a plane without feeding me first. What's gotten into you?" This protestation from Digger not only raised the hackles on Rex's neck, it also set two or three other dogs barking in a crazy frenzy—probably in sympathy for Digger.

Rex muttered, "Sorry, boy. I'll make it up to you, I promise," as he beat a hasty retreat from the frowns of the baggage clerks. He didn't envy them trying to settle their charges after that. He had no time to placate them, and he already felt terribly guilty about Digger's hunger and sense of abandonment.

Looking over the unappetizing selections in the first

vending machine he came to, Rex was visualizing trying to find a juicy steak or roasted chicken, whichever he could find first in Vietnam to make it up to the dog when an overhead announcement made a bad situation worse. His flight was delayed because of a mechanical problem. Rex hurried to the information desk and asked if they knew how long. The answer wasn't reassuring, in fact, unhelpful would have been a more accurate description as the shoulder-shrugging clerk said, "No, sir, we have no information at this time. And we don't know when we will know more. Perhaps an hour, perhaps two… could be more."

Rex quickly realized that throwing his toys out of the crib wouldn't fix the plane, so he turned his thoughts to Digger. An hour wouldn't give him time to retrieve the dog from baggage. In fact, there was a chance he was already aboard the plane. He asked about that, and again got noncommittal, vague, and unhelpful answers—frustrating.

This is not going well.

He requested to speak to someone who could tell him whether the animals were aboard the plane yet, whether they would be given water at least, and whether he could be permitted to feed his dog during the delay. Every question was met with a blank stare or one of what felt to him like at least five body language variations of "I don't know."

But every person has a limit to their patience, and for Rex, anything that could impact on Digger's well-being was the no go zone. He slammed a closed fist on the counter, causing the two airline employees behind it to jump. He looked the woman he was speaking to straight in the eyes and started speaking softly and measuredly, "Listen carefully. My dog is a service animal. I demand the opportunity to see to his safety. If he's sitting in his cage inside a hot aircraft for much longer, his life is in danger."

The two clerks spoke to each other rapidly in a language Rex didn't know. Tamil, perhaps—one of the three official languages of the island nation of Singapore. Then the woman turned back to him and spoke softly. "My co-worker will call down and ensure that your dog and the other animals aboard have water and ventilation. I'm sorry, sir, but that is the best we can do. You are forbidden to return to the area."

Rex was still anxious about Digger's safety, but he wouldn't help the situation any if he got himself arrested. He worked to control his anger and frustration, pacing it off while he waited for the overhead announcement to inform him how much longer the flight would be delayed.

He paced for two hours, growing increasingly worried about Digger and about beating the yacht to the finish line —the dock in Ho Chi Minh City's port. At last, the announcement came. There would be another two-hour delay. Passengers were advised to enjoy the airport's restaurants and duty-free shops before checking in again.

That was the last straw for Rex. He stepped away from the nearest person and called Rehka on the satphone, despite the early hour in Mumbai. "Rehka, I'm sorry to wake you, but are there any other flights leaving here in the next two hours? My plane has mechanical issues, Digger's been in baggage for hours without food, and I'm concerned about him. If I can get him out of there, I'll just take another flight."

"Good morning to you, too, Ruan," she said. "I will see what I can do." She ended the call before he could apologize for his abruptness.

Shit, on top of all this, I've now blown it with Rehka, as well. You better get a grip on yourself Dalton, you're acting like a spoiled brat.

Thankfully, the restaurants were now open. He secured half a dozen McDonald's egg and sausage biscuits, downed two himself with a cup of coffee, and headed to the baggage area, despite having been told to stay away. On the way, he composed himself. He was convinced that if he could make nice with the employees, he wouldn't be arrested. Fortunately, that proved to be true. Perhaps his low blood sugar because of an empty stomach was part of his earlier grumpiness.

Rex found a baggage clerk whose ethnicity looked to be Chinese and asked politely in Mandarin if he could arrange to have some food delivered to his dog. He explained the dog hadn't had any food today, and because of the delay was probably suffering from hunger.

The clerk turned out to be sympathetic and promised he'd personally deliver the food to Digger. Rex told the man what to say to Digger when he fed him and how to avoid losing his fingers—Rex crossed his own while giving the man the instructions.

A few minutes later, the man came back smiling. "Your dog said thank you," he quipped. Rex could imagine it. A starving Digger, hearing the command "mind your manners" sitting down politely as the clerk gingerly held a sandwich between his fingers and poked it through the cage wires, and the man snatching his hand back when Digger's large mouth opened to take the treat.

He'd taught Digger the command after nearly losing his own fingers a few times. He'd never tried it when Digger was this hungry, though. It was with relief that he offered the volunteer a tip for his bravery and humor. However, the man refused the tip curtly.

"It was my pleasure, sir."

Rex recognized he'd offended the man. He apologized.

"He has water?" Rex asked.

"Yes, sir. Orders came down to give all the animals some water. We also opened the baggage compartment doors to give them some air. It's warm, but the air is circulating. They are not in distress. However, I am curious. You speak with no *guówài* accent. How is this possible?"

Rex gave his usual shrug. "It's just something I can do," he said. "I don't know why."

Rex was glad Digger had the good luck to be cared for by an employee who apparently liked dogs. He stopped worrying about that but was still concerned whether he'd be able to get Digger off the plane if Rehka came up with a different flight.

As he thought about it, he also wondered what the heck was taking her so long. As if by telepathy, his sat phone chirped ten seconds later.

"Hello, and good morning, Rehka." He smiled as he said it, knowing the smile would change the pronunciation of the words and signal that he was more cheerful.

She answered in kind. "We're a little happier now, are we?"

He grinned even broader. "Yes. Food in our bellies, and I'm no longer worried about Digger. He's in good hands. And please accept my sincere apology for my inexcusable manners earlier."

"No problem, Ruan. Apology accepted. I know you're in great stress over there."

"You can say that again. Since I woke up this morning, nothing has gone my way. What's the good news?"

"There isn't any, I'm afraid. The last alternative flight to Ho Chi Minh City left about ten minutes before you called me. There isn't another for three hours. I didn't book it, since you said your delay would be two hours, but I can if you want. There were plenty of seats available."

"No, I guess this one will have to do. At least they gave us a time frame. If that changes, I'll call you back. At this rate, though, the yacht's going to be there before I can arrive."

"I'll cross my fingers, Ruan."

"Thanks. I'll be in touch."

Half an hour later, the overhead speakers announced that boarding for his flight would begin in ten minutes. He thanked the employees who'd helped Digger and hustled back to the boarding area.

Even after boarding and the doors were closed, the plane didn't take off immediately. The captain explained over the intercom that they were waiting for a runway, as their flight was unscheduled for this time. The interior had grown hot and the passengers were starting to complain when the plane began moving. At last, they were backing away from the jet port and taking their place in a long line of aircraft waiting to take off.

By the time they were in the air, Rex calculated that he'd be at least two hours late to get to the dock after the estimated arrival time of the Java Princess. Mid-flight, his fears were relieved, though, when Rehka informed him by text message that he'd better hurry straight to the dock, giving him the number. She'd heard the captain making berthing arrangements and telling the port authorities that his ETA was another two hours. With luck, Rex would be there just in time to see Margot debark.

Chapter Thirty-Five

Ho Chi Minh City, Vietnam

The string of bad luck had ended during the flight. When they landed in Ho Chi Minh City, Rex went as quickly as he could to the baggage area. Fortunately, he had only his carry-on, so collecting Digger was his only errand there. He found two smiling Vietnamese women flirting with Digger. He was relaxed and giving one of the women an adoring dog smile, probably trying to coax them into giving him some of the candy they were chewing on. Rex couldn't help but grin at Digger's antics. Rex thanked them for their kindness to his dog, and then he took possession of his goofy buddy and rushed to find a taxi.

He had the taxi stop a few hundred yards away from the dock where he wanted to be. He wanted to make sure Margot, if she was still there, wouldn't observe his arrival. Keenly aware he'd tracked down a woman who, for whatever reasons she had, wanted to remain hidden, he wanted to confront her, if he had to, on his own terms. He'd try to observe and understand what was happening, and then decide if he'd let her know of his presence.

However, if he was too late—if she was already off the yacht and on her way somewhere else—he might have lost her again, which meant he'd have to go to Da Nang to try and find her there. At least Rehka had captured her cellphone number when she spoke to her brother. It would be possible to pinpoint her location when she switched it on. He just hoped she wouldn't be so security conscious as to get another phone or simcard.

The taxi stopped, and he paid the driver. He commanded Digger to follow him at a distance, and the dog immediately obeyed and dropped back.

Rex turned and headed for the correct dock at a jog, slowing only when he was close enough to see the Java Princess, docked where Rehka said it would be. He slowed to a casual stroll, put his dark glasses on, pulled the baseball cap low over his face, and altered his gait slightly in case Margot happened to notice him from a distance. There wasn't a lot he could do about hiding Digger. He looked back to see where the dog was, and it took him almost a minute before he spotted him about hundred yards back, moving almost stealthily between the people and vehicles.

Clever boy.

One big black dog looked much like another from a hundred yards away, so unless she saw the two of them together, Margot probably wouldn't notice.

While he was careful to escape her notice, Rex was on the lookout for Margot leaving the yacht. He could see, once he got a bit closer, that a gangplank had been extended.

Not good, that means she could have left already.

Keeping his eye on it, he took up a seat under a large

umbrella outside a small dock-side restaurant making sure he had an unrestricted view of the yacht and ordered a fruit juice from the waitress.

Digger joined him silently after a couple of minutes.

"Good boy. Hide," Rex commanded. Digger moved in under the table and dropped down on his belly. Rex kept his eyes on the yacht, noting the name Java Princess in ornate lettering on the bow. Finally, after all the days of searching, listening, and today's delays, he was just a few yards from the yacht that had whisked Margot away, leaving a mystery in her wake.

He'd been watching no more than five minutes when a distinguished-looking older gentleman preceded a woman down the gangplank, holding out his hand for her to steady herself as she followed. It was Margot, and he presumed the captain of the yacht. She'd done nothing to disguise herself, though Rex thought she'd acquired a much deeper tan since he'd last seen her, about two weeks ago. He supposed two weeks on an ocean-going yacht would account for that.

She was more beautiful even than he'd remembered. Was he imagining a glow to her skin, or was the cliché about pregnant women glowing fooling his eyes? Apart from that, she didn't look pregnant. She was as slim as ever, and she moved with the same lithe grace as always. Margot exhibited a confidence that indicated to Rex she was here definitely of her own accord.

Which left the core question—why hide this way?

Digger must have sensed the change in Rex's chemistry because without Rex noticing, he had crawled out from under the table, gave one look at the yacht, must have spotted and recognized Margot, and started whining softly.

"Digger, quiet," Rex whispered. "She has no idea that we're here."

Digger gave him a tilted-head glance, then turned his attention and focus back on Margot. Rex muttered, "We're only going to scout, boy. We'll contact her later, and only if it's necessary, otherwise you and I are going back to Rehka, and from there we'll decide where we're heading next."

He didn't have a clue how much Digger would understand of his explanation, but the dog's ear twitched at the word 'scout'. Even so, Digger must have recognized that it wasn't a command, not yet anyway. He sat, quivering, his tail wagging incessantly from excitement and intently focused on Margot and her companion, who had made it some yards down the dock area toward town.

Rex tossed more than enough cash onto the table to pay for his order and commanded Digger to heel as he stood to follow the receding couple.

I'll just follow her for a while and not let her know I'm here.

Nothing in her demeanor as she left the yacht, nor in her body language now, as she was walking side by side with the older man and talking to him, indicated she was under duress of any kind. Watching from a distance for a while wouldn't harm anything. If he decided she was okay, then that would be the end of it. He'd leave without contacting her, allowing her the privacy she'd worked so hard to ensure.

If she wanted to be anonymous, and she was safe, he would be happy. He fully understood what it was like to live a life of anonymity, and he was not going to barge into that if that was her wish, though he thought she could have done it in a way that wouldn't have excited international alarm and the presumption she'd died. But he didn't have a leg to stand on in that thought, and he knew it. Hadn't he done the same thing, although under different circumstances? He had his legitimate reasons, and maybe so did she. He couldn't know without asking her, and he'd probably never get the opportunity to do so.

He was still perplexed as to why she didn't want to make her pregnancy public, but that was her prerogative. She didn't owe him an explanation, and he wouldn't demand one.

He'd followed at a discreet distance until he saw his targets get into a taxi. He immediately dived into another, with Digger landing unceremoniously in his lap, and uttered the age-old cliché, "Follow that cab!"

When the taxi didn't move, Rex understood his mistake. He'd spoken English. He switched to French and rapidly explained he wanted to follow the taxi that had just left. The driver smiled, started the meter, and shot out of the parking space like a rocket.

Rex amended his request. "Not too closely. I don't want those people to know I'm following them."

This time the driver grinned broadly and winked. He slowed down and moved over a lane, exhibiting some knowledge of street craft, as he dodged between vehicles while keeping Margot's taxi in sight.

Rex assumed he had the wrong idea about why they were following, but it didn't matter. All that mattered was he not lose Margot before he determined whether to contact her or not.

Chapter Thirty-Six

Ho Chi Minh City, Vietnam

By the end of the day, Rex paid off a very happy taxi driver, who'd driven him all over town, waiting while either the captain of the yacht or Margot stepped out of their vehicle for a shopping errand and then got back in.

Digger had been restless until Margot and her companion stopped in front of a restaurant and dismissed their taxi. Rex figured he had enough time to let Digger out for a walk, but he didn't want to risk losing them. He rigged Digger up with his harness, camera, and comms unit, and opened his iPad to keep an eye on Digger while he waited at a table at a restaurant across the street.

"Go on, boy. Do your business, and then come back. I have to stay here."

Digger gazed at Rex, head tilted.

Rex said, "I know, we haven't done this in a while, boy. Go on, bathroom." Digger woofed softly and trotted off.

Rex hoped Digger would pick a spot where the results

wouldn't be too much of a health hazard for the populace of the city, since he wouldn't be there to pick it up. Although, looking around him at the dirty streets and run-down buildings, he wasn't too worried that anyone would take much notice if Digger were not discreet about the place he picked as a toilet. But there was little choice. It was either send Digger off like he had or risk losing Margot if she came out of the restaurant while he was gone. Sometimes, especially when trying to go around without being seen among people, as was the case now, having a canine partner was a little inconvenient. But there were ways around it, and Digger's extraordinary senses and skills more than made up for the few times it was inconvenient.

Rex divided his attention between the restaurant door and his iPad, switching his gaze back and forth every minute or so. Digger was making his way into an alley but then started nosing about some garbage. "You must remember, dogs are scroungers. They'll eat anything that looks or smells like food," Trevor used to tell Rex.

"Leave it," Rex said. Digger's ears twitched, and he shied away from the pile of garbage. Rex stole a glance at the restaurant door, waited as a group of people left to be sure Margot wasn't among them, and then turned his attention back to the iPad.

Digger seemed to be in a garden, as there were what looked like fronds of some tropical plant all around him. He must have found a residence or park. He nosed around the stems of the plant. The video feed went still indicating to Rex he'd probably found his place and was doing his thing. A minute or so later, Rex experienced a dizzy spell as Digger had apparently turned quickly. The video feed went blurry as Digger must have been trotting or running somewhere now, probably exploring the area where he was. Rex was getting anxious that Digger wouldn't return before Margot left the restaurant. He couldn't get into a taxi and leave, or Digger wouldn't be able to find him. If Margot left before Digger was back, he'd have to let her go and risk losing track of her for now.

But it was only a minute or two before the video feed showed Digger was moving again, and some of what it showed looked familiar. Digger was on his way back. "Hurry, boy."

He kept his eyes glued to the restaurant door, now that he was confident Digger would be back soon. And soon enough, Digger was at his side. It was none too soon. Rex signaled a passing taxi, and as soon as he and Digger were inside, he explained to the driver that he was to follow another taxi but had to wait until he pointed out which one. The driver seemed a bit befuddled but didn't complain, the meter was already running. Margot and the captain came out carrying boxes by strings tied around them and hailed a taxi. They got in and sped away from the curb.

Rex said, "There, follow that one." But, just as his driver sped up, Rex exclaimed, "Wait!" He was thrown forward as the taxi came to a quick stop. Rex had caught sight of another taxi speeding past his and then abruptly slowing to stay behind Margot's.

What's this?

"Go ahead, but slowly. Follow the taxi that just passed us, not the first one."

The driver broke out in rapid French, apparently speaking to himself but obviously meaning Rex to hear his complaint.

"Follow this taxi, no, follow that taxi. Make up your mind."

Rex grinned. The driver had a point, but if there was

someone else following Margot, it put a twist on the already bewildering turn of events.

Who is it, and why?

As the strange procession kept going, Rex recognized that Margot's taxi was headed in the direction of the port, and he was now one hundred percent sure the other taxi, with two men in the back, was following Margot's. The other taxi followed closely, letting him know that either the driver or the followers were not particularly street-craft conscious. They made no attempt to evade discovery, which made it easier for Rex and his driver to do so. Since the unknown followers were between Margot and him, he only had to evade the notice of her followers. And by the looks of it they were focused on Margot, giving no indication that they were looking out for anyone who might be following *them*.

In due time, Margot's taxi entered the port district, and at that time, Rex decided it would be best to ditch his ride and head for his former observation spot on foot. The other taxi appeared to follow Margot's, so he assumed they'd eventually get close enough for him to determine who they were, with Digger's help.

He set off at a jog, keeping to the darker spots and shadows thrown from the moonlight or occasional street-lamps. Digger followed closely without being told. Because he had on his harness and comms unit, the dog knew he was working now, and was alert to Rex's commands, body language, and emotional state.

When they arrived at the dockside restaurant, it was closed, but the tables and umbrellas were still out, chained to each other. Rex chose a table near the building that was deep in the shadows and sat down to watch the yacht. He assumed Margot and the captain had already boarded it, as he could see only one taxi, which had its engine running.

Although Rex could hear the engine, it was parked far enough from the yacht that Rex assumed the sound wouldn't alarm the yacht's occupants in any way. He waited to see if it would leave or just remain there.

As he waited, he felt the vibration of his satphone in its holster on his hip. He retrieved it and answered in a hushed voice.

Rehka asked how the weather was, and he answered it was dark, which caused her to laugh.

"Why are you whispering?"

"Odd development, here. Someone else is following Margot. They're about thirty yards away, in a running taxi. Worst fieldcraft I've ever seen. I'm just waiting to see what they do next, and if I can discover who they are."

"Oh. Well, maybe this will help. I just picked up a conversation on the captain's cellphone that someone will be collecting Margot in three days. She's planning to stay on the yacht until then."

Rex literally felt his anxiety level drop. "That's great news! That means I won't have to worry about losing her, and I can concentrate on finding out what these other people are up to if I have to."

"Okay, good. Let me know if you need anything else."

"Will do."

———

Twenty minutes later, the drone of the taxi's engine had begun to wear on Rex's nerves when the back doors of the vehicle opened, and the two passengers got out. They closed the doors as quietly as they could and stepped to the side as the taxi rolled away, made a U-turn, and sped off.

An observant man by training, profession, and self-preservation, Rex studied the men intently as soon as he could see them. His first impression was that they were Caucasian, not Asian. One was tall and had the physique of a retired wrestler, with broad shoulders, a hulking sort of gait, and, not to put too fine a point on it, he was spectacularly ugly. Rex changed his idea of the man's former career to boxer when he noticed one cauliflower ear and a bulbous nose that leaned slightly to one side. He was bald.

The other gave Rex the idea that he must be the senior in rank. He was much smaller, perhaps five-foot-ten, and his slender build suggested office work rather than the boxing ring, and if the man's looks were anything to go by, probably had more brains than his companion. In contrast to the other man, he had a full head of light brown curly hair, and had nondescript looks that could have blended with a crowd anywhere in Europe but definitely not here in Asia.

Their distinctiveness had Rex briefly wondering why they'd been chosen to follow Margot, whatever their purpose was. He shrugged. *Whatever, they wouldn't be hard to keep track of.* He mentally labeled the first one 'Brawn', and the second 'Curly.'

Rex and Digger watched carefully as the men made their way closer to the yacht by fits and starts. It was obvious they wanted to conceal their presence. Nevertheless, Rex mentally criticized their fieldcraft as they continued to show carelessness.

Rex's original instinct that Margot was in danger had been off the mark, but the perception of danger was back in full force again as it was clear something was indeed going on, and he was almost convinced she was unaware of it.

His decision whether to contact her and let her know he was there or not had been made *for* him. No matter why she had deliberately disappeared, it was apparent he wasn't the only one who had an interest in her. But before making contact with her, he had to find out who these men were, if possible.

Rex dropped his hand to Digger and scratched behind his ears, running his hand over the ear with the comms unit to be sure it was still in place. When Digger looked up at him, he tapped the side of his nose and felt Digger's alertness ramp up a notch. He pointed discreetly at the two men, who were by now almost opposite him across the street and moving closer to the Java Princess.

Digger crept out from beneath the table and began trotting toward a spot near where the taxi had disgorged the men. He stopped and sniffed at spots in the street, wandered back and forth, but always on a tack that would lead him near the men. If they'd been watching, the men would have seen a stray dog looking for something to eat among the litter. They wouldn't notice that the dog was working its way toward them.

Digger's fieldcraft is far superior to theirs.

When Digger made his way to the opposite side, his tactics changed. Rex split his attention between the dog moving in and out of shadows and the iPad screen that showed what Digger was seeing. Soon, the two pairs of legs belonging to the men following Margot came into view. Then the angle changed. Digger would be on his belly, crawling silently toward his target.

He'll be within inches of them before they notice him, if they ever do.

Rex looked up at their position and even he couldn't see Digger, the dog blended so perfectly with the night.

But as he watched, one of the men must have sensed movement behind him. Digger was only a foot or so away. As the man turned, Digger adopted a cringing attitude. Through the comms unit, Rex heard the man speak gutturally, but he couldn't hear what the man said or what language he said it in. The man kicked out, missing Digger by inches as the dog let out a yelp and whirled away.

Digger gave the perfect impression of a stray cur as he scurried away with his tail between his legs, his body hunched in self-protection. Once he gained a deeper shadow, closer to where the taxi had waited, he straightened up and turned to look at the two men. He watched alertly for a few minutes, and then sat down to wait for Rex's next command.

"Good boy. Return," Rex ordered. Digger resumed his stray-dog act as he meandered toward the restaurant. Rex watched the men to be sure they didn't watch the dog, but their attention was firmly on the yacht.

Digger arrived in due time and wriggled happily as Rex praised him sub-vocally. Digger heard the praise loud and clear, the comms unit and his superior hearing interpreting the sounds of Rex's words even though they were barely audible to a human. "Good boy! Damn, you're a good actor. We should go to Hollywood and make you a star! You're the smartest dog in the world, did you know that, buddy? You're a very clever boy."

Digger basked in the praise. As a matter of fact, Rex believed Digger knew he was the smartest dog in the world. His happy grin proved it.

When the yacht's interior lights went out, Rex felt it was safe to try to get a few hours of sleep in. He'd put Digger on watch, and if the two men across the way decided to make any moves, the dog would pick it up and alert him.

"Digger, guard." Rex said, pointing to the two men.

Digger dropped to his belly, front legs outstretched, back legs bunched beneath him, head up. His head was pointed in the direction of the two men, and Rex decided to leave the camera on, so he could check the situation now and then. It would only take a tap to wake the iPad and see the feed.

He found the softest spot available, a scrap of lawn surrounded by shrubs next to the restaurant's entrance, put his backpack down for a pillow, and promptly went to sleep. Sleeping patterns when in an operational situation differed from those when not in a tense situation. It was not a deep sleep, it was more a state of restful alertness. It was a skill honed over the course of his years of training and on many missions. Rex came out of it without a startle reflex and was instantly one hundred percent aware of his surroundings when Digger nudged him two hours later.

The two men were approaching their position at the restaurant. Rex whispered, "Hide!", and Digger slunk off around the side of the restaurant, staying low. Rex turned over and, nudging the backpack in front of him, inched further into the shadows of nearby trees cast in the moonlight. When he felt he'd better stop moving, lest the men notice, he slowly turned his head to see if it was as he suspected, the two men who'd been following Margot earlier.

He caught a lucky break when, as if they'd heard something behind them, they both turned to look toward the yacht. Rex took the opportunity to twist and turn so that he could look at them directly but was even further under the tree, nearly right up against its trunk and curled around it so he blended with it.

Then he heard one speak.

Russian!

Because it was one of the languages he spoke fluently, Rex understood every word. The one who was speaking told the other that their leader would be there soon, and they should move away from the line of sight from anyone on the yacht. "We'll meet her further down the docks."

Her? Hmmm. So, Curly isn't the leader after all.

Rex clicked the mic on his comms unit to signal Digger to come out as the men turned left and proceeded down the street toward where their taxi had waited. Digger came, still crawling on his belly, and nosed Rex to let him know he was there.

"Good boy." Rex pointed to the men and said, "Track. Hide." From this compound command, Digger knew to follow the men but stay out of sight. It would be nice if he stayed close enough to hear what they were saying, but it wasn't imperative. Rex would be able to tell quite a lot from the video feed.

As Digger moved out, Rex watched on the iPad, his attention divided between the screen and his thoughts about the Russians.

Why in hell would Russians follow Margot? Is there some kind of shady spy business going on here? Is Margot involved in it?

The feed showed the men walking confidently down the wide paved area that was part of the long string of piers that protruded from it into the water, interspersed with buildings or stacks of shipping containers that hid the piers behind them from his perspective. The pavement between where Rex still lay concealed and those structures was about as wide as a four-lane city street back home, and showed evidence of carrying vehicular traffic regularly, like the taxis Margot, the Russians, and he had used to get there.

As he'd told Rehka, the Russians' taxi had waited about thirty yards from his location, but they now were beyond that point and still moving. From the angle of the video feed view, Rex could tell that Digger was walking along his side of the street, presumably staying in concealment because he was almost parallel with the Russians and gazing at them steadily as they moved.

Before they'd gone much farther, movement on the edge of the screen told Rex that someone else had arrived. Probably the person the men had been expecting, since they stopped and waited as a car came into view. Rex was frustrated to see that the car had stopped between Digger and the men he was following. However, he could still see their heads over the roof of the car. While he watched, the door opened, and one person stepped out and swung the door shut. It was a woman, judging from the long blonde hair that cascaded down her back and the short raincoat that revealed bare legs and spiked heels on her shoes.

She walked around the front of the car to join the men in conversation. In the poor light available to Digger's video camera, it was impossible to make out facial features, yet something about her seemed familiar. But Rex couldn't place her. Once she was engaged in conversation, Rex commanded Digger through the comms unit to close in on them, so he could listen to the conversation.

"Close in, boy. Hide."

Instead of crawling through the moonlit street on his belly, Digger walked across with no attempt at concealment, but meandering again. Rex shook his head in admiration.

Digger you're one damn smart dog.

The men would think nothing of seeing the 'stray'

they'd seen before. If they did, at worst they'd chase him off. But no one looked at the dog. The woman's back was to him, and the men's attention was fully focused on her.

Rex hadn't been able to make out much of her appearance. The blonde hair shone in the moonlight, so he was sure of that. The glimpse he got when she got out of the car indicated a slender woman, but the raincoat had a full skirt, so it was hard to tell just how slender she was. He didn't get a good enough angle to have a good look at her facial features, and now in the video feed they were too small to get a better idea.

As Digger gained the hiding spot represented by the car, and belly-crawled around it from the back to get close to his targets, Rex could make out the low murmur of conversation, but not the words. And then, when Digger rounded the right rear fender, suddenly, the words were clear, and he could make out the woman's features in profile.

It was with profound shock that Rex recognized her.

Ida Engberg!

More confusion settled in his mind.

What's that obnoxious Swede doing here? What does she have to do with the Russians? What's she got to do with Margot?

But it took less than a minute for the penny to drop. From the conversation, and her body language, Rex realized she was it. Their leader. As he eavesdropped on more of the conversation, a cascade of memories fell into place. Ida had been spying on Margot on Vanuatu all along! She wasn't Swedish at all, but Russian.

Another one who pulled the wool over my eyes. Although I can't say Digger didn't warn me about this one. He never liked her.

The one thing he gleaned from the conversation that gave him a sense of relief was that she was telling the men to stay out of sight and just keep an eye on Margot for now.

Whatever is going on here, it's not a kidnapping scheme—not yet. And probably not a collusion scheme either.

Ida's instructions to the men were just to keep her in sight and wait for further directives.

As if trying to figure out why the two Russians were following Margot and not coming up with any logical explanation wasn't maddening on its own, the surprise appearance of Ida on the scene was threatening to send Rex into a really foul mood. There were moments when he had a good mind to walk over to the Russians, knock their heads together, and get the story out of them. Appealing as the thought was to him, the frustration was that he had no idea what Margot's role in this was. By all indications, she was unaware of their presence, but he couldn't be sure. Unlikely as the notion sounded, and mindful of Margot's role in French politics, he had to admit there was a slight possibility he could be interfering in some very important government business, which was the last thing he wanted to become involved in.

What are these further instructions Ida referred to? Are they planning to make contact with Margot at some stage? What are they waiting for?

Chapter Thirty-Seven

Ho Chi Minh City, Vietnam

When Ida got back in the car, Digger quickly moved out from under the rear bumper and followed the two men, who had turned and started back toward their observation post. But no one appeared to spot him.

Ida had made a U-turn and was driving away, when Rex spotted another vehicle, parked about hundred and fifty yards away, pulling out and following her vehicle. As it was passing under a streetlight, he could make out two people in that car.

Ida's backup? Margot's backup? More surveilers? Surveilers surveilling the surveilers? This is getting more unusual by the minute.

More unanswered questions. But at least Rex was now convinced there'd be no danger for Margot tonight. He halted Digger's progress and slipped behind the restaurant, making his way behind the buildings to the exit while staying on his side of the street. When he got closer, Digger joined him, and when they got beyond a curve in the pavement, Rex broke into an easy jog.

His intention now was to find a cheap hotel, get a few hours' sleep in a bed, have a shower when he woke up, and be back at the restaurant before dawn. It was going to be an interesting morning, he suspected.

Rex found a surprisingly clean-looking small hotel with its lights still on just a block from the port entrance. He'd gotten five solid hours of sleep, showered, and assured Digger that they'd have breakfast at the restaurant where they'd been observing the night before.

He felt a sense of anticipation for the day. Today, he would probably contact Margot and tell her about the parade she was leading unbeknownst to her. But first, he'd try to understand who was following Ida. If that required having a private chat with the Russians, so be it.

First things first, though. The good news was the restaurant was open for breakfast, with pho, a noodle soup, the featured, and in fact, the only offering—beef, chicken, or vegetable pho. The not-so-good news was Rex already knew Digger wouldn't enjoy it as much as he would. In fact, to get anywhere near enough of the nutrients he'd need, Digger would have to have two or three servings.

Digger looked at the beef pho Rex offered him, and then back at Rex as if to say, "You must be joking, mate. What the hell is this? Two nibbles of beef, some weird green stuff, and water?"

"Try it, boy. You'll like it. It's good, see?" Rex took an overfilled spoon of his own soup, slurped it noisily, and then uttered a genuine, "Mmmm!" Digger must have bought it, because he lowered his head to the bowl discreetly placed under the table for him and started licking and gulping his portion too.

Rex suppressed a smile when he saw the look of bewilderment on the server's face when he returned to take the two empty bowls and ask if there was anything else, and Rex ordered two more of the same plus a cup of tea.

This time, the bowl in front of him was just window dressing as Digger rapidly finished his second bowl and stuck his nose on Rex's lap demanding the third one.

This dog is reading my mind. How did he know I ordered it for him?

Rex switched the bowls quickly and sipped at his tea while Digger polished off the third bowl of pho in less than a minute. There still hadn't been enough protein in the entire meal for the dog, but Rex would supplement it later, as soon as he could, with half a roast chicken. He'd eat the other half himself.

During the entire time, Rex had been aware that if Margot made an appearance, he'd have to ditch the meal and follow. He was wondering how Digger would react if he was told to forget about the food and follow Margot. Fortunately, Rex didn't have to find that out today, Margot only appeared half an hour later as he was sipping his second cup of tea after paying the bill. She was alone on the gangplank and made her way to shore.

Without the captain by her side, it would've made it convenient to approach her, were it not for the tails.

Despite Margot's colorful scarf that he'd be able to see a mile away, he couldn't just get up and follow her. First, he'd have to give the Russians the chance to fall in behind her, and then he'd have to wait and see if there was anyone following the Russians. He still had no idea who was in that car that followed Ida the night before. Whoever it was, he'd have to give them a chance to show themselves.

He didn't have to wait long before he spotted them, two more Caucasians from the look of them. Rex quickly decided that these men were not there in support of the Russians. They employed different surveillance and counter surveillance techniques than Curly and Brawn. Second, they were observing Margot and the Russians. He couldn't be certain it was the same two people he'd seen only in shadowed silhouette the night before.

Mademoiselle Lemaire, are you aware of the procession you're leading through the streets of Ho Chi Minh City? Two Russians, two men of unknown origin, a former assassin, and a big black dog? The only things missing to make this a carnival are screaming crowds, streamers, and a big brass band.

It was indeed a parade, of which Margot seemed completely unaware. Of the missions of the three sets of followers, the only one whose purpose he knew was his and Digger's. The others remained a mystery, particularly because neither of the others was making a move on Margot, and neither did the first and second group seem to be aware of the other or him and Digger. Rex grinned as the thought crossed his mind that if some cosmic watcher had been viewing it from above, it would make a great silent-films comedy.

Despite being asked by Rex about the meaning of all of this, not even the all-knowing Digger had any ideas—or none that he wanted to share with Rex.

For several hours, the three groups followed Margot as she enjoyed a leisurely walk punctuated by visits into various shops, and the only contingent who seemed to be aware of it all was Rex's. He noted she went into a shop specializing in modern Western maternity clothing. The Russians didn't seem surprised, but it caused some consternation between the second set, judging from the all-but-silent, intense conversation, complete with big arm gestures and violent shaking of heads that ensued.

While Rex waited for Margot's reappearance, he decided it would be good to know who the second set were. Accordingly, he sent Digger to get a little closer so the comms unit could pick up the language they spoke. By the time Margot reappeared, he knew they were speaking French. He recalled Digger and set off to follow again as the procession resumed.

French? No real surprise there—after all, she is French and an important one at that, well at least to the new President, it seems. So, what is the role of those Frenchmen following her in all of this? Protection? From whom and what? Surveillance? Well, that's obvious but to what end?

Could they be DGSE? If so, Margot could be involved in something BIG here. Good or bad? Maybe it isn't about her pregnancy at all.

So, what could it be? Some underhanded dealings with the Russians? But that doesn't make sense. In that case, why would the Russians tail her without her knowledge? Is there some kind of secret deal about to go off between the French and the Russians and Margot, the French emissary? But why choose Vietnam for such a meeting? Here the French and Russians stick out like sore thumbs.

Shit, Rex Dalton, you are one paranoid son of a bitch. Well, that might be so, but that's no reason to get careless, either.

As the day wore on, there were no further revelations.

Rex's logic couldn't account for all the factors, no one was talking and providing more clues, and Digger was no help in unraveling the mystery at all. Rex took a fistful of Digger's fur between his shoulders and tugged gently, then let go of it and scratched the spot vigorously, his apology for unfairly thinking his companion had been no help. It was because of Digger that he knew the identities of either set of followers.

"Sorry, buddy. Look, this is pointless. Let's break off, go get you something to eat, and wait for a chance to talk to her, shall we?"

Digger's attention turned eager when he heard the word 'eat'. He grinned his trademark grin and wagged his tail once in either direction. It was a clear sign he approved of Rex's plan.

To be certain he knew when Margot returned, Rex got that roast chicken he'd been thinking about since breakfast and returned to the same spot where he and Digger had kept vigil before. The restaurant served nothing but pho, and while that was a very tasty dish, it just wasn't filling enough for him or for Digger. But to placate the owners for bringing his own food to eat at their tables, he ordered a bowl for himself anyway.

At mid-afternoon, and with nothing in her arms to show for her hours-long shopping trip, Margot returned. Rex searched the opposite side of the street and spotted the followers; the Russians almost parallel with him on the other side, and the French about a block behind them on the same side of the street. They'd made themselves at home on a shelf-like protrusion of one shipping crate that was topped by others in an arrangement that left a nook between two crates in the next layer. It was far better concealment than the Russians had chosen, and it gave Rex the impression that the French followers were better at their jobs than the Russians, who seemed to him a bit amateurish at the best of times.

Chapter Thirty-Eight

Ho Chi Minh City, Vietnam

Hours later, the sun had begun to sink when Rex saw the captain and another man, he presumed to be the first mate, leave the yacht in a jovial mood. They were talking loudly, laughing, and nudging each other. Rex thought their mood signaled a night on the town.

This could be my opportunity to get to Margot to try to clear up these mysteries.

He'd have to wait for darkness, though.

In another fortunate break, he saw the Russians split up, the big one following the captain and his companion. Then the French did the same. That left only two to contend with if the need arose.

While he waited, he thought about how to approach the yacht. He'd seen no indication of security patrols or cameras the night before. He and Digger hadn't been bothered by anyone, but he couldn't be certain there were no cameras trained on the vessels moored to the piers. Before he risked approaching the Java Princess, he'd need to know. He freed the satphone and called Rehka.

After the usual protocols and a few pleasantries, Rex asked, "Can you let me know if I have to evade any security cameras to get on that yacht? I'm planning to go onboard in the next three to four hours."

"I'll check it out," she replied.

An hour later, she reported that there were indeed security cameras, but there was only one person apparently monitoring them from a central location. She'd found one person in the monitor room, and he didn't seem very attentive to the bank of monitors. He seemed more attentive to the bottle of Mekong whiskey on his desk and the girlie magazine he was reading. "In another two to three hours he might not be able to even see the monitors," Rehka laughed.

"I still wouldn't want to take a chance, though. Can you record a loop and send it to the right monitor when I tell you to?"

"Sure thing, boss."

An hour after that, she called again and told him she was ready to switch the feed to her loop on his signal.

"Good deal. I'm going to wait another hour, at least. There's still too much activity on the docks, and I still haven't figured out how to get on the yacht without the others noticing."

"Why do you care if they notice you? They don't know who you are."

"Good point. Okay, let me just check a few more things. Wait for my signal."

Shortly before midnight, Rex and Digger stealthily approached Brawn's position to find out what he was doing and were not entirely surprised to hear the loud snoring sounds coming from his position under a palm tree. The empty vodka bottle next to Brawn explained the Russian's condition and assured Rex that he was not going to wake up soon. If he woke up, which didn't look like it would be soon, it would probably be with the mother of all headaches—not alert and fighting fit.

Next, Rex and Digger furtively went around to the Frenchman's position. He was awake and alert, so Rex and Digger watched him for about half an hour and established that he'd worked out a routine to stay awake. The routine included him sitting down for a while, then moving to a different spot where he would sit down again. Every now and then he did a few stretches and pushups or walked about as if on a patrol round. Nothing he did gave Rex the idea that the man posed a threat.

Chapter Thirty-Nine

Ho Chi Minh City, Vietnam

It was nearing one a.m., and the full moon hadn't risen yet when Rex sent Digger on a final round to check out the Russian and Frenchman before he made his way back closer to the port entrance. He then walked down the middle of the street, feigning casual confidence, toward the yacht. He'd left Digger concealed in the restaurant bushes with his comms unit and camera on, so he could monitor the situation outside while he was on the yacht.

When he got to the right pier, he walked up the gangplank as if he had every right to be there. He expected Margot would be surprised, probably shocked, and if she didn't know about her entourage, almost definitely angry. He crowded close to the cabin door before knocking. As soon as she opened the door, he pushed his way in and closed the door quickly.

As Rex expected, chaos immediately ensued as Margot started screaming and ran from him. Rex moved quickly to restrain her and get her to stop screaming and calm down. But that was easier said than done, because she obviously hadn't recognized him and must have been thinking of him as an intruder who meant her harm. By the time he caught up with her, she had run into the galley, seized a large pan, and swung it wildly at him.

He evaded it easily, shouting, "Margot! Margot, it's me, Rowan Donnelly!" while dodging the second swing.

When he straightened back up after ducking under her swing, he saw she'd stopped trying to crown him with the pan and was looking at him in utter astonishment.

"Rowan? How…? What…?"

Rex felt bad about scaring her like that. He started to apologize, stuttered, and stopped. Feeling like a total idiot, not knowing what the right thing would be to say in the moment, he just grinned at her. Finally, he got his voice and said, "Put down the weapon of mass destruction, and I'll explain."

As she set the pot back down on the counter, he could see the recognition had finally reached her brain, and her expression turned from shock and astonishment to pure fury. "You'd better have a good explanation, you creep!" Her eyes were blazing. "You've been stalking me. Haven't you? You pervert."

Rex had expected her to react with aggression, but being called a creep and a pervert, he didn't. "Margot… please…"

"Don't you Margot me! What the hell are you doing here? I'm…"

In an effort to not annoy her any further by looking her in the eyes, Rex turned his gaze from her to the floor for a fleeting moment. He heard her move and was just in time to see her hand moving toward an electronic control on the wall. In a flash, he'd covered the small distance between them and grabbed her wrist.

"Let go of me, you bastard!"

"Margot, calm down. Please listen to me. I think you might be in danger. I'm not here to hurt you or interfere in your plans. Just let me explain."

Her eyes narrowed, indicating another realization had just dawned on her.

"How do you know I'm Margot?"

"You've got to be kidding me! I make friends with this nice woman, who told me her name was Jacqui Madrolle, while on holiday in Vanuatu. One day, this friend of mine, Jacqui, made a breakfast date with me, but stupid me was soon to find out she had no intention to keep the date. She went missing. And being such a good friend, I was worried, reported her missing, and the next thing I know, Digger and I found ourselves in police custody being accused of complicity, if not engineering the disappearance of the Press Secretary of the President of France, one Mademoiselle Margot Lemaire. Of course, I had no idea what they were talking about until I finally realized my good friend, Jacqui Madrolle, was one and the same person as this Margot Lemaire they were going on about.

"Oh, and by the way, it was thanks to your friend, Ida's deliberate lies to the police that I was a suspect in your disappearance for several hours.

"After the police told me who you really are, I googled you and discovered what a big fool you've made of me. You, Mademoiselle Margot Lemaire, have caused a world-wide incident. Not to mention how much you've disappointed me." Rex took a deep breath and was about to launch into another rant to tell her that she'd also succeeded in reinforcing his dim view of politicians, but then noted the tears streaming down her face.

"I'm sorry. I didn't think," she whispered.

"No, you obviously didn't."

Margot's shoulders were now shaking as she surrendered to the sobs.

Rex's heart went soft as he also remembered that she was pregnant. He took a step closer put his arms around her and pulled her against him. "Margot, sorry about that. Those were the last words about that matter you'll ever hear from me.

"Let's rather talk about the reason why I am here, okay?"

She nodded and sniffed.

"Did you know you have two sets of tails following you everywhere? One group of two Russians and one group of two Frenchmen."

"No, of course not! Why would anyone follow me? Why would *you* follow me?"

Rex huffed in frustration. *Come on, lady, focus!*

"I followed you because I thought you might have been kidnapped. The police were convinced you'd gone for a swim and met with an untimely death."

Margot shuddered. "I'd *never* go for a swim in those waters! You know that."

"So you told me, and I believed you, and therefore that's exactly what I told the Vanuatu police and the French detective from Paris as well. They didn't believe me and insisted you either committed suicide or drowned by accident. Whatever the cause, as far as they are concerned, you're dead. But it's obvious the Russians and French on your tail know different."

"So, how did *you* know I'm not dead?"

"Because I believed you when you told me you're afraid to go into the sea, and I was sure you didn't commit suicide. So, I asked Digger to find you. He tracked you to the docks, and a little questioning of a few witnesses convinced me you'd gotten on a yacht, but I didn't know whether it was voluntary or not. So, I followed you."

Margot's expressive face had gone through a range of emotions since he'd first shoved his way in. Right now, it was back to bewilderment at his statement. "How?"

"Never mind that now. The question is why are the others following you?"

"Rowan, I know after all I did to you there's no reason to trust me, but please believe me, I had no idea that anyone was following me. I don't know who they are and why they would be following me... Do *you* have any idea?"

Rex then painstakingly explained that he'd become aware of the first group not long after he'd arrived the day before, and he'd determined they were Russian.

Her eyebrows flew up as if she'd heard about the Russians for the first time. She was clearly still dealing with the shock, and her brain was struggling to keep up, process, and retain everything.

Rex went on to tell her he'd discovered Ida Engberg was directing the Russians, which caused her to drop her jaw, and then, that two French-speaking men were following the Russians. By now, Margot had dropped onto a nearby lounge chair, pallid and shaking like a leaf in the wind.

Rex went to her and put his hand on her shoulder and said, "So, Margot, I want you to look me in the eye and tell me... if you know... Who are these people and why are they following you? Are you in danger? Or do you really know about either or both groups, and you're lying to me again?"

"Again? When have I ever lied to you?" Her indignation was genuine, he thought.

"Um, I don't know, *Jacqui*, let's see… when have you lied to me?"

She had the grace to blush. "Oh, that. Well, that wasn't specifically lying to you. I was just trying to be incognito on Vanuatu, so I could enjoy my holiday. I told everyone that was my name."

"I get that. And in that case, how did Ida know you were someone of importance? She was spying on you even then. You realize that, don't you?"

Margot shook her head. "This is … this is… just too much, Rowan." She started crying again.

Rex put his arm around her shoulder again and waited.

She wiped her tears with the back of her hand. "I don't understand. Ida's Swedish. Why would she be directing Russians to follow me?"

"If it's any conciliation, she also had me believing she's Swedish, until I heard her speak to the Russian men last night out there on the pier. Believe me, she's not Swedish, she's Russian…"

Margot pointed to the outside in the direction of the pier. "Are you saying those men are all out there watching *me*. Right now?"

"Well, at the moment, there's one Russian and one Frenchman out there. The other two followed the two men who were with you on the yacht earlier, I take it the captain and his first mate, into town."

Margot stared at him for a long while before she spoke again. "And how do you know they won't turn up here any moment?"

Rex smiled. "Don't you worry about that. Digger is watching them and will let me know if they come closer."

"Digger! Digger is here? Outside?" Margot's face was beaming.

Rex grinned and said, "Yeah, he's out there. He told me to say hi."

That little interlude about Digger was the turning point. From then on, Margot seemed to get hold of herself, and the conversation started flowing much better.

Rex continued with his questioning. "And you don't have a French security detail? You don't know who they are, either?"

"No, on both counts."

Rex knew the answer to his next questions, but he wanted to hear them from her. "Margot, why are you here? Why was it necessary to slip away in secrecy?"

She blushed again but lifted her chin as if in defiance. "I'm pregnant."

Rex managed to hide his relief that she wasn't hiding it from him. "Thanks for being honest, Margot. I know that you're pregnant."

"So that was a test?"

Rex nodded.

"But how did you ..."

Rex held the palm of his right hand up as a stop signal. "Again, not of importance for now, Margot. What I need to know is, since when is being pregnant enough reason to mislead people and fake your death and cause all this trouble?"

More than a few seconds passed while she avoided eye contact. She seemed to have an internal struggle with what to say, before she finally looked directly at him. "When it's the child of a married man, someone whose indiscretion might affect the fate of an entire nation and the European Union."

It was Rex's turn to be shocked. "You don't mean…"

"Yes. The child I carry is the President's."

"Oh, shit," was all Rex could say.

"Indeed," she commented with heavy irony. "Merde. I was stupid, there is no excuse for it."

When Rex found his voice again, he said, "Still want to hit me over the head with that pan or throw me off the yacht?"

Margot shook her head slowly without looking at him. "No," she whispered. "But Rowan… I… I've caused so much trouble. I thought I did the right thing to disappear and to protect the President and my country, but now…" the tears were streaming down her face again.

"Margot, I'm able to help you…"

"How can…, what…"

"You know the answer by now." Rex grinned slightly.

She nodded. "Yes, of course, not of importance for now. Right?"

Rex nodded. "So, let's put our heads together, figure out why these parties are following you, and then come up with a plan. What do you say?"

"I say thank you, Rowan. You are very kind to have put yourself to all this trouble for a passing acquaintance."

It's kind of what Digger and I do. Rex didn't voice his thought, neither did he respond to her praise. "Now, why do you think these people are following you?"

"I can't imagine. I don't know any state secrets or anything. All I can think of for now is that it's got something to do with my pregnancy. During the campaign there were rumors about me and the President," she said with a certain measure of bitterness. "That's why I disappeared without a trace. I didn't want it to become known and ruin his presidency. Despite our affair, he really is the best thing for

France right now. I believe that, and I love my country. Besides, he has a family who doesn't deserve to suffer because of our stupidity. I was starstruck, it was never love, and it's certainly no excuse to destroy him or his family, much less France. So, I decided to put aside my political ambitions and raise my baby quietly."

"That's admirable, Margot, if self-sacrificing." Rex paused. He knew the answer to the next question he was going to ask, but again he wanted to hear if from her. "How did you make the arrangements? You don't strike me as the deceptive type."

She laughed mockingly. "No? Well, if I am, apparently, I'm not good at it, since I've got three different sets of people who seem to know all about my movements and have been following me. I'm surprised the press isn't here in full force, sticking a microphone in my face. But in answer to your question, my brother helped me. I guess he's no better than I am at it."

Again, Rex suppressed the sigh of relief he felt. "Your brother? Is that the older gentleman who appears to be the captain of this yacht?"

"Henri? No, but he's a friend of my brother, or perhaps a friend of a friend. I didn't ask too many questions. I phoned my brother from Vanuatu when I found out I was pregnant and asked him to help. He arranged everything else, including a new identity for me. Henri says the papers aren't very good, though."

"Good enough to get you into Vietnam," Rex murmured. "Be that as it may, now we know how the Russians know about your movements. As a senior official in government, you must know about tapping of phones that's been going on across the world for years."

Margot frowned.

"The name Edward Snowden ring a bell?"

Margot's hand flew to her mouth, and she nodded.

Rex continued, "Well, as you can imagine, anyone close to the top levels of governments are targeted by default. You would have been high on their list—don't doubt that for one moment. And do I have to tell you this is happening all over the world, not only in Russia? Everyone does it. You get on a phone and you can be assured someone somewhere is recording it."

Margot was shaking her head. "My stupidity has no bounds, it seems. I knew all about this but just never thought it could be happening to me."

"They most certainly would've been tapping your phones and those of anyone with whom you spoke."

"Like my brother... oh, my God! Not only did I phone him from Vanuatu to make all the arrangements; I also spoke to him just as we left Singapore."

"Yep, you can assume they've known about your plans from that first phone call you made to your brother. They'd never had a challenge to follow you. I bet they were waiting for you here. The question is, what's their purpose? Just to bring down France's government by getting proof of a scandal? Would it come to that? What could they gain by that? If we can figure that out, we'll have our answer. I overheard Ida telling your tails not to interfere with you—just keep track of you and wait for further instructions."

Margot was staring into middle space when she spoke. "But are these Russians on assignment from their government, or are they private citizens with some agenda we can't guess? And how would the French know I'm here? Surely, they aren't tapping my and my brother's phones, too. Are they press, maybe? But if so, how did they find me?"

Rex didn't think most press agencies would have had the

technical know-how to track her the way he had, and he didn't particularly want to go into that or raise more questions from Margot about how he did it. For now, he'd keep that to himself. However, she had a valid question.

"Don't be so sure that your government wasn't tapping your calls. As I've said before, there is evidence that all calls of all people are somehow tracked. Maybe not all of them are recorded, but they'll know who called whom. As for you, your position in government and closeness to the President, in official capacity I mean, you can bet your bottom Euro on it—they would've tracked and probably recorded them, as well.

"As for the Russians, I don't know if they are government sanctioned. I doubt it, because their methods aren't very professional. I spotted them a mile off.

"The French are better. I'd say they probably are government. When I saw them, I'm sorry to say this, but I thought they might be following you and the Russians because they suspected you of collusion or spying."

"What?! How could you even... I would never... Why would they think... *mon Dieu*, I have it!"

"What?" he prompted.

"The Russians! They want to push Giles to sign the gas pipeline agreement, despite his campaign promise to follow his predecessor's lead not to sign it. We talked about it at length during the campaign, and we agreed it's not in France's interest to enter into that agreement. But why would they think I had any influence over his decisions?"

"Did anyone else know about the affair?" Rex asked. "Your theory is plausible, but only if they have some idea that controlling you would cause him to change his mind."

"Not really. There was speculation. There always is when a man and a woman collaborate closely. I was his campaign manager, you know. But no one ever let us know they had proof."

"Not your friends, not your brother, no one?"

"No. Unless… Could it have been Ida? She was in my hut on occasion. Oh, mon Dieu, she must have seen the positive pregnancy test! It was in my bathroom. Of course, that's it! Not tapping my brother's phone at all. And Rowan, I have never told him who the father is! They don't really know, do they?"

"I suspect they've figured out where there's smoke, there's fire. It may be pure speculation on their part, but it's true, isn't it? Gaining control over you would force Aguillard's hand, one way or another. All they really have to do now is start a rumor and let the media do the rest. You can't deny you're pregnant, and it's already clear you're not going to have an abortion…"

"I'll never do that—have an abortion. But I can't let them use this to get that pipeline. Do you know what that pipeline would do to my country? Or, for that matter, what it would do to the European Union? Even NATO would be affected. But I would think if that was their motive, they *would* have kidnapped me already. What else could it be?"

Rex was silent as he thought through the threads of what she'd shared and what he knew about the followers. She was right, of course. Kidnapping her and threatening Aguillard with her demise or with producing her when she was more visibly pregnant to break the scandal would be more effective than just following her around. And it still didn't explain the French involvement.

There was one glaringly obvious solution—not foolproof, but it would take the wind out of the Russians' sails. Rex didn't expect Margot to mention it, but he was sure it would've crossed her mind. If not already, it would soon. He could stand up and claim the child was his. Given the gravity of the situation, he would have no problem doing it. But there were a few stumbling blocks. One being that he hadn't known her long enough to make the math work for how far along she was. Another was he'd have to give up his anonymity and have his face splashed all over the media across the world, and that was a nonstarter. Yet another was a fleeting thought of an Israeli woman living in Italy that crossed his mind. The question he had to ask himself was if his personal interests should outrank the damage to France, the EU, and NATO?

Wait, hang on there, Dalton. Don't get ahead of yourself. First get her to safety, then sit down on your ass and think through it carefully.

The only way to find out what her followers wanted would be to have a chat with them and ask. But that he could only do once he'd seen her to safety.

He became aware that she was staring at him, waiting for him. "Okay, here's what I suggest we do. We have to break up their plans, whatever they are..."

"How would we..."

"We should get you out of their sight, tonight."

Margot had evidently been thinking along other lines as Rex had his silent conversation with himself. "You know, I don't have any idea what Giles would do if he knew of the baby. He's an enigma. Very determined to have his way with France and her future, but he's warm and personable to his friends. I don't know whether he'd fall on his own sword and admit to the affair and that the baby is his, or whether he'd cling to power and sign the agreement to keep the scandal from becoming known."

Rex pointed out that either one would get the Russians their pipeline. Another special election would almost certainly get the opposition's party into power, and the new

President would sign the agreement anyway—that's what Aguillard's opponent had promised during the election campaign.

Margot, grimly pragmatic now, said, "There's even a possibility he would want me dead. If I'm gone, then all his problems are solved. No more scandal, no more threat to his marriage, and no more leverage for the Russians."

In his mind, Rex quoted Stalin darkly. *Death solves all problems—no man, no problem.* "But surely he wouldn't…"

"I simply don't know anymore. From what you've told me so far about my countrymen following me and how the government would've been listening to my telephone calls, surely the President *must* know all about my pregnancy, and he surely knows how I got pregnant. Those French guys out there are likely here on his orders.

"Rowan, I'm worried. Giles can be ruthless when he's up against a wall."

"I don't think that's why the French are here," Rex replied, "though they may well be government agents. If the Russians had been ordered to kill you, they could easily have done so already and disappeared. But I think their purposes would be served more readily with you alive. Either way, we can't allow either group to take you. We need to get you out of here without them following."

"I can get my brother to help."

"No, Margot. That's what compromised you in the first place. I can help. But you'll have to trust me, and do precisely as I tell you."

"I don't have much of a choice, it seems. But may I ask what expertise you have in these matters?"

"You know the answer," Rex replied tersely.

"Yes, of course, not of importance for now. Right?"

Rex grinned. "You're a quick study. We're going to get through this just fine."

"I trust you, Rowan. I'll do as you tell me, and I hope one day you'll be able to answer all those questions that are not of importance now."

Rex made no reply. He was busy outlining a plan in his mind.

Chapter Forty

Ho Chi Minh City, Vietnam

After a few minutes, Rex thought he had the answer, but he needed to know that he had Margot's buy-in. She'd had enough trauma tonight that her acquiescence to his demand that she does what he tells her might have been on the spur of the moment and not what she really felt.

"Margot, what do you want to do now? What would you do if you became aware of all this, but I wasn't here to help you?"

"Knowing what I know now, I would've been in a panic. Maybe I would've phoned, no couldn't do that… I don't know Rowan. I really don't know. I guess I would've been sitting there in a corner crying my eyes out. Maybe I'd follow through with my plan and go to the convent where my brother arranged for me to stay during my pregnancy and the birth. But… now that I know what's going on, that might just put those people in danger."

Rex nodded.

"Rowan, what can I do?"

Now he was convinced she was sincere. "How about we get you out of this country and to another safe place instead?"

"That seems to be the only logical option. But how can I do that? I can't contact my brother for help. What…" she paused and looked at Rex, and it was clear she had just realized something important. "Did I hear correctly? You used the word 'we' when you suggested to get me out of the country?"

Rex grinned and nodded.

"You can do that, too?"

Rex scoffed. "Of course, I can." He winked.

"How… okay scratch that. Not important to know for now. But you must have other responsibilities. Why? You barely know me. I can't ask you to do this for me. I'll just have to take my chances."

Rex heaved an exasperated sigh. "Woman, try to get this through your head. If I didn't want to help, I wouldn't be here."

"Are you sure you don't want to tell me how you can do all this?"

"I'm sure."

"What do you want me to do?" she asked. "While you make the plans, I mean? Should I go to a bank and withdraw some money tomorrow? Do I need cash?"

"You don't need anything. I'll take care of it," Rex answered. "Just stay put while I get things started. Right now I want you to pack a small bag with your absolute necessities, with the emphasis on absolute necessities. Nothing else. Whatever you need we will get you when we get there."

"Where is there?"

Rex smiled.

Margot knew that look by now and answered her own question, "Not important to know for now?"

"Yep, you've got it."

"Rowan, I insist on paying. I have the money to arrange everything, just not the skill."

"Margot, stop! We don't have time for that now. We'll sort out the money later. Go pack your stuff and get ready to leave, and wait for me to come and get you. I'm going to take Digger and scout our options for getting you off the yacht. I'll be back soon."

He left a chastened Margot to her packing, hoping against hope that she at least followed directions about how much she could take and hoped she wouldn't do anything stupid such as phoning her brother.

I need to get that damn cellphone off her and destroy it.

Exploring the inside of the yacht, he discovered an exit that would put him on the other side of the cabin, away from the eyes of the followers. However, there was a bright light from a pole on the pier that might as well have been a spotlight trained directly on the door.

Looking behind him to make sure Margot wasn't within earshot, Rex took out his satphone and called Rehka again. "Can you do your trick with the security cameras again? I need to get Margot off the yacht unseen. Also, there is a light out here that's going to make it difficult to get out of here unnoticed. It'd be great if you could do something about that."

"To get the loop on the security cameras going will be quick. I looked at the lights earlier, and that shouldn't be a problem either. Stay online. I will make that happen right away."

Rex waited. It wasn't much more than ten seconds when

she came back on the line. "Okay, the security cameras have been taken care of, you can go for it. You have fifteen minutes. Just say when you want the lights off."

"Thanks! Okay, you can do the lights now. After I've got Margot off the yacht and we're in a safe place, I'll get in touch to let you know what's going on. It could be in an hour or so. In the meantime, please start looking at flights from here to Mumbai for Margot as well as Digger and myself. Don't book anything yet, just send me a list of all available flights for the next two days."

"Okay, will do. I'll wait up for your call. Take care, Ruan."

It was only then that Rex did the math in his head and realized it was almost as late in Mumbai as it was here. "Thanks, Rehka. You're the best."

"I know it," she said, her voice altered by the grin he suspected she had on her face. "You use that on me every time you ask for the moon."

Ten seconds later, the light that had been lighting up the exit went out, along with several others in the immediate area.

Good girl.

Now he had no issues disabling the watchers if necessary.

First, though, he and Digger needed to check on the Russian. He went out the same way he'd come in and gave Digger the hand signal to follow him as they went cautiously to check on the Russian. They found him fast asleep and snoring worse than ever.

No wonder. A full bottle of vodka would do that to anyone.

To check on the Frenchman required more caution. Rex and Digger took evasive maneuvers as they approached his position, Rex keeping an eye to their rear and flanks while

Digger crept forward. Now and then, Rex would pause and let Digger creep further out while he watched the video feed on the iPad. They were almost to what Rex thought of as the Frenchman's main spot, the nook in the storage containers, when Digger's camera finally picked up movement in the watcher's position.

Rex commanded Digger to stop and hide, while he moved up to the same spot, moving slowly until the Frenchman stood, turned his back, and stretched. Rex took the opportunity to rush quietly forward to Digger's position and watch with his own eyes instead of relying on the camera. The Frenchman set off on his established rounds, and Rex knew this was his chance. He'd have to hurry to get back to Margot and get her out of her yacht before the Frenchman returned to his post.

"Digger, keep watch," he whispered, before rising quickly to his feet and speeding back to the yacht.

Rex tucked the iPad into his shirt and went back inside to check on Margot's progress. He found her standing still, a designer backpack looped by the strap over her shoulder. She'd taken his 'pack light' instruction to heart, and that boded well for getting her to cooperate for the rest of the plan.

"Got your papers?"

She nodded.

"Okay, let's go."

He grabbed her hand and they left through the same door he'd come in. He hustled her across the street to the concealment of the trees and bushes around the restaurant where he'd spent so many hours observing the yacht. Then he retrieved the iPad to see where Digger had gotten to.

"What's that?" Margot asked.

Rex didn't have time for a long explanation, so he just

said it was an iPad and he used it to keep track of Digger. When she opened her mouth to say more, he gave her a slight shake of his head. She made a show of zipping her mouth shut. Rex could imagine that wasn't the end of it. "I'll explain later," he conceded.

With his main focus to get Margot away as quietly and quickly as possible, he would not confront the watchers. Rex gave Digger the command to return to him. Just then, the lights came back on, casting long shadows where Rex and Margot waited. Digger was caught in the middle of the street and poured on speed. Seconds later, he was all over Rex, standing on his hind legs trying to lick Rex's face and wagging his tail. Rex whispered, "Good boy. Okay, boy, off! That's enough."

Digger eagerly turned his attention to Margot, but before he could welcome her back to their pack, Rex commanded him to sit. "We're still working, Digger. You'll have your chance to greet her later. We need to get out of here now." He pointed in the direction he wanted them to go and said, "Scout-hide."

Digger immediately adopted his military bearing and trotted off with caution, looking from side to side. Rex followed his progress on the iPad screen, and when Digger was about ten yards ahead, he signaled Margot to get up and follow him.

Rex took Margot's hand and stayed in the shadows as they made their way to the exit. Once out of the port area and on the streets, Rex was relieved to join the crowds milling about in a cacophony of music, laughter, shouting, and honking vehicles. Everywhere they turned, there were motorcycles cruising the streets with a man driving and a woman passenger. Some were parked alone or in groups, with the drivers and passengers drunk, laughing and clinging to each other, and more than a few times they were engaging in very public displays of affection.

It made Rex wonder if those that were on the streets were also drunk, but everyone seemed happy. Despite several near misses, pedestrians crossed the streets while disregarding the motorcycles and cars streaming by bumper to bumper.

The ideal environment to hide in plain sight.

"Margot, see how the women have their heads slightly bowed as we pass them. Follow their lead. I think most of these people are too drunk to notice us, but we do stand out a bit. Keep your head down." Fortunately, it wasn't far to his hotel, where he intended to stash her while Rehka did her magic and found them a flight out.

In short order, they reached the hotel. The clerk at the desk gave Rex a wink as they walked through. Rex was momentarily indignant on Margot's behalf, but as he thought about it, this was the perfect cover. Her head was down, her silky black hair swung forward, obscuring her face. From the desk clerk's point of view, she could be a local prostitute, and Rex still had hold of her hand. He winked back.

He hustled her up the stairs, slipping around between her and the clerk so her decidedly non-Asian features couldn't be seen. When they reached the next floor, Margot was out of breath.

They hurried into the room and Rex quickly closed the door behind Digger and propped a rubber wedge-shaped door-stopper under the door so that it couldn't be opened from the outside.

Margot dropped her backpack on the nearest chair and

bent to praise Digger. "Who's a clever boy? Yes, you are so clever, aren't you Digger? Did you miss me?"

Digger lapped it up, his mouth opened in a wide grin and his tongue getting a lick to her face in now and then, with Margot trying to dodge them. "No, I don't need a kiss, thank you, Digger."

Digger paid her protests no mind as he dodged in and out frantically, evading her hands that were trying to fend him off to lick her face.

"Rowan, aren't you going to rescue me?" she squealed.

He snapped his fingers, but it didn't faze Digger, who continued to express his joy at being with Margot again.

At last, she stood. Rex had enjoyed the show from the corner of his eye while he pulled out the satphone and dialed Rehka. She'd answered while Margot was still dodging Digger's kisses. He'd told Rehka they needed to pull out all the stops to supply Margot with a new forged passport in a hurry. The sooner he could get her out of Vietnam, the better.

"Where do you want to send her, Ruan?"

"I'm bringing her to you, where we can plan what to do next without all the unwanted people blowing down our necks."

Rex made a mental note that the name was going to be a bit awkward, with Rehka calling him Ruan and Margot knowing him as Rowan. Then he thought again. They'd probably be speaking English, the only language common to all of them, and the two women's accents would account for the slight difference in pronunciation. Or he could just mention to Rehka in a quiet moment that Margot knew him as Rowan Donnelly. Rehka would understand. He relaxed.

The next bit of awkwardness might have been that there was only one bed in the room, but Rex quickly dispensed with that, when he said, "You should get some rest. You take the bed, and I'll take the floor."

To his relief, Margot didn't argue. She went into the bathroom and came back out a few minutes later wearing no makeup and wrapped in a hotel robe. She turned her back to him as she slipped out of the robe and under the covers.

"Where's Digger going to sleep? Does he usually sleep on the bed with you?"

"Occasionally. Not always," he answered.

"Well, he's welcome to get on the bed if he wants."

Rex smiled. "Let's ask him. Digger, where do you want to sleep? With Margot on the bed, or with me?"

Digger had turned his attention to Rex and then looked at the bed and Margot. He padded over to Margot, pushed his wet nose against her cheek, then turned and went back to Rex, curled up next to him, sighing, and closed his eyes.

"I guess that was a goodnight kiss from Digger," Margot giggled and turned out the bedside lamp.

Just when Rex thought she'd gone to sleep, she asked, "Is now a good time for you to tell me all those things you said weren't important before?"

"Maybe," he said. He was cautious, certain he couldn't answer all her questions. "It depends on what you want to know."

After a short silence, when he imagined she was picking her questions carefully, she asked, "Well, what about Digger? He's very clever, but sometimes you sound like you're giving him orders, like someone in the military. And he acts like he understands them. And what's this business with the iPad. I could see what looked like security camera footage on it. What's the story?"

Rex sighed. She was far too observant. "Well, you're

partially right. I told you before that he's a service dog. It's true. He's my emotional support animal. But he was trained as a military dog before that. So, yes, he's very clever, and he does follow orders when I give them in a certain tone as if he were still in the military."

"What about…"

"Margot, we've got a long day ahead of us, and not many hours to sleep. That's enough for tonight, okay?"

"Okay," she said in a small voice.

Ten minutes later, she whispered, "Rowan, are you awake?"

He pretended to sleep. A few minutes after that, his eyes popped open in the dark. The captain of the yacht! Would he raise an alarm when he found Margot gone? Would he be too drunk to notice before morning? Rex gritted his teeth.

It's too late to worry about that now. We'll deal with it in the morning.

Chapter Forty-One

Ho Chi Minh City, Vietnam

Dawn found Rex stretched out on the floor next to Digger at the foot of the hotel bed. Margot almost stumbled over his legs as she sleepily made her way to the bathroom. Her movement woke Digger, who yawned widely, emitting his signature squeak at the most intense part of the yawn. And that, in turn, woke Rex. He noticed Margot's retreating figure and closed his eyes again for a few more moments sleep before she returned.

Forty-five minutes later, the scent of soap and shampoo woke him again. He opened his eyes to find Margot seated in a chair and watching him. She smiled.

"Good morning."

Rex yawned and answered, "Good morning, yourself. Did you sleep well?"

"Probably better than you did. If we're going to be here another night, I insist you take the bed."

"We'll cross that bridge when we come to it." Rex sat up

and immediately remembered his concern about the captain. "Hey, will the captain raise an alarm when he finds you missing?"

Margot's expression changed from her indulgent smile to one of concern. "Henri? He might. He'll probably phone my brother."

"I think we'd better do something to stop him from doing that. You can't call him on your phone, and I'd rather you didn't return to the yacht. Maybe write him a note that you met a friend last night after he left, and... I don't know —you went off with her for a couple of days... No wait— that might cause problems as well. I'll call him on my phone and you talk to him."

Margot started to ask the obvious question, why is your phone safe and mine not? But Rex pre-empted her question with a waving index finger. She knew the answer—not important to know for now.

As soon as Rex heard the line open, he thrust the phone into Margot's hands.

"Henri? Is that you?"

Rex had set the phone on speaker, so he could hear both ends of the conversation and help Margot if she was at a loss for words. He heard the captain say, "Yes, I just said so, didn't I? Margot? Is that you? Where are you calling from? Aren't you in your stateroom?"

Rex relaxed, *the captain hadn't yet missed Margot.* That was good. And he sounded rough. Hangover, probably. They must have woken him with the call. He probably hadn't even looked at the caller ID, but that would have done him no good anyway. The number was spoofed. If he called it back later, he'd get a message that the owner of the phone was unavailable at the time.

"No, Henri, I'm onshore. Some friends of my brother

turned up last night unexpectedly. I'm with them. I'm going to spend a few more days here with them, and then they'll take me to Da Nang."

A heavy sigh wafted through the speaker, and then he answered, "Okay, no problem. Did you take your things?"

"I'll come back for them day after tomorrow. I'll call before I come out. Is that all right?"

"We'll be here for a few more days, yeah."

"Thanks, Henri."

"A pleasure to serve, sweetheart. Take care."

She was still smiling when she handed the phone back to Rex, who clicked the End Call icon quickly.

"Okay, with that out of the way, next we need to get you some new papers. And before we do that, we need to age you, and get you some appropriate clothes for the persona you'll be with your new passport."

"Age me? How?"

"A little makeup, some temporary white in your hair, unless you'd prefer a wig. Glasses, and I think we'll make you an elderly Eurasian woman, so some appropriate clothing."

"Definitely a wig!" she exclaimed, ignoring the rest. "Do you know what it would take to put gray in this black hair?"

Rex grinned.

Margo held her hand up as if she was a student in a classroom indicating she knew the answer to a question asked by the teacher.

Rex raised his eyebrows.

"I just remembered the people from the convent are supposed to pick me up today."

"Then we should get word to them also that your plans have changed. But before that, I need some breakfast. How about you? We have a lot to do today."

"I'm ready for breakfast, but I don't think you are," she pointed out.

Rex looked down and realized he was still in the gym shorts and t-shirt he'd slept in. "Oh, yeah."

A few minutes later, he emerged from the bathroom with wet hair and dressed in jeans, t-shirt, and his usual Timberland boots.

Margot looked at him and shook her head.

"What?"

"You were in there about five minutes, in that time you shaved, showered, shampooed, and dressed?"

Rex grinned. "Yeah well, I'm in a bit of a hurry, and I'm hungry. I usually do it in six minutes."

"Don't tell me you actually time yourself?"

Rex just laughed and opened the door for her as they headed for the hotel restaurant and got a table. No one seemed to mind when Digger crept under the table and lay down at Rex's feet.

Rex found the phone number for the convent online. While they waited for their breakfast to be served, he called the convent and pretended to be Margot's brother, Bert as he mournfully informed them that she had suffered a miscarriage and would no longer need to be there.

His expression conveyed deep grief. He acted it so well that Digger got up from beneath the table and laid his head on Rex's lap, a concerned wrinkle between his expressive 'eyebrows'. It was all Rex could do to remain in character as Margot clapped both hands over her mouth to keep from laughing at him.

When he'd ended the call, Margot burst out, "*Mon Dieu*, that was perfect! I'm sure they will light a candle for the baby."

Rex reassured Digger he was fine and sent him back

under the table, where a few moments later he was enjoying a treat of scrambled eggs and Western-style bacon.

After breakfast, Rex took Margot back to their room, explained to Digger that he had to guard her, and then went shopping alone for the supplies he'd need to pull off Margot's transformation.

He came back with a gray, human-hair wig, a pair of slim-legged, black pants in her size, and a simple, white button-down shirt he thought she could wear untucked to create a bit of mystery about her figure. The conical straw hat made her laugh.

"Why the hat?"

"It's all the rage among the older women. It's too bad you haven't put on a little weight yet. I could have done a lot with that. But changing your body shape is a little beyond our time limits right now. Oh, and here." He handed her some wire-framed glasses with non-prescription lenses and an oversized pair of sunglasses. "You'll wear the sunglasses when we're outside, and the others for your passport photo. Now sit still while I make you into a woman twice your age."

"I can put on my own makeup," she protested.

"Have you ever aged yourself?" he asked.

"Well, no."

"Then sit still and let an expert do it."

She opened her mouth and closed it again as she already knew his standard answer to her intrusive questions.

While putting the makeup on her, he had to put in a conscious effort not to start laughing as he remembered some of the hilarious bantering among them when they went through the make-up training sessions at CRC. Some of the recruits thought learning to put on makeup was an utter waste of time for tough guys like them. 'If you can't shoot your way out of it, you sure as hell won't paint and powder your way out of it," one wisecrack reckoned.

Rex, however, was one of those who paid close attention, and later on, there had been more than once when he was grateful he did. One such an occasion, that had him smiling from time to time when he thought about it, was when he dressed up as a big-bosomed blonde, red lipstick, high heels and all, and slipped past a contingent of mean-looking, heavily armed, testosterone-filled security guards in Romania without a request for proof of ID, only their licentious stares.

In about twenty minutes, he'd transformed Margo so well that it was all but impossible to pick up the false wrinkles in her neck, the crow's feet, or the bags under her eyes as phony. He'd slightly tilted the look of her eyes, and now she looked like an aging Eurasian beauty. Not even crow's feet or wrinkles in her neck could erase the underlying structure of her lovely face, but he did shade under her cheekbones to exaggerate their height.

When she looked in the mirror, she was in awe. "Is this what I'll look like at sixty?" she asked.

"Not exactly, but close enough," he answered but refrained from adding, *and you'll still turn heads.*

When he'd finished with her, he made a few changes to his own appearance, in case they bumped into Ida by accident. He didn't think much was necessary. It was a long shot they'd even see Ida, in the first place. If she did turn up, seeing him out of context, she wouldn't necessarily make the connection. He had the kind of looks that one encountered everywhere and took no notice of. A pair of thick-rimmed, black, plastic glasses with flat lenses and a sprinkle of powder in his hair to turn it a bit gray would do the trick. He could only hope that if they were so unfortunate to get near Ida she wouldn't recognize Digger. However, Rex was not too worried about that. Ida would have to first recognize Digger, and then she'd have to recognize Margot and himself through their disguises.

"What now?" Margot asked.

"Now we wait for a telephone call, then we get your new passport, and then we get on a plane out of here."

"Where are we going?"

"Mumbai. We'll stay a few days to sort things out, and then we'll get you on your way to a place where you can wait for your baby in peace."

Half an hour later, Rehka called with the name and address of a forger and told Rex they had an appointment with him in an hour. When they left the hotel, Rex went first and hailed a taxi. Margot followed a few minutes later so she wouldn't have to wait on the street for the taxi or for Rex, and risk someone noticing the disconnect between her elderly-looking face and her youthful clothing.

Along the way, they had time to stop at a second-hand shop and pick up a suitcase for Margot's meager possessions. She'd look more like the older Eurasian lady she was pretending to be without a designer backpack slung over a shoulder. While they were there, Rex decided a cane would help, and instructed Margot to hunch over it as she walked.

When they arrived at the forger's address, Rex dismissed the taxi and went in with Margot to negotiate a rush job and payment. They wouldn't need a complete legend, he explained to the man, just the Vietnamese passport. Rex impressed on the forger that the passport must have a number that would pass database parameters.

For a premium of fifteen percent over his regular fee, a price Rex thought very reasonable, the man promised to have the passport ready later that afternoon. Rex paid the required ten percent deposit and said they'd return for it, and the transaction was complete except for the photo, which the man took himself.

In the meanwhile, Rehka had sent a text with a list of flights that had side-by-side seating for two from early in the afternoon to mid-day the next day. Rex selected one leaving at nine p.m. that night and texted the choice back to Rehka.

The three of them had a late lunch at a sidewalk café, a test of sorts for Margot's disguise. Not even the server did a double-take. Even in the light of day, the makeup was so expertly applied that it passed muster. Margot seemed to be having a ball playing the old woman. She'd added a slight limp to her gait.

Digger seemed to think their walk was for his benefit. On the leash, he trotted forward as far as Rex would let him, then fell back to heel for a while, greeted children with a happy smile, and behaved politely when adults tried to approach him. The latter was rare, but sometimes people would coo at him and try to pet him. He was aloof but didn't snap at them. He seemed to understand he was to act like a normal dog.

Late that afternoon, after returning Margot to the hotel for a nap and leaving Digger with her, he returned to the forger's place and picked up the passport. It was an excellent job. The man had used an existing valid Vietnamese passport and very craftily only replaced the photo. Rex had been trained in the art of forging passports—not how to do it, but how to spot the fake ones. On this one, even under the magnifying glass he couldn't find any flaws. Margot was now Suong Gould, mother Vietnamese and father from the

UK, and according to the customs stamps she'd traveled to quite a few different countries around Europe and Asia, including India.

In the few hours they had left before leaving for the airport, Rex refreshed Margot's makeup and outlined the rest of the plan over a room-service dinner.

As planned, Rex left the hotel room first and went down to check out. Margot, in her disguise, followed a few minutes later, walked past Rex and Digger, paying them only cursory attention on her way to the lobby, where she looked at her watch and then out the front door as if she were waiting for someone to turn up.

Although Rex was busy with the clerk, he was fully aware of where Margot was and what she was doing. Fortunately, the clerk on duty this evening wasn't the same one who'd seen Margot enter with him in the early morning hours.

The plan worked perfectly, though Rex noted Digger looking after Margot with a tilt to his head, as if to say, "Where's she going without us?"

As soon as Rex finished paying, Margot stepped out and hailed a taxi.

Rex followed short on her heels, got into the next taxi waiting in line, and told the driver to follow the one that had just left but to make sure he was not too close. He greased the driver's palm with two twenty-dollar bills to ensure he had the man's full cooperation.

Chapter Forty-Two

Ho Chi Minh City, Vietnam

About fifteen minutes into the trip, Rex had begun to relax and think they'd get away clean, when a bold move in the traffic ahead caught his attention. A taxi had careened out of a side street and was now between his and Margot's. His driver didn't seem concerned, but as they kept going, making several turns, the interloper taxi made the same turns.

"Can you get next to that taxi that almost cut you off?" Rex asked.

"Sure."

"Please do. I think it might be friends of mine," Rex explained.

The driver worked his way into the next lane while Rex kept an eye on the target. It took several more lane changes, but within a few minutes, they were parallel with the other car. Rex ventured a direct look at the passengers. He'd have recognized the one nearest him anywhere. Brawn—one of Margot's Russian followers.

How the hell did the Russians pick up the trail?

His mind went into overdrive. It could have been any number of ways. Maybe Henri had betrayed her. Maybe there were bugs in her cabin or the yacht lounge, so they'd known all along. But then they would've turned up much earlier, wouldn't they?

Nope, can't be any of that... Damn! Must be that cursed cellphone of hers again. Shit! I should've destroyed it last night already.

I need to get rid of these Russians before we get to the airport.

They'd come to a spot where there were few street-lights and the buildings appeared to be industrial, maybe warehouses. He was about to ask the driver to get ahead and cut off Brawn's taxi when it sped up, flanked Margot's taxi, and began crowding it to the side of the road.

"Shit!" he yelled, startling the driver and causing him to swerve. "Quick! Catch up to them!" He'd had the presence of mind to switch to French after his decidedly Anglo-Saxon outburst, but the driver had already increased their speed. Seconds later, the driver slammed on his brakes and Rex was out the door, just steps from where Brawn's taxi had performed an expert PIT maneuver, causing Margot's taxi to fishtail and reverse directions before coming to a stop. Rex was one step behind Brawn, but Digger was two steps ahead, engaging Curly, who'd also been in the taxi but concealed from Rex's view by Brawn's bulk and was getting out on the opposite side.

Behind him, his taxi driver twisted around and grabbed his backpack, threw it out of the car, and sped away, evidently preferring to lose his fare than stick around and get involved in scrap. Seconds later, another car sped away, but Rex couldn't take the time to determine whether it was Margot's taxi or the Russians'.

Leaving Digger to take care of Curly, Rex tackled Brawn from behind, expecting to knock him down, but that didn't pan out. Brawn stayed on his feet and whirled with Rex clinging on. It was an untenable position.

As Brawn blundered about, Rex worked his left arm up under the Russian's chin and squeezed, cutting of his airway. With his right fist, he began punching the Russian in the kidneys. Brawn staggered and began to fall backward, clearly an attempt to pin Rex down below him. Rex pushed off the giant and sprang lightly to his feet, poised for a take-down maneuver.

The Russian roared and turned to rush at his assailant, but Rex easily avoided the lumbering beast and danced around him, getting in kicks and jabs where he could. But it had little effect on him. If he let the Russian get a hand on him, it would be all over. The man could probably crush him like an eggshell. The Russian charged toward him, roaring with rage. Rex took a step to the side at the last moment and kicked him in the side of his right knee. He heard the snap followed by the Russian yelling out in pain, but to Rex's surprise he remained on his feet, turned, and stormed in again. Just then he heard a gunshot and Digger yelping.

"Digger!" He screamed at the top of his lungs.

It was enough of a distraction to Rex to allow Brawn to hit Rex with a swinging fist in the side of his head. Fortunately, at the very last moment, Rex was able to get most of his head out of the way. Nonetheless, the residual part of the blow was powerful enough to make him see stars and send him reeling backward.

Brawn growled and snarled in Russian "I'm going to

take you apart boy, in small pieces, and feed it to the fish." He dropped his head, extended his arms, and plunged toward Rex.

Digger's yap had put Rex in a murderous mood. He shook his head, danced back, and when Brawn was within striking distance, he twisted to the side and landed a vicious kick to the Russian's throat. The jar to his extended leg sent a shock-wave all the way to his hip.

That had the desired effect. Brawn fell like a rotten tree in a high wind, clutching his throat and gasping for breath. Rex quickly moved in, kicked him once in the groin which folded him over, and followed it up with a sleep-inducing kick to the side of his face that broke the Russian's jaw in two places. Brawn's body went limp. He was going to have liquid meals for a long while.

Rex immediately turned his attention to Curly and murmured while he was running toward the other end of the taxi, "If you've injured my dog, you're dead."

Rex was relieved to see Digger had Curly by the arm, worrying it to keep Curly off balance. In the hand of the same arm in Digger's jaws was a snub-nosed pistol Rex recognized as a Russian-made PSS-2, the modernized version of the MSS 'vul' silent pistol. With its short barrel and wide handle, it looked like a child's drawing of a gangster's gun. But it was no less deadly than any other gun. Digger had no doubt saved his life by keeping Curly from firing it while Rex was busy with Brawn.

Rex rushed at the struggling pair and swept Curly's feet. He was in no mood to be nice. He took out his anger on Curly by kicking him in the side, taking the wind out of his lungs and breaking more than a few ribs in the process. While Digger continued to hamper his shooting arm, Rex kicked Curly in the face, leaving his nose a shattered, blood-spurting mess. He was lining up another kick when Curly sighed once. Then his eyes rolled back, and he stopped moving—lights out.

Rex caught his breath, took one step to get to Digger, and dropped to his knees next to him. He was bleeding. "Come here, boy. What…" He stopped speaking and had to swallow a lump in his throat as he saw that Digger had only been grazed by the bullet. He got up and kicked the pistol away from the Russian's limp hand and made sure the scumbag was not in need of another kick, but he was unmoving. Further examination of Digger's wound gave him the relief that it was not much more than a skin-deep gash on the upper part of his right hind leg. It would no doubt heal with a bit of antiseptic salve—no need for medical intervention.

He still had his arms around Digger, talking to him when he became aware that Margot was kneeling in front of him, crying hysterically and trying to hug him.

"Margot, get back in the taxi, hurry! Before he drives off."

She shook her head and reassured him she'd given her driver a large sum to hand her his keys, so he couldn't speed away as the other two had as soon as the fight started. Rex couldn't blame them. There'd be consequences soon, though. He needed Margot to get away and catch that flight. It was more important that she got on the flight than for him to get on it.

"Okay, let me up," she said.

He stood and pulled her to her feet, then gave her the hug she so clearly needed. "You *have* to make that flight, and I have to hang back and question these punks when they wake up, and maybe I'll have to deal with the police, as well. You *must* get out, Margot."

He pulled out his satphone and opened it to find a picture of Rehka. "This is my assistant. Her name is Rehka. She'll meet you in Mumbai. Go with her, you can trust her with your life. She knows all about you, she knows what you look like, and she'll keep you safe until I can join you. Go on, hurry now, or you'll miss your flight."

Margot started protesting, but Rex had no time for that. He swept her off her feet into his arms and carried her to the taxi. She kept on screaming and kicking, and he kept on telling her to shut up and calm down. After what felt to Rex like eternity, he got her to the taxi. Mercifully, she had stopped opposing him and started listening. He helped her to get inside the taxi, kissed her on the top of her head, and said, "Remember Margot, you promised me you'll do exactly as I tell you to do. Now is the time to do it."

She nodded through the tears.

Rex closed the door and tapped on the roof for the driver to go. Just as the taxi started to move, though, he snatched the door open again and the driver slammed on the brakes.

"Give me your phone."

"What? But I might…"

"Margot, that's how they knew where to get you. They've been tracking you through that phone. Did you switch it on when you got into the taxi?"

She nodded. "I'm… I… didn't… sorry…"

"Okay, not time for that now, just give it to me." He held out his hand and snapped his fingers a few times.

With manifest reluctance, she extended it, and he took it quickly before she could change her mind and waste more time. With the seconds ticking by, he dropped the phone on the pavement and ground it under his heel.

A small squeak of dismay from Margot was all the protest she made.

"I'll see you in a day or two. Margot, there is no one that will follow you now. All you have to do now is execute our plan, but without me. You've got your boarding pass, your suitcase is hand luggage, so you don't have to check in, go straight to customs and go through. Go to your departure gate and wait for your flight to board. That's all you have to do, it's easy. Just do it."

Her white face looking back at him with concern was the last he saw of her. He thought she might be crying again. But it was too late to remind her to refresh her makeup when she got to the airport. With luck, airport security wouldn't notice that the bags under her eyes were dripping down her cheeks or smeared as she'd wiped her tears.

Have a safe flight, Margot.

Rex assumed the police would be there soon, since both his and the Russians' drivers had sped away, and would no doubt report the incident, or maybe they won't. They'd probably want to have nothing to do with it. However, before the police arrived, if they arrived, he hoped to revive at least one of them for questioning. When he turned back, he saw Digger sitting with his front paws on the pistol Rex had kicked away, staring at Curly, who was beginning to come around. Brawn was breathing, but barely. Rex suspected he had a crushed larynx, broken jaw, and crushed nuts, and would need medical attention soon if he was to live.

He shrugged. Nothing he could do about that at the moment, that's if he even wanted to do something about it. Maybe the police would be there in time to save him.

Meanwhile, he'd get what he could out of Curly, who seemed to be the more intelligent of the two anyway.

"Why were you following my friend?" he asked.

Curly only moaned. A few minutes later, he hadn't gotten much more out of the injured man when a car pulled up. Expecting it to be cops, he stayed where he was and only looked up when a pair of 4-inch spiked heels entered his view. He looked up.

Ida.

The look of shock and bewilderment of recognizing Rex and Digger was unmistakable on her face. The few seconds it took her to process seeing him and pull her gun, gave him the time he needed to grab the one from between Digger's feet and scramble for cover behind her car, yelling for Digger to hide, too. Despite his injured leg, Digger was already on his feet and running toward the car as Rex told him.

Gunshots rang out as Ida recovered her wits. Fortunately, those first few shots were fired wildly and gave both Rex and Digger time to reach the vehicle. Rex took up position behind the engine block. Digger was at his feet behind the front tire, safe for the moment.

When it came to killing women, Rex was a sexist. He'd never killed a woman and hoped he'd never have to, not even tonight when one was shooting at him. However, he couldn't let her continue shooting at him and Digger, she might just get a lucky hit. He needed to scare her.

He got up in a crouch, rested his hands on the hood and fired off two shots into the ground a few yards in front of Ida, which made her cease firing and start backwards. Two more shots over her head and Ida got the message. She fired one more round in Rex's general direction, turned, and took off for the building whose parking lot they'd come to rest in when the Russians' taxi had run Margot's off the road.

Rex was about to follow Ida when he noticed Curly had regained consciousness, had crawled over to Brawn's position, and was searching his unconscious body. No doubt, looking for a gun.

The next moment, to Rex's surprise, Curly, from his prone position, started shooting at the shadows of the building concealing Ida, instead of shooting at him behind the car.

That kick in the face must have scrambled his brains. Suits me just fine, if he's not shooting at Digger and me.

Rex quickly saw the opportunity presented by Curly's confusion. Therefore, he also fired a few shots in the direction of the building, keeping it high. This obviously emboldened Curly who started firing more rapidly at the building.

Another two shots fired in quick succession by Curly elicited a high-pitched scream. Then he stopped shooting, probably realizing that scream came from a woman.

Rex grinned when he heard a few Russian expletives emanating from Curly's position. The next moment, he saw the Russian stagger up and lurch toward the building.

Nope, you're not going anywhere, asshole.

Curly's back was turned to Rex, who landed on him in a flying tackle that smashed him face-first into the ground. Digger was there, too, grabbing Curly's shooting hand in a crushing bite. The gun dropped from Curly's hand, and he tried to get up to fight. Rex had to hand it to him, despite his small stature and office-looks, this guy was one determined Russian. As he swung around, his jaw met with Rex's haymaker, which broke his jaw and knocked him out cold for the second time in less than five minutes.

Rex called Digger off, grabbed Brawn's gun off the ground, and ran to the building to see if he could find Ida.

He found her sitting with her back against the wall. Her gun was about two yards away. She had her hands over her stomach and blood was trickling through her fingers. She was barely conscious and moaning.

Rex knelt in front of her, ripped her blouse open from the bottom, and saw the tiny entrance wound in her lower abdomen. The size of the entry wound belied the severity of the injury.

He turned her over gently to see there was no hope. The exit wound gaped enough for Rex to see that the slight upward trajectory of the round had shredded her liver.

She was dying.

Rex knew he had to get the answers from her quickly, if he was to get them at all. He couldn't be here when the police arrived, which also meant there was no time to wait around for the two Russian thugs to regain consciousness, so he could question them.

"Ida, tell me why you were following Margot."

Her eyes fluttered open, and from the widened pupils, Rex knew she was afraid. The look in her eyes was one Rex had seen many times. It was the look of fear of someone who knew death was staring them in the face. "I'll stay here with you. The ambulance is on its way," he lied.

"B…blackm…" she faltered.

"Blackmail? Who? The French President?"

She closed her eyes and gave a tiny nod.

"Who's behind it, Ida?"

"Rus…"

"Your government? Russia?"

A gush of blood erupted from her lips, but she shook her head. "Rus…neft…"

242

"Russneft, the gas company?"

She gave a small nod.

Rex knew Russneft was a privately owned Russian natural gas company. He also knew that there was a lot of speculation about just how privately owned they really were. Intelligence analysts were of the opinion that it was all just window dressing—trying to show the world that private enterprise was thriving in Russia. But in reality, Russneft's strings got pulled from inside the Kremlin.

"Why did you want to take Margot?"

"Marg… escaping. Orders, take… her."

"Has the demand been made already? Is that why you were supposed to take her?"

"mmhm… don't… le'… esca…"

With her last word unfinished, Ida's body suddenly relaxed and her head would have lolled to the side if Rex hadn't been cradling it. She was gone.

As if on cue, Rex heard sirens in the distance. He gently eased Ida's body to the ground and then signaled Digger to follow. They ran silently between the buildings and back toward the more populated areas. Rex was relieved to get independent confirmation from Ida that Margot was definitely not in cahoots with the Russians. He knew a bit more now, but it only corroborated what he and Margot had speculated. But none of it explained the French presence at all. Before he left Vietnam, he should get those answers as well, and hope it wouldn't require the mayhem that had happened here tonight.

Chapter Forty-Three

En Route to Mumbai, India

While Rex had been busy with the Russians, Margot had followed his orders. She surprised herself when she found herself in a state of calm and her mind starting to work rationally. She started by urging the taxi driver to hurry her to the airport. Then she extracted a solemn promise from him that he would not go to the police or talk to anyone about what he saw tonight. To seal the deal, she shoved a bundle of US dollar bills, which she only later realized was almost a thousand dollars, into his hand. With that out of the way, she took a moment to think of the next most important thing before she got to the airport.

Makeup! She got her makeup out and touched up her face as best as she could in the back of a speeding taxi and managed to not make a mess of it. She understood instinctively that a disturbed appearance and even small indications of panic would draw attention to her, and then it would be all over. Carrying a forged passport and a disguise to go with it would get her thrown in jail, possibly accused of espionage or suspected terrorism. And with the knowledge she had now, she wasn't too sure that the French government would do anything to get her out of there if it happened. They'd probably deny that she was even a French citizen.

You're on your own, Margot. Keep your head on your shoulders and think straight.

She took the next few minutes to practice some deep-breathing techniques she'd learned during the campaign to center herself and release the panicky emotions. The techniques had served her well then, and they served her well tonight. When they arrived at the airport, she felt she was as much in control of her emotions as she could hope to be. She paid the driver the fare, since the money she'd given him before was for his silence, praised him profusely for his help and kindness, and gave his hand a nice squeeze before she got out and made her way into the departure hall.

She even remembered to hunch slightly over her cane as she made her way through customs and to the departure gate.

It was only when she sat down at a small coffee shop close to her departure gate after she had cleared customs that she became aware that she was starting to breathe normally. She didn't even spare a moment's thought that ordering a double espresso and a very sweet pastry might actually not be the best food to have for her over-tensed nerves. Enjoying every bit of it, she took small sips of the coffee and tiny bites of the pastry to make the feeling of relief that started washing over her last as long as possible.

When I'm on the plane, I'll allow myself to worry again.

An hour and twenty minutes later, the plane was in the air, and when it reached cruising altitude and the announcement came that refreshments would be served, she reclined her seat, closed her eyes, and allowed her mind to wander.

What is Rowan doing? Is he safe? Is Digger?

The one thing she was sure of was that Rowan Donnelly was no history teacher or journalist or travel blogger. The things he'd done to those Russians were only possible if he'd been a trained soldier. Not just a normal soldier, a highly trained soldier—Special Forces. In her tomboy days as a teenager, she and her brother had liked to watch action movies, and it was the impossible stunts the action heroes pulled off that entertained her. But she knew, what she saw tonight was not choreographed movie stuff, not put on for her entertainment. It was the real thing—to save her from the claws of the Russians. Rowan had acted from pure instinct, it looked like. The kind that could only come from hours of training and real combat experience. The way he took down that gorilla of a man, twice his size, was something she would not have believed possible if she hadn't seen it with her own eyes. And what surprised her about her emotions was that she felt no revulsion about Rex's viciousness.

A tiny smile played on her face as she promised herself, *Rowan Donnelly, I'm going to find out who you really are.*

Before long, the rebound from the adrenaline spike left her drained of all energy, in need of a nap. A smile broke across her face as she could've sworn that she'd felt a little fluttering inside her womb. Impossible, it was too early, but it certainly felt like it. She placed her hands on her lap.

Don't worry little one, you're going to be safe. No one is going to hurt you.

The drone of the aircraft engines helped her nod off, and she slept for most of the seven-hour flight.

When she woke, unrefreshed as only air travel sleep can

produce, her thoughts had returned to Rowan. Did it really matter who Rowan was, or what his motives were? The fact of the matter was if it hadn't been for him, she'd now be in the hands of those Russian thugs. She couldn't imagine that would have had a positive outcome, not for her baby, not for her, not for the French President, and not for France. That much she was sure of, and that Rowan Donnelly was the one who'd prevented it.

That settles it. I promised him I'd do as he said, and that's what I will do. At least until we unravel this and know what's really going on.

She followed the rest of the passengers out of the plane and through the airport to the baggage claim area, where Rowan had told her Rehka would meet her despite her lack of checked luggage.

She spotted the beautiful Indian woman right away. In a country where a preponderance of women Rehka's age were very attractive, Rehka stood out like a beacon of light. And she was smiling so widely, Margot knew she must have recognized her as well. Her thoughts were confirmed when Rehka immediately started toward her.

As they met, Rehka reached for Margot's suitcase with one hand, while thrusting the other forward to shake hands. Overcome with gratitude that she'd made it out of Vietnam safely, and the other woman was there to meet her as promised, Margot let go of the handle of her suitcase and threw both arms around Rehka for a hug instead.

She felt Rehka's hand patting her back as she murmured, "Hey, you're all right. You're safe with me, and Ruan will be here soon. Come on, let's get you to my apartment."

Margot let go and straightened herself, feeling abashed. "I'm so sorry! I didn't mean to…"

"It's all right," Rehka interrupted with a big smile on her face. "Believe me, I know exactly how you feel."

"Thank you for meeting me, Rehka. You don't know how much I appreciate it. Have you heard anything from Rowan?"

"Yes. He and Digger are safe, and they'll be on a plane this way within the next…" she paused and looked at her watch, "three hours."

Margot sighed in relief. *"Dieu merci."*

Rehka didn't speak French but she understood what Margot just said and nodded, "Thank God, indeed."

The women made their way out of the airport, Margot once more in character as the old lady shown in her passport, until they reached Rehka's little car and got in. For the first time in two days—or was it three?—she felt safe.

Chapter Forty-Four

Ho Chi Minh City, Vietnam

Rex managed to evade the police and start back toward town. He first found a quiet place and had a closer look at Digger's wound and was relieved to see that it had stopped bleeding and that he was probably more troubled by it than Digger was. He petted Digger saying, "Good boy. Looks like we're both still fighting-fit. What do you say we go find those Frogs and hear what their story is?"

Digger gave a soft woof in reply.

As the area changed from industrial to light industrial, he began looking for a taxi, but at this time of night, they were few and mostly already in service. One or two refused to stop for him, whether because of Digger being with him or because he looked a little rough and it was late, he couldn't say.

Rex now had a bit more insight about the Russians' motive, but the French involvement remained an elusive loose end. Yet, it was important to know what they had in mind to help advise Margot on the best course of action when he got back to Mumbai. The only way to find out was to ask them, and the scrap he'd just had with the Russians had put him in the right frame of mind for getting it from them.

As he was walking back in the direction of the city and trying to wave down a taxi, his thoughts turned to Margot. With no way of checking how she was doing, he could only hope she'd been able to get control of herself and not raise any suspicions at the airport. He was confident her passport would stand up to scrutiny. All she had to do was to be her normal charming self, and she would glide through all the checkpoints without hassles.

"She'll be all right, mate." Rex said in his best imitation of the late Trevor's Aussie accent, while looking at Digger.

Digger just smiled back at him.

"Yeah, thanks buddy. I thought that's how you'd feel about it."

At last, a taxi pulled over, and the driver waved for him and Digger to get in. He asked to be taken to the port entrance. He'd seen no sign that the French were involved in tonight's Russian operation. He had no idea where they were staying, so his only hope of tracking them down was that they would still be keeping a watch on the yacht. He reasoned that they might or might not have realized that Margot had gone missing the last day or so. Notwithstanding, in order to reestablish contact with her, they'd probably be keeping a watch on the yacht in case she returned. If not, he'd have to decide whether he should abandon the idea to talk to them and get on the first plane out to Mumbai or spend more time trying to find them.

I'll cross that bridge when I come to it, he decided.

After being dropped off, he led Digger to the same

restaurant, across the street from the yacht where they'd been hiding before, and commanded him to stay. This was going to be a more delicate operation than the one involving the Russian hooligans. He also didn't want to put Digger through any more trauma, though he was sure the dog was going to be very disappointed if he discovered later on there'd been a fight he was not invited to. Also, he didn't want the French to see him and Digger together and recognize them in the future.

He explained all this to Digger, as he always did when he needed to talk through his mission plans before going into action. Although he knew the command to stay would be enough for Digger. He just took comfort in the dog's look of understanding. He grinned at his belief that Digger could understand everything he said. He knew that wasn't true, but Digger sold his apparent understanding of it well. For the first time since he'd inherited Digger and his night-vision gear, Rex wished the roles could be reversed so that Digger could use the iPad and he the camera. He was about to do a job that Digger could do better, but the circumstances demanded it.

After assuring himself that Digger would stay, leaving his gear except for the night-vision goggles which he took with him, Rex crept toward the stack of shipping containers where he'd seen the Frenchman two nights ago. He reminded himself that the guy might be on his 'rounds' and to wait if he didn't find anyone there at first. That was if it was the same guy as before. He'd previously timed the absences, and they seemed to be random, but usually within a fifteen minute to half hour range. So, if Rex didn't find him in his usual spot, he'd wait an hour before giving up on it.

It sure would be convenient if they haven't given up. Finding them

again might be a bit of a chore in a city of over eight million.
Assuming they're even still in the city.

His thoughts took less time than his slow progress toward the containers, and he soon was thinking only of his memory of the area. A lot could change in a day in a busy port. The night was clear, and he could easily see that the container stack was still there, but had its configuration changed a bit? Had some been added, or removed? He couldn't be certain. He crept a little closer and settled into a shadow cast by the stack itself.

Here was where Digger's superior night vision and the ability to see quicker and smaller movements would have come in handy, not to mention his sense of smell. At first, he could see nothing in the nook where the Frenchman of two nights ago had made his observation post.

Movement from his right alerted Rex. He knew he was all but invisible, dressed as he was in black cargo pants and jersey he'd changed into before leaving the restaurant's grounds, along with a black balaclava.

He started to move toward the spot where he detected the movement. He hoped to get the information he needed with as little violence as possible, definitely not any killing— if he could help it. But he knew he was dealing with highly trained men, DGSE more than likely, and highly unlikely to be submissive. It was bad enough he'd left behind one confirmed dead Russian, another probably dead, if he hadn't received medical attention quickly enough, and another badly injured. They saw his face, and they saw Digger and would be able to give the police a description. Getting out of Vietnam could very soon become extremely difficult if the police acted quickly and launched a full manhunt for him.

He let out a cautious sigh of relief when he caught sight

of the Frenchman settling into his nook. It was the same guy as before. Rex thought this guy must have been the junior of their team, hence he pulled all the late-night shifts.

So, the French were not tracking and monitoring Margot's cellphone. Interesting. I'd have sworn they were better at this than the Russians.

Rex just shrugged. It didn't matter now. What mattered was to find out why they were watching her. It had to be done quickly so that he could be on his way.

Rex backed away from his place of concealment and took a wide route to circle around behind the Frenchman's probable field of view, then approached at an angle that would allow the shipping container to conceal him until the last possible moment.

As he approached the point where he'd have to show himself, he realized there was only one way to do it— surprise and overwhelming force. A tactic that'd been drilled into him during his CRC training, and it worked exceedingly well when applied correctly at the right time.

This was one of those situations that called for it.

From about three yards away, Rex exploded into a full run. He saw the Frenchman jump to his feet in the last split second before impact. Rex hit him with his shoulder in the solar plexus with so much force it lifted him off his feet and dropped him on his back into the narrow space between the containers. Rex followed through with his momentum and landed on top of the man in a sitting position with both his knees pressing into the man's abdomen. The space was so narrow, the Frenchman's shoulders and arms were pretty much pinned down by the container walls. Rex realized there was no room for him to throw a proper punch. So, he grabbed the man by the front of his shirt, pulled his upper body up, and hit him in the face with his head. It wasn't a major blow, but powerful enough to break the Frenchman's nose, tear up his eyes, and send his head back to the ground with an audible thud. His body went still.

Rex got off him and pulled him out of the narrow space by his legs and propped him up against the front door of the container in a sitting position. He searched him and found a silenced Glock 19 and two spare magazines, a tactical fixed-blade knife, the man's passport, and wallet. Rex replaced the passport and wallet, took a step back, shoved the knife into his own belt, and kept the gun in his hand—pointed at the unconscious man.

A minute or so later, the Frenchman let out a moan and opened his eyes. He shook his head which spread the blood streaming from his nose all over his face. His eyes were still a bit glazed, but eventually he was able to speak.

"Who are you? What do you want?"

"Answer to question one; depending on how well you cooperate with me, I might be your worst nightmare or just someone who passed by here. Answer to question two is actually twofold; one, I want to know who do you work for and two, why are you following Mademoiselle Lemaire?"

Rex kept the pistol pointed at the Frenchman who took a few moments to answer. Rex admired his restraint. Someone less well-trained would have been babbling indignantly. It was good reason for Rex not to underestimate this guy. He must have concluded that Rex was someone like himself, but more skilled, to have gotten the drop on him.

Only the tiniest flicker in the Frenchman's eyes betrayed his surprise at the question. He countered. "Who is Mademoiselle Lemaire?"

Casually, Rex raised the gun and pointed it to a spot between the man's eyes. "I'm on a very tight timeline here. Don't play games."

The Frenchman's eyes went cockeyed for a moment as he looked down the barrel of his own gun, then he shifted his gaze to Rex's eyes and must have gotten the message. "I am here on orders from my government." He pressed his lips together as if to avoid saying more than he should.

"DGSE?"

The man made no reply.

"I'll take that as a yes. But for the sake of your own health I'd suggest from now on you answer my questions."

Rex backed farther away and gestured with the gun for the Frenchman to get up. "I know you aren't alone. Take me to the others, and we'll have a chat about your orders."

With a lift of his chin, the Frenchman slowly shook his head. "*Non.*"

Rex grinned and pointed the gun to the agent's left knee. "Oh, I think you will. The only question is how much damage are you willing to endure before you do it? Why not save yourself the trouble?"

The man must have realized that the gun pointed at his face was a bluff, this guy wasn't going to kill him, not yet, but the gun pointing to his knee was a different story. This guy was going to pull that trigger and shatter his knee at any moment.

"You will be tried for treason for this!"

"Treason?" Rex was amused.

"You are French—from Paris, I can tell by your accent. You're interfering with the work of a government agent. I'm on a mission of national importance and your meddling in this matter is treason."

"Hmm, I see. Well, you might have a bit of a legal problem with that charge, I'm not French. But look, this is a waste of time. Will you cooperate, or are you ready to take a knee for France?"

With an air of complete bewilderment, and probably capitulation, the agent gave the signature Gallic shrug—raised shoulders, hands half way up, palms open, and a pout on his face, as if to say, *have it your way.* "I will cooperate."

"What's your name?"

"Louie."

"Okay, Louie, where are you staying?"

"A motel about two blocks from here."

With the gun, Rex motioned for the agent to start moving, "Go on, now, head out to your motel." He spoke into the mic to Digger. "Stay. Hide."

The Frenchman turned and started walking but stopped when he heard Rex and looked back, confused.

"Not talking to you, *monsieur.* You move. Carefully," Rex added and nudged the Frenchman in the back with the Glock.

When they reached the exit and emerged into the city proper, Rex rolled the balaclava off his face to sit like a beanie on his head and closed the gap between them, concealing the pistol from casual view.

"How many of you were sent on this mission?" Rex knew there were three of them.

"Only two of us."

Rex grabbed him by the shoulder but didn't allow him to turn around and see his face. "Louie, for a trained DGSE agent, you have piss poor field craft skills. I've been following you and your buddies for a few days already. I know there are three of you. So, don't lie to me ever again. Okay?"

Louie nodded and started walking again.

"So, let's try that again. How many of you?"

"Three," came the reply immediately.

"You're sharing a suite at the motel, right?"

"Yes, two bedrooms."

"And you drew the short straw because you're the junior and therefore have to work the night shifts and sleep on the couch."

Louie didn't make a reply, but he stopped as if to ask, *how the hell did you know that?* But he must have remembered that Rex said he'd been watching them for a few days already. He just nodded and started walking again.

Rex grinned. His deductive reasoning was spot on so far and obviously had Louie off balance as to how much Rex really knew about them or not.

"Okay, Louie, now I want you to describe the layout of the apartment to me. But be very careful and very precise. I still have a very itchy trigger finger on this Glock of yours."

Louie sighed in defeat and started describing in minute detail every feature, including the estimated measurements of the apartment.

When they were about hundred yards away from the motel, Rex told Louie to stop so he could give him some instructions. "Okay, here's how it's going to go down. We're going to the door of your unit, you'll swipe your card to get in and give any passcodes or signals to tell them everything is okay.

"Now, just in case you are contemplating any funny business, I will have *your* pistol in your back. You'll be the first to die. If you survive that part, then as soon as the door is open, you'll tell them not to touch their weapons, to put their hands up and keep them up. Got all that?"

Louie swallowed and nodded.

"No Louie, I want to hear you say it."

"Yes, I got it."

"Good. Now just to make sure you got it right, repeat it back to me in your own words."

"I open the door with my card. I tell them to not touch their weapons, to put their hands up and keep them there."

"And if you don't do it. What's going to happen?"

"You're going to shoot me."

"Yes, Louie. You've got that right, and the important thing to remember is you'll be dead after I shoot you."

"Yes, I've got it."

"Excellent. I see you're a good listener. Let's go."

Rex grinned again. He knew that if he did it like he'd described it to Louie, it was probably one of the worst plans he'd had in a long time. But as long as Louie thought that's how it was going to go down and acted accordingly, there was a more than an average chance of success. After all, it already worked well earlier with Louie—surprise and overwhelming force.

The streets were clogged with the usual revelers making a lot of noise.

Well, that will work in my favor if I have to make some noise to get the truth out of these French assholes.

When they entered the hallway of the motel complex, Rex closed the gap between him and Louie and made good on his word that the gun would be pressed against the Frenchman's back.

He increased the pressure of the gun's muzzle in Louie's back when they arrived at the door of the unit, while Louie retrieved his electronic card from his wallet and swiped it through the slot in the door lock. Rex could hear the sound on the TV coming from the inside and grinned.

Everything is working in my favor so far. I hope it stays so for a while longer.

With his left hand, Rex quickly pulled the balaclava

back over his face. He told Louie to drop his pants, and when he hesitated, Rex pushed the pistol hard into his back. This persuaded Louie to do as he was told. When his pants were around his knees Rex told him to unlock the door. He waited until Louie pushed the door handle down and the door started opening, then placed his boot on Louie's butt and pushed hard.

Louie tumbled into the room. Rex followed him and kicked back with his right foot to close the door behind him. He took a quick step to get up right behind Louie, and cold-cocked him with the pistol. Louie's legs started to give way from under him, but Rex grabbed him from behind with his left arm around his throat, kept him on his feet and aimed the pistol over Louie's shoulder at the two Frenchmen sitting on the couch watching TV, beer in hand.

Rex stood in the dimly-lit room and took in the scene in front of him. He had to suppress his urge to laugh when he saw the absolute shock and bewilderment on the faces of the two men on the well-worn sofa, their weapons stacked on a coffee table in front of them. They were stunned into paralysis, mouths ajar, unable to move or speak.

"*Bonsoir*. My apologies for barging in like this, but unfortunately, I'm in a bit of a hurry." Rex decided not to ask them to turn the TV off. For starters, the remote sat on the table right next to their guns, and he didn't want to give them any ideas by asking one of them to reach over and switch the TV off. In any case, the TV wasn't so loud that they couldn't hear each other, and the noise would help to disguise any noise they were going to make if a brawl ensued.

He let go of Louie who sagged to the floor. Rex put his foot on Louie's neck and started talking to the two conscious but stupefied men. One was tall, probably around six feet, the other was short, probably around five eight or so. "Now, who wants to go first? I want the truth, the whole truth, and nothing but the truth about why you're watching Mademoiselle Lemaire."

When the two men remained silent, Rex said, "Oh, I see —you want some encouragement." He leveled the pistol at the right foot of the tall one, seated on his left and said, "I've got fifteen rounds in the magazine, so we'll start with the right foot, then the left foot, right knee, left knee, etcetera. I'll work my way up until you're dead, then start with your friend, and when Louie joins us again, I'll carry on with him."

"I will tell you!" The tall man shouted.

The short man elbowed him viciously, but he ignored it. "We are here on orders from our government. We were to find her and take her back to France for questioning on a matter of national security. That is all we know!"

"So, why didn't you take her the day she arrived? You've been following her since she got off that yacht on day one."

The two men exchanged glances, and the short one now spoke up. "We noticed others following her. We wanted to see if she met with them."

"The Russians?"

The two men exchanged quick glances of surprise again and nodded in sync.

"And if she did?" Rex asked.

"Then we would have evidence with which to confront her," said the short one.

"What matter of national security?" Rex continued.

"We were not given much detail, but by the looks of it, she could be in collusion with the Russians. They're probably SVR agents."

The SVR was the Russian Foreign Intelligence Service, successors of the infamous KGB.

"Well, you guys must be stupid or blind to believe that those Russian goons could be SVR agents. Or is it a matter of you desperately wanting them to *be* SVR, so that you could at least pin something on Mademoiselle Lemaire?"

They both started protesting.

"Okay, so then I'll assume you are dimwitted French agents. I always thought France's DGSE agents were selected for their brains and trained well. Seems to me, I stand to be corrected."

The two men were obviously insulted in the extreme but there was nothing they could do about it other than bite on their tongues.

"Okay, now back to Mademoiselle Lemaire. Who gave you instructions and what information were you given before you embarked on this Vietnam excursion?"

The short one answered, "The Director of DGSE gave us instructions, which came from the Minister of Defense, who got his from the President."

Ah so the President knows. Well, that answers that question then.

"What were you told?"

"That Mademoiselle Lemaire is endangering France by colluding with agents from a foreign country. That we are to apprehend her and bring her back to France."

"Anything else?"

They shook their heads in sync.

"And that was good enough for you? You didn't ask for more information?"

The two of them produced the Gallic shrug in unison, and the short one said, "Look, that's what we were told, and that's why we're here. We'd been given very specific instructions not to hurt her in any way and just bring her back to France."

Rex concluded that he was not going to get more information from these guys. Not because they wouldn't give it, but because they knew nothing more. "Okay guys, I would've liked to hang around and have a beer with you, but I must be on my way now. Maybe next time.

"But before I go. Just so you don't waste too much of your taxpayers' money sitting around here waiting for Mademoiselle Lemaire to turn up, she's left the country again. Said something about not liking the weather and then all these stalkers, Russians, French, and who knows who else. I suggest you guys saddle up and ride out of town. I am sure there are some other real bad guys elsewhere in the world more deserving of your attention than an innocent woman."

"But… we have instructions… we can't…" the tall one started.

"Guys," Rex interjected, "seriously, if I find you anywhere near her any time after tonight, you will be three very sorry frog eaters. Believe me."

They made no reply.

Rex moved toward the table with the weapons and gathered them in his arms. That was when the short one made the mistake of trying to stop him. Dropping everything he had in his arms, Rex met the charging Frenchman with a Krav Maga block, used the man's own momentum to propel him through the air headfirst into the kitchen wall, and braced for the next charge.

The tall one came at him with his head down like a charging bull. Rex waited for him, and when he was within range, delivered a kick to his face, which flipped him right over on his back. Lights out.

The short one had semi-recovered from his encounter with the kitchen wall and charged in. Rex met him with an uppercut that broke his jaw and laid him out on the floor on his back. The fight was over.

Louie was just starting to stir, he'd be up in about another two minutes. Rex would be long gone by then. He didn't want to mete out more punishment to the three of them. After all, they were citizens of a NATO country, an ally of the United States.

Rex straightened his shoulders, gathered the weapons again, and said, "I'd advise you guys to pack up and go back to France. The wine is good, and the women are beautiful." But he suspected none of them heard what he said.

Rex left with the pistols and knives. He started taking the weapons apart as he walked and dropping them in trash receptacles as he passed them on his way back to the harbor to collect Digger. He made sure to wipe his prints off every piece before discarding it.

With the weapons all gone, he pulled out his satphone and pushed the speed dial for Rehka. "Rehka, Margot should be well on her way to you now. We had a bit of a hold up here earlier, and I missed my flight. So, I'm going to need the next one out. Can you please have a look and find me one?"

"Are you okay, Ruan?"

"I'm great, haven't felt so good in a long while."

Rex also gave her a description of what Margot looked like in her disguise.

Rehka knew not to ask more questions. "You've got it, boss. I'll get back to you in a few."

The call came just as he reached Digger's location. "What have you got for me?"

"There's a flight leaving in three hours. Can you make it?"

"Thanks. Book it. I'll do my best."

Feeling assured that there'd be no more trouble from the French, Rex nevertheless took a circuitous route to the port. He had retrieved his backpack and Digger, changed back into more normal-looking clothing in the concealment of the bushes, and then headed back to the busy streets to find a taxi.

Within a few minutes, he and Digger were in the back of a taxi, and he gave the driver instructions to take a roundabout route to the airport, though he was conscious of the passing time. Once he was convinced he wasn't being followed, he had the taxi speed down the highway to drop him off at the airport and prepared to board his flight to Mumbai.

Rehka had asked him whether he'd rather wait for a confirmed seat or try to grab a standby spot, and he'd opted for confirmed because he couldn't be certain he would be able to get Digger on the flight at the last minute if he chose standby. There was no way he'd be putting Digger into baggage and then not getting a seat himself, although Rehka could be there to meet Digger on the other side. However, even though it required a wait, he was able to find a seat in the waiting area with his back to the wall and a clear view of the rest of the area. If any suspicious characters showed up, he'd spot them. He had only two hours to wait after putting Digger into the care of the baggage handlers. Between that and the flight time of almost eight hours, it would be a long wait for Digger but nothing he hadn't endured before. It would have to do.

Chapter Forty-Five

Mumbai, India

Some nine hours later, Rehka met him at baggage claims at Mumbai airport, where he was waiting for Digger to clear customs.

They hugged, and he kissed her on both cheeks, French style.

Rehka blushed a little but obviously enjoyed it.

"Where's Margot?" he asked.

"The poor woman was exhausted. She is asleep in my bed. She's okay, Ruan, and I really like her."

"Phew," Rex sighed. "Thank God for that."

They spent a few minutes asking how each other was doing before Digger's cage arrived, and he started whining when he saw the two of them.

With Digger out of his cage and on his leash and having been allowed to greet the two of them, they all headed for Rehka's car.

Shortly after they were on the road, Rehka asked, "Ruan, why does she keep referring to you as Rowan?"

Rex cleared his throat. "It's probably just her pronunciation of my name."

Rehka, took her eyes off the road for a moment and looked at Rex. "Ruan, come on. I'm not that stupid. Out with it…"

"Okay, Rehka, you're right. She knows me as Rowan Donnelly. I'd appreciate it if you'd go along with it."

"I have no issue with that, Ruan. Only now I wonder if Ruan is your real name."

"No, it's not, but I'd prefer it if you'd go along with that, as well. Just trust me when I say I'm not doing it to deceive you. But for your own safety, it's better if you don't know who I really am. Can we agree about that?"

"Yes, we can agree, Ruan. To me, your real name doesn't matter. You're still the best, most loyal, and trustworthy friend I ever had. I got to know you as Ruan Daniels, and that's what your name will be to me forever. And don't worry, I will make sure not to let her know that I know you by a different name."

Rex sighed inaudibly. *That was much easier than I thought it would be.* It wasn't the time or the place to get into his history or why he traveled under different names. Someday, maybe, if the need arose, he'd tell her everything. Not now. He also asked her to wait for a report of his adventures, so he wouldn't have to repeat himself when he told Margot, and she was good with that. They had enough other matters to discuss.

At her apartment, they found Margot up and about, looking for the means to make a pot of coffee. Rehka took over and told Rex and Margot to wait, and she'd bring them some coffee and a snack if they were hungry. Digger's ears perked up.

"Uh, Rehka? I think Digger sensed we're talking about food, and he's probably starved."

Digger's ears swiveled at the sound of his name, but his attention remained on the door to the kitchen.

"I have something for him," she called. "Digger, come here, my friend. I have some chicken for you."

Digger definitely recognized chicken. He was up from his spot at Rex's feet and into the kitchen before Rex had a chance to answer.

Rehka's attention was drawn to Digger's wound when he shifted uncomfortably while eating, and his hair parted to show the gash. She gasped, and her hand flew to her mouth. "Ruan, he's wounded!" she cried.

Rex rushed into the kitchen to hush her. "Remember, it's…"

"Rowan, I know. I'm sorry. But Digger…"

Margot wandered in next. "What's wrong with Digger?"

Rehka was on the floor, cradling the dog, who was straining to get to the food he couldn't quite reach because of Rehka's embrace. Rex was telling her it was nothing, just a scratch, but Rehka would have none of it, and as soon as Margot saw it, she was equally disturbed.

"Rowan, what happened?"

"Let's just all settle down. I'll tell you what happened when we let Digger eat in peace."

Rehka let him go and rose to her feet. "He at least needs antiseptic for it. I'll get some."

While she went for the ointment, Rex urged Margot back into the sitting room and returned to find Rehka smoothing a white ointment on the flesh wound while Digger continued eating, unconcerned.

"Rehka, he's just going to lick that off. Come on, he's fine."

She shot him an annoyed glance. "Go sit with Margot. I'll be there in a moment."

A few minutes later, Rehka emerged, carrying a tray with a carafe of coffee, cups, and some sweet pastries. She set it on a nearby table and poured coffee for Margot first, offering her cream and sugar for it. After repeating the process for Rex, she passed the plate of pastries, got herself a cup, and then sat down opposite them to hear Rex's report of what had happened.

Digger followed, settled down beside Rex, and proceeded to lick off the offending white stuff, just as Rex had predicted. Rex saw the women noticing it and decided not to rub it in by saying, 'I told you so'.

"Margot, I assume you've filled Rehka in on what happened on the way to the airport." He waited for her nod. "And I assume you had no trouble, since you arrived here all right."

This time, both Rehka and Margot nodded.

"Okay, here's what happened to me after you left the scene. Curly and Brawn..."

"Who?" Margot interrupted.

"The Russians. Those were my nicknames for them. Anyway, after you left, the small one, Curly, started to come to, and I was getting ready to put him out again, when a car pulled up with Ida in it. Well, the woman we knew as Ida. I don't know if that was her real name. Probably not. Anyway, the details aren't important, but she started shooting at me. I got hold of Curly's gun and started shooting back, but I made sure I didn't hit her. She must have gotten a fright when I started shooting back and ran toward the buildings. By that time, Curly came to, found

Brawn's gun, and started shooting also, but not at me. He was shooting toward the building. He must have been confused about who was shooting. Long story short, one of his shots hit her and, well, it was a fatal wound, Margot."

Margot's hand flew up to cover her mouth, her eyes big with shock. A tear spilled, and Rex thought he knew how she felt. Despite what they'd learned about Ida's treachery recently, Margot must still think of Ida as her friend from Vanuatu.

"I'm sorry, Margot. I'm sure I have not killed her and had no intention of doing so, the matter was taken out of my hands. I managed to overpower Curly again and ran over to where I heard her scream after being hit by Curly's shot to see if I could help her. I found her, but she was dying. I tried to comfort her and also asked her a few questions while I held her in my arms."

Margot nodded and dashed a tear away from her cheek. With an air of determination to put it behind her, she asked, "Did you learn anything? Do you know why they were following me?"

"Yes. I've had to fill in some blanks. They were following you because Ida's employer, Russneft, wants that gas pipeline to France pretty badly. Ida was sent to spy on you, as you know, but her employer must not have wanted an international incident such as a kidnapping would have caused. It seems they've sent a blackmail letter to your President, and they were prepared to snatch you to back it up if he didn't cooperate. When they tracked your location after you turned your phone on last night, it didn't take them more than a minute or two to determine you were headed for the airport, and the rest you know. They were going to prevent you from escaping, and probably this time they'd have gone ahead and kidnapped you."

Margot nodded again. "I assumed as much."

"Okay, there is more."

Margot frowned and looked at Rex. "What?"

"I also had a chat with your countrymen who were following you, Margot. They didn't seem to know much, except that they were supposed to intercept you and take you back to France as soon as they could." Rex didn't bother to detail the nature of the 'chat'. Margot didn't need to know that.

He continued, "They hadn't made their move yet, because they were waiting until you moved to Da Nang, and yes, they knew why you were going there. They figured it would be easier to grab you there without making too much of a fuss. But then they noticed the Russians following you, and then they thought that you were collaborating with the Russians. They were going to move their plans forward as soon as you turned up at the yacht again. They were still watching the yacht when I went back there."

Margot showed distress, not only in her expression, but in her body language. She had put down her cup of coffee and wrapped her arms around her body tightly, hunched forward, and was rocking gently back and forth. "Why?" Margot asked. "Who told them to take me back to France, and for what purpose?"

Rex took her hand to calm her. "I'm sorry, Margot. I asked, and they didn't know, but we can make an educated guess. They were DGSE. They told me they got their instructions directly from the Director of the DGSE, who got his instructions from the Minister of Defense, who got his instructions from…"

"Giles," she spat.

Rex nodded "Yes."

"What now?" she asked. The desperation had returned to her voice.

"Now we relax and start planning. They don't know where you are, and there is no way they'll find out. It's important that you don't leave this apartment, neither should you use the internet or a phone."

Rex paused and looked at Margot. "Do we have a deal about that?"

"Yes, Rowan, we have. I've learned my lesson about the use of phones. I don't know how I could I ever repay you or make it up to you. I shiver when I think what could've been if you hadn't turned up."

"There's nothing to repay or make up, Margot. Put that out of your head, and let's start planning what we're going to do next." Rex looked at Rehka and nodded ever so slightly for her to say something.

Rehka smiled. "Okay, Margot, first of all, you and I are going to my room, and then we're going to take your measurements so that I can go out and buy you some decent clothes. No girl can think properly if she's dressed up in clothes that make her look sixty years older than she is."

Margot started laughing.

Chapter Forty-Six

Paris, France

Giles Aguillard paced as he waited for news. The last report he'd received about Margot was that the DGSE agents had her in view, but there was a complication. The Defense Minister brought him the news in person because he didn't want any phone records, hadn't explained the complication, and Aguillard didn't ask. *Plausible deniability,* that political construct dictated that if she turned up dead, in truth, he would know nothing about it. All he did know was that they expected to have her in custody today.

His confidant, Lucien Laurent, watched him as one watched a tennis match, turning his head back and forth as Aguillard passed him going one way and then the other. Laurent's silence was annoying, but Aguillard controlled his temper and said nothing.

When will that idiot of a Defense Minister get back to me with news?

Blocks away, the idiot in question was getting unwelcome news from the Director of the DGSE.

"What are we to do? My agents have failed."

"What do you mean by failed?"

"I will let their words tell you." He handed the Minister his secure phone after setting it up to play the recording. The Minister pressed play, and they both heard the agent relate the facts. "Mademoiselle Lemaire is alive but gone. There is a man helping her. He spirited her out of the country, but we do not know where. The man found us somehow, and we do not know how. All we know is that he impressed upon us that we were to return to France, or else."

"Or else… what?" the Director's recorded voice asked.

"Sir, his words were something to the effect that if he found us anywhere near her any time after tonight, we will be three very sorry Frenchmen, sir."

"Did you get a look at this man? Can you describe him?"

"He is about one meters eighty or so but that's all we can say. He was wearing a black balaclava."

"And am I given to understand that this man, on his own, was able to overpower the three of you?"

"Sir, it's… well…"

"Yes or no?"

"Yes, sir."

"I can't believe my own ears. One man, not even a big man, can take on three of my top agents and kick their asses. Did any of you even manage to lay a finger on him?"

"Well… no sir, but… but… he surprised us, *and* he was armed."

"That's even worse. Why were you without your weapons? How could he surprise you? What the hell were you doing? Sleeping or drinking or… no, let me not even go there. What an embarrassment."

There was no reply from the agent on the phone.

"So, what now?"

"All we can do is to start searching for her again. Unless we can find this man and question him. But… well… we don't know…"

"Yes, yes, I know you don't know what he looks like, and you're scared shitless of him."

"Sir, we believe it would be better to return to France."

"You've got that right. Get on the first plane and when you land here, come straight to my office. I've got a good mind to transfer the three of you to the Paris police and ask them to assign you as parking wardens."

The Minister handed the phone back as the recording ended. "This is not only an embarrassment, its incompetence if you ask me, Director. One man defeats three of our secret service agents. I want a full, and I mean full, report on my desk two hours after those clowns of yours have landed."

"I will report to the President, but you know I don't even know where to start. On second thought, give me back that phone. I will let him listen for himself."

The Director gave the phone to the Minister and showed him the passcode and how to retrieve the recording. The director tried to salvage the situation with a "Good luck, sir." Which he regretted the moment the words had left his mouth.

"Good luck, you said? Good luck. Let me tell you, Director, good luck is not going to cut it. What you need is a miracle, and not just a small one. I am talking one on the order of magnitude described in the Bible, when the sea parted before Moses and the Israelites."

The Director was staring at the floor and nodded slowly.

What the Minister didn't say was, *I'm also going to need one of those miracles.*

"Mr. President, I knew you wanted to hear the news straightaway. I have the Defense Minister's secure phone with a recording of the agents who were assigned to the mission explaining why they have failed."

"Failed, you say? How is that possible?" Aguillard's frown would have turned most men to stone, as if they'd gazed on the face of Medusa of Greek mythology.

The Minister quailed. "I do not know, sir, but the agents' own words will tell you. Here is the phone. The recording is on speaker. If I may?"

Aguillard had to collect himself, then said with exaggerated calm, "Oh, please do. That is exactly what I wish you would do."

After hearing the recording, Aguillard thought about having them ordered to stay and question this mysterious man, of whom, it was clear, the agents were for some reason more afraid of than they were of what would happen to them and their careers if they returned to France. More afraid of him, in fact, than they were of the President of the country they were sworn to serve. But the remembered the agents had no idea who the man was or where to find him.

Perhaps bringing back the guillotine would be a good idea.

Instead, he dismissed the Minister and turned to Laurent, who had remained silent the entire time the Minister was with them. He'd forgotten his annoyance with Laurent.

"Lucien, what shall I do now? Do you have any ideas?"

Laurent stood. "There is one consolation, my friend. We have not heard from the Russian blackmailers again."

"But that only means they may have taken her. And that would be a big problem."

"Mr. President…"

"Oh, for Heaven's sake, Lucien. This is no time to stand on ceremony."

"All right, *Giles*. Why borrow trouble? Either they have her, or they don't. If they have her, there is nothing you can do but wait to hear from them.

"But it's also possible that she is with this mysterious masked man, and that could be a good or a bad thing. Again, we have no idea what his appearance on the scene means. And again, there is absolutely nothing we can do about it until he contacts us—if ever. In the meanwhile, all we can do is to pull out all the stops to try to find her."

"Perhaps her brother knows something?" Aguillard asked.

"Perhaps. But I think I might have a better idea…"

"I'm all ears, Lucien, don't make me wait."

Laurent held his hand up. "Then stop interrupting me. I suggest we request a summit meeting between you and the President of Russia. The negotiations for the terms will take quite some time, and if the Russians have her, they may believe it is progress toward their goal. They can't help but think, because of the timing, that you'll use that summit meeting to discuss the terms of the gas pipeline agreement. In our request, we could even hint at that. That should buy us some time to find Margot and keep them off our backs for a while."

Aguillard immediately agreed. "That's brilliant! Whether it is the Russian government or some private interest who's behind this, our request for a meeting will surely fool them into thinking we are capitulating.

"While you attend to that, I'll call in our top law enforcement and security agencies to redouble their efforts, and I'll suggest they also request the help of every one of their counterparts in the western world to find Margot."

Laurent nodded.

"It's agreed then. This is the best course of action. Make it so."

Laurent had one more comment. "Just make sure you understand that if the Russians indeed have her, then at that summit you'll be expected to sign the agreement or resign."

"Yes, that much I've figured out," Aguillard replied in a whisper.

Chapter Forty-Seven

Moscow, Russia

Fyodor Koslov, CEO of Russneft, the Russian company that so desperately wanted a gas pipeline through France, experienced a rush of adrenaline that caused an icy feeling to slip across the back of his shoulders. It was that kind of feeling commonly expressed as someone walking over one's grave, as he read the note hand-delivered by a Presidential Security Service agent. The SBP agent waited for him to read it, and then said he'd been ordered to wait for Koslov to escort him to the Senate building, where the President's official working office was located.

This is bad.

Koslov didn't have to examine his conscience for anything he'd done wrong—this was about the disastrous end to his team's Vietnam mission.

But that was hardly my fault. It was the men... That may be so, but you know the adage, you can delegate authority but not responsibility.

Koslov wasn't entirely innocent, of course. He enjoyed privilege well beyond the average Russian citizen. Part of the 'new' Russia, at forty-five-years-old, he was unmarried, wealthy, and able to rely as much on his good looks as his money to support his decadent lifestyle. His light-brown hair hadn't yet begun to turn gray, and his blue eyes were described as 'piercing' by his sycophants and 'dreamy' by his paramours.

Deep down, he knew he was nothing more than a pawn in the President's game of chess, both domestically and internationally. It would be fun while it lasted, and he was intelligent enough to know it wouldn't last. Someone else, likely an enemy of the current regime, would eventually be in power, and he would be out. But he had contingency plans. When that happened, he'd be comfortably hosted by some other country, courtesy of the money and other assets he embezzled from Russneft and squirreled away regularly.

It was a matter of an hour's drive from his office to the office of the President, during which Koslov's apprehension grew. Although the wait in the anteroom outside the President's office was only fifteen minutes, it felt like many lifetimes before he was ushered into the opulent presidential office.

Surely the President would have kept me waiting longer if he'd been angry?

He was even more relieved when he saw the President's smile, though something was off about it. It was more the smile of a predator than that of a friend welcoming a friend.

"Fyodor, thank you for coming so promptly," the President said.

It sounded almost kindly, but Koslov had made his assessment and knew better.

As if I had a choice, he thought.

The smile became even thinner and colder as the President's voice turned to ice. "Please explain to me what happened in Vietnam. Your report said your men lost Mademoiselle Lemaire. How is this possible?"

Koslov stammered, "As you know from my report, there was an incident, during which a trained special ops agent along with his military dog severely injured one of my men, who sustained brain-damage, he seriously injured another, and killed the woman you detached from the FSB to lead the mission."

"Ida Sokolovna, one of our most valuable agents." The President left out the part, *and one of my mistresses.* "She was only on loan to you, Fyodor. I hold you responsible for her death."

"But..."

The smile was gone now, replaced by a mask of pure disapproval. The President's cold stare was fixed on Koslov's eyes as he said, "Don't try to deceive me, Fyodor, I've read your report and made my own inquiries. Sokolovna was killed by friendly fire. *Your* man killed her, not some mythical super-agent. I hold you responsible for that, as well as for hiring incompetents in the first place."

"Yes, Mr. President... I... I... apologize but I... didn't try to..."

"Fyodor, I've decided to give you one more chance to redeem yourself. You will hire a better team to reacquire the target, and I trust I don't have to stress to you the importance of not making another mess of it?"

"No, Mr. President. I understand I will go to work on it right away. I will not disappoint you, Sir."

"There will be no more waiting and watching. She is to be taken alive and held until we need to show her to that

French upstart. Oh, and do us all a favor. When you find that super-agent, make sure he never becomes a problem again. Understood?"

"Yes, sir."

As Koslov left the President's office, he knew two things; one, he was on a very short leash, and two, he had no idea where to start looking for Margot Lemaire. Those were the thoughts that made him shiver as he already felt the cold Siberian wind of the gulags between his shoulder blades. Although those places and facilities apparently didn't exist anymore, no one who knew what was really going on in Russia would dispute that the FSB was only the new name for the old KGB. Anyone in high positions and even in low positions knew in Russia people still disappeared, just like in the old days—especially those that opposed the President and from time to time also those that disappointed him.

Chapter Forty-Eight

Mumbai, India

Rehka returned from her shopping trip with new clothes, which Margot declared were perfect. There were comfortable clothes for lounging around wherever they decided Margot should go from there, and a couple of fashionable sets of business attire that were cleverly gusseted to accommodate Margot's soon-to-be expanding baby bump. Margot was now set for anything that might come next. Except that she still looked very much like herself.

"We're going to have to do something about your looks if you're going anywhere in Europe," Rex remarked. It wasn't the most elegant way to put it, but Margot knew what he meant and took no exception.

"What if I go blonde?" she said.

"I thought that would be an ordeal," he said. "You said before..."

"Well, it won't be good for my hair, all that bleaching,

and I'll have to keep it touched up. But I suppose if I also cut it short, it will recover."

Rehka went online and found a number of sites about the latest hairstyles and showed them to Rex and Margot to look at and pick one while she went back out and bought some hair bleach, a few dyes in blonde shades, haircutting scissors, and a plastic drape to protect Margot's clothes. When she got back, she said, "Who's going to do this?"

Rex stepped up. "I've cut hair before."

Both women stared at him in astonishment. "A woman's hair?" they asked in chorus.

He declined to explain. Grinning, he just said, "Just trust me. Margot, which one of these styles is it going to be? Make your pick, sit back and relax, and let's see if I can pull it off."

Margot and Rehka protested as if they were identical twins as they explained that a woman's hair is not a 'let's see if I can pull it off' matter. A lot of light-hearted bantering followed, but Rex won the argument when he said, "Okay, if any of you clever girls have an option that does not include leaving this apartment, now is the time to tell me."

In the end, Margot shrugged, sat down, and sighed. "Okay, go for it, just try and keep the damage to a minimum."

"Well, there is always a way out of it if I *do* make a mess of it…" Rex said.

"Yeah. Do you care to tell me what that would be?" Margot asked.

"Buzz cut…" he replied matter-of-factly.

"Rowan Donnelly! You're a dead man if you do that to me." Margot warned him with a big smile. Amidst a lot of wittiness, hours later, Margot got a glimpse of her new look. Her new haircut was chic, short, and swept forward to change the shape of her face, and her hair was a shade of golden blonde that complemented her tan.

With a very serious face, Rehka said she was so enchanted with Rex's handiwork she was considering doing that to hers. His look of dismay that she'd cut her long, thick, black hair made her giggle.

Rehka produced the *coup de grâce*, a pair of oversized glasses with thick, black, plastic frames. The combination completely changed the shape of Margot's face, and she was certain her own brother wouldn't know her if he passed her on the street.

For the moment, she agreed with Rex that it was best not to involve Bert.

However, she did want to be near him, if at all possible, without jeopardizing her secrecy. She sensed she'd need his support and the companionship of his wife, her sister-in-law, in years to come to raise the baby without a father. Having considered all the factors and getting Rex's and Rehka's input, she decided on Switzerland for her next destination. Geneva was only an hour's drive from her family estate, close to Lyon.

Rehka researched every birthing facility in Geneva and found the best-reviewed, a private clinic. Once Margot approved it, Rehka began corresponding with doctors and estate agents in the area in Margot's new name until she'd made all the arrangements for prenatal care and a place to live.

Another consideration was a new passport. Neither of her old ones now looked like the new Margot, and Rex had a suggestion for her next persona.

"Why don't we make you Margot Donnelly? I can pass for your husband or brother, whichever you prefer, or whichever is expedient in the moment."

Margot shrugged. "I don't see why not. If you're good with it, so am I." She didn't say that it was a thought that had crossed her mind more than once the last few days.

"It was my idea, of course I am okay with it," Rex replied.

It was settled. Once she'd had a chance to put on some makeup and admire her new hairstyle once again, Rehka took her picture, cropped it to the correct dimensions, put it all on a thumb drive, and took it to a print shop to print. Then Rex went to have a new passport made for her.

While waiting for the new passport for Margot, Rex went out and bought another satphone. He quietly asked Rehka to configure it so that it would only have his number. He handed over his old one, which would now have Rehka's number and the new phone's number. He asked her to keep it quiet, because he wouldn't let Margot know about it yet. He just envisaged that there might be a situation when he would need to be able to contact Margot, or she him, when he was not nearby. He would see if it became necessary— better to be safe than sorry.

The next day, Margot and Rowan Donnelly, accompanied by Digger, flew together from Mumbai to Geneva.

Chapter Forty-Nine

Geneva, Switzerland

Margot's ready tears began trickling down her cheeks as their taxi driver delivered them to a small villa on the outskirts of Geneva. Surrounded by trees, it appeared to be a remodeled farmhouse that had been reserved when the city overtook the acreage that belonged to the farm. It was set perhaps half a kilometer from its nearest neighbors and separated from them by a privacy fence of at least two meters. The neighboring houses were grand, obviously a newer development, but the villa Rehka had rented for her was cozy-looking, charming, and surrounded by trees for even more privacy.

The yard was a bit unkempt, and Rex told Margot he'd clean it up, but she shook her head. "Don't worry about that. I love gardening!"

"Okay, we'll work out who does what chores around the house later. Let's first see what it looks like on the inside and if you like it," Rex suggested.

They wasted no time doing just that, and it turned out Margot loved it. The rooms were furnished comfortably, and the first floor was adequate for Margot's needs, so she wouldn't need to climb the stairs toward the end of her pregnancy when it would have been a chore to do so. The inside had been partially remodeled, so that the master bedroom and its attached bath boasted clean lines and modern colors. The sitting room and its furnishings were of a different era, as was the kitchen, but everything was of the highest quality even though dated. Margot declared herself well-satisfied with Rehka's choice.

There were separate living quarters upstairs so Digger and Rex could be close by to keep an eye on Margot, at least until Rex was certain she hadn't attracted new followers.

"We have everything we need here, except groceries," Rex said. "Why don't I go and get some and come back this afternoon with a rented car for us and take you to an early dinner? In the meantime, you can get a rest, figure out where everything is, and settle in a bit. What do you say?"

"That sounds like a fine plan," she answered.

Leaving her to explore what would be her new home for the next six months, Rex returned to the waiting taxi and asked to be taken back to the center of town. Rex had the taxi drop him and Digger off in a park near the shopping district. He found a bench and, observing others with their dogs, let Digger off his leash with an admonishment not to pick a fight. Digger gave him a look he could have sworn was scornful before trotting off to make some new friends.

Rex took out his satphone and called Rehka. After the usual greetings, he said, "Well, we arrived, and Margot loves the villa. You did a great job."

"Thanks! I've also arranged a car for you."

"You're a star, Rehka. You've thought of everything. Thanks for that. What's the address? I'm going food shopping, and then I'll take Margot out to dinner. I'm not sure how she'll respond to my cooking, and she can use a rest tonight."

She gave him the address and asked if there was anything else she could do.

"No, Rehka, I think that's all. Thank you! You've made it very easy for us. I think I'll go do that grocery shopping now. Thanks again. I'll give you a call now and then to let you know how things are going."

"Ruan, how long do you intend to stay with Margot?"

"I'll play it by ear, Rehka. Maybe just a month or two to make sure she's settled in and doing okay on her own. But if necessary, I might stay until the baby is born."

They said their goodbyes, and Rex called Digger back, interrupting what might have become a romance with a full-sized poodle who seemed to think Digger was the handsomest dog she'd ever seen. But Rex would have sworn that Digger was relieved to be rid of the pushy, French canine female. Rex hailed a taxi and gave him the address where his rental car was waiting.

When he got the rental car, he discovered Rehka had indicated he'd pay cash, avoiding a paper trail. She really had thought of everything.

Rex smiled when he saw the car, a PEUGEOT 308 station wagon, a spacious 5-door with enough space for Digger in the back.

I guess Margot would be thrilled to at least be driving around in a French car again.

"Okay, buddy let's go find a market and get some food," Rex told Digger as he opened the hatchback door.

Digger didn't have to be told again, he jumped straight

in, sniffed around, and sat down looking to the front in anticipation.

After that first night, when Rex had taken Margot for an early dinner and shopping, they worked out a daily routine.

In the mornings, Rex would feed Digger, and then the two of them would take a five-mile run before knocking on Margot's door. Then he would start preparing breakfast for them. In the afternoons, they would take long walks.

For days, they'd been chatting about everything but the elephant in the room—Giles Aguillard's intentions and what she wanted to do. Rex didn't push it. After her ordeal in Vietnam, he wanted her to have time to rest and recuperate, and he knew she would talk about it when she was ready.

On the third day after they arrived, Margot had her first appointment with the doctor who would provide her prenatal care and deliver the baby. Rex was a bit nervous that she'd want him to accompany her.

Margot must have sensed his uneasiness and took the opportunity to have a bit of fun. "So, Rowan, can I take it that you'll be chauffeuring me to the doctor's clinic today?"

"Ah... yes... of course I will... be happy to do that."

Margot started laughing. "Don't worry, I was just pulling your leg. I am not disabled, I can do this myself. You and Digger go about your business. I'll fill you in when I get home."

A few hours later, Rex was sitting again at the kitchen table and watching her bustle about. "What did the doctor say?"

"He said I'm pregnant," she teased.

"Really? Is that what he thinks it is? I would never have guessed that."

Margot stopped laughing. "All right, I'll tell you. He did an ultrasound and established that I'm about sixteen weeks along, which is a bit more than I realized. I thought maybe twelve. Other than that, I'm healthy, and the baby is doing fine."

"Did you find out the gender of the baby?"

"I asked, but the baby didn't want to play along, kept its back to the scanner all the time, so he couldn't tell. I'm okay with not knowing. I'd rather be surprised, even though I have a strong intuition the baby's a little girl."

"Anything else?"

"He gave me a prescription for pre-natal vitamins." She showed him a pharmacy bottle full of pills of a size he thought a horse might have trouble swallowing. "He said the nausea shouldn't come back, and that I'm fine to carry on any normal activities I feel like doing."

Rex suddenly felt an urge to protect and pamper Margot. "I'll take over the meal preps from now on. Then you can get off your feet."

She turned around to face him. She had a smudge of flour on her nose and a wooden spoon in her hand, looking like a harried housewife, but a beautiful one. "Do you know *anything* about pregnant women, Rowan Donnelly?"

Sheepishly, he had to answer, "No, not really. I mean, I was old enough to remember my mother pregnant with my brother and sister, but I was very young at the time, maybe seven or eight or so. It seemed like she was always tired."

"You probably only remember the last couple of months. Right now, I'm full of energy, and I feel like I could build a house and then build the furniture to go in it."

Rex's jaw dropped. "Seriously?"

"No, silly. But I think it's hormonal that women seem to want to become homemakers and feed people and sort of feather their nests when a baby is on the way. By the way, my doctor wants you to come to the next visit, so he can get us signed up for pre-natal classes."

Rex's jaw dropped. He'd been noticing for the past few days that Margot seemed to be filling out, not only a slight roundness to her waistline, but her face was fuller as well.

And… well, best not to go there.

"Me?!" He cleared his throat after the exclamation came out as a high-pitched squeak. "Pre-natal classes?"

Her smirk told him she'd done it even before she confessed.

"Well, I may have told him my *husband* will be my birthing partner."

Rex blushed. He could feel the heat reddening his face as he hemmed and hawed and finally said, "Husband, you said? But I've never… No, wait. Yes, of course I will do it. But what do husbands do at these ah… pre-natal classes?"

With his discomfort on full display, she couldn't help but have another quip at his expense. "Maybe you should be asking what they do *to* the husbands there."

As frightening as the whole idea was for Rex, it was obvious she was enjoying every moment of it, and he was good with it—this was the Margot he'd met first, full of fun and a little mischief.

Early evening on the same day, Rex decided that it was time to talk about Aguillard, and there was no way to sugarcoat it. "Are you ever going to tell Aguillard the baby is his?" And to his surprise, she was not upset about it. She must have been mulling it over, too.

"I've been thinking about that." She sat down at the table. She'd put a made-from-scratch chicken pot pie in the oven to bake for their dinner and poured him a second cup of coffee. She had green tea.

"I'm pretty sure he knows, and that's the reason he'd have the DGSE try to take me back to France. He's worried I'll go public with it.

"Of course, it's all speculation. As far as I understand the situation, he would've had no idea that the Russians were also on my tail until the DGSE agents would've told him. And of course, when the DGSE agents discovered the Russians, it played right into their hands—it gave them a reason to apprehend me, because I'm in cahoots with the Russians. That's what the agents told you, is it not?"

Rex agreed. "So, what's your thinking? I mean, at some stage you'll want to show your face again and go back to France, I take it. For now, it seems, there are a few people who know you're alive, but the rest of the world believes you're dead."

She nodded. "Yes, I've been thinking a lot about that, and you're right—I have to resurface sometime, and I don't think I can put it off for much longer. If I wait much longer, I'll never be able to give a believable explanation for my disappearance. It's already been what, twenty days or so since I've gone missing from Vanuatu."

"Twenty-four," Rex replied.

"I've been thinking I want to contact him and let him know that I don't expect anything from him, won't make political waves, and that I'm no threat. I just want to reappear, give the public an explanation, and have my baby in peace, raise her in peace, and stay away from the limelight, for now."

"You wouldn't return to politics?"

"Well, I would, if I could explain this baby. But not for at least six months after she's born."

Rex nodded and thought for a moment. "So, how are you going to explain the baby?" He had been thinking about that for many days already, and he'd made up his mind. If it became necessary, he was prepared to take on the role as father of the baby. Whether they'd have to get married could be determined later, and if that's what was required, then he was okay with it, as well. But he didn't want to put it out there as an option, not yet.

"I don't think it should be a major issue. One option is to just explain that I wanted a baby but wasn't ready for a relationship and therefore went for artificial insemination during the last month of the campaign. It's not an unbelievable explanation. Yes, I know the media might have a field day speculating and guessing, but unless they have blood tests done that's where it will end—conjecture.

"But that's not the real issue here, is it? The problem is the President of France has got his secret service out looking for me, and I don't think it's with good intentions. And then of course, the Russians. I can just imagine if they were to get hold of me what they'll want to coerce out of me."

"Yep, you've got that right. Until we know what Aguillard has in mind it's better to ensure that you're safe. As for your idea of artificial insemination, that can work. It's not an entirely unbelievable option. So, now we need to get in touch with Aguillard and tell him to call his dogs off. How do you want to communicate with him?"

"I'd rather do it in person."

Rex nodded. "It makes sense, but it might not be easy to

set up and might expose you to much more danger than I'd like."

"I understand, but I want to look him in the eyes when I talk to him."

Rex nodded.

"I'm sure between the two of us we have enough brains to work something out." Margot smiled.

"Yeah, well, I'm not sure I've got as much of those as you have. But for what it's worth, I am happy to contribute all the brains I have. So, to start with, we have to figure out how to get a message to him without betraying your whereabouts."

Late that night, while thinking about the day's events, Rex found himself examining his feelings about posing as the father and attending pre-natal classes. He was happy to support Margot in any way he could. But this chain of thought made him wonder if a guy like him, with so much blood on his hands, could ever contemplate being a father in truth.

What kind of father would I be? As a former assassin, what kind of father could I be? Is it even fair to a child if all you have is a history of death and destruction?

Nonetheless, despite his misgivings about his aptness at fatherhood, he was prepared to take on the role to keep Margot safe.

Chapter Fifty

Geneva, Switzerland

"I've been thinking about how to get a message to Giles," Margot said at breakfast the next morning. "What if we send it through my brother to Uncle Lucien?"

"Uncle Lucien? Does he know President Aguillard?"

Margot smiled. "Gosh, if he doesn't have contact with the President, France is in serious trouble! Lucien Laurent is the Prime Minister." She chuckled. "He isn't really our uncle, but he's an old and close friend of my late father. We called him Uncle out of affection and respect."

"Oh, I see. Yeah, I suppose they'd know each other," Rex answered. "But I thought we'd established that you can't contact your brother."

"I've been thinking about that, too. Rowan, Bert must be worried sick. Whether this plan of mine would work or not, I must let him know I'm all right, somehow."

"Okay, so now to work out how to get in touch with

your brother, and when contact has been established, to impress upon him the necessity to keep it a secret."

———

Margot insisted Bert would recognize her even in her disguise, if he could also hear her voice. Rex thought it would be safer not to reveal her face in her new guise but wasn't certain a recording of her voice would be enough to convince Bert the recording was genuine and not coerced. In the end, he agreed to a video but suggested she leave the glasses off, and maybe wrap her hair in a scarf.

Rex went out and found a store that carried flash drives with the correct connection for the iPad USB-C port and bought a couple, along with an adapter for standard USB. He set up the iPad and recorded two videos, both without a script, so Margot's delivery would be natural and unrehearsed.

The first was Margot talking to her brother. In it, she apologized for the trouble and worry she'd caused him. She said she was sorry also that she'd refused to tell him who the father was, and unfortunately, for the sake of his and his family's safety, she could still not tell him.

She went on to tell him her reasons for not coming forward with the news in the first place, and then she told him about the Russian and French DSGE involvement. She went into detail about how she met Rex on Vanuatu and how they'd become good friends and how he'd saved her.

"Bert," she went on, "it has become dangerous for you as well as for me. We believe they discovered my where-abouts because our phones are tapped, definitely by the Russians and almost certainly also by our own government. I need you to do one more thing for me, and then my friend, Rowan, who will be delivering this message to you, will protect me until I can reach an agreement with Giles.

"The other flash drive Rowan will give you is a message. I'm asking you to deliver it to Uncle Lucien to take to Giles."

After that, she had Rex join her in the frame, so Bert would know he was the friend she mentioned in the video, introduced him as Rowan Donnelly, and said a tearful *au revoir*. She hadn't seen her brother for a long while, and she didn't know how long it would be before she'd see him again.

Rex patted her on the shoulder and let her turn to him and cry on his chest for a few minutes before fixing her makeup for the second video.

In that one, Margot addressed first Laurent, whom she asked simply to show it to Aguillard, and then Aguillard himself. The message to the latter was brief. "Giles, I would like to meet with you face to face so that we can come to an agreement about our baby. As you no doubt are aware, this is a matter that holds wide-ranging implications, not only for yourself, but also for our country."

Chapter Fifty-One

Lyon, France

Rex left Digger with Margot to protect her and drove across the border to Lyon that very night. Before approaching the farmhouse, as Margot described it, his plan was to observe it and the surroundings for a while to see if there was anyone else keeping a watch over her brother. The farmhouse turned out to be a three-hundred-year-old stone mansion.

Trust Margot to keep her own counsel about family wealth.

Rex took his usual precautions, wishing he could have cloned Digger as he could have used the help. Checking the entire perimeter of the house and grounds without being seen himself was more than a chore. It was the work of almost the entire night. It was strange, but he could detect no one watching Bert. He would've expected the French and the Russians both would be around in the hope that Margot might turn up there. Or maybe they just relied on electronic surveillance, which could include bugging phones and internet usage and maybe also bugs in the house, maybe even cameras.

Dressed in dark clothes and balaclava, and after assuring himself he couldn't have missed live watchers, Rex approached the house. As it was an hour before dawn, and by all indications, the Lemaire family, Bertrand, his wife, and two kids were asleep. He was also glad there were no dogs.

Margot gave him detailed drawings of the layout of the house and buildings as well as the garden. The luscious plants surrounding the house made it difficult to see what was going on inside, but at the same time, it offered Rex good cover as he sneaked up to it.

Margot told him that Bert was an early riser and that he was usually up about an hour before sunrise when he would make coffee, pour it into a stainless-steel travel mug, and then do the rounds on the farm, inspecting everything and planning the day's tasks.

Rex was bargaining on Bert keeping with his routine and waited for him outside the backdoor in the shadows of a large oak tree, which could not have been younger than a hundred years. It could have been much older, given that those trees were known to have a lifespan of up to seven hundred years.

Of course, Rex would have preferred to rather arrive during the day, and like a normal visitor, drive up to the house, knock on the front door, introduce himself, state his business, and have a conversation with Bert.

Right on time, an hour before dawn, Rex saw the kitchen lights coming on, and about fifteen minutes later, a man matching Margo's description of her brother stepped out through the backdoor with a stainless-steel travel mug in his right hand. In the brief moment when the kitchen light was still shining on him when he exited, Rex could see the family traits—this was Margot's brother, no reservations.

He was a sinewy, dark-haired man of about six-two or so. Rex could see that he would be a tough man with a lot of strength from the hard work on the farm—not to be trifled with when it came to a physical encounter.

Surprise and overwhelming force, he said quietly to himself, *but not so much force that it would injure him.*

Rex waited behind the big trunk of the tree for Bert to pass, and when he was about two meters away, he moved in quickly and noiselessly and put his right arm around Bert's neck from behind and his left hand over his mouth. At the same time, he swiped Bert's legs with his right leg. As expected, that was enough to drop Bert to the ground, and Rex landed on top of him holding him down, keeping his arm around his neck and hand over his mouth.

Rex's strategy worked like a charm. Bert was not a trained fighter, and the sudden attack must have paralyzed him because he lay there quietly, not putting up a struggle. Not yet. But Rex could feel Bert was tough as nails. If he were to get his wits back, he'd be able to put up some serious resistance that would compel Rex to use more force, and that was the last thing he'd like to do.

I better state my case quickly before this guy comes to his senses and puts up a fight and makes a big noise.

Rex kept his head out of the way of Bert's head in case he tried to head-butt him and whispered urgently, "I'm not here to harm you, Bert. Promise not to raise an alarm, and I'll let you up and explain. I'm here about Margot. I am sorry to have scared you like this."

As soon as Bert heard his sister's name, he mumbled something and went still.

Rex said, "Bert, I'll remove my hand from your mouth,

but please don't make a noise. I have news about Margot. She is safe and not in any danger. She sent me to talk to you. Do you understand?"

Another muffled sound followed, which Rex took to mean Bert agreed and removed his hand from the man's mouth.

"Who are you? And what is this about Margot? Where is my sister?" he fired off, the anger unmistakable in his voice.

"I'm a friend of Margot's. I have a message from her. We need to get to a quiet place where we can talk."

Rex sensed that Bert was considering his odds and tightened his hold. It must have convinced Bert that he had little or no choice in the matter.

"All right. I will listen. But if you have harmed..."

"Save it. You'll see she's unharmed, and I'm genuinely a friend."

"We can talk in the cellars," Bert said.

Rex let go of his grip around Bert's neck, stood, and took two steps back giving the man space to get to his feet. Bert turned toward the cellars and Rex followed him. It was less than fifty meters away. Bert opened the door to the cellar and a set of stairs that must have been almost as old as the house. The stone steps led to a cool underground area redolent with the aroma of fermenting grapes.

"Will this do?"

Rex assented, and Bert put down the flashlight on a rough-hewn counter along the wall. He struck a match and lit a lantern, setting it on the counter and turning to see Rex, who still had on the balaclava.

"Friend? What kind of friend wears a mask when he introduces himself? Am I going to see your face?"

Rex peeled off the balaclava. "The kind who doesn't

want others seeing him. My apologies again for scaring you out there. I trust I didn't injure you in any way."

Bert sneered. "Yes, you scared me. No, you didn't injure me."

"Okay, that's great to hear," Rex said. "Let's get down to business. The mask was to hide my face from the people who mean harm to your sister and might be watching you and your family and your property. In other words, I considered the wearing of the mask as prudent, for your sake, your sister's, as well as my own."

Bert began to protest, but Rex cut him short with a chopping gesture. "Save it. Let me show you what I've brought, and then you can ask all the questions you want. I don't promise to answer all of them, but you'll be convinced your sister is safe. You'll see why the precautions, also."

Rex pulled the iPad from his backpack and set it up.

Bert watched with evident curiosity, and then gave a start when Rex turned on the video, showing Margot's face, framed by the scarf with which she'd wrapped her hair. He leaned closer, as if to see her better, though the video was clear, and the voice recording came through sharp and clear as well. When it came to the part where Rex had joined her on camera, Bert looked closely at Rex's features in the dim lantern light and must have concluded he was seeing the same man.

He nodded. "Who are these people following her, and why?"

"I'll let her explain the why herself, when the time is right. The people following her are the same ones who tapped your phone and found where she was going in Vietnam. Some are Russians, and some are DGSE. They were hoping you'd lead them to Margot, and they still may be hoping that, though I didn't see any signs of them tonight.

However, your house may be bugged. You must remain calm and make sure that no one, not even your wife—*no one* must know that Margot made contact, except for Lucien Laurent and the President."

"Lucien? Why him?"

"She's got a message for the President, which she wants Lucien to take to him."

"What is this message?"

"It's on another video." Rex gave it to him in a sealed envelope and asked that Bert honor Margot's request that he not view it, but instead take it to Laurent himself as soon as possible. "It's a matter of national security."

"Who is the father of her child?" Bert asked.

Rex shook his head. "I don't even know. Margot and I have agreed that I won't ask, and she won't tell," Rex lied without blinking an eye. "It's best that I don't know, and it's also best that neither you nor anyone else knows. But also keep in mind that, these days, there doesn't necessarily have to be a man involved in getting a woman pregnant."

Bert looked at Rex with a 'huh' expression on his face for a second or two, and then said, "Ah okay, I see what you mean. But I am surprised that she never told me. And if that's the case, what's the big deal with her being pregnant then? I mean, why has her being pregnant become a matter of national security?"

Rex shrugged, "I have no idea why she didn't discuss it with you. As for your question about national security, both Margot and I are trying to figure it out. That's the reason she needs to talk to Lucien and the President. What we do know are that there are forces at work that are bigger than any of us. The Russians obviously want to use it for some nefarious purposes. As for the DGSE, that's what Margot wants to find out from Lucien and Aguillard."

Bert was still staring at Rex in disbelief. "Well, I have my suspicions…"

"So do I, but you must understand the importance of not mentioning them to anyone. I mean *anyone*."

Bert nodded. "Yes, I will honor her wishes."

"Thanks. She will be grateful."

Rex then took out the second satphone, the only one in the world besides Rehka's that had his own satphone's number programmed into it, and explained how it worked. "You'll have to be the go-between communicating securely through this phone with me."

Bert shook his head. "I never thought that when my sister went into politics it would involve me at some stage. But thank you for keeping her safe. Tell her not to worry about anything. I'll do as she asks."

Rex looked at the signal strength on the satphone he gave Bert and saw that it was good enough to make a call from the cellar. He told Bert that he was going to get Lucien on the phone so that Bert could talk to him and make arrangements for an urgent meeting.

Bert agreed.

From memory, Rex typed in Lucien Laurent's secured mobile phone number given to him by Margot earlier, and when he heard a sleepy male voice answering, he handed the phone back to Bert.

"Lucien, it's Bertrand Lemaire," he said.

"Bert! Why in God's name are you calling so early?"

"I can't say, Uncle Lucien," Bert said, emphasizing the *uncle*. But I need to see you today. It's very, very important."

"Are you driving or flying?"

"Flying, but I still have to book it."

"Okay, let me have the details when you've done that, and I will arrange for my chauffeur to pick you up at the airport and bring you straight to my residence."

Bert hadn't considered what he should tell his wife, he asked Rex.

"I'd say be as honest as you can without telling her everything. In other words, just tell her you've been called to Paris to meet with Lucien, it's about Margot, and that you don't know anything else."

Bert grinned. "The only honest part about that is that this is about Margot. But I think that'll have to do. My wife is okay. She loves Margot like her own sister."

Rex stayed behind in the cellar while Bert went to explain to his wife about his urgent trip to Paris.

As Bert expected, his wife was alarmed when she heard the news but was also very supportive.

Fifteen minutes later, Bert dropped Rex off at his car which he had parked about two kilometers from the farmhouse. They shook hands, wished each other the best, and Bert drove off to the airport to try to get the first available commercial flight, or if necessary, he'd hire a private charter.

Rex drove around in Lyon and surrounding areas, doubling back a few times and taking sudden turns, and when he was sure he was not being followed, he headed back to Switzerland, taking a different route than before.

Chapter Fifty-Two

Paris, France

Two and a half hours later, after managing to get a seat on a domestic flight from Lyon to Paris at the very last minute, Bert was seated in Prime Minister Lucien Laurent's residence, known as *Hôtel de Matignon* in the seventh arrondissement of Paris.

It was a palace-like building with an illustrious history, constructed between 1722 and 1725 by Jean Courtonne and Jean Mazin. Since then it had changed hands a number of times, Napoleon Bonaparte being one of the most famous of the owners. There was a time when the city council of Paris wanted to convert it into a museum, but eventually it became the official residence for the Prime Minster of France. It was said to have the largest private garden in Paris. Over the years, since it became the official residence for the Prime Minister, a tradition was established that every new prime minister who moves into the residence plants a tree. The only prime minister who didn't follow the tradition was Jacques Chirac who served as France's prime Minister from 1974 to 1976.

"I don't know what this is all about…" Bert began, "but the message is from Margot."

It had been a little more than a week since Aguillard had received the inconvenient, worrying, and infuriating news that his top DSGE agents had not only lost Margot Lemaire but had been bullied, cowed, and thoroughly embarrassed by someone they thought was a countryman but couldn't identify.

While matters of state kept him busy, his mind, most of the time, was occupied with Margot and the damage she could do to him, his marriage, and his country. Some of his thoughts were egotistical in nature, some of them were totally irrational, and all of them only served to increase his trepidation.

When Laurent requested an urgent meeting to discuss 'personal matters', he was in such a state of flux that the only logical conclusion he could reach was that the time of his downfall had come. Resigned to imminent disgrace, he had his chief of staff clear his calendar for the afternoon after agreeing to Lucien's request.

He looked at the ornate Louis Quatorze clock on his office mantel. The trumpeter figure atop it seemed to herald doom. The face indicated it was almost time for the meeting. Aguillard had a strong impulse to seize the heavy object and throw it through one of the office windows as if destroying the clock would freeze the time, and he wouldn't have to go through the ordeal he was sure awaited him. Fortunately, Laurent turned up right on time to save the priceless object from an ignominious end.

"Well?" Aguillard prompted without a greeting.

"She wants to meet with you."

Aguillard's heart plummeted, but Laurent put out a hand. "Giles, I don't think she wants to cause trouble."

"And what makes you take such a sunny view of my downfall?" Aguillard asked.

Ignoring the implied accusation of disloyalty, Laurent went on. "First, let me tell you how I received the message. You know, of course, that the Lemaire children are like a niece and nephew to me. Our families are very close, and their father was my best friend before his death."

"Yes, yes. You are fond of Margot."

"Not only Margot, but her brother, Bertrand. He contacted me after her disappearance in Vietnam, very worried. I told him we had not heard from her. Giles, it pained me to deceive him. But that matter has been put to rest. Bertrand paid me a visit today. The long and short of it is he has heard from Margot, and her message was that she would like to meet with you to assure you she will not cause trouble."

Aguillard brightened a bit. "And you trust him?"

"With my life," Laurent answered simply.

"How are we to arrange this meeting?"

"Bert and I are to act as go-betweens until the terms are satisfactory to both you and Margot. I am happy to serve in that context if you agree."

"What choice do I have? This matter is driving me insane, wondering when the other shoe will drop. By all means, arrange this meeting. Just be certain I cannot be followed by journalists or Russian spies. That would easily snatch defeat from the jaws of victory."

And thus, began an elaborate dance of power play between two strong-willed people just to reach agreement to meet with each other.

The negotiations would probably have been much quicker and more efficient if Margot and Giles could talk to each other directly—maybe. With both of them hard-headed, it probably had an equal chance in ending in a stalemate. So, frustrating as it was for the go-betweens, they all knew it was the best strategy.

At the outset, the President was adamant to establish the upper hand. So, his first salvo, relayed through Laurent, was that he would not meet Margot in secret and demanded that she present herself in Paris to explain herself.

Rex talking on behalf of Margot, through her brother, told Bert, to tell the Prime Minister to tell the President to think carefully about his demand, and maybe to be a bit more realistic about how much clout he had in this situation. If Margot would've allowed Rex to formulate the reply, he would've been a bit more direct and would've told the President to go jump in a lake, but in all likelihood it would have been something much more discourteous. As it were, he was, just like Bert and Lucien, only a messenger and therefore passed it on as Margot dictated.

Next, Aguillard cited her deliberate attempt to defraud him and the people of France by faking her death and her suspicious 'dealings' with Russian agents in Vietnam. So, according to him, she was the one who had to reconsider the sway she held.

In the end, after a lot of back and forth, it came down to Margot putting her foot down when she said, "No, I will not go to France. Tell him the baby will not be born in prison. The meeting *will* be in Switzerland, or there will be no meeting."

Rex called Bert and dictated the words of the message

to him. It included words to the effect that Margot had a considerable distance of between seven and ten hours flying, a long one for a woman in her condition, to travel to attend a meeting in Switzerland. Thus, making sure no one would suspect where they were.

Bert who knew they couldn't be too far away from where he lived just chuckled while he took down the message.

"Okay, I'll get on the phone to Lucien right now. Please give Margot my love," Bert said.

Rex said, "Give it to her yourself," and handed Margot the phone. A few minutes later, she gave it back with tears in her eyes. "Thank you so much, Rowan. It means so much to us to have heard each other's voices."

Rex smiled gently. It was such a small thing to do for her happiness.

A couple of hours later, the satphone rang again. It was Bert, and he had the happy news that the meeting in Switzerland had been accepted. Now what?

"Date, time, and location," Rex answered.

In Paris, Aguillard and Laurent conferred about how to get themselves out of the country without having a gaggle of reporters follow. After considering many options, including Laurent's suggestion that Aguillard announce a personal retreat day, they settled on the coming Sunday, four days hence. It was a day when he would not be expected to be seen by the public, his constant media entourage, or any other government official. Only his security guards would be let in on the secret, and they were notoriously close-mouthed about Presidential movements.

Rex had used the intervening time to consult with Rehka about a place near Geneva to meet. She'd suggested a private airfield.

When Bert and Rex next talked, they discovered both parties had been thinking along the same lines; with much secrecy, a skeleton security detail, and in a private plane Laurent would rent for the purpose in the name of a non-existent entity. Rex gave them the name of the airfield, and it was agreed that Laurent, Aguillard, and three security guards, one of whom would be the pilot, would fly in for the meeting.

Only one more point of contention came up, and that was that Aguillard didn't want to get out of the plane. And on Rex's advice, Margot was adamant not to get into the plane. This point required several phone calls back and forth, and the President tried his tough-guy tactics again until Rex had enough of it, got on the phone, and dictated another message for Bert to pass on.

"Tell him this, and say it word for word, Bert. He knows, Laurent knows, you know, and I know, that Margot has and had nothing to do with Russians. She never met with them, didn't even know they were following her until they tried to kidnap her. She will not be put in a position to be kidnapped by the French now. Tell Aguillard that she doesn't trust him, and with good reason. He has one chance and one chance only to turn this mess around, and that's to meet with her, on her terms. She held out the olive branch, and he'd better take it."

"You want me to say all that verbatim?" Bert asked.

"Just change the pronouns, Bert. That's the bottom line."

"Will do. May I speak to Margot now?"

Rex gave Margot the phone.

It wasn't another half-hour before Bert called back with good news. "They have accepted the terms. They'll taxi into the hangar as you've suggested and meet with her there."

"That's fine, so long as the President's men get out on the tarmac, they must be at least five hundred meters away from the hangar, and they'll stay there until the meeting is over. The pilot takes the plane into the hangar, but he does not leave the plane when it gets into the hangar. Only Laurent and Aguillard come out, and then the door is closed."

Bert conveyed the final demands to Laurent and phoned back to confirm they had agreed to it.

At dinner, Rex asked Margot, "How are you feeling?"

"Much, much better," she replied with a big smile on her face.

Digger looked up from his dinner bowl, stared at Margot, and broke into his signature smile, which made her laugh.

"It's almost as if he can understand our conversation."

"Don't doubt it for a minute," Rex answered. "Sometimes, I could swear he can even read my mind."

Chapter Fifty-Three

Geneva, Switzerland

Rex had shared with Margot his expectation to be at the meeting to protect her. She at first protested that it wasn't his fight, but a look from him quelled her objections.

"I won't interfere unless they start something, Margot. I know these are private matters between you and Aguillard. But I'm not comfortable to leave you alone in their company. So far, they've not given me any reason to trust them. I can't risk your safety. I hope you understand."

"I do, Rowan, and I'm grateful for your help. I don't know how I'll ever repay you for everything. It's just... well, I'm embarrassed."

"No need, Margot. I want you to stop fussing about that. Consider me part of the woodwork."

She smiled. They were all ready to go, including Digger. Rex had already checked the location and surrounding areas out the day before and took careful note of where everything was. He still wanted to get there at least two hours ahead of schedule so that he could make sure that no one else was lurking around, there was nothing that would've stopped the DGSE to send in a few of their agents ahead of the meeting.

Two hours later, right on time, they watched as a sleek Beechcraft G36 Bonanza landed gracefully and taxied toward the hangar they'd been directed to. Rex and Digger had scouted it for anyone who might be hidden and waiting for the meeting to start, clearing it and the well-appointed meeting room inside before the jet landed.

Rex and Margot were watching through the window as the plane came to a stop about five hundred meters from the hangar, the door opened, the steps were lowered, and two men in suits and dark glasses, no doubt armed, got out, looked around, and nodded to someone up in the plane. They took up positions next to each other on the tarmac, one facing the hangar and the other facing outward.

"So far so good," Rex mumbled.

When the plane approached the hangar, Margot went into the meeting room as pre-arranged, while Rex and Digger watched the plane enter the hangar. Rex activated the mechanism that automatically closed the hangar door.

Laurent came first, and then Aguillard came down. His face showed arrogance and no fear, but Rex noticed he kept his hands and arms slightly spread away from his body.

Rex waited for Aguillard and Laurent to deplane and the door to close again before he went into the meeting room and through to a small kitchen off the meeting room to wait for Margot's signal to come out.

Rex could hear and see the greetings as Laurent came forward to where Margot stood and tried to hug her. It was an awkward moment, with her standing stiff and unyielding. After a few seconds, Laurent stepped back, a curious combination of grief and embarrassment in his expression.

"Margot," the President said, with a curt nod serving as greeting.

"Giles. Before we begin, I would like to introduce you to my bodyguard and his partner." Rex stepped forward on cue and stood silently, his arms crossed as Margot went on. "Meet Rowan Donnelly and his partner, Digger."

"This was not part of the agreement," Aguillard started. "And why would you need a bodyguard when you meet with me?"

"Giles, you've got three of them to meet with me. But if you feel intimidated by one man and a dog, get back on the plane and go back to Paris. And as for your question why I need a bodyguard, I had to hire them after you set the DGSE on me and tried to pin collusion with the Russians on me as part of your effort to cover-up your share in all of this."

Aguillard made no direct reply to that. Instead, he went on the offensive. "How could you have been so careless?" His arms were crossed, the picture of a closed-off attitude.

Rex sighed. *This is not going to be pretty.*

He was right. Margot immediately snapped, "Me? You're the one who…"

"How do you even know…"

"Giles Aguillard! Don't you dare say it! I'm not going to join you in the sewer of your mind. One more word of that nature and I walk out of here, and the next thing you'll have on your hands is a paternity suit," she shouted.

Both were already red in the face when Laurent stepped between them. "Please! Both of you. We're here to find solutions and make an agreement, not to insult and threaten each other."

Margot took a step back, tears threatening to fall. Aguillard maintained his stance, but Laurent tapped him on the chest. "Giles, stand down."

To Margot, he said, "It takes two to tango, young lady. You're not insinuating that he raped you, are you?"

"No, of course not, but do you think it's acceptable for him to suggest that I'm trying to frame him as the father?"

"No, of course not." Laurent looked at Aguillard and shook his head in admonishment.

Aguillard went on the attack again. "Nevertheless. You have put me in an indefensible position, politically."

Margot was shaking with anger, and ice dripped from her words. "You left out the bit about personally, Giles. And that's the most important part because that's what this is about, Giles. Not France or the baby or our party, no it's all about Giles Aguillard and how he can stay in power.

"I have done nothing but try to protect you, though you don't deserve it, you bastard. I disappeared so our secret wouldn't come out. I did it to protect your marriage, your good name, and France. And you return the favor by setting secret agents on me and even trying to pin treason on me."

As she spoke, Aguillard became redder and redder, and had his retort ready even before she finished. He spoke over her last few words when he said, "All I wanted to do was get you to France and safety, and nothing else."

Margot was about to respond when Laurent cleared his throat, causing everyone to look at him. "Giles, I'm sorry, but if you insist that what you just said is the truth, I'd like to point out that you not only had an adulterous relationship with Margot but now also have a similar relationship with the truth. If you'll recall, I was there when you briefed the Minister of Defense. You certainly did want her abducted and brought to France against her will."

Aguillard harrumphed and muttered that he'd had her best interests at heart.

Margot scoffed. "You certainly have a unique way of showing it."

Aguillard huffed again, and in a loud and aggressive tone, admonished her for her disrespect.

This was the point where Digger had had enough of this stranger yelling at one of his pack. He pulled his upper lip back, took a step toward Aguillard, and growled, causing the President to stumble backward almost falling on his ass. After recovering awkwardly, and not yet ready to relinquish his stance, Aguillard looked squarely at Rex and said, "Control your dog, or I'll call in my guards and have him shot."

This was the point where Rex also had enough. Up till now, he had kept his displeasure at the argument to himself, respecting Margot enough to let her fight her own verbal battles, but a threat to Digger by this obnoxious man was what pushed him over the top.

He drew himself up to his full height and spoke in a soft but measured tone, full of menace. "I don't care who you are, if you injure my dog, you'll be one sorry son of a bitch. And let me give you some more good advice. Stop threatening Margot, behave like a President not like a jackass, and my dog will stop threatening you. I've been patient with your rudeness to Margot, and so has my dog, but if you want to get out of here with your ass in one piece, your insolence ends now."

Aguillard reacted with equal anger. "Are you threatening me?"

"No, I don't threaten people. I give advice, and I make promises, and I don't make them unless I can keep them. You're just about to experience it if you don't settle down."

For a moment, it appeared Aguillard was on the verge

of apoplexy. Rex assumed he'd never been spoken to in that way by someone he considered a nobody. No doubt, since he'd become President, he was surrounded by bootlickers, but if this meeting were to continue, he'd have to change his attitude, or Rex would change it for him. Digger still had his hackles raised, which Rex assumed was in reaction to Aguillard turning his invective on him.

Laurent stepped in again. "This serves no purpose. What's done is done, and both of you are at fault. Giles, for your own good, stop being an asshole for a minute. Margot, you called this meeting. What did you want to say to Giles?"

"I *was* going to tell him not to worry. But if he's going to be a bastard about it…"

Aguillard turned red again and opened his mouth, but Digger placed himself between him and Margot and growled. Laurent answered before he could recover and start again. "Stop this name-calling immediately. Your father would've been appalled at your behavior."

Margot turned sad eyes on her uncle and pressed her lips together.

Laurent said, "Let's start over. He will not have to worry about what?"

"I just want to retire from public view and raise my baby in peace," she said. "There are ways we can keep this out of the media. But with Giles deciding not to get in touch with me but rather have me abducted or arrested by the secret service, that's not going to happen.

"Giles, I believe in you. I believe in your platform. Remember, I *wrote* your speeches for you. I had nothing to do with those damn Russians. You *do* know that. Admit it. Why would you accuse me of anything to do with them? To kill me? To save your own ass, when I never threatened you with anything?"

"How was I to know you wouldn't appear later, obviously pregnant, and threatening to make it public or approach my wife or make a deal with the Russians?" Aguillard hadn't dropped his entitled tone, but he stopped talking when Rex took a step forward.

"Giles, if you had just stopped for one moment and thought rationally, you would've sent me a message, not your DGSE agents. There was a time, and that was not long ago, Giles, after I discovered I was pregnant until I found out you had sent DGSE agents after me, when we could have sorted this out between us with just a few hand-delivered messages or a face-to-face meeting.

"As for your wife, I never asked you to leave your wife for me. And let me tell you a little secret Giles, even if you did, I wouldn't have married you.

"Finally, why did you think I'd disappear if not to keep this pregnancy secret?"

"And what else? To name this child my bastard?" Aguillard snapped.

"Nothing. I'd never want *my* baby to know what a bastard her father is. You owe me nothing but to leave me alone and let me raise her in peace."

Sighing heavily, Laurent once more intervened. "Can we please stop going in circles? You two have now firmly agreed that you don't like each other anymore, and I don't think anyone has any doubt about that. Giles, I suggest you man up and apologize to Margot for setting the DGSE on her, and then let's sort out the rest of it. Margot, you *will* accept his apology."

Margot nodded slightly, obviously not entirely happy that she had said everything she wanted but probably realizing it served no purpose to continue spitting fire.

Aguillard hesitated, but a moment later, he grudgingly said, "All right. I apologize. I shouldn't have done that."

Margot said, "Damn right…" but stopped at a quelling look from Laurent.

Rex said, "What's the rest of it you mentioned?" His question was disingenuous, because he and Margot had positive affirmation from the Russians that she was the bait in a blackmail scheme. So, it was no surprise what Laurent said next.

"I received a blackmail message to deliver to Giles, threatening to produce you and evidence of your pregnancy and link him to it if he didn't reverse his stance on the gas pipeline the Russians want. You must realize that would not be good for France, for our allies, the NATO nations, and certainly not for Giles. Or you, Margot. If you two are finished hurling insults at each other, we need to move on and see how we can recover from your joint stupidity without destroying our country in the process."

Rex nodded, "Yeah, we heard about that."

"What do you mean? Where did you hear?" Laurent asked very worried.

Rex grinned. "One of the Russians who followed Margot in Vietnam told me."

Aguillard and Laurent looked at each other, bewildered. Aguillard recovered first. "You better explain what you had to do with the Russians."

"No, you've got that wrong, I don't *have* to explain anything to you. But just to put your mind at ease, I'll let Margot explain how it came about that I made contact with them."

Aguillard and Laurent turned their gazes to Margot, and she explained what happened that night in Ho Chi

Minh City when they were on the way to the airport, fleeing out of Vietnam.

Aguillard and Laurent listened in silence, and when she was finished, the two of them slowly turned their gazes on Rex, new-found respect clearly visible.

"So, as you can see Giles, I *did* have need of someone to protect me because my own government wouldn't give it to me."

"I'm sorry, Margot," Aguillard mumbled softly.

Margot was on a roll and continued, "Come to think of it, I have a few more things to say. You haven't even thanked Rowan for what he's done for me, for you, and for France by preventing those Russians from kidnapping me. Obviously, that has broken their stranglehold on you. They don't have me and neither do your DGSE agents."

"Yes," Aguillard responded. "But did he tell you he also assaulted and seriously harmed three DGSE agents?"

Margot turned a questioning look on Rex, who shrugged and said, "Well, I wouldn't exactly have called it serious harm. And you must keep in mind people tend to exaggerate things like that, especially if their jobs are on the line."

She then turned to Laurent with raised eyebrows, who answered her unspoken question by telling her what the Minister of Defense had told them.

For the first time since the President and Prime Minister had entered the meeting room, Margot smiled. "Well, I saw him in action against the Russians, so I feel very sorry for your agents, though they don't seem to have suffered as much as the Russians did. And Giles, you'll probably want to look into the training the DGSE agents receive, because if a man who is a history teacher can take on three of France's DGSE agents and kick their asses, I think there is a training problem at DGSE. Wouldn't you say?"

Rex saw from the twinkle in her eye that she no longer believed his lie about his profession, which he told her in Vanuatu. He had to suppress a chuckle, and Digger looked from him to Margot as if to say, "What just happened?"

Aguillard was speechless. Even Laurent had to realize the talks had turned a corner, and Margot now had the upper hand. She must certainly have realized it, Rex reflected, as she now went on.

"Before we move to a final agreement, I want you to state in your own handwriting that Rowan will not be prosecuted for any of his part in this. Uncle Lucien, I want you to witness it."

Aguillard offered to give a pardon.

Margot fixed him with a raised eyebrow and hard stare and said, "You must think I'm stupid. A pardon means that he's done something wrong, and that is not the truth. In fact, I no longer want just a guarantee he won't be prosecuted. I want you to give him a letter that states he acted in the interest of France when he protected me. You will word it as a letter of thanks, praise, and commendation."

Aguillard must have finally realized he had nothing left with which to negotiate. He promised to write it, but that was not good enough for Margot. She adamantly refused to discuss anything else without the letter in her hand. At that point, pressured by Laurent, he surrendered, sat down, and wrote the letter. Margot looked it over, saw that it included everything she'd demanded, and pronounced herself satisfied on that score.

Then Laurent suggested they brainstorm how to put to rest once and for all the threat posed by Margot being found alive and her pregnancy exposed to the public. While she remained in hiding, the Russians could even use her disappearance to foment rumors and start a media frenzy. Laurent suggested the only way to keep it from happening was for her to come forward with a reasonable and believable explanation of her disappearance.

Margot and Aguillard both protested that, until Laurent said, "Hear me out. What I propose is that Margot come forward at a press conference and say she has been on an ocean cruise on a yacht and unaware of the stir she's caused. She isn't showing yet. She can plead exhaustion from the campaign and that she still needs a break and would appreciate privacy. Nothing needs to be said about the baby. Then after the baby's birth, when she's ready, she comes back to work."

"I didn't say anything about going back to work. I'll go and do the press conference, but then I want to be left alone to raise my daughter in peace. And Giles, I will expect another handwritten letter from you guaranteeing it."

Rex smiled to himself. She was still convinced the baby was a girl.

Aguillard said, "But you are my press secretary. The media misses you. You must come back!"

Margot shook her head. "I don't want to be *your* press secretary anymore, Giles. Besides, working that closely together would only start the rumors again."

Rex thought the arguments would start again, but once more, Laurent's cooler head prevailed. "Margot, you have always had political ambitions, since you were old enough to realize there was a government at all. You have the talent for it, you've proved it. The people like you, the media likes you. You're a natural, Margot. Don't let that go to waste.

"Please don't try to tell me you are now content to be a private person, a mother and nothing else." He held his hand up as she bristled. "Yes, being a mother is an important job, and I know you will throw yourself into it and do the same excellent job you did for Giles' campaign.

"I even understand your reluctance to take up your old role. But remember, Giles offered you a deputy ministry originally. Won't you consider returning, after say a year, and accepting that job? You won't have to work closely with him, and you'll have the freedom to raise the baby as you see fit."

"I don't need a bribe to stay quiet, Uncle Lucien."

Aguillard had the grace to keep his tone friendly when he answered, "It isn't a bribe, Margot. It was a genuine offer the first time, and it is a genuine offer now. You are far too capable a woman to deprive France of your service. Please accept. I will pledge not to bother you, not to take an unseemly interest in the baby, and not to threaten you again. I was out of line."

This time even Digger seemed to accept the apology as genuine. For the first time since he'd put himself in front of Margot, he sat down and let his tongue loll out of his mouth.

"It's settled then," Laurent said. "You'll return to Paris with us now, and we'll hold a press conference to explain that you are not dead as assumed but had only been on a private vacation and unaware of the assumption. You will say you need some private time, and then you can return to wherever you wish to have the baby. You will come back to Paris when you are ready to take up your new duties."

"And Aguillard will put his promises in writing," Rex added.

"Yes, of course."

Ten minutes later they had agreed that Margot and Rex would go back to their 'hotel' to pick up their clothing and return to the airport. The two security guards on the tarmac would then drive the rental car to Paris, while Margot, Rex, and Digger would fly there with Laurent and Aguillard.

When they got on the plane, Margot was in her disguise with her chic new haircut, blonde tresses, and oversized glasses, so no one would recognize her when they arrived in Paris.

Margot would be the guest of the Prime Minister at Hôtel de Matignon. Rex wanted to stay out of sight, therefore he and Digger would find themselves a hotel nearby.

When they were in the air, Laurent said, "It is too late to arrange the press conference for today. Giles can get some publicity out of it, so I think we should make it a big celebration."

Margot knew how these things worked and that politicians were always on the lookout for anything that would give them exposure to good press. Because he'd been forced to declare a period of mourning for her, having her show up at a poorly-attended press conference would make him very unpopular with the press. And though he was still enjoying the honeymoon phase of his Presidency, with the press for once supporting the popular opinion rather than trying to change it, it was a good idea to exploit that good relationship for as long as it lasted.

Therefore, Aguillard insisted that he must tease them with an announcement that he had something stupendous to share, something monumental—something that they would not want to miss. But he wouldn't say what, only that it was very good news.

Chapter Fifty-Four

Paris, France

That evening, the airwaves were already abuzz with speculation. Could the President have signed a new trade agreement that would improve the economy? Had he and allies discovered who was behind the terrorist attacks that plagued the country? Was there a breakthrough in countries signing on to the world agreement to fight global warming?

Laurent chuckled as each new theory emerged. The stations were clueless.

Rex found a modest room for himself and Digger in a hotel near the Élysée, where the press conference was to take place. He sat down on the hotel bed and flipped through a few TV channels, watching with amusement the wide speculations.

Those who knew didn't say, and those who said didn't know.

Soon he decided that sleep was more important and turned the TV off.

Digger tried to get on the bed with him, but Rex had

promised the desk clerk that his dog would not be a problem. Rex quietly told him, "Sorry, boy. You'll have to make do with the floor tonight. I'll make it up to you tomorrow."

The following morning after breakfast and giving Digger an exercise run, Rex made a few subtle adjustments to his appearance, including donning very dark glasses and extending the folding white cane he'd purchased in Geneva. He leashed Digger and rigged him up with his harness and fitted him with the comms units, just in case, though he left the camera and iPad in his backpack. He joined the crowd as simply another bystander, albeit blind, waiting for the press conference to begin. It was scheduled for eleven a.m.

The mood of the crowd was like that of a child waiting for his parents to wake up on Christmas morning; happy, expectant, and impatient all at once.

Imitating a blind man, Rex had to remember not to look directly up at the giant TV monitors that had been set up in the square. Instead, he watched at an oblique angle, his head cocked as if to hear better. The pre-conference talking heads were still speculating, building the impatience of the crowd.

Right on time, Aguillard emerged from the palace and mounted a temporary stage set up in the square. Applause and cheering broke out, but the crowd quieted as he raised his arms.

"My fellow citizens," he began. "It is my great joy to announce that a tragedy we all mourned only weeks ago has turned into jubilation. I know you were all deeply saddened to learn of it, as was I. Therefore, you will be happy to know that one of our own has been found, alive and well, the news of her death simply a grave error. Please join me in welcoming our own Margot Lemaire home!"

As he spoke, the crowd collectively held its breath until the name was revealed. There was a moment of stunned silence and then a roar of joy and approval went up that surely shook the rafters all over Paris. Maybe the Eiffel tower shook a little, as well.

Digger started barking until Rex quieted him with a firm command through the comms unit. It took several minutes for the President to quiet the crowd and tell them that Mademoiselle Lemaire was there in person.

On cue, Margot came out and walked up the stairs. Rex saw that she'd dyed her hair back to its natural color overnight. The short cut still looked good. He smiled when he thought, *as far as I'm concerned, she would've looked good even with a buzz cut.* He hoped the color it was now was just a rinse, so she could go blonde again when they got back to Geneva and into hiding.

She had gained the podium and was smiling at the crowd as they cheered. Rex noticed tears on the faces of nearby onlookers. It touched him how popular she was. Well, she deserved it. She was a wonderful woman, that was for sure.

The crowd quieted to hear Margot.

"Dear friends and countrymen. I am here to apologize, deeply and humbly, for the grief I inadvertently caused you and the President. It was never my intention to do so. Looking back at my actions now, I regret it. I acted without thinking about the angst my sudden disappearance might cause. Please accept my unreserved apology. As you know, President Aguillard's campaign was an arduous one, taking place over such a short but intense time. As his campaign manager, I became extremely exhausted, and as his press secretary, the pressure only increased—to the point where I was advised by my physician to take a long vacation. I am still not recovered.

"Nevertheless, I feel it is my duty to tell you where I was for those weeks, and it is a simple explanation. I had the opportunity to take an ocean cruise on a yacht belonging to a friend of my family. A chance opportunity with a small window for acceptance. And what was most appealing of the trip was that I would be incommunicado for the entire duration. For all this time, I've been unaware of the storm that my disappearance created, and I'm so sorry that my impulsive decision cost anyone any measure of grief.

"And now, I must ask for your forbearance. President Aguillard has graciously accepted my resignation from my post, as I still need some private time to rest and recover—on doctor's orders. My successor is quite capable. You will not miss me." Here, she gave a brilliant smile as a protest went up from the crowd.

"Never fear. I will return to serve the Presidency and my country. I will have the opportunity to see you again, my friends. However, for now, I bid you *au revoir*."

Shouts of "We love you, Margot!" and "Please don't go!" went up from the crowd. A few "Return soon!" and "Vive la Lemaire!" shouts could be heard as Margot waved and left the podium and the stage and vanished into the shadows of the palace doors.

Aguillard stepped up to the podium again and said a few more words to rally the crowd and return them to the happy mood they'd enjoyed when they heard Margot was alive. He announced that when she was ready to return, there would be a place in government for her, though he would not ever overwork her again. The last was said with an air of rueful amusement, like a joke, and the crowd ate it up. When the President, too, left the stage and Margot's successor announced that he would take a few questions, the crowd began to disperse.

Rex moved a little closer to monitor what was being asked and answered, but the press secretary was being quite circumspect, stating, "I don't know. Let us please respect mademoiselle's privacy," to most of the questions.

The journalists living in Aguillard's pocket went to work immediately and stated that now everything made sense and that the whole episode just served as a lesson for everyone not to jump to conclusions. They also interviewed the President's personal physician on TV, and he stated that although Mademoiselle Lemaire didn't say so, it was quite possible that she was suffering from one of the debilitating conditions known as fibromyalgia and chronic fatigue syndrome. The only therapy was a healthy diet and lots of rest.

An hour or so after the press conference, Margot met Rex at a coffee shop near the palace. She'd changed clothes into a new outfit, complete with a large, floppy hat and big sunglasses to disguise her face. The best part, though, was the big pregnant belly protruding from her otherwise slender body. Rex grinned broadly as she walked up, kissed him in typical French style, on both cheeks, and sat down.

Digger wasn't fooled by her disguise, he immediately moved next to her and rubbed his head against her arm. She laughed and scratched his ears and back.

"No one apart from Digger would recognize you in that," Rex remarked. "You had a good idea, there."

"I may as well get used to the look," she said, smiling back at him. "It won't be very long when I don't need this prop for it." She patted the 'belly bump' prop he'd found for her at a theatrical shop early that morning when she'd told him about her idea.

"I'll bring the car around. I take it you want to go back to your uncle's home?"

"Yes. Aunt Sophie insists that I spend the night. That's all right, isn't it?"

"It's entirely up to you. After all the excitement, maybe it's a good idea. We can drive back to Geneva tomorrow." He would have preferred to whisk her away back to Switzerland today, but it didn't really matter. His reasoning was that the Russians were snookered, and the DGSE would not trouble her again. However, he'd still take precautions to keep her privacy, but he believed the threat to her safety was now moot.

Little did he know how wrong he was about that.

Chapter Fifty-Five

Moscow, Russia

Very early on Tuesday morning, the day after the French news conference, Koslov was once again escorted to the Russian Presidential palace for what he believed was going to be the end of him as CEO of Russneft because he failed his President yet again.

He'd watched the news from France with growing unease as he came to the conclusion that with Margot Lemaire's reappearance in France and her explanations, the battle for the pipeline was over—they lost. And he had no illusions that the failure would be pinned on him.

The thing was, he didn't possess a criminal mind nor that of a detective or a spy. He had no idea how to run an operation such as had been expected of him by the President. He felt it was grossly unfair to expect him to do it. But then, he also knew that those defenses would have no effect on the President. He had no uncertainties that he was about to be handed his ass, and not on a silver platter.

However, in retrospect, he could kick himself for not doing enough to intercept the accursed woman before she reappeared on her own, in front of all of France, no less! Now he was certain he was headed for a Siberian 'vacation'.

He hadn't known the FSB agent, Ida, had been one of the President's mistresses, though he should not have been surprised. It seemed many beautiful women in mother Russia, of whom Ida had been one, had enjoyed the favor of the President at one time or another.

The rumors...

He tore his thoughts away from such speculation. It would do him no good. To keep them away, he thought of the unfortunate agent who'd been brain-damaged by the unknown superagent. Ivor had been a professional boxer, he'd been told. There were those who said the brain damage was hardly noticeable now, as his brains had been scrambled already from a few hundred too many punches to the head. However, the doctors assured him that Ivor's brains were in much worse condition now than before. But with a broken jaw, wired together to immobilize it, it would have been near impossible to be certain whether he had sustained brain damage or not.

Koslov shivered when he found himself envying Ivor, but he had to admit, it would've been better to be a little brain-damaged than having to spend the rest of your life in the Siberian ice desert.

At least the other man he'd hired, code named Kudry, short for Kudryavyy, his nickname for his curly hair, had recovered sufficiently to serve as a go-between for hiring another team. He was to have brought them to meet Koslov today, but the presidential summons had interrupted that appointment. With luck, the President would accept

Kudry's efforts as progress. But luck had little to do with what went on in the President's office, Koslov knew.

Twenty minutes after being escorted into the President's office and not been asked to take a seat, once again, Koslov left counting himself among the luckiest people on the planet.

He breathed an audible sigh of relief. He'd dodged the bullet again and had one more chance. Just one handicap stood in his way. The President had flatly refused to lend him another FSB agent. "You got the last one killed," he'd said, unfairly in Koslov's opinion. "I cannot risk another, not the least because it cannot be known that I have a personal or governmental interest in Russneft, which, as you know, is privately held. You will do this on your own, or you will answer to me."

As soon as Koslov got back to his own office, he summoned Kudry. The message instructed him to bring his new team. When they arrived, he gave them the assignment almost word-for-word as the President had given it to him.

"There is no time to waste. The target has surfaced in Paris, but her remarks at the press conference tell us she will once again disappear. This time, you *must* find her, and do so quickly and take her. I want her in custody no later than three days from now."

Kudry tried to argue. "But sir, how are we to find her so quickly? And how will we spirit her across the border? This is a bigger job. We'll need more money and more people."

Koslov fixed him with his coldest expression. "You mismanaged the last assignment. You have this opportunity, and only this one, to rectify your ineptitude in Vietnam.

"Use your brains. Acquire the CCTV footage from Paris from yesterday and find out where she went after the press conference. Take her and bring her here by private aircraft.

I will take care of the details for entry. Above all, keep in touch! I want a report every two hours, without fail. Is that understood?"

Kudry nodded, he was not a happy man. He saw the payment he'd received for the first mission evaporating as he was required to hire a hacker to gain access to the closed-circuit cameras in the French capital. While he waited for that to bear fruit, he'd sent three of his newly-hired men to Paris to be ready when he got the information about where Margot had gone after the press conference.

Within hours of the time he'd met with Koslov, Kudry had his first breakthrough. Margot had been spirited away in an official government vehicle from the press conference to the *Hôtel de Matignon*, the Prime Minister's residence. Less than an hour after her arrival at the residence, a pregnant looking woman with a large, floppy hat, and big sunglasses left the property and got into a taxi.

Kudry's hacker was able to trace the route of the taxi to a street café where this woman met with a man. The hacker had the wherewithal to zoom in on this man, and that's when Kudry recognized the face of the man he'd hoped never to see again—the man who broke his ribs and nose and rendered him unconscious twice in less than five minutes. The same son of a bitch who'd permanently disabled his comrade, Ivor, condemned *him* to take his food through a straw for the next few months, and killed the woman who'd been leading their team. He refused to acknowledge that it had been his bullet. He'd been confused, his head ringing from the kick to his face, in pain, and disoriented; and all that, he laid at the unknown assailant's door. He was expecting to also see the dog that almost ripped his hand off during the encounter in Vietnam on the images provided by the hacker but didn't. He didn't have time to ponder on that—he had to get to his team in Paris.

To the hacker, he said, "That's the man that attacked us. He's still protecting her. Keep at it, and find out where they went from that café. I'm on my way to Paris shortly."

Chapter Fifty-Six

Paris, France

It was about five hours later, when Kudry joined his team in Paris and learned that the targets had gone from the street café back to the Prime Minister's residence and apparently had spent the night there.

Further footage revealed that it was early on the morning after the press conference, the day when Kudry had arrived in Paris, that a white PEUGEOT 308 station wagon had left the Prime Minister's residence. The footage was clear enough to show two people in the vehicle, but it was impossible to recognize their faces.

After a couple of hours of footage had been analyzed, they had a direction of travel for this vehicle—southeast, toward Margot Lemaire's ancestral home of Lyon. Kudry contacted his street team and told the four of them to fly to Lyon and rent an SUV when they get there, drive out to Bert's farm, and set up a surveillance post until he could get there.

Kudry spent another two hours going over more footage with the hacker and gave him more instructions before making a phone call to a contact who owned a private jet with the request to be flown to Lyon right away. He named his price and Kudry accepted.

By the time this is over, I'm going to be broke, but at least I might still be alive.

An hour later, they were in the air, headed for Lyon.

Half an hour into the flight, he received a call from one of the team members in Lyon. They had landed, rented an SUV as instructed, and had established a surveillance post but ascertained that there was no sign of the PEUGEOT, Lemaire, or her mysterious protector.

Kudry had a strong urge to punch something, but the only thing in reach was the instrument panel. He reckoned if he punched that, one of two things would happen; the plane would crash, killing him, or the pilot would shoot him on landing.

Kudry called the hacker and gave him the news and new instructions. "Go back to the CCTV records. Check every intersection with a major highway from the last place you saw that car. Keep me posted."

Soon the hacker had a different story to tell. It seemed that the car hadn't turned south at the turnoff for Lyon after all. It had continued, and there was a record of it crossing the Swiss border at an unguarded checkpoint about twenty minutes from Geneva. He also gave Kudry the registration number of the PEUGEOT, which he had finally managed to capture from the security cameras at the border.

Kudry negotiated with the pilot to change the flight plan and take him to a private airstrip near Geneva. Six hundred

Euros later, he phoned his team in Lyon and told them where to meet him.

———————

Geneva, Switzerland

By the time Kudry had joined his team at the private airstrip in Geneva, and they were all in the SUV, the hacker had provided him with more details about the PEUGEOT. It was owned by a car rental company on the outskirts of Geneva. It was rented to one Rowan Donnelly, and the deposit had been paid in cash.

"Let's pay a visit to the rental agency and find out a bit more about who rented this car," one of his men suggested.

"No, you idiot, we'll phone them." Kudry castigated.

Swiss rental agencies aren't as security-conscious as Swiss banks—all it took was a call in which Kudry claimed to be a traffic cop checking on the legitimacy of the rental involved in a minor accident. The clerk at the agency, on request from the 'police officer' she was talking to, was glad to give the name and address and cellphone number of the person who'd rented the car so that the 'officer' could double check it against the information given by the driver. Her only concern was whether there was major damage to their vehicle. She was delighted when she was told the other car had gotten the worst of it.

Chapter Fifty-Seven

Geneva, Switzerland

Rex, Digger, and Margot had arrived back home two hours earlier. He'd sent her to rest while he took Digger for a run. When he returned, she was still sleeping, so he called Rehka and gave her a report of the happenings of the past few days. Then he started dinner.

He was about to call Margot to the table when he got a call on his regular cell phone. It was a local number. He answered.

"Mr. Donnelly, we have had a police report that you were involved in an accident in our vehicle. You were asked to report it, but we are about to close for the evening. Please bring the car in for inspection first thing tomorrow morning. We will exchange it for a different car while we make any needed repairs."

Rex was instantaneously alarmed. *A police report?* "I'm afraid there's been some mistake," he answered. "I have not been involved in an accident."

"Sir, please do not compound your failure to report with noncompliance. There was no mistake about the license plate number."

Rex went on full alert. "Did the officer give you the make and model of the car?" he asked.

"Yes, sir, he did."

"And when was this report made?"

"About half an hour ago."

"Okay," Rex said. "Thank you for the call. I will be in first thing in the morning."

He ended the call. "Margot!" he called out. "We've got a problem."

Margot was wide awake and had a concerned look on her face when she joined him in the kitchen.

Rex quickly explained to her about the phone call he just had and that the only people that came to mind were the Russians. They were the only ones who could still have an interest in Margot's whereabouts. He had no doubt that the woman at the rental agency would've given the 'police' his mobile number and address. Although, the address he gave them was of a hotel in the city, they would quickly find out it was a ruse. All that was needed to track him down was his cellphone. If the woman was correct in her estimate that she received the call from the 'police' about half an hour ago the caller would've had enough time to pinpoint their exact position in less than five minutes. By now, Rex was convinced it was the Russians, and they could be outside the house already.

"How do you know it's the Russians?" Margot asked.

"There's no time to explain, Margot, I need to get you to safety immediately."

Kudry's hacker was able to pinpoint the location of Rex's cellphone within minutes after getting the number. One of Kudry's team entered the GPS coordinates into his smartphone and brought up a map and directions. It was a forty-minute drive from their current location.

On the way, Kudry tried to warn his men about the mad beast that had attacked him in Vietnam. "It's huge, its black," he said. "And it's vicious. You must shoot it on sight."

"But sir, so far we haven't seen any sign of a dog with the man and woman. He must have left it behind, or perhaps it was a stray dog in Vietnam."

"I'm telling you, there *is* a dog. It obeyed his commands." But Kudry got the impression his words fell on deaf ears. He had no time to argue with them—he'd warned them, and that was all he could do about it.

At their house, Rex spent a precious two minutes deciding where to stash Margot. He didn't want her in the house if he could avoid it and finally settled for the root cellar not far from the kitchen door in the back yard. "Are you claustrophobic?" he asked.

Margot told him she was not, but when she saw where he expected her to wait, she asked, "Why not upstairs in your quarters?"

Rex didn't want to frighten her any more than she already was, but he didn't have time to argue. "I don't want you trapped up there if they enter the house. I expect them to be armed, and just like in Vietnam, they won't hesitate to use their weapons."

"But Rowan, if they're armed…"

"Margot, just get in there, we don't have time. Digger and I can take care of this."

Margot heard the urgency in his voice and bundled into the cellar without further objections. It turned out to be a nicely-appointed but dated bomb shelter, circa 1960s, by her estimate. To Margot's relief, it was clean, and there were no spiders in sight.

When Margot closed the cellar door behind her, and he heard the lock turning, Rex called Digger and ran back to the house and upstairs to his bedroom. He quickly retrieved Digger's surveillance harness and equipment and fitted it. He donned his photographer's vest which he'd always had with him in his and Digger's equipment bag. The vest had many pockets and hiding places, ideal to carry all kinds of weapons, spare magazines, cable ties, pocket knives, piano wire, duct tape, and such, even a small first aid pack.

He ran down the stairs, switched off all lights in the house, and went back out through the back door with Digger right on his heels.

Outside, he had a quick look around, kneeled next to Digger, ruffled the dog's ears, and said, "We're on, buddy."

Digger looked at him in anticipation. Rex turned Digger's face to his and rubbed his nose against Digger's and said, "Clever boy, scout and hide."

As Digger disappeared into the darkness among the garden plants, Rex plugged the wireless earphones into his ears and started the iPad.

He felt naked without a firearm in a situation like this

where he knew his adversaries would probably be heavily armed. But there was no time to dwell on that. He had been trained to kill with his bare hands, a toothpick, a paperclip, a broomstick, and anything up to knives and guns. And on many occasions, just like in Vietnam, his enemies supplied the guns, once he got his hands on one of them.

In the kitchen, he used the small penlight to find two steak knives and a butcher's knife and crawled to the lounge where he stashed the weapons under a sofa, then hid behind it. Once he was ready, Rex fell naturally into the waiting that characterized so much of the operational time of his profession.

He was neither anxious nor bored. Alert but relaxed, he could have waited for hours.

Chapter Fifty-Eight

Geneva, Switzerland

But this time, he had to wait less than five minutes when Digger alerted, apparently on a smell, since Rex couldn't see any human figure on the iPad monitor.

"Digger, down. Wait for my signal." By now, Rex was so convinced that Digger understood plain English, he often added sentence-long commands to the familiar ones Digger had been trained by his first partner, Trevor, to respond to. Rex also knew Digger would act on his own when the situation warranted it.

After a few minutes, a low growl reached Rex's ear via the comms unit.

"What is it, boy? I can't see them."

And then he did. Digger had apparently stood up. Four, no, *five* men were approaching the house along the long driveway from the street. Were there more? Rex would not have made so open an approach, but these men were bunched as if their business was legitimate, and they were just paying a friendly visit.

Digger's next soft growl was accompanied by the squeak that usually came at the end of one of his anxiety yawns. Rex interpreted it as Digger having recognized the scent of one of the men. The figures he could see in the night-vision camera's feed were of average size, none of them big enough to be Brawn from Vietnam. But the last man, the one he hadn't seen at first because he was lagging behind, that man had a limp. Could it be his old 'friend' Curly? He'd know soon enough.

Because the house sat on a few acres of wooded land, the walk up the driveway was a long one. Rex reckoned he had five minutes. But he needed to know whether there were others approaching from different directions.

"Digger, leave it. Scout," he commanded. A soft whine indicated Digger's reluctance to leave the targets he'd spotted, but the camera feed soon showed he was moving again, trotting around the perimeter of the grounds as trained. Rex figured at the speed Digger was going, he'd cover about half the perimeter in the time the five men would take to reach the house.

He didn't expect them to knock politely on the front door when they did.

Rex saw that Digger was speeding around the perimeter, which was an indication to Rex that the dog knew there were no other intruders on the way to the house—only the five he'd spotted before.

It was a puzzle to Rex how the Russians could be so stupid as to come in a bunch rather than approaching from all sides.

Not a military-trained bunch, another rag-tag criminal operation.

"Digger, return," Rex said with a low voice.

Rex couldn't see the men, but by his estimate they would reach the front door momentarily. His iPad was about to become a liability because of the light it put out. Rex pushed the screen's off button and shoved the iPad under a throw rug under the sofa he was hiding behind.

Rex heard them fiddling with the lock of the front door for a few moments and then the door opened, slowly. The Russians were talking among themselves in low voices but made little effort to be quiet. He heard one of them, who was about three paces away from his hiding place, saying, "I told you there was no dog. It would have barked."

Boy, are you scumbags in for a nasty surprise.

Rex was waiting on Digger's imminent arrival and the advantage the shock and surprise of the dog's appearance would give him before going into action. And that moment arrived right on time, just as a heavy boot narrowly missed his body behind the couch, Digger came flying through the open front door. Rex lashed out with a leg, and as his victim dropped to the floor, he karate-chopped the man in the jugular before he even had a chance to cry out.

At almost that same moment, someone cried out. Rex was on his knees, looking over the couch, and saw Digger had engaged the man who shouted. There was no time to think about it; there were three others to disable.

With no more element of surprise, Rex jumped to his feet and ran through crossed beams of the attackers' flashlights to turn on the lights in the lounge. The sudden brightness of the lights left the three men dumbfounded for a second or two before one of them aimed a pistol at Digger.

Rex took two steps and hit him with a flying two-legged kick in the chest that sent him reeling backward and deflected the gunshot from the silenced pistol into the ceiling.

The man he'd dropped first was gurgling, his larynx crushed. He was out of the picture. The second man had lost his pistol in his fall. Rex kicked it out of the way and followed it up with a kick to the face which knocked him out cold, and whirled to meet the remaining two, who were stupid enough to charge at him in tandem. He lashed out with one foot, connecting with the soft belly of the first one.

"Oof," Rex heard, as he turned his attention to the second man, who seemed more competent as well as fitter. But Rex was a moment too late. A punch rocked him backward, and he tripped over the guy who'd tried to shoot Digger.

He registered a vicious snarling and someone crying out in pain as the man he'd belly-kicked scrambled to his feet and waded in.

Rex had stumbled backward after tripping, and he was still off-balance when the one who'd punched him came at him again. Rex seized a lamp from the table that had broken his fall and swung it in a wide arc, connecting with his assailant's head, but doing less damage than he'd hoped. The lamp had broken into pieces—what remained of it was useless as a weapon.

But the blow to the man's head was enough to give Rex a chance to regain his balance, and he was ready for the next charge. The softer guy got to him first, so Rex head-butted him, and a gush of fresh blood cascaded over the guy's mouth and chin. His eyes went blank as he reached for his injured nose and dropped to the floor, revealing the tough one, who was once again preparing a charge at Rex.

A sharp yelp from Digger momentarily distracted Rex. He had just enough time to catch a glimpse of a familiar face, Curly's, and he had a knife in his hand, before the charging assailant was on him with no time for Rex to move out of the way. The man connected with him in the solar plexus with his shoulder, carrying him backward, past the table and onto the floor, and landed on top of him with so much force it almost took Rex's breath away. A street brawl ensued, with Rex taking punches to the face and chest. Rex blocked most of it with his arms while trying to dislodge the man straddling his chest. He quickly managed to gain leverage by getting his feet under the man's knees and heaving backwards, tossing the guy over his head to land on the floor behind him.

Rex twisted quickly and lunged from his hands and knees and landed with his knee in the guy's liver, which caused him to grunt in agony. Rex pushed off him, landed a kick to the same place his knee had just injured, and the guy went still.

Rex stood up and looked at the carnage. Two out cold, one maybe dead. The first one was no longer gurgling. The last one moaning and holding his side, unable to get up. And Curly still in Digger's death grip, stabbing at Digger over and over but missing as far as Rex could tell.

Rex rushed over and picked up the Russian's weapon, about two paces away, turned, and pointed it at Curly's head. He told Digger to stand down. Rex looked Curly in the eyes and said, in Russian, "Stupid asshole, you've lost again. Get it through your thick skull, you'll never have the woman."

His finger tightened around the trigger, Curly's eyes widened. For a few moments, Rex was tempted to pull the trigger but didn't. Instead he let loose with a vicious kick to Curly's face which rendered him unconscious. Curly was not only going to need extensive surgery to his jaw, he'd probably also need a full set of dentures.

Rex finally turned to Digger and found he had several

bleeding wounds in various places over his body. A quick check assured him, to his relief, that none of the wounds were life threatening.

Rex sat down heavily beside his wounded partner and gathered the dog into his arms. "Digger, you're going to make it, boy. It's all over. You can relax now." Slowly, he eased Digger onto his side on the carpet and said, "Stay. Don't move, I'm going to get Margot. We'll be back in less than a minute." Digger replied with a soft whine and his wagging tail thumping the floor a few times.

Chapter Fifty-Nine

Geneva, Switzerland

When Margot entered the room and saw the carnage, her hand flew to her mouth to stifle a scream. When she saw the injuries Rowan and Digger had suffered, she could no longer control it and cried out in alarm.

Rex put his arms around her and said, "Margot, there could be more of them. We have to get out of here as quickly as possible."

She was shaking, but she nodded and said, "What do you want me to do?"

Rex retrieved the first aid kit from a pouch of his tactical vest. "You can tend to Digger's wounds while I tie up and gag these men. After that, we have to gather our stuff and leave."

"Where do you want to go? Are you going to leave these men here?"

Rex shook his head. "No, I won't leave them here. We'll never get a chance like this again to find out who is behind all of this and why. That'll be powerful information in the hands of Aguillard when he has to deal with the Russians. I want to take them over the border and hand them over to the French authorities for interrogation. I am thinking of going to your family farm."

To Rex's surprise, Margot was calm and collected. She nodded and said, "Makes sense to me. Let's do it. I might need some direction from you when doctoring Digger. I've completed only a basic first aid course, and that was many years ago."

"No problem. He should be okay. He'll let you know when you hurt him."

Margot went to work on Digger while Rex checked the five men in turn, discovering they were all alive. With the cable ties he had in one of his vest pockets, he tied their feet and then their hands behind their backs, took their boots and socks off, and used the latter to gag them, then secured his handiwork with duct tape wrapped over their mouths and heads.

When he was done, he stood and looked to see how Margot was doing. Digger was licking her arm while she very tenderly applied antiseptic ointment to each of his wounds and spoke comforting words softly to him. Digger hadn't made a single sound to indicate that he was in pain.

Margot wiped the tears from her eyes with the back of her free hand and said, "Thank God you're both alive. I've stemmed the blood flow from his wounds, and none of them seem to be deep. I think he's going to be okay."

Digger raised his head from the floor, turned from his side onto his belly, and let out a soft woof.

"Yep, that's it, boy. You'll be out jogging with me in no time."

Margot got up and took a close look at Rex. "What?" he asked.

"Just checking if you're in need of any first aid."

Rex grinned. "Just a few bruises, I'm good. Now I want you to bring the car around from the garage to the front door while I keep an eye on them."

Margot took a few steps toward the kitchen to get the car keys, stopped and asked, "Do you think there'll be enough space for all of us?"

Rex just grinned. "It's going to be a bit tight for them, but we'll be okay."

Margot turned and went to collect the car.

Fifteen minutes later, they were ready. Rex had let the back seat of the station wagon down and packed the Russians in like sardines in a tin. Digger was in the space on the floor behind Margot's seat. She'd put a blanket on the floor for him, and he seemed to be comfortable.

Behind Rex's seat, on the floor and in the space under his seat, they shoved in the few personal belongings they didn't want to leave at the house. Rex had explained that he'd have to talk to Lucien to send in some DGSE agents to clean and sanitize the place as soon as possible, preferably before the sun came up. He looked at his watch. It was 10:00 p.m.

En Route To Lyon, France

The Russians in the back of the PEUGEOT couldn't have been comfortable, since the car had never been intended for five men to lie side-by-side, even with the back seat folded down. Rex had put the less-injured men on the bottom and had arranged Curly and the guy with the crushed larynx on top, in the gaps between the bottom three. Nevertheless, those two had to be weighing heavily on the others. Not long after crossing the border toward Lyon, they began waking up, moaning and groaning, and by the sounds of it, complaining about the 'seating' arrangements.

Rex hadn't heard Curly's voice yet, and he knew the one with the crushed larynx wouldn't be able to make any sounds, other than maybe a grunt, if that. Rex wasn't certain he'd survive, since his airway was clearly obstructed. If he did, there might be brain damage from hypoxia. But Rex couldn't be bothered too much. He didn't have any problems justifying the injuries to any of them, including Curly, whose jaw was completely destroyed. Rex figured they deserved what they got. They were the ones who'd invaded Margot's temporary home, armed, and with evil intent.

When the noise from the back grew loud enough to be annoying, he yelled, in Russian, "Shut up back there! You were full of bravado when you entered the house to attack a defenseless woman, now you sound like a bunch of old women with wet knickers. Don't make me pull over and silence you, again."

The moaning and groaning ceased, and it made Rex remember when he was a kid, bickering in the back seat with his brother and sister, and his mother would say, "Don't make me pull over!" It made him smile, but at the same time it caused him a pang of missing his family, dead now for more than ten years. If these scumbags were terrorists rather than common thugs, they'd be dead when he finished his interrogation. The French authorities would get none of them.

Margot flinched when he yelled. She began in a gentle

voice, "Rowan, they're not comfortable, and they're injured. Should we…"

"No, Margot, we should not. Have no doubt, their instructions were to kill Digger and me and take you alive to force you to cooperate with them. They deserve this, and worse. It's the second time the guy with the broken jaw has tried to kidnap you and injured Digger in the process."

She put her hand to her mouth. "He was one of them? In Vietnam?"

"Yes, he was the one who shot Digger."

She paled and nodded.

"Okay, I think it's time to get your brother on the phone and let him know we'll be there soon." She dug in the pocket of his utility vest and got the satphone out.

When she'd done so, she asked, "What are you going to do with them, Rex?" Her tone was fearful.

Her tone made Rex wonder if she thought he might want to kill them and leave them buried among her brother's grapevines. "I've been thinking about it, and don't worry, I won't kill them. I have some questions for them, and then we'll turn them over to the authorities."

Just then, a loud moan from the back interrupted her answer and annoyed her instantaneously. She turned around in the seat and spoke sharply. "Shut up, he told you!"

Rex grinned to himself. She was much tougher than he'd have thought a month or so ago when he met her. He admired that. She'd need to be, to raise a child as a single mother and fulfill her role as a deputy minister in the French government.

Rex turned his thoughts to what he could do to secure her a measure of peace and quiet in which to enjoy her baby and return to her career. And it didn't take him long to conclude for that to happen, this shit from the Russians had to end now. That thought led him to a firm decision. He was going to have a chat with these hoodlums before he handed them over to the French authorities. Then, once he got the information out of them about who gave them their instructions, he was going to Russia, or wherever the culprit was, and have a chat with him or her as well. The only person he wouldn't touch, although he would have dearly loved to do so, was the Russian President. Rex had no desire to go down in history as the man who started World War III by roughing up or killing the Russian President.

He knew all too well that once the goons were in the hands of the French authorities, he would have no access to them, and he would get no answers. Therefore, the time to get those answers was now, as soon as he got them to Bert's estate. After he had what he wanted, he'd ask Bert to call Lucien and arrange to have them picked up and put into custody.

The Russian government would, of course, immediately kick up a racket about their citizens and would probably spin it so that it would sound as if they were attacked in Switzerland, of course, 'without any provocation', and abducted to France. Although everyone in the car knew the truth, Rex knew only he and Margot would tell the truth. But neither of them could come out and do it. She, because she'd already hedged the truth to buy some time and couldn't afford to be in the public eye again so soon, and he, because he didn't dare appear in the public eye at all.

It pained him to admit it, but Aguillard would have no choice but to let these assholes go, and they'd probably be back in Russia within a few days.

Chapter Sixty

Lyon, France

Half an hour later, Bert and his wife, Adele, met them in front of the farmhouse. Bert laughed as he picked his sister up and swung her around, setting her on her feet for a big hug when she laughed. "It's so good to see you!" they exclaimed in unison, and then the round of hugging started again before it was Adele's turn, after which Rex was introduced to Adele.

Rex then let Digger out of the car, and Bert caught sight of him. "This must be the famous Digger that my sister has told me so much about!"

Rex grinned and made the introductions. Digger winced a bit when he sat down and lifted his paw to 'shake', but he made no sound.

With a big smile, Bert shook the offered paw and then his brow wrinkled. "He's hurt. How…"

By that time, Rex had crossed to the car again and

opened the tailgate. "We need a place to keep these guys secure, and I'd like a bit of time with them, in private."

Fortunately, Margot and Adele were standing in front of the car, so, Adele didn't see the cargo in the back. Bert asked Adele to take Margot into the house, and when the women were a few paces away, he motioned to Rex to follow him to a different cellar than the one he'd used to talk with Rex the first time they'd met. This one had little open space and was fortified with rough-hewn wood beams to brace the low ceiling. Rex assumed there was something heavy above, full wine-barrels, maybe. The cellar was chock-full of them, resting on cross-beams and stacked two high on their sides, maybe sixty or more in the space. "Will this do?" he asked.

"Perfect," Rex said. "If you don't mind, I could use a hand getting them down here and secured to these support beams."

"Precisely what I had in mind," Bert answered.

It was close to midnight when the Russians were all inside the cellar and Rex asked Bert to leave him alone with the captives. Rex thought perhaps Bert might not have the stomach to witness the interrogation, which suited him just fine, and besides, he didn't care to have witnesses.

"I'll let you know when I'm done," he said. "I reckon our conversation will take about two hours, and then you'll have to call Lucien and get him to send DGSI agents to pick them up."

The General Directorate for Internal Security, DGSI was tasked with counter-espionage, counter-terrorism, and the surveillance of potential threats on French territory, in other words, the French equivalent of the American FBI.

Inside the house, while Rex was busy with his prisoners, Bert and Adele questioned Margot about her health and wellbeing, what had happened to her over the past few weeks, and eventually the inevitable question, "Who *is* this Rowan Donnelly?"

Margot couldn't really answer that question, because she didn't know. She'd already discarded his cover story that he was a history teacher. She had more than enough reason to believe he was some kind of specially-trained black ops operative, and Digger was a trained military dog. Maybe someday, say in thirty or forty years, he'd explain. In the meantime, she had learned that her questions wouldn't be answered, so she no longer asked them. What she did know was that she didn't care what his real name or his history was and that she had, over the last few days, come to realization that she loved him.

She didn't tell them any of that. She just shrugged and said, "Digger introduced him to me in Vanuatu, and we became friends."

"Digger introduced you?" Adele asked with skepticism.

Margot smiled and explained how it happened and how they became friends and how Rowan didn't buy the story that she'd drowned and went looking for her and how he'd saved her in Vietnam and again now in Geneva.

Adele had a twinkle in her eyes and winked when she said to Margot, "Sounds to me like the type of friend a girl can only dream about?"

"You've got that right. But… I… well… let's see what happens." Margot was blushing, and Bert started laughing.

"Well, Margie," he knew she hated it when he called her that, "I guess you're old enough now to… wait hang on for just one second… is *he* the…"

"No Bert, if only it was him…"

Chapter Sixty-One

Lyon, France

Three of the prisoners were wide awake and perhaps anticipating their questioning, as they looked apprehensive. The man with the crushed larynx would need medical attention before the night was out, Rex thought. Curly was groggy and in severe pain. Rex assumed he'd be the one with the most information, and perhaps the one most willing to part with it, but interrogating him was going to be tricky—he couldn't form intelligible speech.

Rex returned to the car and got a notebook and pen out of his effects. Curly's injuries notwithstanding, he clearly was the leader of this gang, and Rex intended to get answers. He returned to the cellar and asked a general question in perfect Russian. "Do any of you assholes know who sent you? Spit it out now, and you can avoid the pain of me beating it out of you." It wasn't an idle threat, and from the expressions on their faces, they knew it. But they shook their heads forlornly—they didn't know, but they were all eyeing Curly.

"So, he knows?" Rex asked.

"I don't know if Kudry knows, but he's the one who hired us," one of them said, and the others nodded.

Kudry. Rex almost laughed out loud at that one. His actual nickname was the same in Russian as Rex had given him in Vietnam.

Now he had no choice but to communicate with Curly, and he called Digger to come and 'persuade' Curly to cooperate. On the ride here, Digger had stiffened somewhat from his wounds. He walked slowly but purposefully toward Curly, stopped about one pace away from his feet, hackles up, growling, and showing his teeth.

Rex would not have thought it possible for Curly to get any paler, but he did, turning several shades whiter as Digger stood snarling at him. "Mph, mph, mph," he uttered.

"You want me to call him off? Then you'd better find a way to answer my questions." Rex untied Curly's hands and let him slide to the ground, his back against the beam to which he'd been bound the moment before. He handed him the notebook and pen. "Who ordered you to abduct Margot Lemaire?"

Curly shook his head violently, and then moaned from the pain. "Mph mph."

"Write it down, idiot. That's why I gave you pen and paper. I won't tell you again, start writing."

Curly seized the paper and pen and scribbled furiously, then held it out to Rex.

Rex took it and read with difficulty the Cyrillic script. "Russneft? Is that what this says?"

Curly nodded and gestured to have the paper returned

to him. Several exchanges later, Rex had the information he needed, though it had taken nearly forty minutes to get what would have been easy to say in five or less.

Fyodor Koslov, CEO of Russneft, the Russian gas company whose proposed pipeline would have been built through France to Paris if they'd had their way, was behind it. But behind that, Curly speculated, was the President of Russia himself. There were many rumors that he was a major shareholder in Russneft, although his shares were held through various front companies which he controlled through a labyrinth of other companies. Whether the gossip was true or not, it was known that the President wielded significant influence over Russneft's dealings. However, it had been the CEO, Koslov, who hired him, paid him, and who threatened him with dire consequences if this second attempt failed. His last message was a plea to be kept in France, where at least he'd live, even if it were as a lifelong prisoner.

"That isn't my call," Rex told him. "Take it up with the French. If it was my decision, you and your men would be fertilizer in the vineyards."

Curly's puzzled frown was his only comment. He must have thought Rex *was* French, maybe part of a security team.

With the information he wanted, he had no further use for the Russians. He went to the house, where he found Bert waiting up for him, and told him he could now make the call to Lucien.

He asked Bert to also request Lucien to send in a DGSE cleanup team to come by and pick up the rental car, take it to Geneva, and clean up both it and the rented house, and return the car to the rental company.

Finally, he asked Bert to also convey the message that a

security detail for Margot be sent, as she would from now on be living on the farm—if he and Adele agreed.

Bert and Adele didn't have to consult each other, "Of course she will be staying with us," Adele said. "We'd love it, and the children will be ecstatic to have their Aunt Margot around, not to mention their cousin when he or she arrives."

With all of the arrangements taken care of, Rex had one more request to make, and for that he took Bert aside and explained that he and Digger didn't want to deal with any of the government agents when they arrive. They would want to stay out of sight.

Bert didn't require any further explanations. He remembered how easy it was for this man to overcome him the first time they met, and he'd seen the condition of the Russians when he helped him get them into the cellar. Those guys looked like they were in hand to hand combat with a pride of lions. He was stunned to learn that it was the work of one man and a dog. This man was a highly trained soldier of some kind—a man not to be messed with. Just like Margot, he knew this man and his dog were not ordinary globe trotters. He had no doubt Rowan had good reason to stay out of sight.

"No problem. I'll take you to the guesthouse, and you and Digger can get some sleep. I'll take care of everything. We can discuss your plans after all the agents are gone. The guesthouse is about five hundred meters away, I'll take you over there, let me just get the keys."

Within no more than twenty minutes after Bert had left them at the guesthouse, Rex was sleeping soundly in a comfortable bed, Digger by his side. But before he'd made ready for bed, he called Rehka. After the usual security checks and pleasantries, he had just one request. "I need everything you can get me on the CEO of a Russian company named Russneft."

Chapter Sixty-Two

Lyon, France

Digger woke up first, with a soft woof alerting Rex that someone was at the door of the guesthouse. Rex pulled on his pants, and while doing so he was glad to notice that Digger was moving a lot better than when they went to bed and remembered that Trevor once told him how much quicker dogs heal from their wounds than humans. He went to the door to find a beautiful little girl of about seven with big brown eyes and long dark hair, waiting for him to open it.

She looked at Rex, then at Digger, smiled, and said importantly, "Mommy says you must come to breakfast." She looked at Digger again and asked politely. "May I pet him?"

Rex smiled. "I'm sure he'd appreciate that. Would you tell your mommy I'll be there very soon? I just want to take a quick shower and get dressed."

She ignored Rex's request and put out a confident hand for Digger to sniff, then scratched behind one of his ears, causing Digger to sink to his haunches and sigh in contentment. Rex left him outside with the little girl and took a hasty shower, put on fresh clothes from his backpack, and rejoined the child and Digger within five minutes.

"What's your name?" he asked her as she led him back to the main house.

"Elise," she replied. "What's your name?"

"Rowan."

"And his name?" She pointed to Digger who was a few yards ahead of them, nose on the ground sniffing out the new environment.

"His name is Digger." Rex spoke Digger's name in English, though they'd been speaking French.

"That's a funny name. Why did you give him that name?"

Rex enjoyed the child's confident and inquisitive yet very polite mannerism and explained to her, in French, the literal meaning of the name, which had her laughing.

"I hope he doesn't dig up my mommy's rose garden, he will be in a lot of trouble for that."

By then they were at a back door, and Elise reached for the knob. "Allow me, mademoiselle," Rex said formally, opening the door for her and gesturing for her to enter while he bowed.

Elise giggled and led the way.

Rex found a warm family scene as Elise led him into the big farmhouse kitchen, where Bert, Adele, Margot, and a little boy of about four sat waiting for his arrival.

"Please, go ahead and eat," he said as he seated himself at an empty spot. "I'm sorry to keep you waiting." He looked at his arm and realized that in the rush, he'd forgotten to put his watch on. "What time is it?"

When he was told it was nine a.m., he was mortified. He hadn't slept that late since he was a kid.

He turned to Bert with a question in his eyes, and Bert answered it immediately. "Our guests have left," he said, flicking his eyes toward Elise and the boy. "And everything else is as you asked."

Rex was hungry, and he thoroughly enjoyed the traditional French breakfast of croissants, tartine, a French bread sliced lengthwise with butter and jam on it, fruit juice, and café au lait, coffee with milk. "Thank you for breakfast, Adele. If you'll excuse me, I have something to take care of before the day gets much older," Rex said. "Margot, I'll see you later?"

"Sure. I'm not going anywhere," she said.

Rex returned to the guesthouse and packed his backpack. His next task was to get hold of Rehka to hear what she had been able to find out about Fyodor Koslov.

"As soon as I started hacking into Russneft's files, they put a tracker on me, and I got out," Rehka explained. "Their security is extremely tight. But in the end, I managed to break through and got the information without leaving a trace."

"Great work, Rehka. Thank you. Please send it over."

She went quiet for a moment, and then said, "On its way, you'll have it momentarily."

Rex thanked her again, and as always, knowing he was going to get himself in harm's way, she cautioned him to be careful.

Rex returned to the farmhouse and asked Margot to join him for a walk in the garden.

Listening to his plan, she was horrified. "Rowan! You can't do that. They'll kill you. Please don't do it. Please."

"Margot, this has to end, now. As long as they think they can act with impunity, they won't stop. Think about it. They managed to find you in Vanuatu, Vietnam, and Geneva. They'll find you here, and they will come again."

"But Uncle Lucien arranged for protection. I'm safe now. They won't be able to come close to me again."

"Margot, I think this thing goes to the top of the Russian government. I'm willing to bet dollars to donuts that the Russian President has a hand in this. They have the resources to get to you if they want to. And they will."

"Rowan! Don't tell me you are going after the Russian President... that..."

Rex took her hand and said, "No, Margot, I'm not that stupid. But with the information I got out of the men last night, I can go after Fyodor Koslov, the CEO of Russneft and get a confession out of him." He didn't tell her that the best information was produced by Rehka.

"What good will that do?"

"Well, I reckon if Aguillard could have a confession from Koslov in his hands when he meets with the Russian President at the upcoming summit, it would level the playing field."

"So, you think the Russian President is going to try to subject Giles to the thumbscrew?"

"I'm convinced he will. The Russians have showed that they're not going to give up. Even if I'm wrong about it, Aguillard will have it as an insurance policy, so to speak."

Margot went quiet and nodded. "Rowan, I can see the

logic, but I am scared. Besides, you're not even a citizen of France. It's not your battle, in fact, it never was. You saved me, and I still don't understand why you did it, although I'm eternally grateful. Now I want you to tell me, why are you doing this? Why put your life in danger for me and for a country you have no obligation of loyalty to?"

Rex found himself staring at her. He had no answer, and he knew he'd better produce one, but nothing came to mind. He could neither tell her about his previous missions while working for CRC, nor the missions after. Since he'd left Afghanistan and set out for a life of peace and quiet, every country he'd been to he'd landed in a situation where there was someone in need of help. Was it his destiny or his curse for the many killings he'd done over the years? Atonement for his sins? He'd thought about it a lot but still had no answer, not even for himself and definitely not for Margot. Instead, he just smiled and gave her the famous Gallic shrug and said, "Maybe it's because I feel obliged to be loyal to my friends and can't stand it when they are treated unjustly."

Margot had stopped walking, she'd turned to him and was studying his face intently. After a long silence, she said, "Rowan, I know you're not a teacher, and I'm sure you're not Rowan Donnelly, but that doesn't matter. Whatever your former occupation and your true name, you are an amazing person, and I have only respect and admiration for you. But, having said that, I can't let you do this..."

Rex grinned and said, "And you will stop me how?"

Margot sighed in defeat. "Okay, admittedly, I can't stop you, but will you at least allow me to arrange a meeting for you with Uncle Lucien, because what you're planning to do could have serious repercussions for relationships between France and Russia if…" she didn't complete the sentence.

Rex half regretted that he'd shared his plans with her. *I should've just done it and told her later.* But he also realized what Margot was saying about repercussions was true. Reluctantly, he agreed to her request to talk to the Prime Minister.

Chapter Sixty-Three

Paris, France

Lucien Laurent was ensconced in a wing-back chair in the President's office. He waited out the President's inevitable temper-tantrum. He understood the man's agitation quite well, as he shared it. When Aguillard settled down, Laurent ventured another tactic.

"If we disavow this Rowan Donnelly, what harm can it do to France?" he asked.

Aguillard's expression threatened another rant, but he conquered his feelings enough to state, rather calmly for his mental state, Lucien thought, "Tell me again what he said, verbatim."

"He said, 'I'm going to go and sort this out, so they leave her and your country alone once and for all. I'm not asking your permission, I'm only informing you as a courtesy, on Margot's insistence. If you have any reason, national or international, I should not do it, you better tell me.'"

Aguillard punched one fist into the palm of his other hand. "I would like nothing better than to get the upper hand over the damn Russians... But if they get their hands on him, they *will* torture every drop of information out of him, and it could backfire on us. We cannot under any circumstances officially sanction his operation against the Russians."

Laurent's secure phone rang at that moment. "That will be him, looking for our answer," he said.

Laurent answered.

Aguillard said, "Tell him no. We cannot have anything to do with it." But then Aguillard got a wicked little grin on his face, and loud enough for Donnelly to hear, he added, "Not officially."

Laurent repeated what the President said to Rex but left out the 'not officially' part.

Rex didn't reply but told Laurent there was one more thing he wanted to say.

"What?" Laurent asked and listened to the reply. "But you must be French... your accent is pure Parisian. No, of course Donnelly isn't a French name, but... I see. Well, you have our stance on the matter." There was nothing more to say.

When the call ended, Laurent said, "He said he isn't French."

Aguillard just nodded and made no reply to that but asked, "Do you think he can do it?"

"Well, he single-handedly subdued the five Russian kidnappers last night, and by all accounts, those guys are in bad shape. Margot assured me he sustained negligible injuries. And if you'll recall, he greatly embarrassed three of our best special operatives in Vietnam and three Russians. Yes, I'd say he can do it."

Aguillard nodded absently.

While he had the President's ear, Laurent assured himself that though Margot's privacy had been breached once again, and her hiding place all but public knowledge, the security orders would be carried out. Guards were in place and would remain in place at the Lemaire estate to ensure that neither media nor anyone else could get within five kilometers of it.

Laurent continued and pointed out that the next prickly problem with the Russians was going to raise its head when they discovered that their citizens were in a French prison.

"One Russian problem at a time, Lucien," Aguillard said with a heavy sigh. "Let's focus on the summit. Donnelly has a point, I'm sure the Russian President is the one who's going to try to twist my arm this time. Maybe we can use the information the DGSI gets out of the prisoners to our advantage."

Laurent nodded and said, "And who knows, maybe you'll even have a recorded confession to go with it…"

Chapter Sixty-Four

Lyon, France

Rex had been committing to memory every bit of the extensive tranche of information about Koslov provided to him by Rehka.

President Aguillard was to meet with the Russian President, Boris Markov, at a summit in Geneva in just three days' time. The subject of the talks was trade and economics, both current and future, but there was rife speculation in Russia that it would be a concession from Aguillard regarding the unpopular Russian gas pipeline to Paris.

Aguillard had steadfastly refused comment to the French media and was feeling the end of the 'honeymoon' period that had kept him popular in the media since his election. Already, protestors were marching outside the presidential palace with placards, the mildest of which said, "No Pipeline." Others threatened dire consequences if Aguillard caved in to the Russian demands.

With the summit only three days away, Rex knew there

was very little time left to act. He asked Rehka to arrange transportation for him and Digger. He decided this was the last time he was going to use the Rowan Donnelly moniker outside of France. His plan was, after he got back from Russia and wrapped things up with Margot, who now had her brother's family and the government of France protecting her, he'd set out on a new adventure, maybe Croatia this time.

The Rowan Donnelly who presented himself at Lyon's airport for transport to Moscow was a different man than anyone he'd met recently would recognize. He'd left Bert's property early enough to do some shopping. When he got to the gate with his e-ticket, he appeared to be in his late seventies, with salt-and-pepper hair, a battered fedora, a cane with a three-pronged foot for stability, and a pronounced limp. Realistic silicone wrinkles completed the look. After one horrified stare at his brown and broken teeth, the gate agent paid him no more attention.

Moscow, Russia

The flight to Moscow was routine, as was picking up his rental car. From Moscow, he drove the thirty-five kilometers to Zelenograd, where the offices of Russneft were located. His hotel, also reserved courtesy of Rehka, was comfortable if dated. The room boasted elegant silvery-beige floral wallpaper that clashed horribly with the ugly red floral bedspread and 1960s-era window drapes. Rex had stayed in worse. It was at least clean, and Digger was welcomed. He wouldn't be staying in it much, anyway, as he had surveillance to conduct.

Rex stayed in character coming and going from the hotel, that day. In the guise of a tourist, he took advantage of a tour of the city to familiarize himself with the locations of the gas plant and orient himself as to direction, roads in and out of the city, and petrol stations. He found excuses to linger in the vicinity of the Russneft offices and waited until he saw the man he recognized from pictures as Koslov emerge.

Koslov met a beautiful woman for dinner and lingered over it, drinking wine with each course, and then switching to what Rex assumed was a vodka-based cocktail before ushering the woman into the back seat of his car and following her in. The driver pulled away from the curb, and that was the end of the surveillance for the moment, as Rex had been on foot.

He returned to the hotel with Digger, had dinner in the attached restaurant, and ordered some meat to go for Digger. Both enjoyed a brief rest, until near midnight, when they left again by the fire escape stairs leading to a quiet backstreet.

Rex's trusty backpack held the equipment and clothing he'd need for the late-night excursion to check out Koslov's estate—Digger's gear, comms equipment, and a set of black clothing, balaclava and gloves, not only for warmth but to make him nearly invisible in the night. Thanks to the intel he'd received from Rehka, he knew where it was and had the layout of the compound and the architectural plans for the home itself.

Digger, of course, came with his own natural black camouflage. And as soon as he noticed Rex packing the backpack, he trembled with excitement. He knew they were going to work tonight.

Rex drove several kilometers toward Koslov's estate, a

compound surrounded by dense forest. The surrounding area was flat for as far as the eye could see, but the forested surroundings provided good coverage for him to get up close. Before getting too close, Rex stopped and changed into his surveillance clothing, rigged Digger's gear, and placed his own comms unit into his ear.

"Ready to work, boy?"

He thought the expression on Digger's face meant, "Mate, I was *born* ready."

He felt the same way. After weeks of concern about Margot's safety, he was determined to bring that to an end in the next day or two, at least from Koslov's clumsy attempts.

For the rest of the night and the next night, Rex gathered information, resting during the day between. He learned about Koslov's patterns, his bodyguards, and his voracious appetite for women. Several women arrived separately during the late-night hours, and none left until near dawn. Rex wondered how Koslov functioned during the day, when he obviously partied hard every night. On the second night, he sent Digger into the compound to get a glimpse through the windows and discovered the interior boasted a room with a hot tub where Koslov was entertaining the night's companions.

As he'd discovered while surveilling Koslov at the restaurants where the man had eaten dinner both evenings, wine and spirits were in generous supply. Koslov appeared to lead the consumption. There were a few moments when Rex began to think his careful observations weren't entirely necessary. Koslov would be easy to overcome and persuade, if he and Digger could get past the guards. But he quickly admonished himself for that—he had enough experience to know that nothing ever works out exactly as planned. He was in full mission mode now, highly alert and attentive to everything around him. And so was Digger after Rex put the comms harness on him.

There were four guards, but only one on duty at any time, and they rotated throughout the night. The only reason, other than having the guards as a status symbol, Rex could think of for the inefficient use of the guards, was that Koslov felt quite secure in his compound and wouldn't have needed guards at all if they hadn't been required to open the gate for his constant parade of women.

In any case, the guard at the gate would be no problem. The problem would happen in the guards' quarters, when he would need to take on the remaining three of them at once. He'd seen all of them by the end of the second night. They were built like weight-lifters—tall, brawny, and twice his weight. Lots of testosterone thanks to the steroids, and fortunately, thanks to the steroids, not much between the ears but aggression.

Chapter Sixty-Five

Zelenograd on the outskirts of Moscow, Russia

There wasn't time to plan a subtler approach than the one he mounted on the third night. He'd waited until two a.m., when the guard on duty at the gate was dozing on the job. The last limo arriving with a woman had left the gate an hour ago, and if the pattern held, she'd be the last arrival for the night. Another guard would relieve this one at four a.m. if it were a normal night. Rex was about to make it an abnormal one.

The summit was hours from beginning, and he had no more time to wait.

Rex hugged the perimeter fence as he made his way around to Digger's position near the gate. Digger had crept up close enough to the guard for Rex to observe him nodding off and then waited at Rex's command. When Rex joined him, he stood, but Rex gave him a hand signal to wait. Then Rex rushed the guard on silent feet and had him in a chokehold before he even woke up.

It was all over before Rex could even call it a fight. The sleepy guard went down like a felled tree, and Rex gagged and ziptied him with ease. His next task wouldn't be so easy, but he now had an advantage he didn't have before. He took the guard's pistol with him when he walked away.

With Digger by his side, he approached the guards' quarters and checked out what was going on inside. As far as he could tell, they were all asleep, but they wouldn't be for long. He and Digger entered the unlocked quarters silently. With his night-vision goggles, he could see the guards sleeping in bunks. Digger waited for his command, but Rex first wanted to search the room for an intercom. Finding it, he ripped the wires from it, which woke the guards. He'd intended it to be quieter.

At that point, all hell broke loose. One rolled off a top bunk, and Digger went for him, only to receive a vicious kick in the stomach. Fortunately, the guard wasn't wearing his boots in bed, so the damage wasn't great, but Digger landed about two feet from where he'd been kicked, yelping.

Rex ripped the night vision equipment off his face, and by the time he managed to do that they were on him. One of them managed to kick the gun out of his hands, and a three-against-one brawl ensued. Rex had to move quickly and keep on moving and striking with punches and kicks at the one closest to him—that didn't give him a chance to take one of them out with a single blow.

One of the attackers managed to get hold of the gun and shot him in the upper left arm. In the heat of the moment, he was aware of the bullet hitting him, and he instantly knew the bone wasn't involved—the shot had been through-and-through. There was no time to pay attention to that or the pain, although the latter only served to make him mad. He had to eliminate the guy with the gun first. So

Instead of moving away from him as the shooter would have expected, Rex closed the gap between them and kicked him in the knee with so much force the man's knee gave way with a loud crack. The man dropped the gun, screamed, and fell to ground.

By now, Digger was back in the fight. The kick he received earlier apparently also just annoyed him as he waded in from the corner where he landed after the kick. He leapt over the guy with the busted knee and went for the one closest to Rex. Two seconds later, the guy went down screaming with an open wound in his ass, lashing out and kicking at Digger who deftly evaded his attempts to get to him.

Rex would have found it funny if he'd had the time, but there was still one guard trying to get the advantage and overcome him. While he engaged the nearest one, Digger went after the one now nursing his knee and tore a chunk out of his calf.

The third guard must have seen his comrades going down in quick succession, and all of a sudden, the deck was stacked against him. He hesitated and took a step back. Rex saw it and followed him, landed a punch to the side of the guy's head, followed it up with a kick to the groin, and as the guy doubled over, Rex hit him with the right knee full in the face. The man landed flat on his back and went quiet—fight over.

Digger was busy with the one who had lost part of his ass. He now had the man's right calf in his mouth pulling and shaking violently, the man blaring with each shake.

Rex took two steps over and kicked the screaming man in the back of the head, rendering him unconscious. The one with the smashed knee was still on the floor, whimpering, and with no interest to get involved in the fight again.

Nevertheless, Rex took out some of the vexation that had been cropping up in him against the Russians since his first encounter with them in Vietnam on this guy. He kicked him in the jaw, which put him away for at least half an hour.

Rex stood over the three men on the floor breathing heavily then looked at Digger and said, "Come here, boy. Are you okay?"

Digger came to him with his tail between his legs and sniffed at Rex's wound. Rex ran his hands over the dog and found no injuries. "I'll be okay, buddy, and it looks like you will, too. Let's get these goons tied up."

Rex efficiently ziptied and gagged them, taking pleasure in using their dirty socks as gags. Digger sat down and watched each of them alertly until Rex had immobilized all of them. The fight, despite the damage done, had lasted no longer than two minutes. And because the walls were thick, and they hadn't had a chance to get to their two-way radios, no alarm had been sounded in the house. Rex was fairly certain that Koslov and company were probably not in a physical state to have heard a bomb explosion in the room where they were partying.

To make sure it stayed that way, Rex found the radios and stomped them to smithereens. Then he picked up the gun he got from the guard at the gate and pocketed it in one of the utility pockets of his pants.

He took the time to get his first-aid kit out of his back-pack and bind his wound to stop the bleeding, and then said, "Let's go, buddy. We have one more Russian asshole to deal with. Hopefully this will be the last one for a very long time—I don't know about you, but I am fed up to the back teeth with these Russians."

Digger replied with a soft woof.

Chapter Sixty-Six

Zelenograd on the outskirts of Moscow, Russia

With no more thought for the guards, who were beginning to stir but were securely gagged and bound and tied up to their bunks, Rex and Digger moved on to the house. As soon as he entered the door, Rex's ears were assaulted by very loud, very bad, Russian rock music.

The party was in full swing.

Rex and Digger made their way through darkened rooms, guided by Rex's memory of the layout and his night-vision goggles. At last, they came to a door that Rex knew would lead to the hot-tub room, where the music was louder than ever.

"Here goes nothing, Digger. I wish you didn't have to see what we're about to see. You're too young to have your eyes corrupted by what I think is going on behind this door."

It was even worse than he imagined, if that were possible. Koslov was on his feet, more or less. However, he was naked, staggering around in a parody of dancing, and urging the girls to get up and dance with him. Unfortunately for him, they were all passed out, just as naked as he was, three of them.

Rex ignored Koslov for the moment, as he was so out of it, he didn't even realize a ninja-clad man and a big dog had joined the party. One of the girls was lying with her chin dipping close to the water in the hot tub. Rex pulled her out and left her lying on the floor beside the sunken tub. If he hadn't, there was a chance she could have drowned. The others were safe, and none of the three looked as if she'd wake up before noon, if so soon. One of them had a rim of white powder around one nostril.

So, it's not just booze, it's drugs, too. Dangerous combination, girls —this stuff will kill you.

Rex turned his attention to Koslov, who had by then fallen to the floor and was crawling toward one of the girls.

"Oh, no, you don't. Party's over, mister. Let's get some pants on you. I don't like talking to naked men."

It was like trying to push a noodle through a straw, Koslov's legs were so wobbly, but Rex finally had the half-comatose man half-dressed.

He secured Koslov to a chair with zipties. The man had a smile on his face, maybe thinking it was one of the girls. With Koslov secured, Rex turned to the girls and tied and gagged them as well. Their discarded underwear made soft gags, and though he had no gripe with them, he justified the necessity with the thought that if they were consorting with a man like Koslov, they got what they deserved.

Maybe they'd wake up and feel ashamed and take stock of their lives and bad habits and make a turn for the better. Rex shrugged at those thoughts, *one could only try. Not my circus, not my monkeys.*

When he turned back to Koslov, the idiot was singing

off-key at the top of his lungs to the horrible music. Rex would have left it on if Koslov had been suffering through it as badly as he was, but evidently the CEO enjoyed it. So, his next task was to find where it was coming from and stop it. There was no one near enough to hear Koslov's inevitable cries of pain that were about to commence. When he found the iPod in its dock, he dropped it to the floor and crushed it under his boot with satisfaction.

Finally, he was ready to question Koslov. There was no time to be subtle. He had to sober Koslov up quickly and get the information he'd come for just as quickly. Nothing was so effective at sobering a man who was drunk and high as severe pain. So, Rex broke the pointer finger on Koslov's left hand.

There was no reaction.

It took him a good half hour of inflicting pain before the pain started registering properly. Rex was almost at wits ends with this guy—he needed that confession, but Koslov was not responsive. He was about to carry Koslov out, put him in a car, and drive him somewhere where he could have more time, when he saw Koslov's eyes shoot wide open. He looked around and saw that Koslov had his eyes fixed on Digger.

Koslov was becoming attentive, and with returning consciousness came the realization of pain.

He uttered an expletive and tried to focus on Rex. "Why'd you do that? Shit, that hurts!" Then he launched into an extensive rant of profanities involving Rex's mother, sister, and if he had a wife, her as well, then he went into Rex's lineage followed by some very explicit but physically impossible sexual acts he told Rex to perform on himself.

While Koslov was going on, the throbbing pain in Rex's arm made him take two Oxycodone tablets out of his first aid kid and swallow them with some wine out of one of the bottles on the table.

Rex let Koslov have his say, as he knew it was helping to get him out of his torpid state. When Koslov finally stopped, Rex called Digger to come closer before saying in flawless Russian. "I needed your attention. Now that I have it, tell me who told you to kidnap Margot Lemaire and why."

Before Koslov answered, the floor under his chair suddenly bloomed with a yellow puddle of urine. Just as Rex had predicted, he'd pissed himself. But to his surprise, it seemed it was not from the pain. His eyes were fixed on Digger, who was snarling.

"Get him away!" Koslov cried. "Name your price. Whatever they're paying you, I'll double it. Just keep that black son of a bitch away from me."

"I don't want money, and neither does my dog, but both of us are riled with you. So, Koslov, it's going to be a cheap round for you moneywise, but you'll have to answer my questions, and if you behave, I will see what I can do about the dog. But I can't promise you anything. He tends to follow his own head. However," Rex leaned forward and whispered, "I've noticed on a few occasions that if he sees I am happy, he won't devour my captives. So, maybe you should try and keep me happy."

"I'll tell you. What is it you want to know? And remember my offer; I'm still happy to pay you. Just keep that beast away from me."

Rex grabbed a chair, pulled it up right in front of Koslov, about one meter away, took his satphone from a pocket in his tactical vest, started the video recording app, and recorded every word, as the confession came tumbling out of Koslov's mouth like a waterfall.

Every time Koslov slowed, Digger gave another snarl, and Koslov sped up. Digger had this act down pat, experience gained from many such interrogations.

"It was the President. I swear, I would not have done it." Rex asked for and got detail, who had hired the thugs he'd twice fought off from kidnapping Margot, why, and finally a surprising admission.

"I don't even want that damn pipeline. Think of me what you will, but I'm a good steward for Russneft. That pipeline will be a cost, not profitable. The President wants it only for political gain, and he doesn't care about the loss to the company. He'll skim his profit off the top no matter what, and the rest of the shareholders will eat the cost. I've been pushing it only because if I don't, I'll be replaced."

Rex finished for him. "And that would mean the end to all this." He swept his arm around to include the house, the girls, and the well-stocked bar at the side of the room.

"Yes, and potentially the end to my life. I'll disappear—like in permanently."

Rex understood. He didn't doubt that what the authorities would find here when Koslov didn't show up for work and they came looking for him would cost him his life, or at least his freedom, anyway. But he couldn't care less about that. His concern was for Margot, and by extension, for Aguillard and Laurent and their country. He had enough to hand to them for a nasty surprise to the Russian President at the summit, should he be so stupid as to try one more time to force Aguillard's hand.

And it was time to go and send it. He assumed he had only hours to get out of Russia before they were discovered. Neither Koslov's guards, nor his partygoers, nor he would suffer permanent damage from being without food, water, or medical care for half a day or so.

He summoned Digger to his side and left the house, leaving everyone as they were.

Let Mr. Koslov explain the scene that the rescuers will find when they arrive.

Moscow was two hours ahead of Paris. Rex looked at his watch, to see that it was now 8:00 a.m. in Moscow. The summit would start at 9:00 a.m. Paris time. He had three hours to get the recording to Laurent. However, he had at most an hour before Koslov's no-show at the office could be noticed and maybe another hour before the CEO would be found at his house. Rex assumed if Koslov were found before his flight took off, he risked all roads and airports being closed. His disguise would stand up to casual observation, but not to a search.

He had to make the flight Rehka had booked for him and Digger. It was going to be tight.

He jogged back to his car, which was hidden nearly half a mile away, Digger keeping pace with him. The pain from the wound in his left arm made him grit his teeth. But there was not much he could do about it until he got to the car where he had a bottle of water and would be able to swallow a few more pain killers.

While trotting along to the car, he phoned Lucien and told him a message with a recording would be coming through shortly. He apologized for the lack of niceties and said he was in a rush, and asked Lucien to use his influence to see if he could help persuade the Air France staff at the airport to let him get on that flight. Lucien promised to do so. Rex ended the call, and then sent the raw video file on its way just when he reached his car.

He and Digger got in, and he stepped on the gas, racing for the airport, hoping and praying the Moscow police wouldn't be out on the roads so early and pull him over for speeding.

Before he got to the airport, he had to stop once again and don his disguise. At the airport, he first had to get Digger to the area where he could get into his crate and checked in. All that made Rex miss his own check-in by minutes. The gate agents were closing the doors to the jetport as he came hobbling up with his walking stick as fast as he could without raising suspicion. They shook their heads. The flight had boarded, and he was too late.

In genuine distress because Digger would arrive in Lyon with no one to meet him, Rex began to protest and wave his cane around, complaining loudly in French that his service dog was aboard, and he must get on the flight. His performance wasn't completely an act, but just then another Air France staff member turned up and whispered something into the ear of the woman talking to Rex. Immediately her attitude changed, she smiled and opened the doors and let him hurry down the jetport to board the aircraft.

Thank you, Lucien, you came through like a real trouper.

He had only minutes before his satphone would have to be turned off for the flight to send one last message to Lucien, with an attachment.

In Geneva, Lucien read the message, "If all else fails." He frowned, *what's the meaning of this?* Then he opened the attachment and started smiling from ear to ear.

The attachment was a photo of a marriage certificate between one Margot Lemaire and Rowan Donnelly, dated a week before Margot's ill-fated trip to Vanuatu.

Chapter Sixty-Seven

Geneva, Switzerland

The summit was about to begin, and Russian President Boris Markov had received the news, a few days before, about the failed second attempt to secure Margot Lemaire. As a very dissatisfied major shareholder, he'd already given the order for Koslov to be 'replaced'.

Markov had a summit to attend, and one more opportunity to get the pipeline agreement signed.

This time, he'd handle it himself, and the threat would be direct, though not so effective as it would have been if he could have produced the woman and her confession that Giles Aguillard was the father of her baby. He'd have a quiet word with Aguillard at the summit to tell him what Russia knew about his indiscretions, followed by the threat to begin expertly leaking the information to the media. Russia had plenty of practice in that, and the fact they'd been discovered at it in other instances only served to emphasize what damage they could do.

However, he knew it wouldn't be as easy as it sounded. The French were masters at diplomacy, and he knew the adage: Diplomacy is the art of telling someone to go to hell in such a way that they'd look forward to the trip.

After the usual folderol of cameras flashing in their eyes as pictures were taken to mark the occasion, both men smiling and shaking hands while muttering their opening salvos between shots, the media representatives were eventually barred from the room, and they were able to get down to business.

As the party who'd requested the summit, Aguillard should have had the first word. But Markov had another agenda and spoke before Aguillard had even opened his mouth.

With a friendly smile on his face, his first lie of the day, Markov said, "I am aware that Russneft is very keen to do business with your country. I, of course, support them, because I think it will go a long way to boost our respective economies, and of course, further improve on the good relations between our countries."

And, of course, make my country totally dependent on yours for our gas needs.

Giles did not express the thought. Instead, he said, "It has been a topic of many a debate in France, and as you know, it's a controversial topic. I am, as you surely are aware, one of those who oppose such an agreement." He didn't say anything else.

Markov didn't allow his annoyance to show on his face, but the atmosphere in the room grew tense.

"So, what will it take to change your mind and support the idea?" he asked.

"Nothing that I can think of right away."

Markov was even more annoyed that the damnable French philanderer didn't even seem worried.

"Not even your position as President?" he said, allowing the coldness he felt to creep into his tone.

Aguillard gave a faint smile. "I'm not sure what you mean by that, but no, not even that. I have been elected to represent France and its interests, not my own."

Markov felt a jolt of satisfaction as he upped the ante. "Not even if it means your involvement in a scandal that will destroy your presidency, your marriage, and your party?"

Aguillard's smile remained fixed, and one eyebrow went up quizzically. "Well, for that to happen, there must be a scandal to begin with, and there are none. Unless, of course, you are planning to create one out of thin air."

This was not going as he'd planned it. Markov began to doubt his intel, but he pressed the point anyway. This time, he went for the jugular. "Nothing will be created out of thin air. Unless you want to call the baby of your press secretary, of which you are the father, created out of thin air."

Giles started laughing. "As you might imagine, I am more than a little surprised to hear about my newfound fatherhood. This would be the second time in human history that an Immaculate Conception took place, except this time there were no signs of it in the stars."

Markov had not expected that reaction. And what was Aguillard babbling about, some kind of superstition? "What do you mean, signs in the stars?"

Aguillard, still amused, smiled. "Oh, if I remember my Bible classes correctly, the last time that happened, there was some kind of bright star showing up in the heavens."

Markov felt the heat rise into his face, and he struggled to maintain his aplomb as he pressed his threat further.

"Okay, so you'd rather have me pass on the information I have to the media?"

"I'm sure the media would love to have a story about such a miracle, and I'm sure they'll give you all the credit for discovering it."

Near apoplexy by this time, Markov snarled, "So, you're going to deny it?"

Aguillard feigned puzzlement. "What is it I should deny?"

At that, Markov lost his composure entirely and shouted, "Listen, Mr. President, you are playing a dangerous game with the wrong man. I can bring you down and break your country if I want to. Just like that." He snapped his fingers.

Aguillard knew he'd gained the upper hand at that point. He raised one eyebrow and let his voice grow cold.

"Is this a declaration of war, Mr. President?"

The Russian's face had gone another much deeper shade of red, reminding Aguillard of the borscht the Russians liked so much. Markov didn't reply, only tried to stare him down.

Aguillard relaxed. This was going his way, and there was no reason to escalate it. He smiled and, bringing the conversation back to the starting point, said, "Okay, Boris, let me help you with your problem. It's obvious you are desperate to have this pipeline. And it's obvious you'll stop at nothing, including blackmail, lies, deceit, abduction of my citizens, and God knows what else. But your problem is, the CEO of Russneft says he doesn't want the pipeline."

"What?! Who told you that?"

"He did. This morning. Do you want to hear him telling me about it?"

The Russian made no reply. Aguillard took it as a yes.

He leaned over and pushed the button on a remote control, which switched on the wall-mounted TV. He pushed another button, and the CEO's face appeared on screen. He started talking.

Markov was livid by the end of it. Aguillard was worried the Russian President was going to suffer a heart attack, and then he'd have a serious problem on his hands.

Instead, Markov stood abruptly, almost knocking over the heavy chair in his haste. "This session is at an end. I will see you after lunch, Mr. President. Don't think you have won."

Aguillard gave a one-shouldered shrug. He stood and held out his hand for the Russian to shake, but Markov brushed past him without an acknowledgement. When he'd left the room, Markov pressed the intercom button and asked Laurent to come in.

"I think that went rather well," he said, smiling, when his friend entered the room. Unbeknownst to the Russian, a concealed camera had transmitted the proceedings to a closed-circuit TV in an adjoining room, and Laurent had heard and seen everything.

"I agree. Do you think he'll be here after lunch?"

"Not a chance. He's got to go home and clean house, and he knows I'll release this video if he rattles so much as a paring knife, let alone a saber."

"How will he save face?"

"He'll send a politely-worded message via his ambassador that he's been called home suddenly, and he'll leave the rest of his delegation to talk about meaningless matters. He's done with this ploy, and he knows it."

When the time came for them to reconvene their talks, Aguillard was amused to see the ambassador ushered in instead of Markov. The man was visibly upset, but he was trying to hide it.

"Mr. President, I must convey my profound apologies, and those of my President. He has been called back to Russia on an urgent matter. He asks that you allow me to continue our trade talks. Unfortunately, I am not up to speed on what was on the table this morning."

"Please do not concern yourself. I will withdraw in favor of my secretary of state, and the two of you may continue the talks. I understand President Markov's position completely. Urgent matters at home, of course."

His eyes twinkled as he continued. "We had just concluded that my answer on the pipeline for Russneft is final. There will be no pipeline. Your President agreed to drop the matter once and for all."

It was at the tip of his tongue to mention the five Russian prisoners held by the DGSI in a Paris jail, but he stopped short.

Let them crawl to us when they find out about it.

Giles Aguillard, although he was a near-narcissist at the best of times, was a very relieved and very grateful man. And there were two names that came up in his mind, Margot Lemaire, who proved to be a much better person than he could ever hope to be and who would be a great President for France in the future; and the second name was Rowan Donnelly. With that man's almost divine intervention, a dramatic disaster was averted.

Chapter Sixty-Eight

Lyon, France

Rex and Margot, of course, were never married. The marriage certificate Rex had sent to Laurent was a fake. Margot had gone along with it, pretending it was a great joke. Although, Margot quietly acknowledged to herself she would have been a very happy woman if they *were* married. And if Rowan Donnelly, or whatever his true name was, would've asked, she would have said yes—without hesitation, even though she knew so little about him. She'd come to love him as her hero and a wonderful man, no matter what his secrets were. But she sensed he still had unfinished business elsewhere, and unless she missed her guess, there was another woman, somewhere. One who might be the lucky woman someday, if he could put his ghosts to rest.

Margot suspected she would never hear the full story, so she firmly told herself it was not to be between them. *I'll survive it.*

However, she wanted his contributions acknowledged somehow, and she told Giles so at the first opportunity.

Giles had called to apologize unreservedly for acting like an ass, his words. Margot forgave him, though she wouldn't ever forget. Their affair was well and truly over, and she would never be so foolish as to become involved with a married man again.

She realized they still thought a lot alike, though, when he told her he would like to convey some honor on Rowan for his efforts to protect her. He would have Lucien call to confer with her on what it should be.

She swallowed a lump in her throat.

She'd had time to think about it while Rowan was in Russia. She'd had enough time to conclude he had something in his past he wanted to hide, but she would not reveal that suspicion to anyone, not even her Uncle Lucien.

"Let me think about it," she replied. "Tell Uncle Lucien to give me a few hours."

"Once again, Margot, my deepest apologies."

Aguillard's apology and his gratitude to Rowan went a long way toward restoring her esteem for him.

"I'll leave it to you and Lucien, then," he said. "I would ask only that your Monsieur Donnelly be willing to meet with me in person to receive the honor you and Lucien come up with. Au revoir, Margot. I look forward to your return to service."

"Au revoir, Giles."

True to her word, Margot gave the matter of how to appropriately reward Rowan focused and grave thought. It was impossible to tell from his accent where he was from.

Certain mannerisms, though, made her suspect he was American, and his skills further convinced her he might have been a former CIA field agent or Special Forces or black ops operator or a spy.

It must have been something terrible that happened in the past that made him so secretive. Maybe he was a wanted man in his own country, although she couldn't think of why he would be. The one thing she knew beyond the shadow of a doubt was that he was an honorable man. And the only way she would ever know more was to ask, but she'd already learned that the only answer she'd get was, 'that's not important to know for now.'

However, it gave her an idea for what the appropriate reward could be. What if they conveyed French citizenship on him? It would have to be in secret, of course. But if he agreed, there would be at least one country on earth where he had a legal name, a legal passport, where he could call it home if he wished, and he could enjoy the protection of the government as it would protect all its citizens.

When Laurent called to discuss it, she was ready. "Convey French citizenship on him, and give him a passport. But it must be in secret."

"But, my dear, why would he want that? Surely, he is a legal citizen somewhere. Do you know whether he would accept?"

"I'll persuade him to accept. He could hold dual citizenship if he wants," she answered.

"Very well, but how will we do it? Especially if it is to be done in secret."

"I've given that some thought, too. You know he was wounded in Russia, yes? Not to mention the injuries he received in Vietnam and in Geneva. But in Russia, he was shot. He's still recovering.

"It's very simple. You use the provision for *Français par le sang verse*, 'French by spilled blood', to convey citizenship on a Legionnaire."

Margot had looked it up. Since 1999, France had been using Article 7 of the *Code du legionnaire*, "Never leave your wounded and your dead behind," as the basis for a law that every member of the French Foreign Legion could, on request, obtain citizenship if wounded. Even their underage children, if these men were killed in action, could apply for and obtain citizenship.

"But, he is not…"

"Oh, for Heaven's sake, Uncle Lucien! Think creatively. His induction into the Legion can be backdated, and his discharge for reasons of having been wounded can be accelerated. Don't tell me that between you and Giles, you can't accomplish something so simple?"

Lucien conceded that it was possible. He'd confer with Aguillard and determine his feelings about it. Margot agreed to do the same with Rowan.

A week later, his arm still in a sling, 'Rowan Donnelly' stood in the presence of both Giles Aguillard and Lucien Laurent in the formal guest reception room of the Lemaire family's farmhouse. The Lemaire family was in attendance, but no one else, at Rowan's request. He had heard Margot's proposition with bemusement, and to her surprise, he'd accepted, but only if Digger received a commendation as well.

The ceremony was simple. At Lucien's direction, he signed first a backdated application to become a French Legionnaire, then the induction papers, and then the honorable discharge. When that was done, he'd stood back while

Aguillard made a short speech to convey his deepest appreciation for what Rowan Donnelly had done in service of France, her President, and one of her most beloved citizens. He'd allowed a ribbon with a flashy medal to be hung around his neck, and then watched as Digger, on full alert, also received a medal hung about his neck on a matching ribbon.

Digger still had some disdain for this man who'd threatened Margot. Like an elephant, dogs never forget, though they can forgive. He'd probably taken his cue from Rex's and Margot's behavior toward the man.

Afterward, Lucien slipped Rex an official passport. Margot saw a brief smile as Rowan opened it and saw what she knew was there—his name as Rowan Donnelly. She was certain he enjoyed the irony.

Adele, with happy tears in her eyes, invited everyone to enjoy a buffet repast that she'd worked on ever since the arrangements were made. For Digger, she had a big steak, and his happiness showed when he allowed Giles to scratch behind his ears and give him a pat.

A couple of days later, Rex walked with Margot on the grounds. He was leaving, but he wanted her to know he would always be there for her if she needed him. In truth, he'd come to admire her courage, and he had a fondness for her that made it difficult to say goodbye. He also suspected she'd developed more than fondness for him, though she hadn't said anything.

Rex knew that sometimes it was better if things were left unsaid.

He hated to leave her without anything but good memories of him, but the fact she hadn't spoken made it awkward for him to express that thought. So, as they walked, with Digger pacing beside them, he told her she didn't need him anymore. Her family would protect her, Aguillard would protect her, and in any case, the Russians had given up their efforts to abduct her.

There was no reason to believe she was in danger anymore.

He handed her a slip of paper with a special email address on it. He'd asked Rehka to set up a secure email box where Margot could get in touch if she ever needed anything from him. "You can reach me here. But, Margot, I'm sure you've guessed that I'm a rolling stone. This is not for ongoing communication. You have your life to live, and I can't be part of it. Message me if it's important or you are in danger."

"I understand, Rowan. If our paths should ever meet again, I hope it will be under more pleasant circumstances. I can't even express how grateful I am to you. If I can ever repay…"

"Unnecessary," he said, cutting her off. "Don't even think about that. And thank you for giving me a reason to call France home. That was very kind."

"You earned it."

After that, there was nothing to say. Later that day, Margot waved as Rex and Digger stepped into a taxi on the way to the airport.

Epilogue

On an evening about five months later, Rex was immediately alarmed when the email account he had given to no one but Margot, pinged. There'd been no activity in the inbox before.

There was no text or subject for the email, only a picture of a newborn baby, looking like most other newborns, red, wrinkled, and a little annoyed at the sudden light.

He smiled and called Digger to look at the picture. The dog was unimpressed, but Rex had never understood exactly how dogs saw digital screens. Maybe if it had been a video, Digger would have been more interested.

The picture had a caption embedded: Rowena Lemaire. It provided her date of birth, but nothing else.

Rex memorized the date and started thinking about a present to send to his namesake.

He replied to the email with an icon of a man doing the happy dance followed by a string of big smiley faces and a heart.

Duty Of Care: Chapter One

John Brandt was a former warrior of the Cold War era, an experienced spook with more missions under his belt than he cared to remember. After retiring from the CIA, he'd formed Crisis Response Consultancy - CRC. He might have been too old, according to the federal government, to be useful as a field agent. But he was not too old to train his own team in the old ways and make a lot of money doing what the 'new' CIA was expected to do but couldn't because of the interference of politicians. Outsourcing to private contractors was the only alternative.

CRC – Crisis Response Consultancy, nominally commanded by the CIA, was a private military contractor under the command of John Brandt. The name, Crisis Response Consultancy, was one of those nondescript names that simultaneously said nothing and everything about the activities of the organization. You had to be one of them to know what crises they were consulted about and how they responded to it. CRC was a Black Ops organization.

Every few months Brandt would take an overseas trip to

visit some of the countries where CRC agents on missions were operating and meet with them, in secret of course. Some of the trips were to touch base with his 'boys and girls' and some were to evaluate them while on a mission.

On these trips he always traveled under pseudonyms, and there were only a few people who knew about it— among them, his second in command at CRC, Chris McArdle, the CIA's Deputy Director of Operations—informally known as Clandestine Services, and of course the agents whom he was visiting.

To attract as little attention as possible, he was usually accompanied by a small group of 'friends' in a tour group, ostensibly interested in sightseeing and the stuff tourists are usually interested in seeing and doing. They stayed in tourist class hotels, ate at tourist class restaurants, and did the things tourists did. In other words, they blended in and went to great pains to attract as little attention as possible. These 'friends' were an old network which he'd cultivated as informants in his days in Russia and France. He kept in contact with them and from time to time used them for surveillance work. They were also among the most talented field agents Brandt ever had the pleasure of working with.

After all this time and so much hands-on experience, they also had the added advantage of being among the invisible ranks of the late middle-aged to elderly. No one paid attention to an old woman knitting a sweater on a park bench, or a pair of old men engaged in a chess match at a picnic table, or a single old man feeding pigeons. An elderly woman waiting for a bus or staring mindlessly at the passing crowds wouldn't excite a moment's curiosity.

What made his 'friends' even more exceptional were that they were lifelong students, now masters, of the science of human behavior. Their particular talent was that they could follow a target for ten to twenty minutes and then predict the target's next or even final destination and be there in advance.

Tailing a subject who had a highly-trained security detail was dicey. It was so amusing to know that the target was taking extreme precautions, long and circuitous routes, and other countermeasures to avoid being followed, only to arrive where they were expected and their 'tails' waiting there for them. These wily old spies could do it without the target's knowledge and get it right with astounding accuracy.

Brandt and his cronies called themselves the Old Timers. He, in his late sixties, and his friends, ranging from his age into their mid-seventies.

Athens, Greece

Day of abduction

They were in Athens, at the Apollo Hotel, Karaiskaki Square, a two-minute walk from Meraxourgio Metro Station allowing for easy rail access from Larissa International Train Station five hundred meters away, and bus access, with convenient reach to Plaka (the Old Town of Athens) and the Acropolis. Being so centrally located enabled Brandt's party to move easily around the city, enjoying the sites of the ancient city and keeping an eye on the agent Brandt was evaluating on his trip.

That night, they all bundled into a taxi and took a food tour of Athens, which took them on a three-hour excursion to ten different restaurants all over the city for a tasting of authentic Greek food. They got back to their hotel at about ten p.m. After the unusually-heavy dinner, the rest of the Old Timers were tired and went to their rooms, but Brandt said he was going to take a stroll before bedding down for the night.

He went to his room first, put on his jacket, and took his wallet. As usual, he looked out the window at the street below to see what was going on before leaving. There was nothing of note.

When he exited the elevator, out of habit, he scanned the lobby and noticed a man with his back to him in a chair reading a newspaper. Besides the chair in which the man sat, there was a couch and two empty chairs. He noted the man was in a strategic position, but that could have just been the most comfortable chair.

However, it's the seat I would've chosen if I wanted to monitor who's coming and going through the lobby.

When Brandt passed him, he noticed the man glancing at him briefly. Brandt nodded, the man nodded back and then turned his eyes back to the newspaper.

The small things. Enough of them and trouble is the next thing on your doorstep. Paranoia? Maybe. That's what kept you alive so far.

He headed for the front door and stepped out. Before proceeding, he stopped and scanned the street outside, first left, then right. There were three cars parked on his side of the street, two to the right and one to the left. Across the street, there were four parked cars. He'd seen them from his room before he'd left. None of the cars had occupants.

Nothing to be concerned about.

He glanced back inside at the man in the chair. He was still reading, showing no interest in Brandt. He ticked the man off his list.

The sidewalks were empty, not unusual for ten-thirty p.m. in this part of the city, where there were only small hotels and apartment blocks. Brandt took a deep breath of the fresh night air, turned to his left, and started walking.

He was about five hundred meters away from his hotel when an African man blocked his way and tried to sell him a handcrafted, collapsible wooden basket. Brandt couldn't understand a single word, but he'd seen peddlers selling those baskets all over Europe. The cleverly-designed baskets were spiral cut and mounted on a circle of wood, with a handle that rotated to lift the bowl part and keep it standing, causing it to drop the spirals into a bowl shape.

Over the years he'd bought them from immigrants trying to make a living in Italy, France, Germany, and elsewhere. He had about a dozen of them in various shapes and sizes at CRC headquarters, serving as vessels for anything from fruit to paperclips.

He sighed, smiled at the man, and said, "I've never bought one of these in Greece before," as he reached into the inside pocket of his jacket to retrieve his wallet.

In the next moment, Brandt knew something had gone terribly wrong. Three men in police uniforms came rushing toward him from the foyer of the apartment building where he and the hawker were doing business. They were screaming at him in English to drop to his knees and put his hands behind his head.

A sting? But…

He heard tires screaming and engines roaring as vehicles came rushing toward him from both sides of the street.

In seconds, he was surrounded by at least eight men and two cars. He was on his knees, hands behind his head, and staring down the barrels of two SIG Sauer P226 guns in the hands of the two men directly in front of him. A third tapped a baton into his opposite hand, and to his left was a man with a Taser X26 gun.

It took him less than three seconds to figure out these men were imposters. The Hellenic police's standard issue handgun was not the SIG Sauer P226 but rather the Heckler & Koch USP 9 mm, or Beretta M9, or Smith & Wesson Model 910, or Ruger GP100. They didn't use tasers, and they didn't wear hiking boots with their uniforms.

Brandt was hopelessly outnumbered, that much he knew very quickly. In days of yore, if it were two or three attackers facing him, he'd put up a fight and would've given himself a better than even chance to beat the crap out of them. But he was sixty-eight years old, and there were eight attackers he could see. There could have been others as well, but there was no point in looking for them. All he could do was to go along with whatever it was these men wanted, for now. He didn't get much more time to think through his situation when the hooks from the taser gun embedded in his chest and his body was jolted by 50,000 volts. He never felt the prick of the needle that was plunged into his neck before his world went dark and quiet.

Duty Of Care: Chapter Two

Arizona, USA

Fourteen months previously

He'd never had a mission go so badly, though he'd lost men before. At least they'd always had a body to bury, or a reliable witness who saw what happened, some closure—they'd never left a man behind, dead or alive. He'd never cried over a loss before, but now he gave in to the grief and let the tears come.

He loved Rex Dalton as if he were his own son.

Those who were not in the know about CRC's business would probably refer to Rex as a consultant. Those who had an inkling of what was going on would have thought of him as a field agent or an operative. His enemies, and some others, would have used the word assassin.

Rex was CRC's most coveted asset; a stone-cold killer with a grudge against bad guys, especially terrorists, who had killed his family when they blew up a train in Barcelona in 2004.

After ten minutes of stunned inaction upon hearing the news from the director of the CIA, Bruce Carson, that Rex and his support team were missing, probably dead, Brandt pulled himself together.

The others had to be informed. He called in Rick Longland, his company's resident psychologist, to help him plan what to tell the others and how to commemorate the best agent CRC had ever had. Rex Dalton inspired great loyalty among his teammates, and a paternal feeling in Brandt. He deserved a memorial, at the very least.

Longland was there within minutes and saw the devastation in Brandt's face. "Dalton?" he asked.

Brandt nodded. "It appears he and the team he took with him may have been ambushed."

"What makes them think it's our men and not the drug lords Dalton was supposed to dispose of?" Longland asked. "Isn't there any hope?"

"Right number of bodies, according to the operational plan Rex submitted before he and the others headed out. Rex must be dead. He'd never leave me hanging like this if he weren't dead or worse."

"What's worse?" Longland asked.

"Do you need to ask? Worse would be if he were in the hands of the terrorists. Remember, the Taliban were supposedly at that meeting. I pray if the team was ambushed that they were killed rather than captured."

"John, I can't tell you how sorry I am."

"What are we going to tell the others, Rick?"

Longland had no answer to the rhetorical question.

Brandt prepared a few remarks, and then he abandoned them when the time came. For the sake of the entire team, he had to be as strong as he ever was in these situations. He decided to inform them at dinner, after he'd had a chance to compose himself. There would be a formal memorial later, when there was a body to bury or at least incontrovertible proof that Rex was really gone. As soon as it appeared that most of the men were finished with their meal and about to leave, Brandt stood up. Everyone went quiet and every eye turned toward him.

"Men, I have some unhappy news. Rex Dalton, whom most of you know, is believed killed in action in Afghanistan. He was a brave man, a great agent, and an excellent soldier. We will all miss him. He wouldn't want you to grieve. Dalton was a man of few words, but those words spoke of his devotion to this country and the missions we take on. The incident was such that there is no body to recover.

"You all know that shit happens, and in our line of work some of us get killed. Nonetheless, Dalton, like you, signed up for this. He knew the risks and never hesitated to take them. None of us is invincible. We bleed and die like any other human. Rex has paid the ultimate price, and I can tell you I know without a doubt he paid it willingly for the safety and betterment of our country."

He turned and left abruptly and with the certain knowledge that Rex had not *willingly* given his life. Not in that sense. He'd willingly gone into danger, he'd willingly gone to the battlefield to fight, but he'd never willingly gone to be betrayed. If he'd failed, it wasn't because he hadn't given it his best shot, he'd failed because of treachery.

Duty Of Care: Chapter Three

Present time

Unknown location

The blow to his stomach would have hurt less had he known it was coming. He could have hardened his muscles. He tried to hit back, and that was when he realized his hands and arms were immobile, wrapped in duct tape to the arms of a chair. The most uncomfortable chair he'd ever sat in.

I'm ready for you now, you bastard. Come on, come at me again.

It was dark—he was blindfolded. He tried to remember where he was, how he'd come to be there, when and how he was taken.

A blow to his jaw rocked his head back.

"Shit!"

He willed his right leg, the stronger one, to move and sweep the attacker's legs from under him, but his legs were also immobilized. Brandt shook and threw his head back, preparing to head-butt his assailant—if he'd only come close enough.

He muttered something, believing he was coherent and snarling a credible threat.

The next blow, contrary to all reason, cleared his head.

John Brandt, The Old Man his underlings called him, found himself in a situation he hadn't encountered since his youth. But he was no longer the formidable hotshot CIA agent he'd been then. Now, even if he hadn't been tied to the chair, chances were, he'd be getting the worst of the beating; back in his youth he would have left his attacker with something to remember.

John Brandt was sixty-eight years old, and if this beating didn't stop soon, he might not make it to sixty-nine. He'd have doubled over with the next blow to his stomach, but yeah, his chest was also duct-taped to the back of the chair.

There was no way to protect himself against the blows he couldn't even see coming. It would have to be his wits that kept him alive, or if not, at least it would safeguard the knowledge in his brain. He knew enough to get a lot of people killed or worse.

The question now was which knowledge this was all about. Bringing his decades of training and focus to bear, he tuned out the physical pain of the blows still raining down on him and assessed his mental condition. The lingering fog around the corners of his mind and the vulgar taste in his mouth told him he'd been drugged.

Had I been questioned?

Had I said anything?

He didn't think so, but the possibility remained.

And then, mercifully, the beating stopped. He estimated the voice he heard next was about a foot to the side and a couple or three feet above his sitting position.

"He should be softened up enough to talk now. Any more and he'll be out again."

The next voice came from farther away. Six feet maybe? No way to tell and no way to use the knowledge anyway.

"Mr. Brandt, I'm sorry to have to resort to these methods, but you haven't been very cooperative so far."

Good. Exactly what I hoped for. Thanks for the confirmation, asshole.

Brandt noted the accent, New York upper-class, but with a hint of something else underneath, indicating it was either affected or perhaps the questioner had lived somewhere else in his youth. Southern?

"I have it on good authority that you were the person who ordered the destruction of our stockpiles of opium product in Afghanistan. What can you tell me about the person or persons who carried out that order?"

Brandt stayed silent. He'd given no such order.

What's this guy talking about?

He got a stinging slap to his bruised cheek. Truthfully, he was confused by the question, and he didn't think it would hurt to say so, though he was shocked at the croaking sound of his voice and the slurred words that he uttered.

"Ah doan nuh wha ur 'alkin bow."

"Oh, I'm certain you know what I'm talking about. We know you had contractors in Kabul at the time. Who gave you the contract? What are the names of your operatives who did it?"

He shook his head.

Wasn't us. That much I know. So, there's nothing you can beat out of me, shithead.

Speaking very carefully, making an effort to enunciate, he answered, "I din' gi' order. Mah org din' do it."

"Gentlemen, I think your assessment was wrong. He

hasn't had enough incentive to talk yet." It was the New York voice again.

Brandt barely had time to clench his core when the next blow knocked the breath out of him. The blows came hard and fast, giving him no warning of where the next strike would hit him, and mercifully everything went dark again.

When he resurfaced, it was to the sure knowledge he was drowning. Wave after wave of ice-cold water hit him in the face, and he swallowed some with each gasp as he tried desperately to breathe.

"Enough," said the voice. It was the one who'd questioned him before. The water stopped, and Brandt sat shivering and shaking as the man began to question him again.

"I'll give you a minute to compose yourself," the unseen man said. "And then, I want to know about the operation that slaughtered our opium suppliers. It happened after the raid your men attempted to perform outside Kabul over a year ago. We know you killed ours in retaliation for them killing yours and that the CIA ordered the destruction of the warehouses. You will tell me who raided the compound of the head of our organization, beheaded him and several of his colleagues, and made off with a fortune in gold and his computers."

Rex Dalton did that.

I 'know' he did, despite all evidence that he's dead. And if they want to know about him, then they too must think he's alive. Well, they won't get anything from me, because I don't know anything. But I can do something to keep them occupied, son. That I'll do for you even if you don't trust me enough to report in.

Brandt took a deep breath and spoke with a labored voice. The effect of the drugs was wearing off.

"Okay, you've got me dead to rights. I cannot tell a lie." His tongue firmly in cheek, he spun a story close to what he thought was the truth. "You're right. We're the ones who took out your guy's – Usama was his name, right? We took out his warehouses on a contract, sure. But it wasn't the CIA who ordered it.

"We're a private company, an international organization, and we don't care who we work for as long as they pay. We take work where we can get it. In this case, it was a Pakistani outfit." Assuming it would mean nothing to his questioner, Brandt uttered one of a few Urdu phrases he'd learned to pronounce well. He was naming the fictional organization, the Urdu equivalent of 'Shock and Awe'.

He went on to explain. "They call themselves Shock and Awe, wanted to break into the drug market in the US and Europe. Apparently, your guy, Usama, wasn't as loyal as he could have been. He'd been talking to them, but the talks broke down, so they decided to take him out of the equation by destroying his warehouses. We did that. But we didn't take *him* out. I have no idea who did that."

It was all a lie, of course. Like any good lie, it held an element of truth. The organization he'd named was real. The relationship with Usama was a figment of his imagination, but his interrogator didn't know that. It would take time to verify everything, and time was what Brandt needed. Time would allow him to prepare himself mentally, and it would give his agents opportunity to find him. He knew that all men broke eventually, and he intended, if he was not rescued before then, to come up with such a whopper that they would kill him before he broke down and talked, endangering all of his agents, many CIA operatives, and— not to put too fine a point on it—many spies and informers across the globe.

A bonus would be if he could confuse and misdirect them to the point where they'd doubt and mistrust their own. He doubted he'd ever know how successful he was at it. At least the lie he just told them had the desired effect. The beating stopped and the questioner left the room.

A prick in his arm was the only warning before he drifted into unconsciousness.

When he woke, he was alone, still in a dark room, but now on a thin mattress in a moving vehicle. Having the time to think, he tried to recall the incident they questioned him about.

Grab your copy...
www.vinci-books.com/duty-of-care

About the Author

JC Ryan is a bestselling author renowned for his intricate espionage, archaeological thrillers, and conspiracy mysteries. With over 30 acclaimed novels, including the popular Rex Dalton K9 Thrillers, Rossler Foundation Mysteries, and Carter Devereux Mystery Thrillers, Ryan has captivated readers around the globe.

Drawing from his diverse professional background—as a military officer, lawyer, and IT manager—Ryan creates compelling narratives that skillfully blend historical accuracy with thrilling adventure. He is celebrated as a master storyteller, known for crafting riveting plots, meticulous historical details, and engaging, multidimensional characters. Ryan's meticulous research lends authenticity and depth to each story, immersing readers in richly constructed worlds filled with intrigue, suspense, and adventure.

Fans of David Baldacci, Lee Child's Jack Reacher, Tom Clancy's Jack Ryan, Nelson DeMille's John Corey, Vince Flynn's Mitch Rapp, Mark Greaney's Gray Man, Gregg Hurwitz's Orphan X, Robert Ludlum's Jason Bourne, Daniel Silva's Gabriel Allon, Brad Taylor's Pike Logan, Brad Thor's Scot Harvath, James Rollins' Sigma Force, Steve Berry's Cotton Malone, and Dan Brown's Robert Langdon will find JC Ryan's novels equally compelling and unforgettable.

When not writing, Ryan enjoys spending time with his college sweetheart, whom he married in 1978. They are proud parents of two daughters, have two sons-in-law, and are grandparents to two grandchildren.

www.ingramcontent.com/pod-product-compliance
Lightning Source LLC
Chambersburg PA
CBHW011418010726
47494CB00011B/2389